Jemima Thompson Luke

The Female Jesuit

The Spy in the Family

Jemima Thompson Luke

The Female Jesuit
The Spy in the Family

ISBN/EAN: 9783337296117

Printed in Europe, USA, Canada, Australia, Japan

Cover: Foto ©Andreas Hilbeck / pixelio.de

More available books at **www.hansebooks.com**

THE

FEMALE JESUIT;

OR

The Spy in the Family.

New-York:
H. DAYTON, PUBLISHER,
36 HOWARD STREET.

INDIANAPOLIS, IND.:—ASHER & COMPANY.

1860.

PREFACE.

THE startling assertion that "truth is stranger than fiction" has seldom been more fully verified than in the details of this volume. The heroine whose extraordinary scheme of deception is here recorded, introduced herself to the Rev. —— as an orphan, with no near relatives but a Jesuit uncle and an aunt, also a "religieuse." She stated that she had been an inmate of various convents in connection with the "Faithful Companions of Jesus" for seventeen years. These she represented as an Order of Female Jesuits. She described herself as having been for two years a postulant in their Order, and as about to be removed to Paris, there to take upon her vows from which there could be no escape. Having long been convinced of the errors of the system, and having accidentally heard Mr. L——'s name and character, she had contrived to get to him in order to throw herself on his kindness for advice. As will subsequently appear, she was received into his family, and thence obtained a situation as a governess. She returned to Mr. L——'s house on account of supposed dangerous illness, and continued there till the discovery of her plots. She is still at large, and has been seen in London. Who and what she is remain a mystery. Whether she is self-taught and self-prompted in the art of deception, or whether the almost supernatural ability she displays, has been acquired in the school of the Jesuits, must be left for the judgment of the reader to decide, and the publication of this volume to elicit.

The statements in the "Introduction" relating to the laws and mechanism of the "Community" which Marie L—— G—— had quitted, and to her escape, were furnished by herself. For these and for her "Autobiography," the writer cannot be answerable. *All the remainder of the book is strictly and literally true.*

The title of "The Female Jesuit" has been chosen *in accordance with Marie's description of the Order* to which she said that she had belonged, and also as indicative of the character of her proceedings. It is the general persuasion of those who are acquainted with the circumstances that she has acted under Jesuit influence, and the following narrative from Hogan's "Auricular Confession and Popish Nunneries," 4th Edition, pp. 90 to 97, in some respects so much resembles the one which this volume records as to strengthen the suspicion, and is for this reason inserted in full.

"Soon after my arrival in Philadelphia," he writes, "I became acquainted with a Protestant family. I had the pleasure of dining occasionally with them, and could not help noticing a seemingly delicate young man, who waited at the table. There was something in the countenance and whole appearance of this individual which struck me as singular. I could see no indication of positive wickedness or signal depravity in the external configuration of the young man's head. The expression of the eye indicated meekness, humility, and habitual obedience,

rather than anything else; but I could see, nevertheless, in the closely-compressed lips and furtive glance, which I could only occasionally catch—and even then by a sort of stealth,—something that puzzled me. I know not why, but I could not like him. There was no cause, as far as I could see, why I should dislike the young man. Constitutionally, I was myself rather fearless than otherwise. I cannot recollect that, with equal means of defence, I ever before feared any one. * * * *
I could never find the eye of this man fixed upon me without an involuntary feeling of dread. I met him often in the streets : he always seemed neat and tidy in his person; he was civil and respectful in his deportment; never seemed to forget that society had its grades, and that circumstances had clearly designated his own. With that he seemed well contented, never, as far as I could see, seeming to feel the least desire of intruding upon that of others. This being rather a rare case in the United States, twenty years ago—at any rate, when it was difficult to get servants who knew their places, struck me as another singular feature in his manner and character, and did not at all tend to remove the unpleasant impressions which his appearance made upon my mind. Not long after this, a messenger called at my rooms to say that 'Theodore ———' was taken ill, and wished to see me. I was then officiating as a Romish priest, and, calling to see him, was shown up stairs to the door of a garret room, into which, after a loud rap, and announcing my name, I was admitted to the *sick* young *man*. He had returned to his bed before I entered, and was wrapped in a large overcloak. I asked him whether he wanted to see me, and for what purpose. He deliberately turned out of his bed, locked the door again, very respectfully handed me a chair, and asked me to sit down, as he had something very important to tell me. He wrapped himself again in his cloak, lay on the outside of the bed, and spoke to me in a firm, decided tone to the following effect :—

"'Sir, you have taken me for a young man, but you are mistaken. I am a girl, but not so young as I appear to you in my boy's dress. I sent for you because I want to get a *character*, and confess to you before I leave the city.' I answered, 'You must explain yourself more fully before you do either.' I moved my chair further from the bed, and tightened my grasp upon a sword-cane which I carried in my hand. 'Feel no alarm,' said this young woman; 'I am as well armed as you are'—taking from under her jacket an elegant poignard: —'I will not hurt you. I am *a lay sister belonging to the order of Jesuits in Stonyhurst, England*, and I wear this dagger to protect myself.'

"There was no longer any mystery in the matter. I knew now where I was and the character of the being that stood before me. I discovered from her that she arrived in New Orleans to the priests and nuns of that city. She had the necessary 'Shibboleth' from the Jesuits of Stonyhurst, to their brothers and sisters, who were then, and are now, numerous in that city. They received her with all due caution, as far as could be seen by the public, but privately in the warmest manner. Jesuits are active and diligent in the discharge of their duties to their superiors, and of course this *sister*, who was chosen from among many for her zeal and craft, lost no time in entering on her mission. The *Sisters of Charity* in New Orleans took immediate charge of her, recommended her as chambermaid to one of the most respectable Protestant families in the city; and having clothed her in an appropriate dress, she entered upon her employment. She was active, diligent, and competent. The young ladies of the family were delighted with her; she appeared extremely pious, but not ostentatiously so. She seemed desirous to please in all things; talked but seldom of religion, but took care that her devotional exercises should be noticed, though she seemed to avoid such a thing. Her conduct was in every way unexceptionable. So great a favorite did she become in the family, that in a short time she became acquainted with all the circumstances and secrets, from those of the father down to those of the youngest child.

"According to a custom universally in vogue among the Jesuit spies, she kept notes of every occurrence which might tend to elucidate the character of the family, never carrying them about her, but depositing them for safe keeping with the Mother Abbess, especially deputed to take charge of them. She soon left this family under some pretext or other, obtained from them an unqualified recommendation for honesty and competency, which, with the previous and secret arrangements of the *Sisters of Charity*, obtained for her without delay a place in another Protestant family. Here, too, she was without fault,—active, honest, and industrious to all appearance. Little did these families know that, while they and their children were quietly reposing in the arms of sleep, this apparently innocent waiting-maid or chambermaid was, perhaps, in the dead hour of night, reducing to paper their conversation of the day previous, and preparing it, at least as much of it as could answer any Jesuitical purpose, to be recorded among the secret archives of the Jesuit college of Stonyhurst, from which they were to be transcopied to those of the parent college in Rome.

"Thus did this *lay sister* continue to go from place to place, from family to family, until she became better acquainted with the politics, the pecuniary means, religious opinions, (whether favorable or not to the propagation of Popery in this country) than even the very individuals with whom she resided. No one suspected her, all believed her innocent and industrious ; the only fault they could find with her was, that she seemed too fond of going from one place to another. For this, however, the *Sisters of Charity* had some salvo or other.

"On arriving in Baltimore, she, of course, called upon the nuns of that city, who were prepared for her reception, and had already a situation engaged for a 'chambermaid whom they expected from New Orleans, and who was coming highly recommended by some of the first families in that city.' She took possession of a place as soon as convenient, spent several months in that city, discharging all her duties faithfully, no one finding any fault with her, except her restlessness in not staying long with any family. Having now become acquainted with the secrets and circumstances of almost every Protestant family of note in Baltimore, and made her report to the Mother Abbess of the nunnery of her order in that city, she retired to the district of Columbia, and after advising with the Mother Abbess of the convent, she determined to change her apparent character and appearance.

"By advice of *that venerable lady, the Holy Prioress*, on whom many of the wives of our national representatives, and even grave senators, look as an example of *piety and chastity*, she cut short her hair, dressed herself in a smart-looking waiter's jacket and trousers, and, with the best recommendations for intelligence and capacity, she, in her new dress, applied for a situation as waiter at Gadsby's Hotel in Washington city. This smart and tidy-looking young man got instant employment: and now we have the *lay* sister in quite a different character. His intelligent countenance—we must not say *her* in future—soon attracted the notice of some of our most eloquent statesmen. He appeared so humble, so obedient, and so inattentive to anything but his own business, and those senators on whom he waited, not suspecting that he had the ordinary curiosity of servants in general, were entirely thrown off their guard, and in their conversations with one another seemed to forget their usual caution. Such in a short time was their confidence in him, that their most important papers and letters were left loose upon their tables, satisfied with saying, as they were going out, 'Theodore, take care of my room and papers.'

Now the Jesuit was in her glory. *Now* the lay sister had an opportunity of knowing many of our national secrets, as well as the private characters of some of our eminent statesmen. *Now* it was known whether Henry Clay was a gambler; whether Daniel Webster was a libertine; whether John C. Calhoun was an honorable but credulous man. Now it was known what value was put upon Popish influence in this country, and what were the hopes of Papist foreigners in the United States. In fact, this lay sister in male uniform, and but a waiter in Gadsby's Hotel, was thus enabled to give more correct information of the actual state of things in this country, through the General of the Jesuit Order in Rome, than the whole corps diplomatic from foreign countries then resident at our seat of government. After relating to me in her sick-room—as the family in which she lived fancied it was—all these circumstances, she deliberately said to me, ' I want a written character from you. You must state in it that I have *complied with my duty ;* and as it is necessary that I should wear a cap for a while, having cut off my hair, you must say that you visited me in my sick-room, that I confessed to you, received the *viaticum*, and had just recovered from a violent fever, in which I lost my hair. My business is not yet done,' said she. ' I must go to New York, where the *Sisters of Charity* will find a place for me as waiting-maid.' It is needless to say with what reluctance any man could comply with such a request as this ; and my having done so, is a stronger evidence than I have heretofore given of the indomitable strength of early education."

Michelet's " Jesuits and Jesuitism" communicates the fact, that Loyola's law, forbidding the employment of female agency, has been expressly repealed, and that some orders of nuns are available for Jesuit purposes. The ladies of the Order of the " *Sacré Cœur*" in particular are said to be " not only directed and governed by the Jesuits, but since 1823 to have had the same rules." The facts quoted from Hogan prove that such a system is in operation.

The writer, however, does not intend to attach even to the Jesuits the odium of a scheme of duplicity in which they *may* have had no share. If it be not so, proof is invited to the contrary, and it is hoped that the publication of these circumstances will bring out the facts, and set conjecture at rest.

CONTENTS.

PART III.

THE SEQUEL.

PART I.

Introduction.

THE FEMALE JESUIT.

CHAPTER I.

PECULIARITIES OF THE ORDER OF "THE FAITHFUL COMPANIONS OF JESUS."

WHEN Ignatius Loyola had been prevailed upon by the entreaties of three ladies to undertake their spiritual oversight, and thus lay the foundation of a community of women, he speedily repented of his compliance, nor could their utmost efforts induce him to resume the trust. He declared that "the control and direction of three women gave him more trouble than the government of a society which had spread itself over the face of Europe."*

But though the Lady Rosella failed, a feminine attempt of more recent date has succeeded, and there exists at the present time in the Roman Catholic Church an order of nuns corresponding in its aims and regulations with the society of the Jesuits.

It was established early in the present century, and owes its origin to a French lady of high rank and large property, who, bringing both to the service of the Church, was constituted by the Pope, foundress of a new religious order. Like the Jesuits, it adopts for its designation "The Society of Jesus," or "The

* Isaac Taylor's "Loyola," p. 189.

Faithful Companions of Jesus." Those who join its community, like the Jesuits, are bound to the most slavish subjection of body and mind; passive and unquestioning obedience being represented as the highest point of perfection. It may be as truly said of them as of the Jesuits, that in their Order "obedience takes the place of every motive or affection that usually awakens one to activity,—obedience, absolute and unconditional, without one thought or question as to its object or consequence. With the most unlimited abjuration of all right of judgment, in total and blind subjection to the will of his superiors, must each resign himself to be led as a thing without life, as the staff, for example, that the Superior holds in his hand, to be turned to any purpose seeming good to him. The Society is to him as the representative of Divine Providence."*

Like the Jesuits, moreover, the members of this female society have no settled resting-place, but are moved from convent to convent, and from country to country, at the will of their superiors, without previous knowledge or choice on their own part, and sometimes at a few minutes' notice.

As with the Jesuits, a perfect system of espionage is maintained over every member of the community, and the utmost secrecy preserved with regard to the movements of the Order. And, like the Jesuits, the chief though unavowed object appears to be the increase and prosperity of the Order, and the accession of new converts by means of the education of the young.

This Society was first established near Geneva, but it has gradually spread itself over France, Germany, Italy, England, and Ireland; numbering upwards of twenty convents, and including in its community about five hundred nuns, novices, and lay sisters. There are also about twelve hundred pupils from the higher orders of society in connection with the convent schools, exclusive of the day schools for the poor.

* Ranke's "History of the Popes." Book II.

The foundress and head of the Order is styled the "Reverend Mother General," or the "Very Reverend Mother," and her provincial deputy the "Reverend Mother." The power of the former is despotic. She can make or unmake laws for the community as she will, and is considered as standing to them in the place of God. When she appears in the morning all instantly kneel for her blessing, and none may approach her but on their knees.

In the absence of the Very Reverend Mother or her Provincial, one of the senior nuns is appointed as Lady Superior to each convent, but her authority is very limited, and she must apply to the Very Reverend Mother for directions in any case not explicitly provided for by the rules of the Order.

This Order has been, up to the present period, steadily progressing. The number of convents is increasing, as well as the number of pupils in each, and many converts to the Roman Catholic faith are annually made from among the Protestant pupils in the schools.

The discipline of this Order is in some respects less rigid than that of other orders, for the service of the sisterhood being required for the purposes of education, it is deemed inexpedient to injure their health by severe fasts and penances. On the other hand, the implicit obedience required, and surrender of all will and judgment, from the most important decisions of life down to the merest trifles, involve a state of mental slavery more trying to an independent spirit than any mere bodily afflictions. The check put upon the natural feelings, and the frequent and sudden removals from place to place, strike at the root of all strong attachments and endearing associations. Those who have been close companions for one or two years in one convent, may in a day be separated never to meet again, and all efforts to trace each other, either by letter or inquiry, be fruitless.

- The members of the community, being for the most part

ladies both by birth and education, of cultivated intellects and refined sensibilities, are just such as are most keenly alive to suffering from these causes, and the history which follows, though it presents no harrowing detail of corporeal inflictions, is probably but one specimen of many who are now in like manner contending with the mental struggles of a reflective and upright mind, and the repressed and agonized yearnings of an affectionate heart.

CHAPTER II.

CONVENT AT I——.

THE convent at I—— belongs to the Order which has been briefly described. It is a large red brick pile of building in the Elizabethan style. The stables have been metamorphosed into a chapel, and the court-yard is beautifully paved with small stones, mingled with crosses and other designs. Without, adjoining the chapel, is a school for the poor, superintended in turn by different nuns and novices. The back of the house is toward the road, and the front opens upon an immense lawn and shrubbery. The grounds are prettily laid out, and are bounded at the extreme end by a branch of the Thames. There are several iron arbors, shaded by weeping ash-trees, under which, when processions are made through the grounds, temporary altars are erected. A grove of beautiful trees rises upwards to an artificial hill, on which a grotto stands. Round the interior of this grotto are fixed a number of little altars belonging to the pupils of the convents, bearing on them images of the Virgin and Child.

On a Wednesday evening, Jan. 17th, 1849, between six and

seven o'clock, while the nuns were at lecture, a young lady, who had been for seventeen years a pupil in the convents of this Order, and who for the last two years had been a postulant, entered the grotto. She knelt, and wept, and prayed in an agony of feeling, which He who searches the heart alone could fully estimate. She had been gradually but fully convinced of the errors of Romanism, and intensely longed for the light of God's truth and the liberty of His Gospel. She had looked forward for some time with increasing dread and disgust to the profession of a nun, yet she could see no escape. She had been educated for a nun. The last wishes of a dying mother had already induced her to become a postulant. She had neither father nor mother, brother nor sister, to whom to appeal. Her uncle was a Jesuit priest, and impatient for her to take the veil. Her aunt brought large property into the Order, and stood high in repute for talents and sanctity as superioress of one of the convents.

From neither of these could she hope for sympathy. The time for her profession had already been on various pretexts delayed, and she could not put it off longer. She could not confide in any of the sisterhood, as they would have been bound by their vows immediately to reveal her secret. She had not one Protestant friend. The penny a day allowed the nuns for charity was the only money she ever possessed. Every article of any value had been taken from her when she became a postulant, and how could she venture out on the wide world without knowing a single person in it, or having the means of procuring so much as a night's lodging. Indisposition alone had prevented her being sent to the continent, in company with two other nuns, a fortnight before; and various intimations, which experience had taught her to understand, convinced her that she was on the point of being sent to Carouges to perform her novitiate. Driven from all creature help, she turned in her distress to Him whose enlightened spirit had visited her, and besought Him, in this her last extremity, to appear for her deliverance. How signally her prayer was answered, she desires to have recorded for the encouragement of others.

CHAPTER III.

THE OMNIBUS.

IT was about nine o'clock on the following morning, when the I—— omnibus drew up at the gate of the convent. Two of its young inmates made their appearance, and asked to be taken to town. There was but one vacant seat inside, so the young lady stepped in, and her companion, who had apparently come with her as an attendant, got outside. The omnibus rolled on, and gradually set down the greater part of its passengers, till four only remained. Among these was the young lady of the convent. It was Marie, whom we introduced in the last chapter. She was reading her Catholic prayer-book, as is the custom of the nuns at all leisure moments, when out of it accidentally dropped a little cross. It was picked up by a gentleman who sat opposite to her, and courteously returned without a remark. Shortly after, the two other passengers got out, and they were left alone. He then entered into conversation with her, and, presuming that she was a member of the Roman Catholic Church, he gradually led the way to what he conceived to be its errors. The gentleman in question was neither young nor handsome, but the expression of his countenance was strikingly benevolent, and his manner most kind and fatherly. The first thought that he might be one of her own Church, seeking to test her fidelity, was soon discarded, and his evident earnestness and sincerity won her entire confidence. She frankly acknowledged her doubts, and stated her circumstances. He expressed his surprise how she or any one could read the Bible aud continue to be a Roman Catholic. She burst into tears, and told him that she had never seen the Bible, and would not be allowed to possess one. He seemed much shocked, and earnestly entreated her to seek advice of some Protestant minister. She told him she had long wished to meet with one, but knew not where or how. He said she could go to some Protestant place of worship, and remain to speak to the minister. She told him that it would not be permitted, and that she could not do it unobserved. He then recommended her to seek one that very day. She expressed her willingness to do so. "To whom should she go?" and he began to think. There was a Dr. ——, a very good man, but he did not know where he lived, and feared it was a long way off. There was a Mr. ——, but he too lived at some distance. There was another minister, a Mr. L——, who had not long been in London ; the chapel at which he officiated was near; she had better go to him. She asked whether she might indeed place confidence in this Mr. L——. He assured her that she might. She thanked him, and resolved to follow the advice of her kind friend and adviser, feeling an impression that he had been sent to her by heaven, in answer to her prayer. The omnibus stopped. He expressed his regret that he could not show her the way, having business in another direction, and bade her farewell.

It was a feast and gala night in the convent of S——, whither Marie was going. Her young attendant's services would be required, so, availing herself of this pretext, on getting out of the omnibus she sent the girl on, promising to follow as soon as she had completed the business about which she had been sent. She, herself, went to execute a commission, and then commenced her search for Mr. L——.

Unacquainted with the neighborhood, and timid from her convent life, she wandered about for three hours, getting into courts and places which terrified her, and receiving one answer from all whom she asked, " that there was no such chapel in the square." It was getting dusk, and fatigue and fasting added to her dejection. At length she met with a girl who knew the place, and kindly undertook to be her guide. It was not in the square, but in one of the many streets leading out of it. She rang at the side door, and asked for Mr. L——, and was told that he was not there, and that he lived between three and four miles off.

If Marie had not been inspired with energy and perseverance from above, she would surely have given up in despair. But she was not to be dismayed, even by this discouraging reply. She inquired farther, and found that there was to be a service at seven o'clock, and that Mr. L—— would be there a few minutes before that time. Resolving to return, she hastened to where she had some other business to transact, and was informed that the lawyer to whom she was sent, would not be at home till after seven. This suited very well, as it allowed time to renew her inquiries for Mr. L—— in the interval, and furnished an excuse for a late return to the convent. She walked about for another hour, to while away the time, and returned to —— street a little after six.

It was Mr. L——'s custom to spend the Thursday in visiting his people, and to take tea with one of them, before going to the service. That evening, as he went his rounds, he felt so unwell that he gave up his usual plan, went straight to the vestry, and asked the pew-opener to send him tea there. He arrived about six. But for this unusual circumstance, he would not have been there till just before the service began, and too late to speak to Marie.

She arrived a little after six, and was shown into the vestry. Her agitation was extreme, and she glanced round as though the walls had eyes and ears, but his calm and gentle manner soon inspired her with confidence. There was not time for any

lengthened conversation ; such as there was, soothed and comforted her. He gave her a little New Testament, the first she
had ever held in her hand, and directed her to come to his
house the next day, if she could obtain her liberty for a few
hours.

From the vestry Marie posted on to the house of the Catholic
lawyer, and thence hastened back to the convent. She had
paced about four hours, and had not tasted food since early
morning. All at the convent were too busy to make more than
general inquiries, and after taking a little refreshment, she retired to her room. She took her Testament from her pocket, and
placed it under her pillow, that it might not be discovered during her sleep.

But sleep was not for Marie. Thoughts of the past, and
dreams of the future, crowded through her excited brain. All
the circumstances of her previous life passed in rapid review
before her, and a lifetime yet to come floated on her imagination. What was to become of her, if after all she did not
make her escape, or how she was to be provided for if she did ;
fears of discovery regarding the past evening, and cogitations
as to how she could get away for a few hours on the morrow,
kept her in such a whirl of thought and emotion, that she would
have been overpowered had it not been for the firm persuasion which possessed her, that the extraordinary meeting
with the stranger in the omnibus was the hand of God pointing
out her way, and that He would not leave her till He had accomplished her deliverance.

Marie was no longer friendless though she knew it not ; there·
were those in whose minds an interest had that night been
awakened which was soon to ripen into warm attachment, and
who talked of her and prayed for her as she lay on her restless
couch.

And where was he who had opened to her the door of hope,
who had seemed to her as an angel from heaven directing her

way? Did *he* think of her and pray for her that night? Did he tell the tale of his interview with her to some dear home circle who could mingle their prayers with his on her behalf? Does he ever think of her now? Does he ever wish to know what became of her? It is her hope that he may chance to see this book, and learn how, while instant in season and true to his Master's work, his Christian fidelity and love were blessed to her deliverance. And if any of the public journals or reviews should notice her little history, she makes it her request to them that they will repeat the circumstance of his meeting with her, and tell him the gratitude she shall ever feel towards him, and how she longs once again to see him and thank him for herself; or how if she may not thank him on earth, she hopes to do so in eternity.

CHAPTER IV.

MARIE'S NEW FOUND FRIENDS.

THE scene must change to a house of moderate size and cheerful aspect at the extreme West End of London.

Its inmates consisted of the pastor, his wife, a sister residing with her, another sister on a visit, and a lively warm-hearted little girl not quite five years old.

The fire had thrice been made up, the slippers had long waited on the rug and the cloth on the table. The wife and one of her sisters had listened in vain, as any footsteps neared the house, for the step they were anxiously expecting, and again and again had the door been opened in the hope of getting a sight of him for whom they waited. Just when anxiety was giving place to alarm at the unprecedented lateness of his return, and they were about to send a messenger to inquire after him, his knock was heard and their fears were dispelled.

He sat down in the arm-chair and seemed unusually silent. "Is anything the matter, dear ? is your mother well ?" his wife asked.

"Oh there is nothing amiss," he answered cheerfully. "First, there were several people to speak to me after the service ; then there was a Sunday-school committee to be held, and when we thought it over Mr. Secretary brought out the Report to be read and corrected. When I got into Oxford-street I had to wait just an hour for an omnibus ; and, finally, your clock is iust half an hour too fast, so the mystery is soon explained. But though there is nothing amiss, I *have* met with an adventure. Give me some supper, and I will tell you all."

So the supper was eaten, and then he told them of Marie's visit to the vestry. They were deeply interested in the story. "But," said Mrs. L——, "I should like to see her and talk to her myself, there have been so many impostors that it disposes me to be skeptical ; I think you are rather apt to be taken in, dear, especially by applicants of our sex."

"Well, I gave her our address and asked her to come, and I hope she will be able to do so ;" and he mentioned several little incidental circumstances which convinced him of Marie's truthfulness. And so they talked till an hour beyond midnight, and retired to rest to wait the issue of the next day.

CHAPTER V.

FARTHER UNEXPECTED EVENTS.

Four o'clock, summer or winter, was the hour for rising in the convent, but on account of her delicacy of health Marie was allowed to rest till five. Long before daylight, on the Friday morning, she rose from her sleepless bed with the question yet unsolved, of " how she was to get leave of absence during the day ?"

She had not left her dormitory when, at six o'clock, the Superioress came to her and told her to go with two mothers (or nuns), who had just arrived from the continent, to the convent at H——. Having twice spent a short time at the convent she could act as guide. The Superioress gave her permission to spend the rest of the day at H——, provided she went on an errand to Regent-street before her return.

Marie was much struck with this unexpected opening, and instantly resolved to avail herself of the opportunity to go to Mr. L——'s. A little after eight she started as guide to the nuns, and reached H—— with them. After resigning her charge, and seeing the sick nuns, she took the omnibus to C——, and another in the direction of Mr. L——'s house.

Being a new neighborhood Marie had great difficulty in finding the house, but the experience of the past day had taught her perseverance. When at length she found the terrace she had forgotten the number, and tried several houses in vain. As is often the case with London neighbors, the name was not known. She went from house to house and found the right.

Meantime, the minister's family had watched and waited for her with anxiety second only to her own. They had joined in prayer that help and guidance might be given to her who needed both. They scarcely dared to hope that she would make her way to them, and many were the regrets expressed that the chances of several mornings had not been left open to her.

The clock had not long struck eleven when a knock, just such as suggested who it was, announced her arrival. She was neatly dressed in black, with nothing else to indicate that she came from a convent. She seemed timid and agitated, and at every ring at the bell, or move in the house, she quickly turned her head with fear lest she had been followed. We may not describe our living heroine even to add to the reader's interest, suffice it to say that five minutes' acquaintance convinced all that Marie was no impostor—no concealed Jesuit seeking to insinuate herself into a Protestant household. Her open and speaking countenance, in which every feeling could be read before it found utterance, every movement unstudied, every expression unpremeditated, none could believe her capable of acting a part.

They chatted with her about her convent life, and ordered some refreshment, and she became more at ease. The minister left the room to return to his study, and his wife slipped out after him. He turned on the stairs and said, "What do you think of her?" "Oh! I am perfectly satisfied; I could not doubt." He was going up, and she ventured to stop him again, and to remind him of a little room at the top of the house which would just do for Marie, if he should think it expedient to offer her a home with them. He willingly fell in with the suggestion; but added, that they should be better able to judge after further conversation as to how far her own mind was made up, and whether she was in immediate danger.

To this they both agreed, and in a little while Marie and Mrs. L—— were called up into the study, for more private consideration of the subject. On entering into conversation with her, they were greatly surprised to find how, unaided by the

Scriptures, and removed from Protestant books, or influence of any kind, she had detected the leading errors of Popery.

The doctrine of transubstantiation had from the first horrified her, as a species of spiritual cannibalism: the worship of the Virgin and saints, and especially of the waxen images of the infant Jesus, had shocked her as idolatry: the daily repetition of scores of useless prayers, and the idle mummery of the public services, had been an insult to her understanding: the revolting questions of the confessional had outraged her modesty: the refusal of her confessor to permit her to read the Scriptures had awakened her suspicions: her naturally frank and upright mind had been disgusted by the mystery and concealment which characterized all the movements of her Order; and her free spirit had risen in rebellion against the spiritual slavery to which she had been condemned, as she had feared for life. With a heart awakened to its spiritual necessities, she longed for liberty to read those pages which would reveal to her the way of eternal life, and panted to approach her one only Saviour, without the intervention of priests or mediators to bar her access. She wanted, she said, to read the word of God, and judge for herself where the truth lay. She would not join the Protestants, for she had yet to learn whether they were right: all the conclusion she had arrived at was, that Catholics were wrong. She had hitherto been treated kindly. She had no complaints to make of anything but "*the system:*" that, and that alone, was abhorrent to her, and from that only did she wish to escape.

Mr. and Mrs. L—— offered her an asylum in their house. They said that she need not return to the convent at all, if she thought her danger imminent. She said she knew that her nun's clothes were making, and judged from several little circumstances that she should soon be sent away. No direct intimation was ever given long beforehand, and she might any day be taken out as for an ordinary walk or ride, and shipped on board a foreign steamer. Should any suspicion of her be excited, such would probably be the result. But she wished to think the matter over, and plan how to leave, as frankly and openly as her safety would permit. She did not like to abscond clandestinely from those who had treated her with uniform kindness; besides, she had been intrusted with a commission to execute before her return, and she thought it was not honorable and upright to leave it undone. So she would return to the convent that night, and contrive to communicate her decision to them by letter. It would be, in some respects, a trial to her to leave those who had been her only friends, under whose wing she had spent seventeen years, and by whom she had regarded herself as provided with a home for life;—to venture out an orphan indeed, friendless and penniless, on a world to her all unknown, and cast herself upon the providence of God. Yet to this course her mind was made up. As the expenses of her education had been amply paid, she was under no pecuniary obligations to the Order. Her happiness both for this world and the next were at stake. The question of time and means alone remained to be settled, and these she must ponder over on her return.

And so, having dined together, they parted. Elizabeth, one of Mrs. L——'s sisters, went with her to Regent-street, and thence accompanied her to the convent gate in S——, saying, as the door opened and she bade her farewell, "I shall see you again soon."

CHAPTER VI.

THE CONVENT IN COMMOTION.

MARIE was not permitted to escape detection as well on the Friday as on the Thursday evening. Some little time before her return a nun had arrived from I——, bringing word that if Marie had returned from H——, she was to go on some other business for the Reverend Mother. Soon after two girls arrived from H—— with the chalice, and from them it was ascertained that Marie left early in the morning. Then arose great wonderment as to the way in which Marie had disposed of herself during the interval; and immediately after lecture she was summoned by the Superioress into the community room, to give an account of herself.

Marie's heart sank within her when she found that her absence had been discovered. Mother Ann, an old nun who was superioress at I——, commenced the investigation, and asked Marie where she had been since leaving H——. She replied, "that she had been to Regent-street for the Reverend Mother."

Mother Ann.—"You could not have been at Regent-street the whole of the day. Who was the young lady with you at the gate? and what did she mean by saying, she should see you again soon?"

Marie.—"A young lady I had met with, and she kindly invited me to spend a few days with her."

Mother Ann.—"That will be impossible. Besides, how do you know who and what she is?"

Marie.—"I am convinced of her being no imprudent or improper acquaintance, and I intend to ask Reverend Mother to allow me to accept her invitation. I mean to claim the privilege of being a few days in the world, before taking the final step."

This is allowable, but is rarely done.

Mother A——, superioress of the S—— convent.—"But where *have* you been, Marie?"

Marie.—"I will answer that question to Mother J——." The name of the Reverend Mother.

Mother A—— asked various questions, with no better success, adding that it was certainly a mysterious business, and that she never heard of a religieuse making acquaintances in the world while out, and that it was contrary to all the rules of the Society.

Mother P——.—"But surely, Mother Ann, you will not allow such an act of disobedience to pass over without penance."

Mother Ann.—"Certainly not." (To Marie) "For your dis-edifying conduct, and the scandal you have caused to this Society, I shall inflict a penance, which I require you now to perform in the presence of this community, according to the rules of this Society; the rest I shall leave to the Reverend Mother, who will solve the matter."

Said Marie to herself, "She will be very cunning to do so."

Mother Ann proceeded, according to law, to quote the rule which authorized her to inflict penance.

' Any postulant, novice, or nun who shall wilfully, or carelessly disobey the Very Reverend Mother, her Deputy, Provincial, or her appointed Superioress, shall, for such disobedience, publicly atone for her fault, if such fault has caused scandal to the said community, by prostrating and apologizing for the said scandal; and if her superiors deem it requisite, they shall require the said postulant, novice, or nun to kiss the floor; and in extreme cases, shall prostrate and make the sign of the cross with her tongue. This penance shall be performed in the presence of the community at lecture, or any convenient time, when the community shall be assembled,' &c. "I shall, therefore, require you to perform the second part of this penance, namely, to kneel down and kiss the floor."

Marie.—"I do not deserve it, and shall not perform it."

Here it may be necessary to remark, that Marie's conscience would not have allowed her to perform this penance. On the last occasion, she had reproached herself for having performed such humiliations to a fellow-creature. Her spirit, too, was roused. She is conscious that something of natural warmth and hastiness, mingled with conscientious resolution. She regrets it on the one hand, while on the other she feels that it helped to carry her through this trying scene.

Her open rebellion astonished the nuns, kind Mother X—— excepted, who, having witnessed a similar scene when Marie was a pupil, observed, "Oh! it is just like Marie; leave her till her hasty temper has subsided. She will be sorry for it afterwards. It is of no use to argue with her now." So the matter ended, Marie leaving the room as Mother X—— was making her speech.

Marie had not been long in the dormitory, when Mother Ann came to her, and in her usual affectionate tone informed her, that Reverend Mother had received a letter for Marie from her aunt, and proceeded to renew her inquiries; Marie again replied that she would explain all to Mother J——. She went down to supper, but could not eat. The novice, whose office it was to read at meals, was dangerously ill, and Marie was asked to read. She took the book, but was unable to articulate a word. Mother X——, who sat next her, took the book, and was permitted to read in her stead. Recreation (or talking time) followed, but it was a gloomy affair. Few spoke, and Marie could not utter a word. All then adjourned to the chapel for evening prayers. Marie longed to get out her little Testament to read, and felt more than ever horrified at the sight of the altars, images, and signs of idolatry around her: and she spent the moments in earnest prayer that she might soon be delivered from her spiritual slavery.

Marie again retired to her sleepless bed, and again her dear little Testament was placed under her head. She slept in the same room with Mother A——, the Superioress. Mother A—— came up a little while after her, and was soon asleep; but not so Marie, who lay silently cogitating on all that had transpired, and planning how to escape with honor and uprightness, and yet with safety.

About two o'clock she heard the door open, and some one softly approaching Mother A——'s bed, and rousing her, commenced conversation in French. It was carried on in a low tone, to avoid disturbing Marie, who eagerly listened to the whole. Mother Ann had come to consult Mother A—— on the number of articles to be taken to France by the novices and others, who were going. Marie heard her *own* name mentioned, and the question asked, how many articles were to be marked with her name.

Mother Ann said there would be a parcel of English books for Marie to take to Amiens for her aunt, who was Superioress of the convent there. Mother A—— observed that there was no hurry about the boxes being made up, as the party would not leave till two o'clock on Sunday morning (or rather Monday); to which Mother Ann replied, that the boxes would have to be sent down to London Bridge on Saturday evening.

This realized all Marie's fears, and convinced her that no time must be lost, as but one day remained before the time destined for sending her to the novitiate, and at all hazards she determined to communicate with her newly-found friends.

Saturday morning arrived, and Marie was sent out on business for Reverend Mother, attended by a girl, who from her vigilance had evidently received a strict charge not to lose sight of her. Her first errand was to the bookseller's to obtain the English school-books which were to be taken to France. On the way back Marie discovered that she had unintentionally neglected to order the principal book. She instantly saw that

this might afford her the opportunity she wanted. She told the
girl she had to be at Mr. C——'s, the lawyer's, at such a time,
so the girl must go back for the book, and meet her at Mr.
C——'s. The girl replied, " Mother Ann told me not to leave
you." Aware that to persist would only awaken suspicion,
Marie agreed to return ; and the girl seeing that both could not
be done in time, consented to divide. No sooner was she out
of sight than Marie set off full speed for the Protestant chapel,
and left a message with the pew-owner, requesting that Miss
T—— would come for her to the convent-gate on Sunday
morning, between eleven and twelve o'clock, when it would be
high mass, and an hour when she thought she could slip out
unobserved. Thence hastening back to the lawyer, she arrived
there before the girl. Her business done, she was returning
with the girl to S——, when the latter exclaimed, " Oh ! what
shall I do ? I have forgotten a letter about which Mother Ann
gave me such a strict charge." This aroused Marie's suspicions,
and in the girl's agitation she caught sight of the direction. It
was to the Reverend Mother at I——, and "immediate" was
written upon it. The girl was obliged to go back to the post-
office with the letter, and Marie, refusing to accompany her,
proceeded homewards.

Marie conjectured that the note to the Reverend Mother regarded herself, and that it would not be safe to delay her escape till Sunday morning, as by that time the authority of
Mother J—— might place some insurmountable barrier in her
way. She had twopence left, which had been given her for
charity a day or two before, and of which she had not yet
given an account. She had also one postage stamp with her.
She turned into a stationer's shop near ————, bought a sheet
of paper, borrowed a pen and ink, and wrote a note to her new
friends, entreating Elizabeth to come for her at six that evening. The people were very civil, and gave her a wafer. At
the shop door she saw a little girl, and asked her if she knew

where there was a post-office. The child replied, that she did. "Are you sure that you know it?" said Marie. "Oh! yes, for I often take letters for my father." Marie then gave the girl a penny to take the letter to the post for her, and made the best of her way to the convent.

The girl who had been sent as guard to Marie was questioned on her return, and the double discovery was made, that the letter to the Reverend Mother had not been posted till one o'clock, and that Marie had been left some time alone. In consequence of this Mother X—— and Mother M. J—— were dispatched to fetch the Reverend Mother without further delay, as no decisive measures could be taken in her absence.

Marie now informed Mother Ann that she should leave at six o'clock that evening. She expected her friends to call for her, and she should leave a note to Reverend Mother to explain. She wrote a note in the presence of one of the sisters, and placed it in Mother J——'s room. Mother Ann asked who would come for her, and she said, the young lady who had accompanied her to the gate. Mother Ann observed that she should not allow her to go, and should take measures to prevent it. Marie replied, that she was of age, and was bound by no vows, and should act as she thought proper, and that if opposed she should call in the aid of the police.

During this altercation the nun in charge of the Infirmary came to fetch Mother Ann to the bedside of Sister Julia, the dying novice. Finding her near death the priest was summoned from the confessional to hear her last confession, and another priest was called to administer the last rites of the Romish Church.

Six o'clock came, and Mother Ann and another mother were at the portress' gate watching for the arrival of Marie's new acquaintance; and about a quarter after six the two priests came in and proceeded to the nuns' chapel. Had Elizabeth arrived at this juncture Marie's departure would probably have been intercepted.

The nuns were soon in commotion preparing for the usual procession of the Host with torches round the convent yard. Six o'clock having passed, they concluded that Marie's friend would not make her appearance, and the Reverend Mother's arrival being every moment expected, they were thrown off their guard.

Marie, knowing that if she lost this opportunity all her hopes were at an end, and concluding that her friends had not received her letter, thought it best to attempt her escape forthwith, while the nuns were engaged in procession. She ran up stairs, put on two gowns one over the other, hastily made up a small bundle of clothes, hurried down, and passed through the community room. Seeing in the lobby a small box of hers which had been sent from I—— on the previous day, ready packed for her to take to France, she requested one of the children of the school, who was washing the lobby, to carry it for her to the poor school lodge. She passed on unobstructed through the chapel tribune to the day-school for poor children; the entrance to which is open on Saturday evening for the distribution of clothes to the poor. She deemed this her safest exit, as being so public, she could, if necessary, have aroused the whole neighborhood.·

Mother J——, who was mistress of the day-school for the poor, was the only member of the community at hand. Being attached to Marie, and seeing her resolutely determined to leave, she offered no resistance. Marie ran out intending to call a cab. How she was anticipated will appear in the next chapter.

CHAPTER VII.

REVEREND MOTHER A LITTLE TOO LATE.

It was Saturday evening at C—— Terrace; the family were assembled at the tea-table, talking over the occurrences of the day, and making preparations for the morrow, when the postman brought in an unpretending looking note. It was not enclosed in an envelope, and seemed hurriedly sealed and directed. Mr. L—— took it, and as he read he drew the lamp nearer, and his evidently increasing interest awakened attention. It was from Marie.

"My dearest friends,

"If you value the happiness and eternal welfare of a soul, which I am convinced you do, send Miss T—— for me this evening at the hour of six. She must, please, ask the man to ring the nun's door bell, that is, the door through the yard we entered last night, and he must say that he has come for Miss G——.

"I have had a most dreadful time since I saw you, but will tell you all when I arrive at —— Green. I am now compelled to make use of an ingenious stratagem to get away. If not discovered, it will pass off very well, and then I will write to them from your house. I have been out this morning, and had arranged another plan, but this one seems the most prudential.

."Oh! my Christian friends, if you knew what I suffer—but I entreat you will be very careful how you speak of me, for I suspect some design, so the sooner I am away the better. I write this in great haste and under great distraction of mind. Humbly and earnestly begging your prayers that God may preserve me,   "I am,

"Your most distressed and destitute supplicant,
                "MARIE."

It was then half-past six, and before Elizabeth could reach the convent it would be half-past seven. What was to be done? the note said six. Perhaps that was the only time at which she could leave unopposed; perhaps half-past seven might be an inopportune hour, and not only fail of success, but subject Marie to discovery and confinement. Yet, on the other hand, she wrote in such distress, that the case must be urgent. Perhaps she might be on the point of being sent out of the country, and this her last chance of escape. If she heard nothing she might think they had deserted her, and be in an agony of suspense, not knowing what next to do. If they waited till Monday they would not then know what hour to choose; so it seemed better to run all risks, and to go for her at once.

Then who should go? Elizabeth had been out all the morning, and was quite over-tired. She had not strong health, and was unused to going about at night by herself. It is no very agreeable undertaking for any young lady to go in cabs and omnibuses at night alone: besides, she knew not what unlooked for reception might await her at the convent. Should her brother go with her? but it was Saturday night, and he was preparing for his Sabbath duties, and he of all others would be most likely to excite attention and opposition. Should one of her sisters go in her stead? But Marie had asked for her; she had been to the house and knew the gate; she was quicker in all her movements than they; and she alone was known to possess that feminine tact and readiness, which would enable her to evade troublesome questions, and cope with difficulties. So the general permission was given; and fatigue and timidity alike forgotten in the excitement of her enterprise, in five minutes more she was equipped and on her way.

There is pleasure in sympathy, whether in a family or community, when various minds are brought together by one common impulse; and pleasure in excitement, when directed to a wholesome object; and pleasure in the active and united exercise of Christian kindness;—and these emotions were experienced by each member of that family circle, and diminished the anxiety, which would otherwise have been painful, of the two hours which followed.

The pastor went to his study, the wife to her room, and the sister to hers, and probably all were at the same moment giving vent to their feelings, in committing their messenger to the care of heaven, and praying that her errand might meet with success.

There was one little room on the upper story, which had been used in turns as a temporary sleeping room, or a summer sitting room, or an oratory, or a reading room, free to all, yet never decidedly appropriated by any, and it seemed to have been kept waiting for some unknown occupant. It had the prettiest view in the house, having fields and pleasure grounds in the foreground, and beyond them a canal, winding more than canals are wont to do, bordered here and there with trees, which just allowed you to see a moving barge occasionally between them; and further still, a well-known and picturesque village on a hill, with the spire of its church rising among the trees. It was as pretty a lookout as one could hope to find in the near neighborhood of a great city.

There was a little bedstead not then in use, and the sisters were soon engaged in drawing it from its receptacle, and preparing it for her who might possibly be its occupant. When ready it was not much unlike a nun's bed, only somewhat wider and softer. A small washhand-stand and carpet, a few chairs, and a rosewood standing desk, on which a Bible was placed, were soon added to the furniture.

Little Lilly enjoyed the unwonted bustle, and must needs "help" to the utmost of her ability; lugging in articles much larger than herself, and expressing most earnest desire for Marie's safety. While preparations were being completed up stairs, her aunt went down to see that the fire was blazing, and the kettle singing, and coffee ready for the stranger.

Meantime let us follow Elizabeth on her expedition. When

fairly on her way in the dark night, she began, she said, to feel terribly frightened, not knowing but that she might get in, instead of Marie getting out.   No thought of turning back, however, was for one moment admitted.   On she went, with more than her usual activity ; and having got over a mile or more on foot, she stepped into an omnibus, and in twenty minutes more reached a cab stand, and was driven to the convent gate, where, to her great joy, Marie appeared and sprang out to hail her. The cabman asked them whither he should drive them.   "To where you took me up," was Elizabeth's ready reply : and off they drove.

Elizabeth changed into an omnibus to avoid being traced, and by half-past eight Marie reached her new home, almost overwhelmed by the excitement of suspense and terror past on the one hand, and joy at her deliverance on the other.   The sound of voices in the hall speedily brought all the family down to meet her.   Her bonnet and cloak were soon off, and she was seated in the easy chair, by a cheerful fire, safe and free, taking the refreshment provided for her.   As the circle sat around and listened to the account of all that had befallen her during the last four-and-twenty eventful hours, it would have been difficult to say which were the happier, Marie or they who welcomed her.   They took her early to her little room, but she was too excited to sleep till the dawn of day.   She woke on the day of rest—emphatically so to *her*.   One of the sisters remained at home with her that she might have entire repose, both of body and mind, for that day ; and occasionally they read together in that blessed book, which she had long sought, and prayed, and wept for, as it seemed in vain.

Between eight and nine o'clock on Saturday evening, a coach and horses waited at the gate of the convent of———, to convey the Reverend Mother to the convent at———, where she probably arrived about two hours after Marie's departure.

Marie having since resolved on the publication of her previous history, will now be left to tell her own tale.

PART II.

Autobiography

OF

THE FEMALE JESUIT:

OR,

SEVENTEEN YEARS OF CONVENT LIFE IN CONNECTION
WITH "THE FAITHFUL COMPANIONS OF JESUS,"

CHAPTER I.

It is a painful exercise to recall the particulars of a lifetime
marked by sufferings neither few nor small—the loss of one
dear relative after another, till I have been left all but alone,
and the mental struggles that have filled up each sad interval.
It is moreover an undertaking of no small difficulty to one
unused to composition to prepare a work for the press; nor is
it without extreme reluctance that I can bring myself to make
reference to those from whom, during a long period of years, I
have received unvarying kindness; and to seem for a moment,
either to them or to others, reckless of their feelings and ungrateful for their care. None but the strongest motives could
have induced me to attempt a task so arduous.

Why then do I thus appear before the public? The motives
that have actuated me, may be stated in few words. I wish
to warn Protestant parents against being tempted, by the unusual advantages of education, to send their children to Catholic
schools. I am anxious, from the experience of my own mental
sufferings, to caution young people against being led astray by
the fascinating representations of a convent life. I desire to
enter my testimony respecting the idolatry practised in continental convents, and the ignorance in which all are kept of the
word of God; and above all, I feel bound to offer on His altar,
who has so wonderfully delivered me, a grateful acknowledgment of that providential interference, which, unaided by external circumstances, first influenced my mind, and then opened

my path. I know not what further designs are to be accomplished by my singular history. It may be that others are to share the benefit, and to be led from the way of error into the path of peace. In repeated illness, and a delicate constitution, I seem to hear the warning, "Whatsoever thy hand findeth to do, do it with thy might;" and not knowing how short my term on earth may be, I desire to improve the life that yet remains, and leave behind me some record which may alike be useful to others and for the glory of God.

CHAPTER II.

THE CONVENT SCHOOL.

I was born in Cumberland Terrace, Regent's Park, London, in November, 1825. My mother was of an old Yorkshire family, the members of which have been distinguished by their devotion to the Church of Rome. My mother possessed considerable musical and poetical talent, and some of the hymns she composed in her youth are still used in the service of the Church. My father was a German. I remember little of my early years, and as they were marked by no events which could interest the reader, they may as well be passed over in silence. When I was seven years old, circumstances caused our removal to the continent, an event which was shortly after followed by my father's death.

The first trial of my life which I was able vividly to realize, was my separation from an only and dear brother, who was a year and six months older than myself. My mother's brother, being then a priest in office at the Court of Rome, used his influence to place my brother in the college of Santa del a Pedrò. My grief in parting with the dear companion of my childhood, may well be imagined. We who had never been separated for more than a few days, were now doomed to be forever parted. I saw him once, after an interval of nine years, for three hours only, a circumstance which will be referred to in the progress of this narrative.

Mamma's next care was to place me in one of those convent schools, with which the different countries of the continent abound. The convent selected by her was one of those to which reference has been made in the introduction to this narrative. Thus early was I enclosed in the very heart of Popery, and where I should have continued to drag on a miserable existence, had not the mercy of God wonderfully freed me from the dark superstition of earlier days, by bringing me to the knowledge of His truth.

Three days after my brother's removal to Rome, I was taken by mamma to the place where I was to commence my education. I was then between seven and eight years of age. It was in the month of May, 1833, when we arrived at the convent of Amiens, a picturesque chateau situated about a mile from the town, the grounds and scenery most beautifully diversified with hill and dale, and commanding a view of the lofty towers of the well-known cathedral.

The nuns were taking their evening repast. I can well remember the feelings of that night. Oh! how my heart fluttered when I heard the sound of the deep-toned bell that announced our arrival. We were received by the Lady Superioress, who was well known to mamma. I was soon introduced to the pupils of the school, then upwards of fifty in number. The greater part of them were English, and many of them were the children of Protestant parents. As the hour for retiring to rest approached, the young ladies, with their mistress, adjourned to the chapel for night prayers. In the chapel were three altars. The centre or high altar, on which was placed the tabernacle containing the consecrated Host. Over the tabernacle was a painting of the Crucifixion of Christ. On each side of the high altar were two small altars dedicated to St. Joseph and the Blessed Virgin, on which were placed an image of each.

The image of the Virgin was much smaller than that of St. Joseph, but had been retained on account of its reputation for miraculous efficacy, many wonderful performances having been attributed to it. The Virgin's altar was lighted up as on special occasions; and according to custom, when any new pupil, whether Catholic or Protestant, arrived, I was led to it, and in the presence of the assembled school, holding a lighted taper in my hand, I repeated on my knees a form of dedication to her service. The prayer was as follows: " Oh! most blessed and holy Virgin, I, Marie, do now choose you, this day and forever, as my mother advocate, and friend. Deign to receive me as one of your adopted children. Obtain for me the grace to imitate your virtues. Grant that I may be humble, and obedient, and persevering in all Christian duties. Oh! most pious, Oh! most clement Virgin, Mother of our Saviour (Jesus), Queen of Heaven, pray for me who have recourse to you. Hail Mary, &c. Oh! Mary, conceived without sin, pray for me. Amen."

Having repeated this prayer, as dictated to me by one of the nuns, I joined with the rest of the pupils in the litany to the Virgin and other evening prayers; at the close of which I was told to kiss the feet of the image. A number of the young ladies did the same. These were the "Congrágânists," which is a society formed among the pupils for the greater adoration of, and devotion to, the Virgin. It is considered a mark of honor to be received as a member of this society.

On returning from the chapel I was met by the Superioress and another nun, who was appointed by the former to take charge of me. The next morning I was awakened by the loud ringing of a bell, which was the signal to rise. While we were dressing, one of the nuns walked up and down the room repeating the beads to keep the children quiet.

When dressed we assembled to hear mass in the chapel at the hour of seven. I felt startled at the first sight of the whole community entering the chapel; the professed nuns in black veils, and the novices in white, with slow and measured pace in solemn procession passing to their appointed seats. After mass we returned to the young ladies' "Refectory," which was a large room opening out upon the lawn. Two or three nuns were appointed to attend, or, as it was called, "serve" the pupils, but were not permitted to eat with them. Strict silence was kept during meals, except on Sundays and holidays. During breakfast a novice generally read a short lecture. When it was over they dispersed for a short recreation, and at five minutes before nine, a bell tolled to summon them to the school-room. At nine, the great or convent bell tolled for the second matin, or third watch of the day, when every one in the house dropped upon her knees and recited the following prayer :—

"Jesus, Mary, Joseph, I give you my heart, my life, my soul! Jesus, Mary, Joseph, may I breathe forth my soul to you in peace? Divine heart of Mary, pray for me! Immaculate heart of Mary, pray for me! Ave Maria, &c."

The school-room was very large, and hung with pictures of St. Ignatius Loyola, St. Francis de Sales, St. Theresa, St. Angela, and many more. Over the mantel-piece was a large crucifix, and on each side a picture of the sacred hearts of Jesus and Mary. At the end of the room was a splendid altar of white marble, dedicated to the Virgin. Her image was veiled and crowned. A chain of pearl hung round her neck, from which was suspended a gold heart, containing the names of those who had made their first communion that year. This altar and image were dressed every day, the degree of splendor varying according to the supposed importance of the day. The pupils were selected alternately from the class of honor to take charge of this altar. On the great festivals of the Virgin, both altar and image were most gorgeously and expensively dressed.

3

There were several altars in the room belonging to the different classes, and also one devoted to the guardian angel. Over every piano was placed a small altar, with a small stone or wax image of the Virgin. At the principal end of every dormitory was a large altar. On every staircase was an altar; indeed every part of the house abounded with altars to the Virgin. These altars were on special occasions brilliantly lighted, and presented a most imposing spectacle. The most beautiful flowers in costly vases were interspersed with a large number of wax tapers in silver candlesticks, and when lighted up, the whole convent appeared illuminated. The entire cost of dressing and lighting the altar devolved on the pupils, who contributed liberally towards them. Lace, velvet, plate, and jewels, vases, flowers, and candles, were supplied in profusion, and no expense was spared. It was thought a mark of predestination to have a great devotion to the Virgin.

CHAPTER III.

FIRST CONFESSION.

It is a precept of the Romish Church, that the children of Catholic parents shall, from the age of seven, attend confession four times a year, until the period of making their first communion, which generally occurs at the age of ten or twelve. Three months after my settlement at the school, I was included in the number of little girls who should make their confession. The day before, one of the nuns took me aside for the purpose of instructing me in the way to confess. The late amiable and reverend Archbishop of Paris, whose death occurred in the conflicts of June, 1848, was then our curé, and my uncle's colleague; he being Grand Vicar, and my uncle Vicar General. A nun introduced me to the confessional. Father Affré, for by that name he was called in the convent, seeing I was afraid, rose from his seat, and taking me very affectionately by the hand put me to kneel at his feet.

After the usual ceremony of blessing a penitent, I repeated the " Confiteor," as taught me by the nun on the previous day. Having little idea of confession, I stoutly maintained that I was never naughty but when provoked, and proceeded to make complaints of a little girl who had vexed me. " My child," he said, " you are to confess your own sins, not the sins of others." He concluded by giving me, for a penance, the Lord's prayer, and a " Hail Mary," to be said at the Virgin's altar immediately after. Then, blessing, he dismissed me.

About this time the feast of Corpus Christi was celebrated with the usual pomp and splendor. We dressed and garlanded for the occasion, and were instructed to take our part in the erection and decoration of altars. I can well remember the impression it made upon me, even at that early age.

My mother had a sister who had been married a short time before my removal to school, and in eleven months after her marriage was left a widow. When younger, she had a great desire to be a nun, but delicate health at that time prevented the realization of her wish. The circumstance of her husband's death, to whom she was much attached, again created the desire to leave the world, and to devote her property and energies, which were both considerable, to the service of the Church. A visit she made to me confirmed this " vocation," she being much pleased with the community. Three weeks after this interview she entered as a postulant, and three years after took the final vows. In this Society she still remains, a zealous promoter of its interests, temporal and spiritual—being, at the time I left the community, Superioress of one of the continental convents.

Between the age of nine and ten, I was confirmed with the usual pomp of the Romish Church. It being customary to take the name of some saint on this occasion, I took the name of Magdalen.

CHAPTER IV.

FIRST COMMUNION.

My uncle was then residing in Amiens, mamma and he thought a little change necessary for me, and determined upon having me with them for a year or two, an arrangement with which I was much pleased. I went every day for a few hours to the convent to pursue my studies. During this interval, mamma was very anxious to have my brother from college for a short time, knowing the pleasure it would afford to both of us, and her maternal love could never feel reconciled to the idea of that estrangement of the nearest relatives, and suppression of the tenderest natural affections, enjoined by the Church: for the devotees of the Roman Catholic religion are not thought to have arrived at the standard of perfection until they feel that they have broken through every tie of earthly attachment.

My uncle evaded mamma's request, on the plea that it was not well to interrupt my brother's studies. The Order had other ends in view. They feared, at my brother's age, to allow him again to join the domestic circle, lest the affections of earlier days should revive, and he should be induced to renounce the intention he then entertained of preparing for the priesthood. From the time of our separation to this period, I had received from him two letters a year; these were afterwards reduced to one annual epistle.

The time was fast approaching when I must make my first communion, a period of anxiety to all who are preparing for so solemn an occurrence. About fifty of us were selected as candidates, thirty of whom were accepted for that year. Three days before receiving the communion we entered upon a strict " retreat," during which we observed entire silence, abstaining from animal food, and employed the time in meditation and prayers. This " retreat" I made in the convent with the rest of my companions.

The day preceding that of receiving the Eucharist, we each went to confession. On this occasion we are supposed to make a general confession of all the sins we can remember to have committed during the whole of our lives. We receive, for the first time, absolution from the priest, and are supposed to be in a state of grace : no member of the Romish church being allowed to receive the Eucharist, unless he has been previously absolved by his spiritual director.

After absolution one of the nuns taught us to practise the proper mode of receiving the wafer, by giving us one that was not consecrated. The head and mouth must be held in one certain position for receiving the Host. The priest puts it on the tongue, making the sign of the cross, and repeating the words " Corpus Christi" as he does so. It must not be touched by the hand or the teeth. Children are therefore always well practised before receiving it, and the whole would strike a Protestant as profane and disgusting.

The next day we all proceeded to the cathedral of Amiens. On the continent the day of first communion is much thought of, and this was additionally distinguished as the feast of the Annunciation of the Virgin Mary, a day greatly celebrated in Catholic countries. We were all dressed in white, and each communicant had on a white veil confined on the head by a wreath of flowers. We proceeded to the screen of the high sanctuary, where we all remained kneeling, and each holding a lighted taper. The late Archbishop of Paris was at that time Grand Vicar of Amiens, and he celebrated High Mass. After the consecration of the Host and his own communion, he proceeded in the usual form to distribute the sacrament or wafer, each one believing that she received the real body of Christ, " and became the living temple of the Divinity."

On the conclusion of mass we returned to breakfast, for communion is always received fasting. My uncle, who was anxious to add to the happiness of the day, had invited the whole of my companions, the young communicants, to spend the feast with me at his château. The day was spent very happily in play, and in the evening we again attended the cathedral for vespers and benediction, when all the splendors and imposing ceremonies of a continental church were exhibited. The procession of the communicants attended by the priests, bearing the sacrament under a canopy, together with acolytes bearing lighted tapers, and the fumes of the censers, all tended to impress the pompous ceremonies of the day upon the young communicants. When the priests arrived at the Sanctuary, vespers were chanted. The imposing service of " Benediction" followed, and the " Litany of the Virgin" was sung.

On these occasions a very splendid canopy and throne are always placed over the tabernacle for the " remonstrance." This vessel is generally made of gold, and contains a consecrated wafer or host. The wafers placed in the " remonstrance" are stamped to represent the crucifixion, and the lights on the altar, being behind the " remonstrance," shows the figure in transparency. The ringing of bells announces that the sacrament is placed upon the throne for the adoration of the people, who all bow with the greatest reverence, striking their breasts with apparent humility, not daring so much as to look at the glittering idol. This ceremony was concluded by benediction being given in the usual form.

The same service is regularly performed in the Catholic

chapels in England, but the public procession of the Host is confined to Roman Catholic countries.

CHAPTER V.

TWO YEARS AT I———.

AFTER two years spent with my uncle, it was decided that I should be sent to England, as a new convent was about to be established in the vicinity of London for the purpose of educating young ladies. I was accompanied by my aunt and seventeen of the community, nuns and novices included. The house to be occupied by the school was a splendid mansion twelve miles from the city, and previous to the purchase belonged to a nobleman. The school commenced with five pupils, including myself, but our numbers soon increased, and in the space of six months we had fifty. At this time the pupils are seventy in number, and alterations are contemplated to admit of the reception of a hundred. Many of the pupils, even in this country, are children of Protestant parents.

On the first commencement of this school the altars and images were not introduced to the same extent as on the continent; but those members of the community who were appointed to conduct the school, gradually, and almost imperceptibly, prepared the minds of the children to erect altars. It was not designed to shock them by too sudden an introduction of Popish observances. At the present time, none of the continental convents surpass that of I—— in the splendor and value of its decorations and images. Every month the community and pupils have their procession round the extensive grounds, the priest carrying the Host, as in Catholic countries, and one of the children bearing an image of the Virgin.

The worldly advantages of a convent education in England, induce many inconsiderate parents and guardians to expose their children to the dangerous snares so early laid for them, by the deep and crafty schemes of Popery. The facilities for acquiring the continental languages, by general conversation with foreign members of the community, present one *great* allurement, tending *greatly* to increase the number of pupils in this Society.

In each of the five convents in England there is the same adoration of the Virgin and the saints, and the same superstitious ideas are infused into the minds of the young. Blessed medals, beads, &c., are constantly imported from the continent. The pupils have also a society called the " poor souls," to which they subscribe weekly, some a penny, others more. This all goes into a general fund to pay for masses, to be said for the souls of poor deceased persons whose friends cannot afford to pay for them. The poorer Catholics apply to the nuns to get a mass said, and the cost is paid out of this subscription. The lowest sum paid to a priest for saying mass is half-a-crown. I was several times appointed treasurer to this Society, and upon two occasions paid as much as two pounds for different masses for the souls of the dead.

The Vigil of All Souls is an evening on which the grossest superstition is practised, and the most ridiculous tales are told. I have frequently on this night heard the nuns say, " O how anxiously the poor souls in purgatory are waiting for the office of the dead to be said," adding a hope that such a one if still in purgatory would be released. They commence the office with most devoted, but misguided zeal, to pray for the repose of the dead ; and I have frequently heard of several who, in the excited state of their imagination, have fancied they have seen little black objects which were souls escaped from purgatory.

CHAPTER VI.

DEATH OF A PUPIL AT CHATEAUROUX.

At the age of fourteen I returned to the convent of Amiens. A few days after my arrival I met with a serious accident, which kept me in bed for nearly three months. Many were the superstitious remedies used during this confinement, such as blessed medals, and water from St. Victoire's well; and my recovery was at last attributed to the use of linen that had been touched by the dead hand of a saint—a relic held in great veneration by the Roman Catholics on the continent. My feelings revolt with horror, when I reflect on the shocking superstition of which I have been a witness and a partaker.

Soon after this illness, my health requiring a warmer climate, I was again removed to another of the convent schools; this convent was at Chateâuroux, about fifty miles from Paris, where I stayed nearly a year. While there a circumstance occurred which I cannot forbear to mention.

In the school was a young lady of reserved and rather melancholy disposition. She had early lost her mother, who was a Protestant, and had subsequently seen some of her Protestant relations. Her retiring and apparently distant habits, prevented her making a confidant of either nun or pupil. When opportunity afforded, she would retire alone to a distant part of the grounds. Anne, for that was her name, was not devout in the observances of the Catholic religion, and never attended confession but when compelled by the rules of the convent, namely, at each Indulgence; and sometimes even on these occasions she was dismissed by the priest because she would not speak a word.

At the time I was at Chat-âuroux Anne was sixteen, and had
3*

been in the convent five years. A short time before I left she was seized with inflammation of the lungs, which proved fatal. The week before her death it was deemed advisable that she should see her confessor, to which she had a great objection. Father P—— visited her, and appointed that afternoon to hear her confession. Before Father P—— arrived, Anne told sister A——, the Infirmarian, that she did not intend to make any confession ; and we were all assembled in the chapel to pray to the Virgin, that Anne might be induced to receive worthily the last sacraments. I shall never forget the excitement of that day. Then I thought it a very sad event, but now I do not doubt that God had caused a purer light to shine upon her, and that she had, even amidst the darkness of Popish error, been a secret disciple of Jesus.

While we were in the oratory upon our knees, many of us weeping, the Superioress entered apparently in great distress. " Pray for poor Anne. She will not confess. Father P——' has been entreating her for the last hour, and she will not answer a word. Promise the Blessed Virgin ten communions, make ten confessions and receive the communion ten times each, for the poor souls in purgatory, if she will grant your requests." Many were the communions promised, but those were of no avail, Anne remained resolute. All that she said was, " that she would confess to her uncle," who was a priest, " if she might see him."   He was sent for, but when he was told of the affair he declined hearing her confession, as she had refused to con- fess to her appointed confessor. The Superioress told us that she was very anxious to confess to her uncle, but I doubt not that she wished to reveal to him the real state of her mind.

The more I reflect on the conduct of this somewhat singular girl, the more I am convinced that she sought the forgiveness of her sins, solely through the blood of Christ. She died a few days after this exciting scene. Not any of the pupils visited her until an hour previous to her death, when we were all summoned to unite in prayer for the dying Anne. I, and five other pupils, with several of the community, remained by her bed-side repeating prayers for the "agonizing." She was insensible to all around her. One of the nuns placed in her hand a crucifix, and in a few minutes afterwards Anne expired. The priest intimated that her disregard of the sacrament had exposed her to the power of Satan, and long held up her example as a warning to us.

CHAPTER VII.

THE NOVITIATE.

Soon after this event I removed to Switzerland, where the community have a large convent, about a mile from Geneva. In this convent is the only noviitate of the Society. Novices are obliged by the rules of the Order to spend two years of strict retreat or noviceship. A separate wing of the building is set apart for the novitiate, and is entirely distinct from that occupied by the pupils.

The novices are superintended by two senior nuns, who are "Mistresses of Novices." Their business is to instruct and pre-pare the former for a life of implicit and slavish obedience. The novices are not permitted under any circumstances to speak to each other, or accept the most trifling article, even so much as a pin, without express permission from the Reverend Mother or Mistress. They are treated quite as children, having no will of their own. Whatever their former rank or station in life, all, when required, are alike sent to perform the most menial offices of the house. I have frequently seen novices brushing shoes, washing dishes, scouring rooms, cleaning the children's hair, &c. The occupations that the nuns would prefer are purposely interdicted, and those to which they feel the greatest repugnance, enforced. This is done in order to break their will, and destroy all feelings of worldly importance.

This discipline commences while they are postulants, and increases in rigor after they become novices. In my own case, drawing being a favorite pursuit, was the one which, when I became a postulant, I was not permitted to pursue. Such is the passive obedience required; and should any novice disobey the command of her Superior, the most humiliating penances are inflicted alike on postulant, novice, and nun.

The two years' noviceship is spent in study, that the novices may be quite prepared for their future duties, viz. instructing the pupils of the school; and they are inured to the practice of "religious obedience" and "holy poverty" by the humiliations before mentioned. The time they spend in other convents as novices is not reckoned into this period; so that some remain novices for four or five years, and sometimes longer. It is in this convent that novices are professed, that is, make their final vows. This is a most solemn and affecting scene. During my stay in this convent I saw six novices take the black veil, two of whom were not more than twenty years of age.

The ceremony of receiving the white veil rarely occurs in the convent of Carrouge. I shall take occasion to describe both hereafter.

It may not perhaps be generally known, that as soon as a lady enters a religious community, she gives up the whole of her property to the Society. It is placed at the exclusive disposal of the foundress, for the benefit of the Order. The nuns do much more than support themselves by the education of the young, so that large sums are continually expended for the advantage of the Church. The Bishop or Vicar of the district in which the convent is situated, has power to call upon the Society for any sum he may deem requisite for the erection of a church or monastery, or for the support of the priesthood. This power does not extend to the Sisterhood of Charity and Mercy, but is restricted to convents of education, so that the Church of Rome has resources amply sufficient for any proposed object.

During my stay at Carrouge, I had a severe and almost fatal illness. I was afraid to die, because I thought I had performed no good works, or had not used any self-mortifications, to satisfy God for the punishment due to my sins (for I was not, up to this period, a strict devotee). I did not then know that the death of Christ had made full atonement, and that IIis blood could alone cleanse me from sin.

On my recovery, I determined to consecrate myself to a life of holiness, by endeavoring to satisfy God with works of super-erogation and strict penance ; and in order to carry out this more effectually, I renewed my dedication to the Virgin, in the presence of the whole school.

While I was at Carrouge, not less than twenty young ladies entered upon their noviceship, seven of whom had been my school companions. Three of them were converts to the Roman Catholic faith. One who was called Sister M—— B——, had, while in the convent of Amiens, been my most intimate friend and companion, but when she became a "religieuse," all communication was forbidden, and she was not permitted to speak to me, though in the same convent, without permission, and then only on general topic ; for it is against the rules of the Society for novices or nuns to have any confidential conversation with any pupil, or with each other ; they are of course at liberty at any time to speak to their Superioress, she being the only one with whom they are allowed to hold private conferences. If a novice is seen speaking to a pupil on a subject unconnected with the duties of the school, it is immediately reported to the Superioress, and she has to undergo reproof or penance for this simple offence. It is made a point of conscience with every nun, novice, and postulant, to report all that she may hear. My conscience never being so tender on this point as others, I have now the pleasure of recollecting that I never brought any nun or novice into trouble.

Being once enjoined to relate the subject of some trifling discussion with one of the novices in the dormitory, in which she was the faulty party, I refused to give the particulars. "You will be obliged to tell when you are a novice," said the nun who was sent to investigate the business. "Well, Mother A——, I will wait till then," and so the matter terminated.

Novices are strictly prohibited all avoidable intercourse with their family and friends. They are only allowed to write to their parents once a year, and they never receive more than three or four letters. If more letters come for them they are kept back. All letters are sent to the Reverend Mother General, or her provincial deputy, and opened and read by her before they are forwarded to the postulants, novices, or nuns ; and all letters written by them in reply, must be perused and sealed by her.

When she is in another country, long delay often occurs in consequence ; and a letter from a dying parent may not be received till after his or her decease. I knew one novice, an only daughter, who did not hear of her mother's death till three months after it took place. The letter conveying the intelligence was written in Scotland, and sent to Carrouge, the head quarters of the Very Reverend Mother, who was at that time in Ireland. It was sent from Carrouge to Ireland, and after inspection was forwarded to the bereaved daughter at Amiens. The letter was given to her as one of ordinary import, and she was expected to go about her customary duties immediately after its reception. This is a specimen of many similar circumstances which occur to my memory. Should the Reverend Mother find anything in a letter that does not meet her approval, it is withheld, and its arrival remains unknown to its owner, unless it accidentally transpires at some future time.

CHAPTER VIII.

TAKING THE WHITE VEIL.

THE winter months being so very severe in Switzerland and my health at that time in a very precarious state, my mother, with my medical attendant, deemed it advisable to remove me from the convent of Carrouge. My aunt, who had been with me a few months at Carrouge, was then at Nice, and thither it was determined at once to send me.

It was in October, 1841, that I reached the convent at Nice, where the Society had a large school, there being upwards of a hundred pupils. A few weeks after my arrival, four postulants were to be " professed," or to take the white veil.

This ceremony I had frequently witnessed, but not having as yet described it, I may as well do so in brief. The ceremony is at all times most affecting and imposing. Before receiving the habit, the postulants commenced that series of rigid preparations and observances known by the term "retreat." For nine days they refrained from animal food, observed the fasts of the Church, and maintained strict silence. Their emaciated countenances and melancholy expression, as we passed them in the cloistered walks, where they resorted occasionally for exercise and meditation, conveyed the impression of mental suffering. One of the four belonged to the noble and illustrious family of the Count de Belline. She was a sweet and amiable girl of somewhat pensive disposition. She never seemed to regain her spirits, and died nine months after her profession, at the age of eighteen.

On the evening previous to taking the veil they make their last general confession to the Bishop, he being the only one allowed, by the laws of the Church, to hear the general confession of those who were to receive the veil. Great preparations were made, and every hand was employed.

The chapel was decorated in its gorgeous attire, the neophytes remaining kneeling before the Blessed Sacrament, as it is termed, until the first "nocturn," or the hour of midnight. They then retire to rest for a short time, to fit them for the solemn duties of the following day.

The convent is quite a scene of gaiety, for the friends and relations of the neophytes are generally invited to be spectators of the scene. The presence of relatives is also frequently required to sign legal documents; the interest of all property belonging to the novices being made over to the church: the principal is reserved till they take the black veil.

At seven o'clock the four novices received communion as usual, and at ten high mass was performed by the Bishop in the presence of a large assembly. After mass the community retired for a few minutes, and re-appeared with the four neophytes beautifully attired as brides, each attended by two pupils as bridesmaids, whose office was to raise her veil on her arrival at the steps of the sanctuary. The organ and choir then commenced the chaunt of "Dominus non sum dignus, &c." At the conclusion the usual ceremonies were performed, and prayers repeated.

The Reverend Mother General then presented the Bishop with the four habits, or dresses, which the novices were afterwards to wear. These he proceeded to bless, and then presented one to each postulant, at the same time cutting off a large lock of their hair. The four novices, who had taken the names of Sister Mary Stanislaus, Sister Mary Winifred, Sister Mary Clotille, and Sister Mary Magdalene, returned to the house carrying their habits. While the choir were chanting the Litany of the Virgin, the novices were being dressed in their new habits by an appointed nun; their hair was cut short round; and when completely attired they returned, each carrying her bridal dress. After a few more prayers were repeated, the novices were asked if they finally renounced the world, and replied in the affirmative. They then threw their dresses on the steps of the altar, and trampled upon them,—this being figurative of trampling upon the things of the world. The Bishop presented them with a crucifix and a rosary. After giving them the Benediction of the Sacrament in the usual form, the ceremony was concluded. The rest of the day was devoted to recreation and pleasure by all parties.

CHAPTER IX.

MENTAL DISQUIETUDE.

The festival of Christmas soon followed the profession of the novices. It is during this feast that the most profane idolatry is practised.

A wax doll, representing the infant Jesus, was dressed in the most costly attire; and a bed of satin, decorated with laces and wreaths of flowers. The Virgin's altar was erected, the covering being of velvet, embroidered with gold. The bed was placed in the centre of this altar, with a large number of vases, &c., containing the most expensive flowers; and wax tapers in silver candlesticks and lustres, added to the splendor of the scene.

At the hour of twelve, immediately before the celebration of the fast mass, on Christmas morning, one of the nuns entered the chapel, and placed the Infant on the bed prepared for it. The candles were then lighted, and the whole of the community and pupils, permitted to attend this service, fell on their knees in adoration to the Infant, repeating the Litany of the infant Jesus. Mass was performed by the priests.

At that time I was often perplexed with the strange contradiction of adoration, for the altar of the Infant was to the right of the high altar, where is kept the consecrated Host. In passing the former, we bowed in adoration to the Infant doll, and again bowed in going before the high altar. I could not receive the idea of Christ being present as God in the form of wafer in the tabernacle, and in the form of an Infant on the altar of the Virgin.

In this convent there was an artificial tear upon the cheek of the wax image, it being customary in Italy to represent the infant Jesus as having been born with a tear of sorrow.

Since that time I have frequently dressed the doll for this occasion, and this occupation was one of the very many circumstances that tended to shake my faith in the Romish doctrines.

The chapel of the convent of Nice being open for public worship at stated periods, I had an opportunity of witnessing the spectacle of an Italian congregation, who, on entering the chapel for midnight mass, all knelt in adoration to the infant Jesus, as it were to pay him homage. I must not forget to mention that in the cross room we had an altar of the infant Jesus, which belonged exclusively to the young ladies.

This doll representing the Infant remains on the altars until after the feast of the Epiphany; and in this interval these altars are every night lighted, the same adoration paid, and the litany daily repeated. At the time I was endeavoring to fulfil the resolutions I had made during my illness, I was, to the utmost of my power, strict in the observance of my religious duties, and sought every opportunity for self-denial and subjection of my own will. I went to confession and communion every fortnight, and also communicated on certain feasts, when indulgences are granted by the Church to those who worthily communicate; but with all these outward observances I never felt the happier: they rather increased my restlessness and fear of death, for I was at that period in a very precarious state of health. Sometimes, in confession, I named these fears to my confessor, who always replied that it was presumptuous in me to expect it otherwise, and that the constant fear of death was one of the crosses apportioned to all mankind. It was a circumstance that often created some surprise, that the " religieuses" should have such a dread of death.

After I had entered the community as a postulant, I frequently heard several of the Society express a wish to die on certain days. Some would prefer Good Friday, because they could hope for more confidence; others would prefer one of the feasts of the Virgin, because they could better claim her intercession, and Catholics believe that whatever the Virgin requests of her Son is immediately granted, and that no petition of hers is rejected.

CHAPTER X.

REMOVAL TO MANOTTE.

My uncle was, in the year 1842, removed by the Pope from his appointment as Vicar General to that of Grand Vicar of Nice.

The duties incident on this change of office required him to spend a greater portion of the year in travelling, and he, therefore, decided upon resigning his establishment of Amiens. This arrangement prevented mamma's longer stay with him, and she resolved upon entering the convent of ———— as a boarder. Her feelings were of late years much inclined to the life of a "religieuse," but that was legally impossible so long as her children remained under age.

The convent of Manotte was the one selected for mamma's future residence, being the most retired. She entered in 1843. When my health permitted it I joined her in this convent, and remained there till the time of her death, which occurred two years afterwards.

This convent was the scene of two of the most melancholy circumstances of my life—the last interview with my brother, and my dearest mamma's death.

My relations, and also several of the nuns, had a great wish that I should become a nun; and for the furtherance of this object a Novena of thirty days to the Virgin was commenced, for the purpose of interceding with her that a vocation might be given me.

When any particular object is desired, the Reverend Mother communicates it to all the convents of the Society, requesting them to commence a Novena to the Virgin or certain saints for so many days, varying from nine to thirty. This Novena is performed as follows:—perpetual adoration before the sacrament, the nuns being relieved in succession, and certain prayers repeated. The one used on this occasion is too long to transcribe. It is called "the thirty days Novena to the Virgin," and concludes thus:—" Oh! glorious and ever blessed Virgin, comfort the hearts of thy supplicants by obtaining for us (specifying the request), and as we are persuaded our Divine Saviour knows thee as his beloved Mother, to whom he can refuse nothing, let us speedily experience the efficacy of thy powerful intercession, according to the tenderness of thy maternal affections. Oh! most Blessed Virgin, besides the object of our present petition, obtain for us, of thy dear Son, our Lord and our

God, a lively faith, firm hope, perfect charity, true contrition, a horror of sin, love of God and our neighbor, contempt of the world, and patience and resignation under the trials and afflictions of this life. Obtain likewise for us, oh! sacred Mother of God, the great gift of true perseverance, and the grace to receive the last sacraments worthily at the hour of death. Lastly, obtain, we beseech thee, for the souls of our parents, brethren, relatives, and benefactors, both living and dead, life everlasting. Amen."

The Novena was joined by most of the pupils of the school, but it was not for some time after that I was at all disposed to join the Society; and then not so much from choice as from the peculiar circumstances in which I was placed as an orphan, that I was at all induced to enter on the first step of a "religieuse."

Much as I have since regretted that first step, I cannot but look back upon it as one link in that chain of providential circumstances which ended in my subsequent deliverance: since, but for that fuller insight into the system which I obtained as a postulant, I could not have been so thoroughly convinced of its absurdities and enormities.

CHAPTER XI.

VISIT OF MY BROTHER.

It was on a gloomy day, in the month of January, 1843, when my studies were interrupted by the agreeable intelligence from my aunt, that my uncle had returned from Rome, and was then waiting to see me in the reception room. I was delighted, and hastened to meet him. On going down the corridor I met my mamma; she was much agitated, and passed quickly by me without speaking.   On entering the room, I was much surprised to find my uncle accompanied by a young gentleman, and to me apparently a stranger.   He rose to shake hands with me, evidently much excited.   I repulsed him for (as I deemed it) freedom, and returned his salutation with a cool movement.

He could no longer restrain himself, but exclaimed in the affectionate language of infant days, " Marie, don't you know me ?"   These words instantly recalled him to my recollection, and convinced me that it was not the voice of a stranger.   No; it was that of my dear and only brother whom I had not seen for nine years.   He had returned from Rome for the purpose of bidding mamma and myself farewell, before making the vows of a Jesuit priest.

It was a final parting in this world, though I little thought it at the time.   He died the following year.   Mamma and I remained in ignorance of our loss till a month after his death. This interview lasted only three hours, for the next morning he left with another priest for Rome, and was professed as a novice at Santa del a Pedrò, on the feast of the Purification, which occurs in the month of February.   I felt the separation from him after this meeting more keenly than before.   This visit was very trying to mamma.   Her inability to suppress her feelings would not allow her to be present on our first interview. This accounted for her agitation in the corridor, and it renewed her maternal anxiety on his account.

CHAPTER XII.

RELIGIOUS DOUBTS.

IT was soon after my brother's visit, that the subject of the Eucharist began to occupy my attention. The doctrine which enforces that Jesus is present in body and soul in the wafer, and that all communicants partake in reality of his flesh and blood was, of all the tenets of Popery, to me the most fearful.

The doubts thus raised I then believed to be a temptation of Satan, and endeavored as much as possible to dismiss them from my mind, but without success. Sometimes when receiving communion I have recoiled with horror, when the priest removed the " Host" from the " ciborium." I trembled at the thought that it was Jesus Christ in his body and blood that the celebrant held in his hands ; and when he put the wafer in my mouth I shuddered, at the idea of a creature eating his Creator. I cannot now write it without the same impression.

At this period I began to inquire (a subject that had never occurred to me before) why the priests drank the wine, or (as Catholics believe) the blood of Christ in the form of wine ; and why the chalice or cup was withheld from the laity. These, in the first instance, being rather a matter of inquiry than of doubt, I did not mention them to my confessor, but asked my parent, who was displeased with my curiosity, and reproved me for my inquisitiveness. I was not satisfied with this rebuke, but shortly after named it again to her and my aunt ; the reply was, " that I reasoned too much, and that I ought not to question the authority of the Church, she being our only guide, and that whatever she arranged or commanded was right ;" and they concluded this lecture by hoping I would not again ask curious and improper questions. But though I refrained from pressing this subject further, I could not forbear pondering it over in my mind.

On going one day to my little sacristy (the sacristan being the place where I kept the ornaments for the altars) I found a little book, whether placed accidentally or intentionally by mamma I do not know. It was a short life of St. Elizabeth of Hungary. In the early part of her life she had experienced the same suggestions of Satan (as they were termed in this book), but escaped this snare by submitting her own will and opinion ;—and suffering herself to be entirely guided by the authority of the Church, attained to eminent sanctity, and the close of her life was distinguished by many miracles. I read this book with great interest; and it, for a time, had the de-sired effect in stifling those convictions of the truth that had just begun to dawn on my darkened understanding. I con-tinued to follow in the same round of religious observances, often frequented confession and communion, but my heart con-stantly sighed after something it seemed to want, and was not truly at ease. My wandering and sometimes agitated mind could not find any object on which to rest. I was a stranger to that peace revealed in the simple truths of the gospel, for among the votaries of the Romish faith the Scriptures are but little known. The attempt to teach religion without the Bible, and to raise the decisions of the Pope and council above those of the inspired volume, demands from her devotees the surren-der of their judgment and will to her authority.

I have met with several young Catholic pupils on the conti-nent who have been altogether ignorant of the existence of such a book, and was myself ten years of age before I understood the meaning of the word Scriptures. I had imagined them to be a mere record of the councils of the Church. The latter are instilled betimes into the minds of the young, but nothing is said to them of the Word of God, which all are alike com-manded to search for themselves.

In the convent-schools of England there is an abridgment
of the leading characters mentioned in the sacred writings, but
even this poor apology for the Bible is withheld from the continental convents; for it was not till I came to England, at
twelve years of age, that I was aware of such a one being used.
In the Missal, it is true, there are several selections from the
Bible for the different feasts for the day, but these are shockingly
perverted statements; and, such as they are, children are not
permitted to use a Missal for some time after their first communion,—the devotions for mass being the prayer-book used
by them at that service. I have for years known that frequently
Protestants bring a Bible with them, but when the nuns examine their trunks, before allowing them to be removed to their
appropriate places, take this and every book from them. It is
considered to contain heretical sentiments. So careful is the
Society of any of these entering the convent, that on one occasion a Protestant History of England, which for a time had remained unobserved, was discovered by a nun, and found to contain Protestant sentiments; it was instantly burnt, and the
young English lady was severely punished. This is but one of
the many similar circumstances I have witnessed on the continent.

CHAPTER XIII.

MAMMA'S DEATH.

Having already alluded to the melancholy circumstance of
my brother's death, I shall briefly go on to state, that this severe dispensation was soon followed by a still heavier bereavement.

My dear mamma had long been suffering from an affection
of the heart; the shock of my brother's death had caused an
acute and serious attack of this disease; she rallied for a little
time, but all my fond hopes of her recovery were soon to be
blasted. I was not informed of her danger, or at least the im-
probability of her restoration, until the night before she wished
to bid me adieu. On the following morning I was summoned
to her room, to see her for the last time previous to her receiving the last sacraments. She had felt much and keenly, the
distressing situation in which I should be placed as an orphan;
and also the impossibility there was of my residing under the
protection of my uncle's paternal roof, as that would be forbidden by the laws of the Church, after the death of my parent.

This increased her desire for me to become a religieuse, and
she knew that everything would be done by the Society, and
by my uncle, to meet this vocation. In several conversations
with me during her illness she expressed this wish, and the happiness it would afford her in her dying hour, to be assured that
I had determined upon this as my future course. I accordingly
promised her one day that I would try the life of a nun, but
preferred waiting at least two years before I entered as a postulant. This promise I fulfilled, though it cost me considerable
sacrifice of feeling and principle.

The morning of the day previous to that of her death, I was
summoned to her bedside, and was told that my parent desired
to take a final leave, as all distractions are avoided by Catholics
after partaking of the last sacraments; and she was so weak,
that, with the peculiar character of her disease, the least excitement might have proved fatal. She was not able to say much,
further than giving me her maternal advice if I should return
to the world; but at the same time expressed the satisfaction
she felt on leaving me with the impression of my becoming a
nun. She desired me to pray for the repose of her soul, and
begged of me to unite my petitions for the repose of the souls

of my father and brother, for whom I must frequently hear mass (that is, offer it up on their behalf), by communicating on the anniversaries of their respective deaths, and enjoined me to have as many masses offered as were possible for me to obtain.

None but those who have witnessed the restless expression of a dying person clinging to this last delusive hope of remission in the grave, can picture the agonizing look of my beloved parent, when she clasped my hand, saying, "*Promise me*, you will do this." Oh! that I could then have directed her to that Saviour whose merits alone could save, and whose blood could cleanse from sin. But I was then ignorant of these sacred truths, and in my misguided zeal promised to do as she required. This promise I kept until the Spirit of God convinced me of the wickedness of the doctrine of purgatory.

I did not see my beloved parent again; she died the following night. Masses were celebrated for her by my uncle and several other priests to whom my uncle had sent, and these are continued yearly. My deceased parent was interred five days after her death, in the church of St. Jose, Manotté.

After my dear mamma's interment, it was decided that I should remain in the Society as a pupil until entering as a postulant, and should also reside, as usual, in the same convent with my aunt.

CHAPTER XIV.

DIFFICULTIES ABOUT PURGATORY.

I REMAINED at Manotté for a fortnight after this bereavement. The next place I visited was the convent of E——, in the south of France, one that I had not before seen. It is in the vicinity of Lyons, and had then been recently commenced.

Owing to some circumstances for which I could not account, my aunt remained but six weeks with me. I was left behind, without any previous notice of her leaving; but on account of the depression and loneliness I felt after my late bereavement, I prevailed upon the Reverend Mother to allow me to return to Manotté, where my aunt was again staying.

About this period I began to feel a desire, or rather curiosity, to see a Bible; for it was by little things that God gradually led me to see the system of iniquity until He thoroughly convinced me, by His Holy Spirit, of the shocking enormities practised and enforced. I could not satisfy my mind with the mysterious doctrine of the Eucharist, and was much perplexed with the subject of purgatory; for my parent's death had caused me to think more about it.

I continued to offer up prayers daily for the repose of her soul. I thought, suppose she were not out of purgatory before the death of those who were interested in her happiness, would she have to endure longer torments because there was no one to pray for masses, and to offer up prayers for her. This suggestion distressed me greatly, for I thought others might fail to remember her in their petitions. Then again it struck me very forcibly that I might go on praying for her, and getting masses said for her, and still continue to feel unhappy about her, when at the same time she might have been released from purgatory, and I ignorant of it. I might have spent thousands of pounds, had they been in my possession, for this purpose, and still be no wiser; perhaps one mass would have released her, and yet hundreds of masses would probably be offered up for her; the thought occurred to me—if these are of avail and acceptable in the sight of God, what becomes of them, for it will not benefit mamma if she is in heaven.

With these reflections, I thought how much I should like to see what the Bible stated on the doctrine of purgatory, feeling assured that if I could only read that book from which the priests had their authority, my mind would be fully satisfied. All that I then wished was, just to read that part that treated on purgatory, little dreaming that there was no such doctrine taught in the simple Word of God.

Oh! if there is one perversion greater than another in the Church of Rome, it is that of Purgatory; it is by that she strengthens and supports this system of iniquity. The very idea of a man bartering, as it were, the souls of his fellow-creatures is horrible; for the rich, who can give large sums of money, are soon released from their torments; but the poor, who are not so fortunate as to get any human person to assist them, their souls must remain a longer period in the place of sorrow.

On mentioning these subjects one day, in the way of question, how it was that masses must be paid for, it being no more trouble to the priest, as he would have to say mass just the same if he was not paid;—the answer given me was, that the Bible declared that "Alms made an atonement for sin." This passage I have now discovered to be no part of the inspired writings, it being a quotation from the Apocrypha, which is not any part of them. I was also told that the overplus of masses offered for deceased relatives were referred to the account of the donors, so that they would avail for them when dead.

I have frequently heard instances in which persons have paid, during their lifetime, large sums of money yearly for different objects, with the prospect of having the sacrifice of the mass offered on their decease. It is this doctrine that embitters the dying hour, as it leaves them destitute of that hope of immediate happiness in the presence of their Saviour, which the Protestant is taught in the Scriptures to entertain.

It is binding on every penitent to confess sins of "thought, word and deed;" it was therefore a duty to mention my views of one of the first questions in the examinations of conscience, which is, "Have you any thought against your faith, and have

you wilfully entertained thoughts tending to heretical sentiments ?"   I named to my confessor the thoughts that occurred
to me, and expressed a wish that he would solve my difficulties
on this point.   I asked him if he would allow me to have a
Bible for a short time, thinking it the best plan to arrive at a
satisfactory statement; but his reproof I shall never forget.
He said, " that if the Church had thought it requisite or pro-
fitable for her children to allow them to read the Bible indis-
criminately, they would have done so ; but the Church, to
whom God has given all power, and whom Christ had promised
to be with to the end of the world and teach her all truth, seeing that men ' wrested the Scriptures to their own destruction,'
wisely limited the disposal of them to her priests, who were the
only depositaries of them."

I felt somewhat perplexed at this rebuke, and thought it
very strange that the Word of God could lead men to destruction, and I wept at so stern a rebuke, for I was both miserable
and discontented with all my religious performances, and was
very unhappy in consequence of my beloved parent's death.   I
felt desolate and without any hope upon which I could really
rest.

There is one circumstance that occurs to my memory in reference to purgatory, that perhaps will serve to show the peculiar views I took upon one subject.   The Romish church asserts,
" that all persons go to purgatory who have not in this world
satisfied God for the temporal punishments due to sin, but the
eternal punishment of which sins have been remitted by sacraments of penance ; that is, they have been by absolution and
the sacraments absolved from mortal guilt, but die in a venial
state."   A question occurred to me in reference to those persons
who would be living at the day of judgment that were not in
a state of mortal sin, yet, according to the Romish doctrine,
will not go to heaven, until they have been purified of their
guilt, without purgatory.   How, I asked myself, could they be

released, for no masses had been said for them? this appeared a great mystery to me. I asked one of my confessors this question, hear the absurdity of his reply: "That the Church supposed God would cause them to feel as much and great torments in a few minutes as years spent in purgatory." It was by such absurd replies as these that all my important queries were answered; but as the Spirit of God continued to enlighten and convince me of the glaring errors of Popery, these evasive answers failed to satisfy me.

CHAPTER XV.

THE DYING NUN.

THE great test of religion is in a dying hour, when all human efforts cease to avail the expiring victim. Should this book fall into the hands of any who may be tempted to be drawn aside by the fascinations and delusions of Popery, and be persuaded voluntarily to resign the liberty of a Gospel dispensation for the bondage of the Romish priesthood; to such I could with all earnestness (as one who has tried and proved it in all its observances both with sincerity and zeal) urge them to reflect ere they take the final step. Let the painful history of one, of whose life and dying hours I was a witness, make as great an impression on their minds as it did on mine; for from this sad scene I may note my first real convictions of the errors of the Church of Rome, and my subsequent conversion to God. I have before stated that I had a great fear of death, and many times when I have laid down to sleep I have been terrified lest I should die before morning. It was the idea of suffering in purgatory, and the fears I had that masses should not be offered up for me, as I had not property to devote to that purpose. During this mental suffering the death of one, to whom I am alluding, increased my difficulties.

E. A. W—— was a native of England, and daughter of Protestant parents: she became a convert to the Romish faith. This event was soon followed by her entering our Society as a postulant, and in three years after she made vows which irrevocably bound her for life. The devotedness and enthusiasm with which Mother Stanislaus pursued the rigid observance of every duty, her zeal and outward piety, combined with a naturally amiable disposition, gave her the appellation of "perfect saint." I often wished I had arrived at that perfection she appeared to have attained.

In three of the convents I had visited she had been one of the mistresses. At the period of which I write, we were at the convent of Manotté. I was much attached to her, and this attachment, as far as convent rules would permit it, was reciprocal.

That winter she was seized with consumption, and lingered for some time. During the last few weeks of her life, her fear of death and mental agitation increased. All attempts to familiarize her with the approaching event proved unavailing; as soon as the subject was referred to (for I frequently said to her, "Mother Stanislaus, when you get to heaven will you pray for me") she would burst into tears, and tell me that I should need to pray for her that she might be released from purgatory.

Being at this time, through ill-health, unable to pursue my studies, I was often the companion of Mother Stanislaus in the infirmary, and frequently for exercise attended her in the day-time, and assisted her in repeating the "rosary," and read with her the "devotions for the sick." But there was not that desire in Mother Stanislaus for the different prayers to be repeated that I have witnessed in other Catholics; on the contrary, I have had to remind her to repeat her beads, to which sometimes she replied, "I am too tired, you say them for my intention."

Owing to her fearful anticipations of death, the Reverend Mother had, as a great favor, obtained a crucifix that had been blessed purposely by the Pope for a happy death. It is customary for all the nuns to keep one against this period; but it was thought if poor Mother Stanislaus had one blessed expressly for her, it would inspire her with confidence.. My uncle took the crucifix to the Pope, and was present during the ceremony of blessing. He immediately forwarded it to Manotté, with a small present of beads and medals for myself; among which was a seal of the Pope's, called the "Agnus Dei,"* or consecrated wax, sealed with the holy seal of the Church, to preserve me in all danger. My aunt, who was then Superioress, told me to take the cross and also my uncle's letter respecting it, and read it to Mother Stanislaus. I was much elated at receiving this commission, sincerely rejoicing to think that I could in any way add to her comfort, for I loved her very dearly.

When I entered the room for the first time that morning I was shocked to find so great a change in her appearance. I went up to her bedside and exclaimed, "Oh, Mother Stanislaus, the crucifix is come, and I have brought it to you : it is blessed purposely for you, that you may have a happy death ; are you not pleased ?" But what a look and answer to my question. She raised her expressive and then ghastly face towards me, and pushing from her my hand which held the crucifix, said, " Marie, I have done wrong ; the religion I have embraced and followed will not support me in a dying hour." She then sank upon her pillow and wept bitterly. I tried to pacify her, but it was of no avail : she continued to weep : I had soon after to leave the room. I gave my aunt an account of the interview. I was not allowed to see her again. She died the next morning.

* This wax is consecrated in the first year of the Pope's accession.

I could not shake off this melancholy scene from my mind: it haunted me by day and by night. I thought if she who was so holy and devoted, and who tried the Catholic religion to the uttermost, found it would not support *her* in a dying hour, what was I to do?

One of the nuns told me that Mother Stanislaus was not conscious of what she said :—that her mind was weak through protracted suffering. This for a time quieted my fears, but my disquietude soon returned. The sacraments of penance became wearisome, and daily more repulsive. I no longer felt the same anxious desire as formerly of frequenting the confessional, for my impression then was, that it was no use mortifying and denying myself every gratification if it would not render me happier when I came to die than Mother Stanislaus. Then I reflected upon one dear to me, now no more, who disowned religion altogether, and became a follower of Voltaire, and I ceased to wonder at the unhappy circumstance.

I cannot refrain from praising God with heartfelt gratitude, that He did not leave me, but wonderfully preserved me from every kind of scepticism, and led me to embrace the truth as it is in Jesus; and, strange as it may appear, I can but acknowledge the mercy and providence of God in permitting me to remain for so long a time with the community in this state of mind, for had I then left the convent, I fear the consequences would have been fatal to my soul's best interests, for I should most probably have imbibed, secretly, infidel sentiments. I still entertained the idea that the Protestant religion was erroneous, for that had been early instilled in my mind, and I had not seen anything in most of the Protestant pupils to prepossess me in its favor. I can now account for the want of piety and devotion when they enter a convent. Had they been children well and religiously trained, they would not have been placed in so dangerous a situation.

CHAPTER XVI.

ENTERING THE COMMUNITY.

It was considered as quite decided that I should enter the community as a postulant, preparatory to taking the veil of a novice, and my studies and pursuits were directed to that object. I felt unhappy when I thought of the subject: I could not reconcile myself to the life of a religieuse in that undecided state of mind.

It was in the month of November, 1846, when I arrived at the age of twenty-one, a period I had previously fixed upon as the time of my joining the Order. A few days after my birth-day I received a letter from my uncle, stating his wish, now that I was no longer a minor, to decide upon any future course; and he reminded me of my dear mamma's dying request, and enforced upon me the blessedness of a life devoted to God and his Church. He also suggested the happiness it would afford me, if by sanctity and mortification I should satisfy Divine justice for the sins of my parents, and be the means of sooner releasing them from purgatory. Several other inducements were mentioned, and his letter concluded with the promise that everything would be done on his part to meet all arrangements.

I was convinced that this was a crisis. I could not bear the idea of leaving many to whom I was much attached, having spent nearly my whole life with them, nor could I decide to be a nun. I could not remain much longer as a pupil, and I had not courage to retract my promise, nor could I again postpone it. I had no female relations, with the exception of my aunt, to whom I could look, for needed maternal care and counsel; and I had seen but little of the world and its customs, having, since the age of seven, spent only two years out of the convent, which circumstance I have before mentioned, so that I was placed in a peculiarly trying position. I had no home, for the laws of my uncle's Order prevented his receiving me (after a certain age) under his protection. This privilege only extends in particular cases to sisters and brothers.

This consideration greatly influenced me to try the life of a religieuse, and I was further influenced by the thought that I need not take the veil after my probation as postulant if I did not like a convent life, or in the event of my mind continuing harassed with doubts.

I did not foresee the difficulties that would await me in escaping from this first step of a cloistered life. When once a poor misguided devotee is drawn into the snare laid to entrap her, and her property and energies to the service of the Church, difficult and dangerous is it to escape; indeed, on the continent, it is almost impossible for a man to extricate himself from it, much more a woman; it is a dangerous experiment for any one to try with the intention of abandoning it, should they not like the life of a nun, for they are wholly in the power of the Church.

Such is the entire secrecy of the proceedings, that the Superiors could send any nun away; no inquiries would be instituted by the other members of the Society, nor would any, but the parties implicated, be the least aware what had become of the missing person. A nun might be imprisoned, and none but those who authorized it would be privy to the affair. Neither can we expect them to shrink from any act of this kind, when their religion teaches them that they render God services by preventing a heretic from contaminating others with his heresy.

The festival of Christmas drew near, when it was expected I should, with five others, be received as postulant, and for this purpose I was removed to Paris. The kindness of the nuns,

their congratulations, and the joyous circumstances attending
one joining the community, lulled my fears and doubts for the
time.   My confessor had tried to persuade me that all my previous doubts were suggested by Satan, who was making a last
effort to prevent my becoming a religieuse.   He told me that
they were marked temptations, and if I conquered them, he
did not doubt that my future life would be eminent for sanctity;
and further stated, that he was convinced mine was a great
vocation, or else the devil would not thus assault me.   I was in
this way flattered, instead of being told how truly sinful I was
by nature and practice, and that I could not perform a pure
work in the sight of that Being who is too holy to behold iniquity.   I was told that my previous good works and life had
merited the approbation of God, who had by the mouth of
His priests declared unto me a vocation.

With these feelings and views, I began to prepare for the
approaching ceremony.   I entered with the others on my retreat for three days.   This season I shall ever remember.   I
would have sacrificed anything so that I might have retracted;
for during this retirement I had opportunities of seriously reflecting upon what I was doing: and on looking back on the
past three years, I felt that I was augmenting my misery so
long as I was not convinced that the Church of Rome was the
true one.   I felt, too, that I was adding to my difficulties in
inquiring into the Romish faith, and I could not really believe
that such a step was meritorious.   But it was too late to decide
otherwise, and I could not then have given satisfactory reasons
for my withdrawment.

The 2d of January, 1847, was the day on which I entered
as a postulant.   This ceremony was not particularly imposing,
all attractions of this kind being reserved till the period of receiving the white veil.   I and my five companions were dressed
in white muslin.   On the conclusion of mass we adjourned to
the outside of the chapel door.   Each one knocked at the door.

The priest and Reverend Mother answered by opening it, demanding our business. Each one requested admission, in the usual form. We were then led up by the priest and Reverend Mother to the sanctuary, and on our knees presented the scissors to the priest, who in return cut off a small lock of our hair. He then gave to each postulant a rosary; and, blessing us, we returned to our rooms to change our dress to that of a postulant, which was a black one. This ceremony is more private than the profession of novices, it being performed in the presence only of a few invited friends.

My uncle, on our return to the chapel attired as postulants, performed the Benediction service; the day was spent in enjoyment with both nuns and pupils. I was, for the first time, admitted to eat with the community; and though I had been so long a resident in the convent I was quite a stranger to their customs and ceremonies at table. When I saw the novice present the book upon her knees at supper, my feelings revolted at this humiliating posture; but how much more did I feel it when I was shortly after required to do the same. I had not at all contemplated the slavery or hardship of a nun's life, for the pupils are quite ignorant of the humiliating penances they have frequently to perform. I was told that evening by the Reverend Mother that I must now begin to practise holy obedience, which implied I must do everything I was told to do without any reasons being given, and must not do anything without permission.

CHAPTER XVII.

DESCRIPTION OF A CONVENT LIFE.

THE next morning I was aroused by a lay sister at four o'clock ; and half an hour after I joined the nuns in procession to chapel. We spent an hour on our knees in silent meditation ; at half-past five a third bell tolled the "Angelus." The following prayers are always repeated during .the tolling of this bell :—"The angel of the Lord declared unto Mary ; and she conceived of the Holy Ghost. Hail Mary, &c." "Behold the handmaid of the Lord." "Be it done unto me according to thy Word."

"Hail Mary, &c.

"And the Word was made flesh and dwelt among us. Hail Mary, &c.

"May the souls of the faithful departed rest in peace. Eternal rest grant unto them, O Lord, and may perpetual light shine upon them. Glory be to the Father, &c.

"Remember, oh ! most Holy Virgin, that no one," &c. &c.

After the angelus the nuns hastened to their appointed duties until the hour of mass, which is generally at seven o'clock. I had now my seat with the community, and joined them in procession to the chapel. At eight breakfast was served in the refectory. I was the first of the postulants that was called to read the lecture during breakfast, it being the duty of novices or postulants to read at meals. The book was given me by one of the senior nuns, who told me I was to take it to the Reverend Mother, and present it in the usual form on my knees, and must also ask for her blessing. I felt very reluctant to do this before about forty of the Society, but after a great struggle with my feelings I did as I was desired. The Reverend Mother then blessed me, and making the sign of the cross over me she returned the book opened in the part assigned me to read. I had then to commence by making the sign of the cross. I continued reading until permission was given me to cease, and then took my own breakfast; not a word was spoken by either novice or nun, the strictest silence being observed. That day two of the postulants were sent to Amiens.

A little circumstance occurred in the morning that will serve to show how much the will is sacrificed. On going to wash my hands, as usual, I was told I could not do that without permission from another professed nun. I was strictly prohibited from speaking to any novice or fellow postulant without leave from my Superior. My first occupation was to ring the bell for the different prayers and arrangement of the young ladies' classes, &c. At a quarter before twelve we were again summoned to the chapel to make our "examen" of conscience : this lasts till twelve. At a quarter before one the angelus was tolled : this was the signal for dinner. The dinner was served in the refectory, the nuns walking in procession, followed by the novices and the other postulants, with myself walking last. On the signal being given we each took our appointed places, the postulants sitting next to the Reverend Mother, this being always their privilege at dinner. No cloth was laid on the table, each one was provided with a napkin in which were enclosed a knife and fork, spoon and goblet. These napkins were tied with pieces of tape, bearing the names of the separate members of the community. The dinner was served by Reverend Mother in strict silence. At this meal was daily read the life of the saint commemorated on each day of the year in the Roman calendar and the Roman martyrology, varying in length to the supposed sanctity of the saint. When dinner was concluded we each wiped our knife and fork, &c., and folded them in our napkins. These were only cleaned once a week, without any consideration of their being used sometimes two or three times a week for fish. This was most repulsive to me, and I have frequently been reproved for my want of mortification when I have been seen to put my knife down with disgust.

After dinner, when the signal was given, we all rose, made the sign of the cross twice, and then adjourned to the chapel in the usual procession, where we remained for a quarter of an hour, and proceeded again to the refectory for recreation. During this hour, the nuns are generally very merry, and on this day were particularly so. The Reverend Mother appeared to be very lively and affectionate towards us. Being always a favorite in the convent, she bade me to sit on a stool at her feet, saying, " I was now her child," for she had promised my dear departed mother she would be a parent to me ; and I must say, that to this time, she had fulfilled her promise. The nuns were all very kind to me, and congratulated me on the great benefits bestowed upon me, and dwelt much upon the happy state of a cloistered life ; but with all this I felt sad, and longed to join my young companions, who were then playing on the grounds opposite. I wished again to feel unfettered and free from that great restraint which I was, and should be subject to. Though I had been an entire resident in the convent for thirteen years, and an occasional one for two years, I had not the most distant idea of the nuns being kept under such restraint and obedience. None but those who are partakers of it can at all imagine the slavery, if I may so speak, to which they are subject. No despotic sceptre is more arbitrary than that of the Reverend Mother's authority and power : her word, and that of her Provincial, are law; the neglect of which, as I have before stated, exposes the delinquent to the most humiliating punishment. Should the conversation at recreation lead to what she may disapprove, she immediately calls them to silence ; they then lose their recreation : no one dares appeal against it. Speaking of confessions or confessors is strictly prohibited : not the slightest allusion may be made to it: the reason of this I could never solve, and it still remains to me a perfect mystery. To ask if a certain priest is a Jesuit is also forbidden; and no member of the Society is allowed to speak of that body, with the exception of the Reverend Mother. Of course there were priests Jesuits, individually known to us; of them we might speak, but not allude to the Jesuits as a body.

The recreation was concluded by the tolling of the bell, which first tolled a few minutes before the hour was past. We all continued talking till the second bell rang, when all rose and made the sign of the cross: this is always done at the commencement and close. We then knelt down, and turning our faces to the image of the Virgin, repeated an Ave Marie and Pater Noster, and afterwards proceeded to our appointed duties.

I went that afternoon to the music room, to sit during the pupils practising, and likewise to attend to the ringing of the bell, for the different arrangement of the classes in the school are summoned by this bell. On this afternoon I lost my fellow postulants; one was sent to England, another to Nice. I heard of all taking the veil but one: the reason assigned for her omission was, that bad health prevented her. One of this number died two months after her profession. I was not permitted to see my young companions before leaving, nor was I aware of their departure until supper,—such is the entire secrecy of their proceedings.

At four in the evening a bell tolled for prayer. The same prayers were repeated as were used at nine in the morning. On the continent we have not tea at five, as in England, but take supper at six or a little after. At five the angelus was tolled, and immediately after the nuns went into lecture. I was told to retire to the chapel, for private meditation. I found this a great relief to my burdened feelings, for I felt the strict silence and restraint to be most irksome to my naturally lively disposition; everything so dull and monotonous, com·

pared with the hilarity of my schoolfellows; and I bitterly repented the step I had taken, and found great relief to my depressed spirits in a flood of tears. I then repeated the rosary for the benefit of the souls of my dear and deceased relatives, and then joined the community at supper. Being the only postulant the book was given to me. After presenting it to the Reverend Mother in the usual form, I commenced reading: it was the life of St. Alphonsus Rodriquez, a lay brother of the Society of St. Ignatius Loyola. On coming to one of the absurd anecdotes, in which this saint's life abounds, I could not refrain from laughing. The Reverend Mother, who could not forbear smiling, seeing me so much amused, silently gave the signal for one of the novices to take the book from me and finish the reading. I was not reproved for this, but was teased about it at recreation. After supper we retired to the chapel for a quarter of an hour; some went to the young ladies to serve their supper and conduct them to chapel for night prayers. At seven the bell again rang for recreation. The nuns who are appointed to see the pupils in bed, lose a greater portion of their evening's enjoyment. When assembled for recreation, one of the nuns said to me, "Oh! Marie; so you laughed at poor St. Alphonsus. I wonder what you will think when you read of his eating rotten eggs in obedience to his superiors." I replied by saying, "I would not have done it." At this reply the whole of the community laughed heartily, exclaiming, "You don't know what it is to practise religious obedience." In this way the hour was spent.

At eight o'clock the complins, or night prayer bell, was rung. There was something very solemn in this part of the day's duties: the nuns all in procession, veiled in black, and the novices with their white veils and caps, diversified the scene; and with heads hung down and slow step walked into the chapel. A novice repeated the night prayers,—all the community responding,—the Litany of Saints, a portion of which is as follows, viz. :—two prayers were daily repeated to the sacred hearts of Jesus and Mary. While these prayers were being said, two extra candles were lighted, and placed opposite the pictures of the two hearts. The one on the right of the high altar was a picture of the heart of Jesus encircled in a crown of thorns, and the one to the left, was the heart of Mary with a sword pierced through. The prayer repeated to the heart of Mary was, "Sacred heart of Mary, the most perfect of all hearts," &c. The lights were then removed to the picture of the patron saint of the convent—St. Philomel: this was the name I took when I became a postulant. Marie Philomel was my religious name. A prayer was dedicated to her. After this all remained in silent meditation for a short time, then a meditation was read, the Reverend Mother pronouncing the blessing: this was the signal for each to kiss the floor, and several of the nuns kissed the feet of the Virgin's image. The portress placed the keys of the house on the Virgin's altar, saying, "O holy Mother, be thou our protector, and preserve us from all harm. Hail Mary," &c.

We then went to our appointed dormitories. Not a word was spoken. It is considered a great breach of religious obedience for any nun, novice, or postulant, to speak after night prayers, without there is absolute necessity for it: we had no lights. Before getting into bed we sprinkled ourselves with holy water, and also sprinkled some on the bed. We again kissed the floor, saying, "Remember, dust thou art and unto dust thou shalt return." When in bed we had to make the sign of the cross, repeating, "Jesus, Mary, Joseph, to you I commend my spirit. Hail Mary," &c.

This is the daily routine of a convent life.

The whole community, if health permits, rise the year round at four in the morning, and retire to rest a little after half-past eight. All must be in bed at nine, when Reverend Mother or her Superior rings the last bell. On Monday night two nuns and two novices, and occasionally a postulant, rise at eleven, and proceed to the chapel to spend what is termed " the consecrated hour," that is, to accompany our Saviour in spirit to the garden of Gethsemane. They retire to rest at twelve.

The following morning before five were performed the "stations of the cross." Lest this term should not be understood by the reader, it may be as well to explain that the " stations of the cross" are performed as follows, viz.—We all knelt on one side of the lower end of the chapel ; after repeating a prayer we all rose and walked across to the opposite side and again fell on our knees, and continued in silent meditation for a few minutes. This represents our Saviour bearing the cross and falling down exhausted with the burden. After this we walked up nearer the altar, till at last we reached the steps of the sanctuary : we all prostrated with our faces to the ground. This is figurative of our Saviour on the cross : and His mother and disciples kneeling in agony around it. In this position we remained for more than a quarter of an hour. To a Protestant it would appear most profane and absurd. We then concluded our morning devotions as usual.

The professed nuns go to communion every morning, unless deprived of a communion by the Reverend Mother or her Superior, which is sometimes done as a penance or punishment. The novices communicate four or five times a week, the postulants three times. Frequently our confessors would deprive us of going to communion by withholding absolution for a time, or sometimes they could restrict us to one communion in the interval of confession.

I had not been with the community more than three or four days, when I was required to give up everything I valued. I found it to be a great trial to part with a miniature portrait, enclosed in a locket, of my beloved mamma, which I had worn since her death. I did think it cruel to tear from me the only relic I treasured : I never experienced any deprivation to be more acute than this, for since my dear parent's death the resemblance of her had afforded me a melancholy pleasure. This was given to my uncle, and I have not seen it since. I was not even permitted to retain my silver thimble: this was taken from me and an iron one given me in its place. They speak frequently of voluntarily resigning every dear and earthly object, but for my part mine was anything but voluntary, I had not the most remote idea that such sacrifice of feeling was required: I had always thought that the nuns might keep little things they valued; I was not told the contrary, and I do not doubt that numbers are in this way deluded. They are not aware of the hardships and trials they will have to encounter, until it is too late to retract, without taking the dangerous step that I did—that of escaping from the snare so deceitfully laid for them.

The next great trial I met with was the separation from my aunt. Of this I was not aware until I had actually left the convent. Three weeks after my entrance into the Society, I was seated in the choir of the chapel practising on the organ, where I had been sent by the Reverend Mother to practise a mass, expecting to play at the following morning at high mass, it being a day of "obligation." With this order no one would have supposed it was the intention of the Reverend Mother to send me away. I had not been in the choir more than an hour, when one of the senior nuns came and told me that Reverend Mother wished to speak to me in her own room. This being the first time I had entered since I was a postulant, the nun instructed me in the way I was to approach her. On opening the door I must kneel, and remain in that position until I was told to go forward: then, on approaching her, I must again kneel and ask her blessing. I accordingly went and did as I was told; but to my great astonishment the Reverend Mother continued writing, and kept me kneeling for a considerable time: she at last told me to rise. I then knelt at her side, and after she had given me her blessing, took my two hands and embraced me very tenderly. After a little conversation she asked me, in a very coaxing and bland manner, if I should like to have a walk with her. I was much elated with the prospect of so great a treat as to walk out with Reverend Mother, and immediately replied, "O, yes." "Very well," she said, "go to sister G—— for the bonnet and cloak I have provided for you."

I had not since I became a postulant been out beyond the grounds of the convent. We were accompanied by another nun and novice. After walking some distance in the city we came to the diligence office. I was a little surprised, and more so when Reverend Mother said, "I am taking you a ride with Mother C—— and Sister M. W——, who are going to Carrouge;" but how great was my astonishment on arriving at a small convent about a mile from Paris, where there is a small community (chiefly invalids), when Reverend Mother got out and a novice from this convent took her place. She told me I was going to Carrouge. I burst into tears at the communication, exclaiming, "I have not wished my dear aunt good-bye." She replied by saying, that this was religious obedience, and by overcoming this trial great merit would be the result. The coach then filled, so that I was obliged to compose myself, though it was with great difficulty.

After five days' travelling, the weather being very cold in crossing the mountains, we arrived at Carrouge. The sudden and unexpected manner in which I had been removed appeared as a dream to me, but I soon ceased to be surprised at such sudden changes.

It is in this way that all are moved from convent to convent. A nun is frequently sent under pretext of taking a walk, when to her surprise she is sent off to some other convent. If the Society have houses only a few miles distant, some are sent perhaps with a message, and when they get there they are told to stay. All the nuns are very suspicious of being sent out, even where there is no intention of "trapping," as they term it in the convent. This affords many a joke during recreation, on the adroit manner in which this trapping is accomplished. With this system not any one is sure a moment; for many times when it appears most improbable and unlikely, that will be the very time they have to leave for another convent. This is done with a view of detaching them from the world.

This sudden removal from those I loved, without being permitted to bid one farewell, was not calculated to reconcile me more to the step I had taken; but, on the contrary, I felt miserable at the idea of spending my life under such painful restrictions.

The sad scene of Mother Stanislaus' death was again brought fresh to my memory; and I thought, if *she* who had spent so many years of living martyrdom should find (when she would most expect comfort and consolation) she had been deceived, and that all the years spent in penance and self-denial could be of no avail in a dying hour: I thought, with agony, oh! if such should be my case. How I envied the freedom of the poor peasant girls as I passed them on my journey to Carrouge. I shall not easily forget the look of sympathy that an English gentleman gave me. He was our fellow-traveller to Lyons; though seated in the same compartment we were not permitted, by the convent rules, to speak to him or any of our fellow-travellers, so that no opportunity was afforded us of making known our feelings to others. I remember his looking very earnestly at me when I had just been wiping away the tears that fell on my cheeks; and then, on seeing me take up my rosary that hung to my side, gave me such a look of pity as now convinces me that he was a follower of Christ. I was very sorry when we parted at Lyons, for though I had not spoken to him, I felt great esteem for him on account of his apparent sympathy, though a stranger to my grief. At Lyons two other nuns joined us from Nice, and accompanied us to Carrouge.

We arrived at Geneva at a late hour, and I was rather surprised to see the convent guides awaiting our arrival to conduct us up to the convent. This circumstance at once told me that our removal was arranged some days prior to leaving Paris.

On arriving at the convent the portress was up ready to receive us, and also the Superior. The latter, and Mother Clotille, the senior nun who had accompanied us, retired for private conversation on Reverend Mother's business. On their return, the Superior, Mother Mary Borgia, conducted me to her dormitory where a bed had been prepared for me. I did not rise the next morning till a late hour, being so much fatigued. In the course of the day the Superioress told me that Reverend Mother desired that I should be sent into the novitiate, if well-enough, the next day; and she also wished her to tell me that I was not, in recreation or any other time, to allude to my former station as a pupil in the schools; that though there would be many amongst the novices that would recognize me, yet, in the novitiate, any salutation or conversation of this kind was strictly forbidden. All worldly communications and inquiries were entirely precluded. I found this injunction very irksome; for on entering the next day I saw two very dear school-fellows who had just commenced their noviceship. They seemed much surprised when I was introduced as a new postulant, Marie Philomel, but did not dare give me a look of affectionate recognition. There were three other postulants then in the novitiate, and fourteen novices. The former spent only an hour a day in this department, but we joined the novices at recreation: the same reserve is then maintained.

The first month of my time was partly occupied in assisting in the poor school; for in most of the convents they have a charity school, varying in the number of recipients from fifty to three or four hundred. These poor children are fed and partly clothed. At Carrouge there were about two hundred. I must not omit to mention that I still continued to pursue my studies two or three hours a day, in order to qualify me better for the duties that were expected to devolve upon me in assisting in the education of the pupils of the different convent schools. My usual hours were from half-past five, directly after morning meditation, to seven, and from nine till ten. After an hour spent in the novitiate, the rest of the day was spent in the poor-school, and the different duties were assigned me.

Ill-health soon prevented me from walking down daily to the poor-school, for it was not at the convent, but in the village, about a mile distant; so after this I had much lighter duty to perform. When I had been at Carrouge about two months, I had again the opportunity of witnessing the very solemn and melancholy scene of three novices making their final vows. No spectators but those connected with the convent were allowed to be present. Were this ceremony made more public, I feel assured it would deter many from taking so rash a step, for there is something so very appalling in the whole service, that it would affect those most wedded to the Romish faith.

The novices were young, the eldest not being more than twenty-five. Sister M—— X——, Sister M—— A——, and Sister M—— I——, were their names. They spent nine days in retreat. The day was ushered in by the tolling of the great bell, which was muffled for the occasion. This is only done in the event of a death, or on the profession of nuns, that is, the taking of the black veil : this is not a day of rejoicing as on the occasion of receiving the white veil.

The three novices made their general confession as before death. On the morning of their profession, previous to the celebration of mass, the Bishop, who always officiated on this occasion, adjourned to the confessional, to give the novices another opportunity of confessing any sin that might have been omitted. After this confession he gave them each pontifical absolution. Solemn high mass was afterwards performed, the celebrants having on black vestments ; the tabernacle and altar were covered with black, as is customary in masses for the dead. When mass was concluded, the solemn requiem for the dead was chanted ; during this, the novices walked up to the sanctuary, attended by the Reverend Mother (who came purposely to Carrouge to be present at this ceremony) and the rest of the nuns, each one carrying a wax taper. A black velvet cloth was spread on the first step of the sanctuary leading up to the altar ; the three novices then knelt upon it, repeating the " litany for the dead," intimating by this that they were dead to the world. After several prayers had been repeated, the white veils were removed by the Bishop ; they then retired to the sacristy ; the hair, which on the former occasion had only been cut short, was then entirely shaved off. When this business was over, the novices returned to the chapel, three of the nuns bearing the rest of a professed nun's habit. The only alteration in the dress is in the shawl, veil, and cap : these were blessed by the Bishop. The shawl and cap were then changed ; the vows, which were previously copied on parchment, were produced by the Reverend Mother. Having never seen a copy of vows made by a nun on her profession, I cannot give the reader the purport of them : they are pronounced in so low a voice as only to be heard by the Bishop and professed nuns. The vows taken are those of obedience, poverty, and chastity. While the novice was repeating these vows, the Host was held by the Bishop closely before her, so that she was supposed to have made them in the presence of Christ himself, to whom she then believed herself espoused ; she concluded by signing these parchments, on her knees, with the Host still before her : the Reverend Mother then signed it. The Bishop then placed the black veil upon her head, at the same time pronouncing her name, and proceeded to give her the Host in the usual form. The other two proceeded wit'

same ceremony.   The designation of "Sister" was exchanged
for that of "Mother," and their names were chosen in honor of
their patron saints.

When the ceremony concluded, the three nuns kissed the
feet of the Reverend Mother, as a profession of their obedience
and homage to her as their Superior. "Dominum non sum
dignus" was chanted; after which, all returned to the house.

This solemn and thrilling scene made a great impression on
my mind, and more than ever tended to increase my doubts.
It also increased my desire to see a Bible, so that I might ascertain if God really required us, in order that we should live
hereafter with Him, to sacrifice the liberty, energies, and property He has given us for higher ends than the secluding ourselves from every means of benefiting our fellow-creatures by
them.   It seemed to me opposed to the venerable character of
God, that He should require from His creatures the renuncia-
tion of all those sources of enjoyment, and the rupture of those
social ties which owe their origin to Him.   I did not feel satisfied to have my judgment ruled by a priesthood, without confirmed proof that it was right to submit to their authority.   In
my next confession I mentioned this desire, more as a subject
of inquiry than of sin against the Romish faith.

When I had repeated "Confiteor," and proceeded with confession in the usual form, I at once asked my confessor why we
were not to read the Bible; that I had frequently requested it
of my different confessors, but had been reproved; therefore I
wished the reason of the Church for so withholding the Scriptures.   He looked at me very sternly, and inquired why I
asked such a presumptuous question.   My reply was, that I
desired to feel convinced that the doctrine the Church of Rome
taught, was in accordance with the Word of God; assigning as
a reason, that my mind had for some time been very much perplexed, therefore I wished to know if I was really right.

This was indeed a daring and bold declaration to make to a

confessor, and was not made without the greatest effort and sacrifice of feeling. I had naturally a great dread and dislike to confession, and it was always attended with painful excitement. My confessor reasoned long with me on the impropriety and wickedness of the question ; and the only reply I could get to this important subject was, as given me on a former occasion, viz. that it would tend to do me great harm, for I was incapable of understanding aright the Word of God ; and again quoted St. Peter's warning on wresting the Scriptures. As a penance for this presumptuous inquiry, absolution was withheld, and several prayers were given me to repeat daily, that God might be satisfied for the great sin I had committed in desiring to search the Scriptures.

I returned from confession more dissatisfied than before with these evasive answers. The unpleasant looks of the nuns that were to follow me, did not tend to conciliate me to it. In my late confessions I had detained the Father sometimes for more than an hour ; on that day I had been about two hours in the confessional. If any one had kept him beyond the ordinary time, the result was that he became impatient and severe with those who followed. This caused the nuns to dislike to go in. Under those circumstances they thought I was scrupulous, so they were on this day more than ever displeased with me. At the next confession I was required to go last, though the postulants usually follow the Superior.

My doubts now assumed a more serious aspect. I felt convinced that there was something wrong in the Roman Catholic faith, and of its inadequacy to meet the wants of a sinner. I could not believe that God would suffer his creatures to be kept in ignorance of the things that belonged to their eternal peace. It was contrary to all reason to believe that God should inspire his prophets and evangelists to write a book that would lead to the destruction of its perusers ; and the question naturally arose, Why the priesthood escaped this destruction ? Then I remembered the subterfuge of the infallibility of the clergy, that it is impossible for them to err in matters of faith. I reasoned the subject over and over again, and at last came to the conclusion, that let the consequences be what they might, I would never receive the veil until I had read for myself a Bible; little thinking that I should be fully persuaded of the pernicious errors of Popery long before the perusal of those holy pages.

I had now commenced a painful mental conflict that lasted through a period of two years; and He who had called me to pass through this trying ordeal, could alone have supported my naturally delicate frame, and brought me out "more than conqueror, through Him that has loved us and given Himself for us," &c.

At the next confession I acquainted my confessor that I still continued in the same state of mind in reference to the Bible, and again repeated my request. He was this time very kind and patient, and appeared more disposed to reason the subject with more calmness than before. He asked me if I had performed the penance he had given me on the previous confession. I replied in the affirmative; adding, that I did not think I had performed it with proper dispositions, such as the Church required. On hearing which he endeavored to impress upon me the great struggle I was now enduring with Satan, that these doubts were temptations—it being Satan's device to lead me astray from the true faith; and urged me, by everything that was sacred, to fight against them; and also enjoined me to spend much time in prayer and devotion to the Virgin, supplicating her aid in this conflict to enable me to overcome these suggestions of Satan. This was my last interview with my Swiss confessor.

CHAPTER XVIII.

REMOVAL FROM CARROUGE.

I LEFT Carrouge the next day, under the following circumstances. Two nuns were leaving for Amiens, and the Superior told me I might accompany them to Geneva. I did so ; but on arriving at the diligence, I was told to get in, for I was to return with them to Amiens. This removal was owing to the state of my health, Carrouge not agreeing with me, and Reverend Mother wished to place me under the care of an experienced surgeon, under whose treatment I had several times previously received benefit.

I was not sorry to leave Carrouge, so that this sudden change was agreeable. This occurred in the month of April, 1847. On arriving at Paris I was prevented from proceeding to Amiens, in consequence of the return of a disease I had a few years before been suffering from—the slight rupture of a blood-vessel. I was very ill for a little time, and Monsieur Dupois, my medical attendant, strongly advised an immediate change to Italy. After a fortnight's stay at the convent at Paris, I again became a traveller to Nice, a convent I have before named. This rather alarming and dangerous illness increased my fear of death, being convinced that the result of it might have been a sudden removal from this world ; and the feeling that I was not prepared to die distressed me greatly. Owing to the danger that was likely to occur on the least hurry or excitement, I was not permitted to attend the confessional for more than a month after my arrival at Nice. My next confessor was an Italian priest, who could only converse with me in his own language. In consequence of this, I found it difficult to mention to him all the doubts that were then disquieting me, so I did little more than make my usual confession.

At this convent they had what they term an " extraordinary confessor," that is, a priest who attended for the accommodation of those who were not conversant with the Italian language. Not feeling satisfied to go again to confession, without entering on the subject that so occupied my thoughts, and knowing that it was very important that my confessor should fully understand the questions proposed, and myself the answers given, to avoid any misunderstanding, I came to the conclusion that it was better I should at once request permission to attend the French priest of whom I have spoken, then a resident at Nice. He was a kind and venerable old man, and the expression of his countenance strikingly benevolent. I frankly told him of all the difficulties then in my way. He listened to me with great patience and forbearance, and endeavored to clear up my doubts in a calm and affectionate manner; but refused my one great request to have a Bible. He warned me that Satan was having a severe conflict with me, and exciting this desire as the great snare for my destruction. In discussing the doctrine of the Eucharist, he quoted to me those memorable words of our Saviour, " This is my body," saying that it was preposterous to think that Jesus meant it was only bread; but when I was permitted to read and search the Word of God for myself, I found it was as reasonable to believe that our Saviour was a door, for he there as emphatically says, " I am the Door." I then asked him how it was that the laity could receive the entire body and blood of Christ in the wafer, while the priest partook of both wafer and wine. He endeavored to explain this mysterious doctrine, by stating that after our Saviour's death, his body could be no more broken, that is, the blood could be no more separated from the body, and that the mass was emblematical of the crucifixion and death of our Redeemer.

The next subject of doubt that occurred was the doctrine of justification by works. In the different prayers of the Romish Church there seemed to be a strange contradiction; for in some the petitioner would express himself as resting solely on the death of Christ for salvation, and perhaps the very next prayer would express the opposite.

I was of course taught to believe that we were fallen by nature, and if Christ had not given himself a ransom for us we must all have perished eternally. So far I was right; but then thought I, why need Christ have died if we are to merit heaven by works of supererogation? I was required to trust in Christ for salvation, and yet to believe I was to perform a life of mortification and penance, in order to satisfy God for my sins, when Christ had already made satisfaction for them. I could not reconcile these contradictions; and when I contemplated the purity and holiness of God, and compared my works with His greatness, I could but exclaim, "God cannot regard these miserable self-imposed penances as a satisfaction for sin." I felt sure that God must have the inward service of the heart, not the daily irksome repetition of a number of prayers, in which the lips only were employed, the very trouble and trial of repeating them unwillingly being considered more meritorious. To say your rosary under feelings of repugnance was considered a very good work. The Roman Catholic religion, followed out in its strictest requirements, makes its devotee a gloomy, anxious, restless creature. There is in her service that which tends to fascinate the senses; but when this temporary excitement is past, her misguided follower is miserable as before. I speak for myself; for when one of the attached adherents to her creed it failed to render me happy. The more I tried to follow out her teaching, the more I felt ill at ease and dissatisfied with my performances. I am convinced, from bitter experience, that Popery can never give comfort to the sincere inquirer, either on a bed of sickness or anticipated death. I have proved this, and am also able, through the mercy and love of God, to contrast it with the liberty and freedom of a purer Gospel. I now enjoy the happiness of trusting alone in the merits of a crucified Saviour, instead of leaving my soul's great interests to the intercession of the Virgin and saints, many of whom I have no real ground to believe ever entered heaven, or. in some cases ever had any existence; and resting my hope of pardon on the will of a priesthood, who may be living a most abandoned life. I can nowhere find.in God's word, that either the intercession of saints is enjoined, or that man is permitted to take upon himself the power of God: I there read that " there is no name given under heaven by which man can be saved except the name of Jesus:" the Bible does not tell me of mediators and mediatrix.

My confessions now assumed a different character, partaking more of argument or controversy than of confession of sin. I esteemed the kind old priest for his patience with me, and his earnest endeavor to remove all my doubts; and trust that if he still lives, these confessions may have awakened his attention to the gross enormities of his faith. The Superioress of this convent I loved very much for her kind and amiable disposition— Mother Genevieve was her name.

One evening, in the month of December, when she had retired to the chapel for private meditation, I was told to fetch her out, letters having arrived from the Reverend Mother. I went to her and whispered my message, when she requested me to fetch them to her. I suppose she anticipated their purport, it being to call her away from that convent. Owing to circumstances requiring her stay, she had been there the unusual period of five years, and both nuns and pupils were much attached to her. When it was found out the next day that she was to leave on the following morning, we were all very much distressed. On seeing her at recreation I said, "Oh! Mother Genevieve, I am very much grieved that you are going:"—she replied very calmly, "and you are going too." I was very much pleased with this intelligence, for I was in anxious expectation of seeing my dear aunt and uncle if I went to France.

I had not seen my aunt since I had entered the community, and had only had a moment's interview with my uncle once since that occasion. I felt desirous of opening my mind fully to him, but this I was never able to do; nor was he at all aware, at least from myself, of my doubts, or my non-attachment to the religious life, until I wrote to him on the subject after my secession.

After a journey of five days we arrived at Paris. I saw my aunt; she was just leaving for Amiens, and I was not more than ten minutes in her company. This was most tantalizing to me; I could not think that true religion required the separation from every dear object of our affections, and earnestly did I desire to know if God really demanded this sacrifice of every endearing tie of affection.

Reverend Mother was then in Paris, in order to be present at the grand high mass that was to be celebrated in the cathedral of Nôtre Dame de Victoires. Our community had the charge of the altar and vestments belonging to this cathedral. When in Paris, I frequently assisted some of the nuns in decorating the high altar for special feasts. The late Archbishop of Paris was then residing at Paris: he frequently visited our convent, so that I often had the pleasure of seeing him. I longed to open my mind and unburden my feelings to him, for I had great esteem for him. I was privileged by him, at his own request, to dress the altar of his private chapel at his own palace, and also to dress the wax image of the infant Jesus. Some would have been much elated at so high an honor, but to me it was anything but pleasing. The doll was most beautifully dressed in a robe of white satin, which I embroidered with gold; its bed was made of crimson velvet, with a fringe of gold and satin to correspond; the canopy was made of velvet, lined with white satin, and this was confined at the top with a small crown of great value belonging to the Archbishop. This was above a week's labor; and many were the silent tears it cost me, whilst others almost envied me my employment. I would gladly have resigned the task to those whose conscience would not accuse their idolatry.

On the eve of Christmas-day I completed all the decorations of the mass altars in the Archbishop's oratory, which had taken me the whole day: having had to put about a hundred tapers in the splendid candlesticks and lustres, and had also to dress the Virgin in her most costly attire, and the choicest flowers that Paris could produce were spread in profusion in very splendid vases. When I had completed the whole it struck me as appearing idolatrous, and for the first time I passed the altar without adoration, for I felt convinced it would not be pleasing in the sight of God.

On passing the altar of the infant doll I could not refrain from bursting into tears, for I was truly miserable. As I was about to leave the door, the Archbishop entered the chapel, and immediately prostrated in profound adoration. Before leaving him he presented me with an indulgence medal; then blessing me, he allowed me to kiss the ring worn by the Bishops and Archbishops on the third finger of the right hand. This is considered a great privilege; for it is thought by Catholics to be a hundred days' indulgence from purgatory.

When I returned to the convent I found all very busily employed in preparing for the grand services of the Christmas-day, one that is anticipated with great delight in the convent, for we had recreation the whole day. Reverend Mother, seeing me much depressed in spirits, and attributing it to the remembrance of mamma, told me I must come into her room directly after lecture. On this interview she talked to me rather severely on the impropriety. [Here a blank occurs in the manuscript.]

CHAPTER XIX.

CHRISTMAS-DAY.

WE retired to rest on the eve of that day earlier than usual, in order to be better prepared for its services. Those members of the community who wished to be present at midnight mass rose at twelve o'clock, when the first mass was celebrated; each priest being obliged by the laws of the Church to say three masses in honor of the blessed Trinity.

In the convent we always had high mass celebrated at this hour. The sweet voices of the nuns, and the melodious strains of the organ, as the well-known hymn, "Adeste Fideles," was chanted before the altar of the infant doll, and the imposing appearance of the altars, which are like one splendid luminary, —appeal strongly to the senses and feelings of the enthusiastic; and they mistake that for devotion, which is merely the effect any other imposing spectacle would produce on the mind of the enthusiast. There is no real religious feeling in such services. I have frequently wept with excitement at such scenes; not that I was seriously impressed with these ceremonies. No; it was nothing more than a mere sentimentality, acting upon my feelings, which I found it impossible to control. In the same manner, very frequently, sweet plaintive music will excite the listener, but no one could suppose these were emotions of a religious character. But to return to my narrative.

Not being in the enjoyment of good health, or in a state of mind to feel much inclined to rise at so early an hour, I did not get up for midnight mass. I had to communicate that morning, having been at confession the day but one previous. I said mass on that day no less than nine times; for the priests, being all unable to say three masses each in the different churches, gladly availed themselves of the opportunity of performing or saying them in the convent chapels. The last one, which was high grand mass, I saw celebrated in all the splendor of continental pomp and grandeur, in the cathedral of Nôtre Dame de Victoires. I went with Reverend Mother at eleven o'clock; and the service, including "solemn benediction," was over about two. We then returned to the convent, where all was hilarity and joy; it being the only day in the year, with the exception of those on which postulants received the white veil, that we were allowed to have recreation for the entire day. There is one duty that rather encroaches upon this enjoyment. The nuns believe that if they say a thousand Hail Marys, they will have any particular wish granted. This observance causes much anxiety amongst the community, lest the thousand should not be repeated, for if one should be omitted the rest would be unavailing. I once tried this but soon gave it up, for I had not the perseverance to go through it.

In the evening we had the benediction and vespers, in our own chapel, but these services gave me no pleasure. I revolted with feelings of horror when I had with the rest to prostrate before the altar, for there was something within, which convinced me I was doing wrong in bowing to the work of men's hands. I did not enter that night into any of the services, but remained a silent spectator. I did not even smite my breast, as is customary, when the Host is elevated at benediction; in the remonstrance it was not noticed, or else I should have been called to account for my omission. My conscience would not permit me to utter the blasphemous acknowledgment to the wafer inclosed in the glittering idol: for while this is done the whole congregation prostrate, repeating three times "Agnus Dei qui tollis peccatur mundis miserere nobis," each time striking the breast.

It would be difficult and almost impossible to describe what passed in my mind that night. I was in a state almost bordering on distraction, for I could not find peace or comfort in any way. I had no idea of simply praying to God without form or ceremony, thinking He was too great a being to be approached with simplicity; but He who knows the hearts of all, knew the desire of mine, and though I did not give those desires utterance, mercifully regarded them, and in due time taught me, by the aid of His Holy Spirit, to approach Him aright.

From that day I was fully persuaded that Popery was wrong; and my awakened spirit began to look more and more into its enormities, and inquired, What could be truth, and where was it to be found? I felt assured it must be in the Bible, and I began to consider the best way of obtaining one. Many were the schemes formed and abandoned. I knew there was no opportunity of getting one on the continent, and I ardently wished I was in England.

I again acknowledge the Providence of God in thus preventing me; for had I possessed a copy of the Scriptures for any time, previous to leaving the convent, it might have placed me in very dangerous circumstances, for it would have been impossible to have kept one concealed for any length of time.

I was now placed in a very peculiar and critical position: I felt miserable in appearing in my faith, and shrank from the idea of deceiving those by whom I was surrounded. If I had openly declared these sentiments I could not, on the other hand, have given full satisfactory reasons for so acting, being still a stranger to the gospel. It was to me a very great load to keep all these things secret from others, with the exception of my confessors; and even to them I did not, for the last few months I spent in the convent, fully confess all the thoughts and troubles that harassed me.

The Christmas passed away without any occurrence worth narrating.   *   *   *   *   *

  *   *   *   *   *   *

  *   *   *   *   *   *

PART III.

Sequel

TO

THE FEMALE JESUIT.

CHAPTER I.

THE completion of Marie's convent history having been prevented by circumstances which will subsequently appear, it is necessary to resume her narrative at the period at which she first took shelter among her Protestant friends.

Her first care was to write to the Reverend Mother, accounting for her disappearance on the ground that her mind had long been agitated by misgivings respecting the system in which she had been brought up, and that she had felt it her duty to read the Scriptures, and examine the subject for herself, before taking final vows. She expressed her thanks for the kindness shown to her through a period of so many years; but to avoid being followed, she gave no address.

Shortly after she wrote at more length to her uncle, informing him of the step she had taken, expressing her regret for the pain she must inflict on him, and stating the overpowering motives and convictions which alone could have determined her on adopting such a course. She requested him to write to her, and to direct the letter to the care of the Hon. Mrs. ——. This address, being a hundred and fifty miles distant, was chosen in order to maintain her privacy, and also to satisfy him that she had fallen into the hands of persons who were able to protect her. This letter was directed and posted to "The Very Rev. Herbert Constable Clifford, G.V.A., Manotté, near Amiens."

During the weeks and months which followed, one or other

. of Marie's friends always accompanied her when she went out.
It was long before a ring at the bell ceased to awaken her apprehensions, and a glimpse of any lady in black at the gate,
used to throw her into the most violent agitation. She was
never left in the house for any considerable time, and the
servants had strict orders never to introduce any visitor to her
alone. Her protectors long concealed her story from all but
their own family circle and a few intimate friends; and even
when in course of time the fear of her being terrified or kid-
napped passed away, they deemed it prudent still to keep her
in retirement, lest public interest and attention should have an
injurious influence on her character. They thought she might
be less able to bear it than one who had been accustomed to
the world, and dreaded lest her humility and simplicity should
suffer through injudicious notice.

Marie soon manifested considerable anxiety to relieve them
from the expense of supporting her, and expressed a wish to
meet with a situation as speedily as possible. They were too
warmly interested in her to be in haste for her to leave them,
nor could it be felt a burden to entertain one whose gratitude
and affection were unbounded. Her apparently delicate health,
and the long period of mental anxiety through which she had
passed, seemed to call for a season of repose : they therefore
urged her for a while to dismiss all immediate anxiety on the
subject. She spent much time in searching the Scriptures, and
tracing out in them all that applied to her peculiar difficulties.
Not knowing where to find her places, she had to learn the
order of the sacred canons as a child would do, and the greater
part of their contents seemed to burst upon her with all the
freshness of novelty. She surprised her friends by the rapid
progress she made in this study, and by her aptitude in apply-
ing different passages to the subjects which had engrossed her
thoughts. For instance, in reading the account of the lame
man healed at the Beautiful gate of the Temple, she remarked

on the expression of Peter himself,—" Ye men of Israel, why look ye so earnestly on us as though by *our own* power or holiness we had made this man to walk,"—as being in striking contrariety to the spirit of the Pope and of the Roman Catholic priesthood..

With the avowed object of devoting this quiet interval to some useful purpose, Marie determined upon preserving a record of the principal events in her life, and in particular of her somewhat singular mental history. This was an undertaking of no small difficulty, for having, as she said, been altogether unused to English composition, except when writing notes at the dictation of the Very Reverend Mother, she knew neither how to form or to' arrange' her sentences. Her deficiency in habits of order and method was another obstacle. Her recollections of the past, as they came to mind, were recorded on sundry scraps of paper of all sorts and sizes, in ink or in pencil, crossed and interlined, as the convenience of the moment dictated. When seated by Mrs. L—— to review her daily or weekly task, it was often the business of nearly half an hour to collect and arrange from desk, pocket, and portfolio, the various parts ; and when fairly stitched together, to prevent the truant pieces from again wandering, they presented an amusing variety of size and quantity. It was a further exercise of patience to decipher the half rubbed out pencil scrawl, or all but illegible ink crossing; and then each sentence had to be re-made, and put in its proper place. She frequently declared that nothing but the hope of doing good would induce her to persevere, and that as this was her *first*, the public might be assured it would be her *last*, piece of authorship. As she proceeded, however, the work of composition became easier, and the latter half of the narrative required very little correction. The introductory account of her escape was written for her by Mrs L—— : *all the incidents re-*

lating to the convent being supplied by herself, and those which related to her arrival, by her Protestant friends.

While the book was in progress, another subject engaged Marie's attention. She expressed herself as dissatisfied with Roman Catholic baptism, and as earnestly wishing to be re-baptized. Her friend Mr. L—— objected, that as Catholic baptism was administered in the name of the Trinity, it was Christian baptism. She replied that *she* could not regard it as such, for it was so mixed up with idolatrous ceremonies, as to assume in her view an idolatrous character. After consulting some intelligent, pious, advisers, and considering that " whatsoever is not of faith is sin," her wish was granted, and after the next administration of infant baptism she was baptized, and subsequently became a communicant.

CHAPTER II.

MARIE A GOVERNESS.

SHORTLY after this decision, and before the book was finished, an opening unexpectedly presented itself for Marie. It was as governess in a kind and Christian family. Mr. and Mrs. S—— had heard her story, and being deeply interested, had resolved on engaging her as governess to their children. They resided within a few miles of her *home*, and she would have frequent opportunities of seeing her friends, and would enjoy every comfort and consideration which her delicate health required. The offer was at once accepted. A few additions were made to her scanty wardrobe, and a few books added to her little library; and with much good advice and many prayers, she quitted her home for one of, in some respects, increased advantages. He:

friends looked anxiously for her first letter, and were pleased to read as follows :—

"April 6th, 1849.

*   *   *   *   *

"In answer to your kind inquiries, I am happy to say that I am very comfortable. Everything is done to conduce to my happiness, temporal and spiritual. In the latter, Mr. S——takes great interest. I have from five till ten at night entirely to myself. Mr. S—— has arranged how I must spend these few hours. I am to pursue my studies under his direction, and he has bought me a number of books for that purpose. When he has given me the plan for the division of my time, I will send you the copy.

"I have two nice rooms to myself. The servants are required to pay me every respect, and they are, so far, very kind and respectful. I rise at six, and go to rest at half-past ten.

"Tell dear Miss T—— I have done some of her purse. I should be so glad to hear from her and dear S——. My heart is often at C—— Terrace ; and sometimes I cannot forbear shedding a tear when I think of you all, and when I reflect how much I owe you.

"I am progressing in the book, and will send you some on Monday, with another letter.

"With dearest love to all, and many, many kisses to dearest Lilly, ever believe me, as long as life remains,

"Your attached and affectionate

"MARIE."

Marie had not been many weeks in her new quarters, when her friends were grieved to hear of the increasing delicacy of her health, and soon after received from herself the following particulars :—

"My very dear Mrs. L——,

    "Since you last heard from me I have become the subject of affliction and suffering. On Tuesday the spitting of blood, attended by a slight cough, returned; and in the evening it became more frequent, so much so, that Mrs. S—— was quite alarmed; and it made me very faint and ill.

"Mrs. S—— thought it very necessary that I should have medical advice; so as you had before wished it, Mrs. S—— decided upon going with me herself the next morning. I was told that there was a threatening of great mischief in the lungs, particularly the right one; but that if I was careful, it could be now soon remedied, and further disease checked.

"Mrs. S—— is so kind to me, and seems quite determined I should attend to every direction; but of course I shall feel it to be a religious duty to do all I can for the restoration of my health.

"I have felt exceedingly unwell all day from the effects of my blister and medicine, and feel also mentally depressed with the thought of my present position—a lonely orphan, thrown entirely on the kindness of friends; and I feel it so very much when I am ill. And yet when I reflect upon what God has done for me, how much need have I to feel humbled in his presence for doubting his providential care over me for the future! Oh! dear Mrs. L——, cease not to ask for me at a throne of grace that this affliction may be sanctified to my eternal good, and that I may be in all things prepared to say, 'Thy will be done.' You have often prayed for me in the sanctuary, at the family altar, and in the retirement of your own room; then may I still desire the same interest, for I much need it now! I feel so very low in spirits, all appears so dark and gloomy to me.

"I cannot express to you all Mr. and Mrs. S——'s kindness to me. The latter has shown it more than ever this week in her maternal kindness and care.

"I shall try after tea to go on with my book. I did a little last night. I go to rest at nine.

"I find increasing delight in instructing my young charge, and rejoice to tell you that they listen with deep interest and attention whenever I speak to them on religion."

Early in June, she wrote—

"I still spit blood, but not so frequently on the whole. For the last two or three days I have been much better.

"Miss M—— went with me to ——, and in returning home I had a sad fright. To my great consternation, who should get into the omnibus but Mr. ——, Reverend Mother's attorney, and Mr. —— the very last priest to whom I confessed. Fortunately I sat near the door, and they went up to the top. We are not sure if I was recognized, for when we alighted I went into the druggist's near to avoid them, and to leave my prescription. They went into a shop opposite. We stayed a little time, but when we had got near home Miss M—— turned round and they were behind us. I nearly fainted with fright when I got in."

Contrary to expectation, Marie progressed so favorably during the summer that her ailments were almost forgotten, but towards the end of August the tidings reached her friends that she had ruptured a blood-vessel, and had lost a considerable quantity of blood. This happened during the absence of Mr. and Mrs. S—— from London, and while she was alone in her room. Feeling very poorly she lay down on her bed, and in a few moments the accident occurred. She fainted; and on coming to herself she felt too ill to rise, and lay there for some time alone. At length she was missed, and discovered in this distressing state with the clothes saturated with blood. Ice was applied to her chest, and the bleeding did not return; but an inflammatory attack followed which farther reduced her strength. Her friends wrote to request that she might have a holiday and return for a little while to them in order to recruit. They received the following reply :—

"September 3d, 1849.

"After I had written to you on Saturday, Mr. —— called and told Mrs. —— how ill I had been, at which she was very much grieved. I showed her your letter. She very considerately and kindly concurs with you that a rest is requisite, and desires me to have a month; and she this morning most affectionately said, that if my health required she would give me the winter. She is engaging a daily governess till I return. She said she should not like to part with me. Mr. H—— wants me to go to the sea-side for a fortnight, but that must be left for your consideration. If you come to-morrow I shall return with you : if not I shall come in a fly.

"My dearest Mrs. L——, I cannot express my gratitude for your kindness. I was quite overpowered with emotion when I read your letter, but I pray God to bless you for your kindness to a lone orphan.

"I am very weak, and my cough still teases me. I have no sleep. I feel grieved to be again burdensome to you for a time. Hoping to see you, believe me with gratitude and love,

"Your dearest

"MARIE."

Marie returned and spent about five weeks at home. She obtained a respirator, and thus protected, walked out daily. She excelled in fancy work, and made presents for many who had shown her kindness, and contributed to Fancy Sales. Reading and music occupied some portion of her time, and with careful nursing and cheerful society her strength and spirits rallied, and sanguine hopes were entertained of her speedy recovery. A recurrence of the accident which had occurred in

———, soon put these hopes to flight. Neither her medical attendants nor her friends considered her capable of any active exertion, and she was advised to relinquish her situation and to spend the winter at home. So strong, however, was her desire to resume her occupation, that her doctors said it would be better to yield the point than to thwart her. They said that another month would quite suffice to convince her of her incapacity for active service, and that she would then return more tranquilly to her home. She resumed her engagements in October, 1849.

Marie's first letter after her return gave a discouraging report :—

"I know you would wish me to tell you all candidly without reserve. I cannot say much as to the state of my health allowing me to discharge my duties without injury to myself. I fear I shall soon sink under them."

A few days after this she wrote again—

"I have been going on with my book this evening, but I felt so low and depressed I was obliged to put it aside.—You know the young lady who is at ———, came from a convent. Before I went away I had chatted to her frequently on the subject, and had lent her several books which she has read. A few days ago she asked Miss ——— to lend her a Bible, which she now reads with deep interest, though she will not own to Miss ——— that it is from motives of inquiry. I called to see her to-day, and desired Miss ——— to take no notice of it, but leave her to read without any comment as to motive. She has read Father Clement. I wish you would tell me of a nice little book I could send her. I am very anxious about her, but do not think it prudent to press the subject too much. I know it requires great caution in dealing with a Catholic.

"Mr. —— called this morning. He told me that I was really consumptive, so must take care. He also said that if I had not rallied with the rest and change, there would have been no hope for me, it being the only thing they had to hope from.

"With dearest love to all, kisses to Lilly and my darling Arnold. (Be sure you let the little jewel have pretty caps, not forgetting the *rosette*.) Write soon, and ever believe me, with very dear love,

"Your grateful

"Marie.

"P. S.—I will send my book."

CHAPTER III.

UNCLE'S FIRST LETTER.

About a fortnight after Marie's return to —— a letter in a foreign hand, with a black border, directed to Marie, reached C—— Terrace. No answer having ever been received from Marie's uncle, it struck her friends that this letter might contain the intelligence of his death, and that, considering her delicate and excitable state, it would be better to open it, and gently break the tidings to her. It proved to be from the uncle himself. It was written in French, and conveyed the announcement of her aunt's decease.

Mr. and Mrs. S—— were requested to allow Marie to come to C—— Terrace for a day, and they readily consented. She came. It was agreed that nothing should be said to her before dinner, and conversation went on as usual. After dinner Mr. and Mrs. L—— took her into the study, and, drawing their chairs round the fire, began to talk to her of her own affairs, her health, the events of the year, &c. They asked if she had abandoned all hopes of hearing from her uncle, or her aunt. In what state was her aunt's health when they parted, &c. &c. At length her attention was awakened by the succession of questions. Turning to Mrs. L——, she said, " Why do you ask ? Have you heard anything ? You have, you have ! Oh ! tell me, tell me ;" and she rose in agitation. " Yes, dear Marie, we have heard ; but do not be alarmed : there is nothing to make you uneasy. It is a letter from your uncle, and for the most part a kind one. You shall read it for yourself." The letter was produced, and with a tremulous hand, Marie seized and attempted to read it. Her agitation was such that Mrs. L—— was obliged to come to her assistance. The letter was as follows :—

(TRANSLATION.)

†

I. H. S.

"LONDON, Nov. 8th, 1849.

" My dear Marie,

" I have for a long time proposed to write to you on the subject of your horrible apostasy from the Catholic faith. Duties of a very important nature have until now prevented me.*

" When the news of your apostasy reached me, I was at Malta. My first impulse was to write you a letter of maledictions, but more recently, other considerations have led me to perceive that such expressions were little worthy of the charity and abstinence of a disciple devoted to the most holy faith. I subsequently tore that letter up, with the determination of altogether abandoning you; but after two or three months' interval, I have felt much disquietude on your account, fearing that I was not liberated from duties towards the Church from

---

* It will be remembered that this uncle was high in office, and in repute among the Jesuits.

which you have apostatized, and to a much loved sister; for your sainted mother committed you to me as a funeral legacy, and she is thus spared the painful emotions that your ungrateful conduct could not have failed to occasion.

" I have felt remorse of conscience in not having fulfilled the responsible trust, in not having taken any notice of your apostasy, or having tried to raise you again to a height from which you have so profoundly fallen. O Marie! I tremble for you. Do you remember the terrible malediction of that Church to which God has given power to punish on earth and in heaven?

"My sorrow on your account is deep. Numerous are the hours that I pass in my oratory, imploring the aid of the Mother of our Redeemer, hours which I should otherwise have devoted to that necessary repose which my duties and my responsibility require. All ungrateful as you are, I love you still, as the only child of a once dearly-loved sister, and I cease not day and night to hope that you may return to the true faith.

" Marie! this has been a great trial to me. I could have borne any trial with resignation except that of seeing a relation so near and dear embrace heresy. How you have been led into error is still a mystery to me. If you had been much mixed up with the affairs of the world, I should not have been so surprised. I could never have believed that a person with so frank and so candid an air as yourself, could have been guilty of such deception : but I must stop, or I shall be betrayed into saying what I shall afterwards regret. God has well fulfilled his threatening of visiting the sins of the fathers upon the children. I feel that He now avenges himself upon you, child of an infidel father! In His mercy He has taken one, but the other remains as a monument of the anger of God. Think and reflect upon his miserable end."*

* The reference here is to Marie's father having adopted the principles of Voltaire, and to the death of her only brother, whilst being educated for a priest.

"How cruel!" she exclaimed; and tears blinded her eyes. She read again, "Your aunt is dead;" and shocked at the abrupt announcement, she dropped the letter. "O Mrs. L——! this is a trial," she said; and bursting into tears, she threw herself on her friend's shoulder, and wept, and sobbed again. She gradually became more calm, and was able to listen to the suggestions which were offered to her, and to resume the reading of the paragraph.

"Your aunt is dead. She was ill six months in consumption, and died in June. In her last moments she spoke much of you, and requested the prayers of the community for you."

The next two sheets of the letter cannot be found, but the substance is well remembered. They informed Marie that her uncle had heard that she was about to publish her life, and that he could not be expected to sanction a step so ungrateful to the community from whom she had received so much kindness. He proposed that she should postpone the publication for a year, when she would have seen more of the Protestant world, and be better qualified to write. If at the end of that time she continued in the same mind, he would then consent that she should follow the dictates of her conscience.

He further told her, that when her aunt entered the community, taking into it the sum of £30,000, she was allowed to leave £1000 in his care, for the use of her widowed sister and children, Marie's mother having given up her entire settlement to pay her father's debts; preferring to throw herself on the world destitute, rather than suffer his name to descend dishonored to his children. That her Uncle Everard had, unknown to her mother, intrusted him with another £1000; and that though her brother's expenses at college and her own at school had far exceeded the interest of this money, he had still retained the principal; and it was to have been paid over to the Order when Marie became a nun. That he was willing *at the end of a year* to settle the £2000 on her, provided she yielded to his wishes respecting her book, and he would also endeavor to make an addition to it. He expressed his confidence that she knew him too well to suppose he intended to bribe her by his offers; and reminded her that the fatherly care he had exercised over her from so early an age, claimed something like gratitude and consideration at her hands. He added that should she, notwithstanding all, persist in her hasty determination to disgrace him and her family, he swore " by the faith of his holy church," that he would never see or speak to her again.

The concluding sheet is preserved, which proceeds thus:—

" I much wish to see a copy of your manuscript, to understand the motives which have prompted you to take the fatal step of apostasy. Will you send me one? If you feel so disposed, do not be prevented by your friends influencing you otherwise. I do not deserve to be despised by one for whom I have done so much. Now that I am about to close, permit me again to remind you, that your future welfare in this life depends on the decision to which you come in taking the inconsiderate step in contemplation, or in waiting till you have seen more of the Protestant world. If you choose the latter, you may lead your friends to suppose that you have acted conscientiously.

" I cannot neglect to remind you, that your eternal happiness depends upon your return to the bosom of that Church, the arms of which are always open to receive the repenting prodigal, who having quitted his mother's house of abundance speedily finds himself in want. Cannot you soon exclaim, ' I will arise, and will go to the church of my mother, and will say, I have sinned against heaven and against thee.'

" That you may yet regain the heart of him who offers up daily prayers on your behalf, is the earnest wish of your faithful and affectionate relative,   H. C. CLIFFORD."

CHAPTER IV.

MARIE'S PERPLEXITIES.

It will be easily imagined that Mr. Clifford's letter furnished abundant occupation for Marie's thoughts, and that she appeared at first almost overwhelmed by the mingled feelings it awakened. These will be best described in her own letters, after returning to her situation.

"Friday Night, 9 o'clock.

" My dearest earthly friend,

" With a mind bordering on distraction, I sit down all alone to unburden my feelings to one who sympathizes in my every woe. Sympathy is sweet to a troubled and affectionate heart.

" I have sat for the last hour ruminating over the circumstances of the past day and its events. I was lost in a train of thought and perplexity. I roused myself, thinking it would not do to give way to this despondency, but earnestly seek the guidance of Him who has so mercifully cared for me. Those who have passed through similar trials can well enter into my feelings of sorrow, in seeing one dear object after another taken from them unprepared for the mighty change. To *me* it is a grief of the *most* poignant kind. I do indeed feel this a heavy trial now that I am alone and away from those who can tenderly sympathize with my peculiar feelings. I seem to realize this bereavement in all its bitterness. I am so bewildered and confused that I cannot settle to anything. I hope to be more composed to-morrow. I felt it such a struggle and trial this morning to begin teaching.

" I shall get the manuscript ready forthwith to send to Manotté. Mr. S—— thinks that very important.

"I do not yet think of my uncle's proposals in any way, wishing to feel more calm before I give him any decision, for I am now just in that frame of mind that it is difficult to think of anything calmly and deliberately, for I am so very confused and perplexed. I am also much indisposed, for my head aches and my cough is troublesome.

"Mr. S—— says that he can get one of his friends, a publisher, to forward the manuscript to my uncle in one of their parcels, so that will be much better than posting it. What do you think? Do write to me. I will write again to-morrow afternoon, for I must tell some one of my troubled feelings. I know you will listen to them.

"Give my dearest love to all, and accept the warmest thanks and love that an affectionate and grateful heart can offer.　　　　　　　　　　　　　　　　MARIE."

The week following, Marie wrote thus :—

"Friday Night, 11 o'clock.

"My very dear Mrs. L——.

"Your very kind and affectionate letters were indeed a great relief to my mind, for I was in such a state of anxiety and suspense, that I really think I could scarcely have kept in any way calm, had not you sent me a letter by this afternoon's post. I was indeed most agreeably surprised in having a letter from Mr. L——. I *shall* value it, for it is the first one he has ever written to me.

"In reference to my uncle's letter, there appears to me to be some very important considerations on each side. On the one hand there are a few things that scarcely reconcile me to falling in with his wishes; and unless these difficulties can be provided against, I cannot do so, viz. Can there be any design on the part of the Jesuit community? I cannot suppose for a moment that my uncle would really sanction any violent means, and as far as he is concerned, I believe the letter to be a very sincere one; but I feel some little difficulty about the manuscript.   In the second place, if my death should occur before the time is passed, what must be done then, because *I wish the book published, and no earthly consideration* WOULD influence me otherwise.   On the other hand, I do think there is *some* respect due to the feelings of my uncle, for he has been a VERY kind relative to me, and I can well enter into his feelings. I know he looks upon my apostasy as a *personal* disgrace to him.   I quite think this, that he is under the impression that I shall one day return to the Church, and therefore he does not wish me to do anything which would stamp me when I did so; and it is also evident he thinks I have acted under the impulse of a moment.   I think that reading my book will undeceive him on this point.

"I should not like to have any trouble afterwards.   If I thought there was the least chance of this occurring, I would not give the subject a second thought.   I must tell you candidly what I feel.   My feelings say it is my duty to agree to his request, because it opens a communication which, if now closed, will forever remain so, unless God changes his heart. We do not know to what good end our friendly intercourse may lead—and it will be a source of comfort to me sometimes to hear from one I love—but I have one great fear of mistaking my own will for convictions, or the right dictates of conscience.   I shall see Mr. L—— on Sunday, so can say more about it.   Now dear Mrs. L——, if you have the least doubt as to the propriety of deciding either way, do not scruple to tell me, for I do not feel capable of settling so important an affair.   I do not care for worldly good; my only wish is to keep the glory of God in view.

"I never had such a piece of worldly business to think of before, so do manage for me.   I have several times wished I had not had any letter till all was over, for it has teased my poor brain so.

"Believe me, in haste, with dearest love,

"Your grateful   MARIE."

"My dear Mrs. L——,

"I have been expecting to hear from you, but I suppose you were too much engaged.

"I write to say, that as I have my book ready, I purpose coming over for a few hours to-morrow or Wednesday. The children are going on one of these days to E——, so I shall be at liberty.

"I want to see you in reference to my stay here. I fear I shall be obliged to give up. I shall be very grieved, but I really have not strength for my duties."

Marie's friends were not surprised by this communication: she had an interview with them, and it was settled that she should return to them at Christmas. In anticipation of this removal, she wrote as follows :—

"My very dear Mrs. ——,

"I have left the drawing-room for a time, for we have several friends here to tea and supper, so I gladly sit down to have a little silent intercourse with one I so dearly love. It is indeed a source of great comfort to me, that when separated from those I love and esteem, I can write without restraint, and tell my every feeling. I do assure you I am now looking forward with great pleasure to the time when I shall again join your affectionate circle.

"I do not, dear Mrs. L——, yet see my way quite clear in reference to the postponement of the publishing. My feelings say, 'consent to your uncle's wishes,' but my judgment says, 'publish.' I have, dear Mrs. L——, a strong presentiment, which I have and do all I can to shake off from me, that my earthly course will soon be run. I have not told you this before, but I cannot get rid of it. I have continually the monitor, as it were, sounding in my ears, 'Set thy house in order, for thou shalt die, and not live.' There are many very serious considerations in this letter, certainly, to induce me to acquiesce in his proposals ; and I *fear* one greatly influences me, particularly while I am here, that of being placed beyond dependency, for to an upright and sensitive disposition this is a great trial.

"Many thanks for the offer of ———'s room, but I shall not leave till Christmas, as I do not wish to inconvenience Mrs. S—— if I can avoid it.

" I have been thinking, that being about to leave, I should like to make the servants a little present. Indeed, I think it is my duty, for they have been so kind to me in illness, that I can do no other than make them some acknowledgment. What if I give them each a print dress? I saw some at ————, near you. Should you not think it too much trouble, I should be so glad if you would kindly buy me three dresses. I can give you the money on Monday, or send it by Mr. L——. I wish to give them on Thursday, it being Ann's birth-day ; so if you consent to my giving them perhaps you will forward them to me by Parcel Delivery. I fear you will think it more than I ought to give, but I will deprive myself of something to make up for the cost."

Mrs. L—— was unable at the time to attend to this little commission, and indeed she felt some doubt about the propriety of giving full scope to Marie's generosity. She thought less expensive presents would suffice.

Meantime the answer to Mr. Clifford's letter was finished, and Marie forwarded it to C—— Terrace for the approval of her friends. It summed up so ably the events of her past life, and traced so distinctly their influences on her mental history ; it contained so good a digest of the principal points of contro versy between the two churches, and stated her own views so frankly and forcibly, yet with such a mixture of tender respect for his feelings, that her friends were much delighted with this unaided effort of her pen. It was directed to "The very Rev. Herbert Constable Clifford, G. V. A., Chateau de St. José, Ma-nolté, near Amiens, France," and posted forthwith.

CHAPTER V.

MARIE'S REPLY.

"LONDON, December, 1849.

"My dearest uncle,

"I need not tell you the emotions of pain and pleasure your letter created—the former caused by the melancholy intelligence of my dear aunt's death. It is a severe trial to a fond and affectionate heart to see one dear object of affection after another taken from me. When I look back upon the last six years, I can but weep when I remember the events that have occurred ; three beloved relatives removed by death, and myself alienated from the only remaining and beloved one. But I rejoice to know that I have realized the truth of that passage in Holy Writ—'When my father and mother forsake me, then the Lord will take me up.' God has, indeed, wonderfully fulfilled his promise, in raising me up parents amongst strangers, and in opening the hearts of many to care for, and sympathize with, the lone orphan. If you love me, which I doubt not you do, you can but feel some degree of satisfaction in knowing that none could better supply the place of fond parents than the kind friends to whom I was directed by the Providence of God. I mean the minister and his dear wife whom I before mentioned to you. Words would fail to express the extent of their parental care and affectionate solicitude ; suffice it to say that I have in both, a kind father and an affectionate mother.

"I said your letter caused both pain and pleasure:—it was pleasure to hear once more from you: I had long given up the hope that you would notice me. I have felt your silence very acutely. *Many, many* have been the hours that I have wept and mourned in my retirement when I have thought of you, and the trial was embittered by the recollection that I was an alien from you. I am not, dear uncle, as you seem to infer, dead to all those affections which were ever ardent to those I loved. No; my heart still glows with love and gratitude to those from whom it is separated.

"You may perhaps think me neglectful in not replying to your letter ere this. I should have done so but that I wished to deliberate the purport of it well, so that I should not write under sudden or rash impulse.

"I conclude from your letter, that you have the impression that I renounced Catholicism under circumstances of momentary excitement, without any previous consideration upon my part. If you read my letter carefully through, you would there find that I stated it was not so; nor was it through the influence of *any* Protestant friends. *No;* it was simply and purely the workings out and convictions of my own mind through a period of two or three years, which brought me to this decision; indeed doubts had arisen some time before my dear mamma's death.

"I am sorry I cannot comply with your request, in sending the copy of the manuscript, for the present: it is not yet ready; but I will just briefly give you the heads of it. Before, however, I go further, I must tell you that I have not made any statement in my book in reference to any personal unkind treatment. On the contrary, I have endeavored to make the reader clearly understand that I was treated with uniform kindness and affection: I think when you read it you will conclude the same.

"In commencing this brief narrative, it will be as well to go back to the time when I had so dangerous an illness at Carrouge. I was then about fifteen. You are aware that up to this period I was not at all seriously disposed, but very neglectful and thoughtless in all my religious duties. In this illness I felt deeply the powers of the world to come, and was much terrified at the prospect of death. On that bed of sickness I made a vow that if God would then spare me, my future life should be devoted to one of penance and good works. In order better to fulfil this promise, on my recovery I renewed my vow before the altar of the Virgin in the presence of the whole convent. I think you know to what extent I fulfilled this promise, for you frequently, in your letters, alluded to it as giving you great comfort in hearing the reports of my mortifications, &c., from my mamma and Reverend Mother. I continued to perform the same routine of religious observances, but I still felt unhappy with the constant dread of death."

Marie then enters into all the workings of her mind in reference to purgatory, the reading of the Scriptures, &c., as described in her own history of her previous life. It is not, therefore, deemed necessary to give this letter at full length. In connection with purgatory she thus refers to her mamma's death—

"I shall not dwell upon that harrowing and distressing scene of the deathbed of my beloved mamma: but can you ever forget that expression of her ghastly countenance when she clasped my hand, saying, 'Promise me, Marie, you will do this,' having previously desired me to hear mass for her, and also to get masses said for the repose of her soul. I can never erase from my mind the intensity and agony with which this request was made."

Here follows the account of Mother Stanislaus, for which the reader is referred to page 96.

"The limits of time and paper will not allow any lengthened detail of what passed through my mind in reference to the Roman Catholic faith, up to the period when it was expected I should enter the community. The mental conflict was indeed intense. I could not bear the idea of being a nun. On the other hand, the thought of leaving those with whom I had spent a greater part of my life seemed to me impossible. Soon after my twenty-first birth-day you wrote to me desiring me to decide upon my future course. In that letter you alluded to my mamma's dying wish that I should become a nun. This, combined with other things, strongly influenced me to try the life of a *religieuse*, and I further thought if I did not like it, or if I continued to have the doubts, and the answers of my confessors failed to satisfy me, I need not remain; but little did I foresee the great difficulties that would obstruct my path. Still I have now abundant cause for gratitude to God that I did take that step, for I was by it enabled to see more fully into the glaring enormities of Popery, and was by it preserved, I fully believe, from falling into the snare of infidelity.

"I cannot now describe to you the feelings of horror I endured when I became a *postulant*. In the first instance I was cruelly deceived, for though I had been with the Society fifteen years I had not the most remote idea of the humiliating and trying ordeal they were called to pass through. I knew nothing of their customs, &c., till I entered the community. You may imagine my feelings of grief, and also surprise, when I was told to give up (with other things) the *only* earthly treasure I valued—my beloved mamma's portrait. Oh! uncle, you say I shall no longer value it. Did you know the tears and wishes that were spent in parting with that dear relic of a fond mother, you would not say so; or if you have still left any consideration for my feelings and affections, you will soon make me the happy possessor of that which, if it were in the power of any earthly good to create happiness, this would to me; parting with which was so great a trial to me, that it appeared as if it were to tear away every fibre of what I loved. I was never told I should be required to do this.

"The daily routine of a nun's life soon became most irksome and wearisome to me. The severing of every tie of affection was contrary to the benevolence of that Being who alone instituted the bond of social enjoyment. The vow of implicit obedience to a fellow-creature was most repulsive. The doctrine that teaches that men are saved by their own good works, began to occupy my thoughts soon after becoming a postulant. I could not reconcile the two great contradictions in the Church of Rome : on the one hand teaching that Christ made an atonement for sins, and then she commands her devotees still to perform certain good works in order to merit heaven. If you will look over any of the prayer-books carefully, you will there see that in some of the prayers it is emphatically stated, ' that we are saved alone by the blood of Christ,' when perhaps in the *very next* prayer there is a gross contradiction,—making our own merits, and those of saints, a plea for salvation.

"These doubts and perplexities I continued to mention in my confessions, but always met with stern reproofs and absurd replies to my momentous questions. The answers of my confessors only tended to increase my difficulties, for I was still firm in my request to see a Bible.

"The doctrine of the Eucharist soon appeared as the most glaring error in the Church of Rome. Long before any doubts on the subject occurred to me, I frequently shuddered at the thought that it was Christ Himself I received in the form of a wafer. The bare idea of a creature *eating* his Creator is *horrible.* I recoil now with horror when I think of it. Oh ! dear uncle, what are your feelings when professing to consecrate that Host ? Do you not tremble with the thought you are taking upon yourself to create God ? I know that the Scriptures state that the last night Jesus took bread with His disciples prior to

His crucifixion, He said 'This is my body;' but He frequently spoke in figurative terms to them. It is just as reasonable to believe Him a door, &c.; for if you have a Bible, you will there find He says, 'I am the door,' 'I am the way,' 'I am the truth,' 'I am the vine;' but I must stop, for I am getting into the maze of controversy.

" I had a long argument, or rather conference, with the good old French priest at Nice, on this doctrine. He was almost the only confessor who listened to me with patience and kindness. But plausible as his answers were, they failed to satisfy those perplexities, which only increased upon each confession. The gross idolatry of the Romish Church shocked my awakened spirit, for I saw it in all its pomp and perfection in a convent life. The adoration of the Virgin was another part of that shocking system of Popery.

" In this state of mind you can but see that it was impossible I could either enter the community as a nun, or yet remain in the Church of Rome. You will now be ready to say, 'Why did I not open my mind to you?' My dearest uncle, many were the times I had resolved to do so, and upon one occasion, when you visited me at Paris, after a severe illness, I had quite determined to tell you all; but when I saw you my lips appeared as if they were sealed, for had the universe been offered me I could not have told you a word. Shortly after this interview I came to England, with the fixed determination that I would by some means gain further information in what was really truth or error, for I had long before vowed I would not become a nun until I had read for myself the Word of God.

" It was in the serious attack of illness that I had in Liverpool, of which you were a witness, that I felt my lost condition and dreadful position as an unsaved sinner in the sight of God. I had not one plea or ray of hope that I should be saved. Had I died then, I must have utterly perished.

" Words would be inadequate to express the mental anxiety I

passed through to the period of my deliverance, which was, through the Providence of God, brought about in the following remarkable manner. I had for some weeks previous been aware that it was the intention of Reverend Mother to send me back to Paris, where I was to receive the white veil, and be sent to Carrouge to perform my noviceship. I should have left the first week in January, with Mother Helen, had not indisposition, or rather Divine interposition prevented it. A few days before taking any final step, several circumstances occurred to convince me that my immediate departure was contemplated.

"The day (18th of January) that these suspicions were fully confirmed, was one spent in a state almost bordering upon despair and desperation. During the nun's lecture I walked in the grounds instead of adjourning to the chapel, as was my usual custom. On coming to the grotto on the grounds, I there threw myself on my knees, and *earnestly* poured out my soul to that Being who alone could be my deliverer. How that prayer was answered you shall soon learn."

Marie here gives the account of her meeting with the gentleman in the omnibus, as detailed pages 6, 7.

"How I escaped, you will have heard from other quarters. I have never seen this gentleman since, nor have I heard anything further of him.

"So far, and I trust ever shall I have abundant cause to praise God for this eventful step in my life. I have proved in the hour of deep affliction, that Christ has been precious to me; and have in such seasons contrasted the dread of a Catholic devotee, with the confidence and hope of the Christian, who feels that Christ is his *only* rock and plea for salvation.

"My dear uncle, you can but see I have had no earthly consideration in this step. On the contrary, I have turned myself upon the world to gain my own bread. I have been since April in a situation as governess. I am now compelled, by the delicacy of my health, to resign a good situation in a kind and Christian family, and return—at least for the winter—to my kind friends, Mr. and Mrs. L——, though I feel great reluctance again to trespass on their bounty. I say there could be no earthly inducement to cause me to take this step. No ; for had I only disliked a convent life, and still remained a Catholic, I should have occupied a very different place to my present one. I have thus sacrificed worldly position and rank.

"You tax me with ingratitude. This heart will cease to beat ere that become my sin. Your kindness will never be erased from my memory.

"In reference to your request of postponing the publishing of my book,—in consequence of the respect, gratitude, and affection I feel towards you, my dear uncle, and also to convince you it is no rash proceeding on my part, I am willing to postpone the publishing of my narrative until I hear further from you. I would not wish you to have the impression that the idea of placing me above a dependent has brought me to this decision. That I leave to your feelings of love and honor, knowing from past experience, that you will honorably carry out your own proposal, so that I may be placed in circumstances more in accordance with the station and honor of the family to which I belong, and be spared the pain of being a dependent upon the charity of others, or of exertions to which my delicate health is unequal.

"I shall be most happy to remain open to any communication you like to make, or answer any questions you may propose. If you again wish to see me, do not let any advice influence you otherwise.

"Many thanks to you for your kind promise of sending me my late mamma's effects. I *shall* indeed value them for her sake.

"You ask me if I am happy? I rejoice to say I am very,

very happy, for I can now look upon God as my reconciled Father, knowing that Christ made a *full* atonement for my guilt on the cross. I can now draw nigh to *Him* without the aid of mediators or mediatrix, and boldly approach a throne of grace, there confessing my sins to *Him*, not to fallen, guilty man. I can now read undisturbed the Word of God, and can look forward, when this my earthly career is run, to a joyful entrance into the mansions of bliss, not fearing purgatorial flames ; and with the apostle I can exclaim, 'For me to live is Christ, and to die is gain.' How can I be otherwise than happy with this hope and prospect ?

"I beg your immediate answer to this letter, for I am anxious to know your sentiments after reading this brief narrative.

"I have no doubt Mr. L—— will be most happy to communicate with you, if you think proper to write to him upon any subject relating to my temporal affairs.

"I assure you, my dear uncle, that *all* my friends, so far from prejudicing me against you, are so liberally disposed, that they have, one and all, strongly advised me to yield to your wishes *as far* as I can without the sacrifice of conscience.

"I beg you will read patiently what I have written, and do not condemn me for doing that which my conscience convinced me was right, and do not judge of me so harshly as to suppose me either guilty of ingratitude or ' *deception.*' I love you still, dearest uncle, if possible, more intensely than ever.

"That you may be led to see the simple truth as it is in Jesus, is the earnest and constant prayer of your dearest and, I trust, still loved niece,

" M—— L—— G——.

"P. S.—You can address your letters as before, if you like, or to me, at ————."

CHAPTER VI.

THE FIRE IN THE HOUSE.

On the 13th of December, 1849, a fortnight before the time appointed for her return, and without any previous notice, Marie arrived one morning in company with Mrs. S——. Her boxes were deposited in the hall, intimating that she was come to stay. Mr. and Mrs. L—— ran out to receive her. Their first impression was, that renewed illness had brought her thus suddenly home, and wretchedly ill she looked. No smile of pleasure dawned upon her pale countenance as she met them. She looked equally ill and miserable. "Oh Mrs. L——," she exclaimed, "I have done wrong, *very* wrong: I want to tell you all;" and Mrs. L—— led her into a back room, while Mr. L—— took Mrs. S—— into the dining-room.

Mrs. L—— made her sit down, and took a seat by her side. "I have fallen into sin," she said : "I have told a falsehood, and I wanted to see you once more and confess all to you, and then return to my uncle;" and she related the circumstances. She had bought some print dresses for the servants at ————, and had said that they were a present from Mrs. L——. When asked by Mrs. S—— where Mrs. L—— had purchased them, she had said, "In the Edgeware Road." But the boy who brought them was recognized by one of the servants as belonging to a shop in the neighborhood : and on inquiry it proved that she had bought them there.

A great grief it was to her friends that one whom they had deemed so particularly truthful, should have been betrayed into the opposite sin. But her sobs and tears, and expressions of penitence and self-reproach could not but excite their pity. There appeared to be no selfish motive about the first falsehood, but rather a wish to give the credit of her liberality to another, and the second falsehood was an attempt to cover the first.

She retired to her room after Mrs. S—— was gone, took to her bed and remained there three days; scarcely ate anything; did not venture to raise her eyes to meet the looks of her friends; and seemed in a state bordering on despair. They spoke to her faithfully of her error, but sought to mingle encouragement with rebuke, and to awaken her hopes that she might yet live to retrieve her character, and regain their confidence.

She told Mrs. L—— that she had once, at the age of thirteen, fallen into the same sin, and had told a succession of falsehoods: that her mother and uncle had been greatly distressed, and had taken every means to bring her to repentance: that they had kept her in solitude for a fortnight, and she had seen no one but her confessor during that period: that she had afterwards become remarkable for her strict adherence to truth, and had never again violated it till recently. She attributed her fall to the absence of confession, and other restraints of a convent life; and that having grown remiss in the duty of self-examination, and careless and self-confident, she had no longer had any check upon her conduct. She appeared at times almost distracted, and her friends found it necessary to treat her with tenderness, lest her health or her reason should give way under her mental struggles.

Some misgivings crossed their minds respecting the sums of money which Marie had collected for different benevolent objects. Before parting, Mrs. S—— had asked her for £10, which Marie said she had collected for a church at ——; and Marie had replied that it was packed up at the bottom of her box, and she would send it. Mrs. L—— sat down by her bedside one day and, without looking at her, turned the conversation towards this subject.

"Marie, dear," she said, "this is the time to clear up everything, and to begin again anew. If anything still rests on your mind I hope you will tell me, and let it be set right. Mr. L——— and I feel uneasy about that money. You are so careless in your accounts, and so generous in your presents, that we are afraid you may have been tempted to use part of it. Now if it is so, only frankly tell me, and we will do our best to save your character, as well as keep your secret. Then you may start with a clear conscience, and a lightened heart."

"No, *indeed*, Mrs. L———," she replied, "the money is all right, and I have nothing else to confess. Do you think I would not tell *you everything?* You may be quite easy, for you know *all*." And hoping that such was the case her friend left her.

Saturday evening arrived, and she was still in her self-imposed solitude at the top of the house. The family assembled for their evening prayer, and before they rose, Marie's voice was heard in loud screams from above. Mr. L——— hastily concluded. Mrs. L——— seized the light, and hastened up stairs, followed by the servants and one of her sisters. On reaching the second landing, they found Marie in her night-dress, with her arms round Lilly, screaming that the house was on fire. "Take baby down, Sarah," was the brief command, and the rest rushed up stairs.

As they entered the room where the little girl had been sleeping, a fearful blaze met their eyes, and the smoke was almost suffocating; but the prompt application of water and heavy cloths soon put out the fire. It was matter of surprise and thankfulness that the flames had not caught the muslin blinds and window curtains, which were close to them, and the bed which was almost as near. In one minute more they must have done so, and in *three* minutes more the flames would have been uncontrollable by private hands. No engines were to be had within a mile and a half distance; and not only the house, but the whole terrace, might in a brief space have been a sacrifice.

Mr. L—— and the other sister had not followed. They thought Marie was hysterical, and that she had enough attendants, so they sat chatting by the fire-light, unconscious of the excitement up-stairs.

Presently the gate-bell rang violently, once and again. Then came a loud rat, tat, tat, at the door, and as no servant came down, Mr. L—— went to open it. " Your house is on fire, sir," said a manly voice, " the people in the road are watching the flames and sparks." The light showed the visitor to be Mr. ——, the occupant of the next house. They sprang up-stairs, and found the flames already extinguished. Then commenced a variety of conjectures about the origin of the fire, but all were at fault. No one had been in the room for two hours. The nurse-maid had been in last, and it was surmised that she might have left a spark behind her. Lilly knew not that there was a fire. Deep in the first sound sleep of childhood, she had been unconscious of the smoke and flame, had seen nothing, heard nothing, till Marie dragged her down the staircase. Part of the wood-work by the window was much burned. Elizabeth's toilet-bag had hung there, and her conjecture was, that when she brushed her hair at six, a spark might have lodged in her brush, and being hastily put in the bag, had been smouldering there for nearly four hours. Marie's account of it was, that feeling her room warm, she had risen and opened the door: that soon after she lay down again she perceived a strong smell of burning: that again rising to ascertain the cause, she saw a light under Lilly's door, and on opening it, the flames caught her view. She dragged Lilly out of her crib, and gave the alarm. In vain were all further surmises and investigations,— the cause seemed fated to remain in obscurity. But excitement and conjecture subsided into deep thankfulness to Providence for the timely preservation of the family. Then came the sense of gratitude to Marie. She and Lilly had been wrapped up in the room below, and it was two hours before, with all the windows open, the suffocating smoke could be sufficiently dispersed to allow of their return to their own story. At length, however, they were again quietly laid in their own resting-places, and Mrs. L—— returned to thank Marie for having saved her child; and Marie looked up for the first time, and the first smile of pleasure dawned upon her dejected countenance.

Marie's spirits seemed revived by the active part she had taken in rescuing Lilly; and on the Monday she rose and dressed. She could not be prevailed upon to come down to dinner. She shrank from meeting Mr. L——, whom she had not seen since the morning of her return. He desired Mrs. L—— to tell her that he should speak to her as formerly, and make no reference to what had passed. Thus encouraged, she ventured down to tea, and in a day or two she seemed to feel that all was forgiven and forgotten.

It was on one of these days that Marie brought to Mrs. L—— the copies of her manuscript. "Now Mrs. L——," she said, " you *must* accept of this, and publish it at the end of the year. I shall not be in want of anything now, and I should like you to dispose of it, and buy a piano for Lilly." Mrs. L—— attached little importance to this gift, not thinking it likely that the uncle would ever allow it to be published : but lest he should, at some unexpected visit, induce Marie to put the manuscript in his hands, she took the precaution to conceal it in a secure and somewhat singular hiding-place.

CHAPTER VII.

THE UNCLE EXPECTED.

WEDNESDAY evening's post brought a letter from Mr. Clifford. Marie was greatly agitated at the sight of the handwriting, and her trembling hand almost refused to hold the letter. She called Mrs. L—— to her side, and they read it together.

(TRANSLATION.)

"My dear Marie,

"Why are you so long in replying to me? I did not expect to be so treated. Had you written the letter, it would have been forwarded directly. I remain in London for some days; how many, this evening's post will decide. I shall probably come to see you, but our interview must be private.

"So you have left your situation. I think you will soon have seen enough of your new friends to be convinced of your error. I know —— better than any of you think. I have suffered much anxiety on account of you, lest you should be turned aside from the right way; for knowing your frivolity, your easy disposition, your thoughtlessness, and your entire inexperience of the world, and also that you are easily led by those who surround you for good or for evil, I cannot but feel some degree of solicitude for you; and I am fully convinced that there is no one who takes so much interest as myself in the right direction of your character, and can counsel you in the same judicious and affectionate manner as the community whom you have so ungratefully quitted.

"I am now with Captain Kenyon, who married one of my cousins, Constantia. I arrived with them from Yorkshire last

Friday. Mrs. Kenyon much wishes to see you. They have both most kindly proposed that you should return with them, and that you should be allowed to enjoy your own sentiments; but this is on two conditions, which future serious considerations will decide. If I do not call upon you within a week, you may conclude that I have left London. I hope soon to see or hear from you, and I am, dear Marie,

" Your affectionate,

" H. C. CLIFFORD."

The prospect of so soon, and so unexpectedly, seeing her uncle, quite overcame Marie. It appeared probable that he would come the very next day. He asked, moreover, for a private interview, and she did not feel sufficient confidence to meet him alone. Mr. L—— had engagements from home for the next day, so after much consideration, she resolved to spend the morrow at a friend's house, and to leave the following note :—

" 5, C—— Terrace, Wednesday Night

" My dear uncle,

"I felt your letter required so much deliberation, that I took some time to consider its purport. I replied to it with very full details last week, and posted my letter on Friday, addressed to you at Manotté.

"Your communication of to-day found me in so weak a state, that I feel quite unequal to an interview for the present. Having twice ruptured a blood-vessel during the last few months, it is necessary that I should be kept very quiet; and feeling that were I in the house, I could not refuse to see you, I have thought it better on the whole to absent myself. I hope in a little time to be better able to bear so exciting a meeting, and should you still wish to see me, if you will fix a time a few days hence, I will endeavor to meet you.

"In my letter last week I felt it my duty to yield to your

request to postpone the publication of my book, but your proposal of to-day I cannot, under any consideration or inducement, entertain, however kindly it may be intended by Mrs. Kenyon. I speak decidedly on this point, and beg you will not again refer to the subject.

"With kindest love, I am, dear uncle,

"Your grateful and affectionate niece,

"MARIE."

It was settled that Mrs. L—— should see the uncle when he came, and receive him with all due courtesy. She felt some slight trepidation at the idea of receiving him alone: the circumstance of his being a Jesuit priest, added to Marie's statements respecting his talents and high position, rendering him rather a formidable visitor. Marie expressed some anxiety for the house to look as well as possible, that he might not suppose she lived in a style unworthy of her family or of him; and to satisfy her, the drawing-room furniture was uncovered, the vases were filled with choice flowers, every chair and every curtain-fold was put in its proper place, and all those little arrangements were made, so familiar to the mistress of a house when visitors of more than usual importance are expected. On Friday Mrs. L—— was at home, and Marie stayed at home too. But Thursday, Friday, and Saturday passed in anxious expectation, and no uncle came. On Saturday evening the following note accounted for his non-appearance :—

✝

I. H. S.

Saturday Morning, December 22d, 1849.

"My dear Marie,

"I had quite decided to call upon you to-day, but this morning's post has prevented me. I received your letter last evening, but cannot yet pronounce judgment on its contents. It is very probable that my next reply will be to Mr. L——; but I cannot yet decide. I hope, however, that everything will be arranged to the satisfaction of all parties.

"If I could follow the impulse of affection, I should soon conclude the pecuniary arrangements; but I must not confer with flesh and blood; I must do the will of my Father in heaven. It is a great struggle between love and religious obedience. Dear Marie, do not divulge this part of my letter. What are your feelings respecting your return to your family? I do not say as a dependent; far otherwise. If this is agreeable to you, I shall be at liberty to grant you a liberal annuity out of my own revenue. Write to me and tell me all you think. Be frank as usual.

"I have seen your good friend Mr. L——, and have heard him preach.

"There is one thing, my dear Marie, which makes me very unhappy. It is the fear lest you should be induced by your inconsiderate and ardent feelings, to contract an imprudent engagement. Do not go much into the world, either for the sake of your health or of your reputation. I have reasons for requesting this.

"I believe that before long you will receive a letter from Mrs. Kenyon, and perhaps a packet from me. I cannot promise you an immediate reply to your letter, for I have other persons to consult. When you write, let me know if you are better. Address to Manotté. It is a great satisfaction to me that your present friends are so good to you. It is more than you deserve after your ingratitude towards those who have shown you so much kindness for so long a period. I learn that Mr. and Mrs. L—— love you much, and that they watch over your health and your reputation. I am not surprised that you have become endeared to them, for all who know you well must love you. It would be a source of infinite happiness to me spiritually, if I could forget you. I often wish that you had died some

years since, for you are my only earthly tie. I should be happy
if I could break the cord which binds my natural affections to
you.

"With many prayers, I am, my dear Marie,

"Yours, most faithfully,

"H. C. CLIFFORD.'

From this note it was evident that Marie's letter had been
well received. The almost tenderness it breathed reconciled
her to the postponement of his visit on the one hand, while it
made her long more to see him on the other.

CHAPTER VIII.

MARIE AN HEIRESS.

A FEW more posts brought the promised letter to Mr. L——.
It thus commenced :—

(TRANSLATION.)

†

I. H. S.

Manotté, December 31st, 1845.

"Sir,

"I think that it will not be necessary to apologize for
the liberty that I take in writing to you, after the obliging permission granted in Marie's last communications.

"The care and direction of a person whom I have so tenderly
loved, and over whom I have watched with a father's affection,
devolves through her apostasy and your generosity upon you
and Mrs. L——. I believe it to be my duty, though by so
doing I may expose myself to the censure of others, frankly to

make you acquainted with Marie's future expectations; but I do not wish that she should hear this part of my letter, for if you knew her disposition as well as I do, you would agree with me in the necessity of concealing this information from her, at least for the present. If Marie is spared, she will become, at the death of an aunt of her mamma's who lives in Staffordshire, the possessor of considerable landed property.

"Thus much I may say,—the lands were entailed by my late uncle, upon the children of his nieces and nephews. There are but four of them, including Marie, who will become heirs to the property in question. I am now in correspondence with the solicitor for the estate, and endeavoring to obtain the lady's consent to settle a portion of the property upon Marie, that is, immediately. I have not yet had a reply.

"My reasons for making this request are as follows:—In the first place I think that, with the assistance of this property, Marie will again take the place and rank which belong to her in society. It would be better for her now to have an income more suitable to this position. The other reason is, that with this in view, you can prevent any unsuitable connection or intimate friendship with undesirable persons. I think you will find Marie a little hasty in this respect. She believes that every person who gives evidence of some good sentiments is sincere. She is very unsuspecting, and being little accustomed to the world is easily imposed upon.

"As far as regards the carrying out of my proposition, I am very anxious to fulfil my promise immediately, rather than to wait the expiration of the appointed time—the end of this year. Marie has doubtless made you acquainted with my position in the Church, and the impossibility of doing anything without the control and direction of persons who are above me.

"If she had acceded to my request in returning to her family, I should then have been permitted to follow the dictates of affection. I am grateful to you for your great kindness towards the only child of a beloved twin sister deceased, and I hope to make you some remuneration for all the expense she has occasioned you; and I hope also that before long, Marie will be capable of rewarding you for your disinterested goodness. The circumstances which induced her to cast herself upon your hospitality, cannot but attach disgrace and infamy to her family. I assure you, sir, no trial was ever felt more keenly by myself than her having thus apostatized from the religion of her ancestors, who have ever been renowned for their attachment to their faith, and some have even been martyrs to the cause of truth. I rejoice that her mamma has been spared this sorrow. I pray sincerely that she may soon see her error, and return repentant within the pale of the fold of Christ. The proposed publication of her life augments the disgrace which she has brought upon us, and adds to the difficulty of my yielding her assistance.

"You will perhaps bear with me if I trespass on your time in making you acquainted with the weak points in the character and disposition of a person whom I have so much studied, and in whom I feel so deep an interest. You will, I am sure, already have discovered that Marie is very excitable, betraying her sometimes into a degree of impetuosity if she is not checked. She is also very ardent and devoted in her attachment to those whom she loves. This sentiment is praiseworthy in itself, but may, if ill directed, lead to evil when the object is not worthy of so sincere an attachment; and there is in her character a lightheartedness and thoughtlessness which tend to make her forgetful of *herself* in wishing to think and act for *others*. This, if not restrained, conduces to a certain degree of imprudence. I do not think that she ever looks forward to the future, but acts on the impulse of the moment. There are many points truly noble and amiable in her, having so total an absence of selfish motives. But to use the expression of the late Archbishop of Paris, who knew her well, in speaking of her to me one day, he said, 'There is in Marie an indescribable charm which every one must love; that simplicity which no one can fail to admire.'

"Captain and Mrs. Kenyon will visit Manotté before long, and I shall avail myself of this opportunity to send Marie's jewels, for I am afraid of risking articles of such value by public conveyance. I should advise Marie to sell the coins, as they are not family property.

"I have not opened my sister's desk since her death, nor shall I do so. If it contains any of her poems, I shall request Marie to return them to me, that they may be published if of sufficient merit.

"I hope Marie will take care of her health, for when in the convent she was much to blame in this respect, being so thoughtless and inconsiderate. I think you will find that kindness and firmness combined will be necessary in the management of your recently adopted charge, for, comparatively speaking, she is still a child in many things. The change has been very great for her, after having been seventeen years in seclusion, to be thus thrown upon the world to act and judge for herself. It is this that makes me tremble for her, lest by her simplicity she should be seduced into evil.

"I shall be obliged to you if you will answer this letter, which will probably be enclosed in Marie's, stating what are your views with regard to the best means of making future provision for Marie; and what sum will suffice for last year, and that which is now approaching.

"I wish to know Marie's deportment towards those who surround her; and all that you think of her health, and if anything can be done which will conduce to its entire re-establishment. I cannot now write to Marie, but will do so immediately after having received some decisive information on the termination of this affair. It is probable that before long I shall call upon you. Present, if you please, my affectionate regards to Marie, and accept, sir, my respectful compliments,

"H. C. CLIFFORD."

It may be supposed that the communication relative to Marie's property awakened no little surprise. It seemed to account, however, for much of her uncle's anxiety about her, and for much of the care and kindness exercised towards her for so many years in the convents of her Order. Her friends scarcely knew whether to be pleased or otherwise, so much did they fear the effects of such a discovery on Marie's excitable and sanguine temperament; and they thought the annual stipend proposed by her uncle quite as much as was likely to do her good. According to his wish they resolved to keep the communication a profound secret, not only from Marie, but also from all her circle. They had some difficulty in evading her inquiries.

"I have had a letter from your uncle," said Mr. L——.

"Oh! have you? May I see it?"

"We will read it to you."

"May I not read it myself?"

"Well, you may read the greater part of it;—almost all; but there is one little point which your uncle did not wish mentioned."

"Oh dear! there must be something the matter."

"No, not at all."

"Then what can he have to tell you that I may not know? It must be something dreadful, and he is afraid of my knowing it!"

"No, indeed it is not," said Mrs. L——. "It is only about the money."

"Well, then, if that is all, why can't you let me read it?"

"Because it would not be honorable after he has enjoined the contrary. So now you must be content. We shall not do it, so it is in vain for you to ask any more."

" I wish you would not be so positive," said Marie laughing. " As it is I suppose I must give it up."

The interdicted paragraphs were withheld, and she was allowed to read the rest. Her replies to her uncle's notes received about Christmas have not been preserved. Mr. L——'s answer to the letter of December 31st was as follows :—

"January 8th, 1850.

" Sir,

" You will, I am sure, appreciate the difficulties I have felt in replying to your letter—difficulties created by the relation which I so unexpectedly sustain towards one in whom you take so deep an interest, the delicacy of the subjects on which you ask my opinion, and the fact that we are personal strangers.

" Marie's own previous narrative relieves me from any lengthened reference to a change which must, I am sure, have occasioned you pain. I should ill deserve your esteem if, holding the opinions that I do hold, I had not, under such circumstances, welcomed her. And yet, when reflecting upon the grief which it has occasioned you, her beloved relative, it is a satisfaction to me that her mind was fully decided before I became acquainted with her. I saw so much of her ardent temperament in our earliest interview, that I should have hesitated to encourage her change, had it been prompted by the impulse of the time, rather than the result of years of reflection. I think it only frank to add my conviction, that subsequent examination has firmly established her in her present views.

" This is all I need say on so painful a subject. Permit me, however, to assure you that Mrs. L—— and myself wish Marie ever to retain and manifest the love which she cherishes for you. We wish her to consult your wishes on all matters not affecting her religious convictions.

" There are two main topics on which you ask my opinion. The first relates to my young charge herself. On this subject

Mrs. L—— is likely to form a safer judgment than myself, and I have therefore requested her to write her opinions.

"The second topic regards pecuniary arrangements. You kindly ask me to name a sum for the past current year. Allow me to acknowledge your consideration for the *past*, but to request that you will not take that into account. I cannot consent to receive any remuneration for the past year. Marie was introduced to me in a way so entirely providential, that I felt it at once to be a case to which the Saviour's command applied. I received her into my house as an apparently destitute orphan, entrusted to my care by Him, and I wish still to enjoy the pleasure without repayment.

"As it is your wish that she should not take a situation, I cannot feel the same hesitation as to the future. You are aware that the cost of a young charge like Marie depends much upon the comforts enjoyed, and that these should be regulated by the resources or station of the party. The usual rate for boarding in private families in London, is from £60 to £80 per annum. Mrs. L—— estimates that she would require £25 at least for clothing. There are always a few extra claims, especially for medical attendance, medicine, &c.; and perhaps in the summer time you might wish her to accompany us to the sea-side. I mention these things that you may judge.

"You ask my opinion as to the best means of arranging a settlement for her. I beg to suggest that the £2000 mentioned in your first letter, if invested in the annuities of the English government, would yield an income quite sufficient without any farther pension. This might be arranged to secure her for eleven years, or even longer. By the first period mentioned, she would probably come into possession of her property.

"Should any difficulty occur to you in carrying out this plan, you can remit through almost any London banker a sum for the current year.

"We fully concur in the prudence of withholding from Marie the knowledge of her prospects at present. She requires to be watched over as one ignorant of the world, and you may rest assured that we shall be very careful as to the society into which she is introduced.

"Anticipating the pleasure of a visit from you at an early period, I am, sir,

"Yours respectfully,
"S—— L——."

CHAPTER IX.

A MYSTERIOUS OCCURRENCE.

It will be necessary to go back a little way in order to introduce an extraordinary circumstance which happened about this time.

A few days after the fire, Marie was removed into her own little room, endeared by associations connected with her *first* arrival. The weather became intensely cold, and brought on her cough to an alarming extent. That night she sat up in bed, coughing almost incessantly, and the servant went in to support her under the violence of the paroxysms. The next morning Marie was taken down stairs to a warmer room for the day. Then every means was taken to raise the temperature of her room for the night. Mrs. L—— stuffed every crevice of the window with wadding, to make it air-proof, and Mr. L—— nailed strips of carpet round the door. Thick curtains were put round the window and bed, and a fire kept burning. A baize curtain was hung outside the door, under which those who went in entered as to a gipsy tent; but with all their efforts they could not get the thermometer above thirty-five, and her medical adviser recommended that next day she should be removed to a lower room. He would have preferred her being taken to Torquay for the winter. Mr. S——, whose family she had just quitted, offered to defray the expenses; but Marie would not hear of such an arrangement. She could not leave her friends at C—— Terrace, and go into voluntary banishment from those dearest to her on earth. "That was her only home. If she was to die, she would die there."

The next best thing was to keep her in as equal a temperature as possible. Exposure to air on the staircase renewed her cough, and threatened the rupture of a blood-vessel. The back parlor, which had been the children's play-room, was considered the best for her accommodation, and it was forthwith fitted up as a bed-room. Lilly cheerfully turned her toys out of the closet, to leave it for Marie's wardrobe. The carpenter was sent for to put up a bedstead. Great pains were expended in making the large and ill-fitting window air-tight; a large fire was made up within, and a large curtain hung without; and she who engaged so many thoughts and anxieties, was led in, and expressed with tears her gratitude for all the concern manifested about her. That room she occupied for three months, and left it, as her health permitted, only to go into the adjoining dining-room. The raised temperature mitigated, though it did not remove her cough, and as she still complained of a tightness on her chest, leeches were applied.

Meantime the meeting at —— drew near, when Marie's £10 were to be presented, and she was gently reminded that it was necessary to send the money. She could not make up the account without her collecting-book, and that remained with Mr. S——. She wrote to him, and it was forwarded. Then she found that she had lost the keys of her box, and the whole house was swept, and a rigorous search instituted. They could not be found, and just at this juncture, a recurrence of the hæmorrhage from the lungs renewed alarm for her life. It came on in the night-time, and the family knew nothing about it till the morning, when they beheld the fearful signs of what had occurred, and Marie lying pale and exhausted on her bed. She had no bell that would ring up-stairs, and had lain there alone and helpless. Medical advice was obtained, and suitable medicine prescribed, but the extreme tenderness of which she complained below the collar-bone, defeated all attempts at examination by the stethoscope. The next evening, when left alone for reading, the bleeding returned. The medical attendant was again sent for, and a blister was prescribed for the tender lung. She was to take everything cold, not to talk, and to be kept perfectly quiet.

Mrs. L—— sat much in Marie's room, and read and worked there, but forbade her speaking, and endeavored to anticipate her wants. As all excitement was dangerous, the subject of the money was for a few days dropped. When a little better, she was told that Mr. L—— had promised to call on Mr. S——, and to settle it that week. She sent for a man to force the box, and said she would dress by-and-bye, and get the money out. She fainted, however, on rising, and was obliged to lie down, and the rupture of another vessel once more drove off the settlement of the business.

At length it became imperatively necessary that the money should be produced, and Mrs. L—— asked her for it. She was still in bed, but she directed Mrs. L—— to her box, and told her to take it. Mrs. L—— opened the box, and a scene of unexampled confusion presented itself. Clean clothes and soiled ones, light things and heavy ones, books, work, Albert lights, lucifer matches, tapes, strings, ribbons, innumerable bits of paper, letters, bonnets, and shoes, were exposed to view.

"You will find the money at the bottom of the box," said Marie, "it is in notes, with the —— tickets."

"In notes! Why I thought you collected it in gold and silver?" said Mrs. L——.

"Yes, but I changed it into notes, for I thought I should like to present a £10 note at the meeting. And there was another £5 note for the Bible Society—three £5 notes in all."

"There are the tickets," said Mrs. L——, as at length she dived to the bottom of the box, "but they are burnt. There are but a few figures remaining."

"Burnt, Mrs. L——! burnt!" cried Marie, "you don't say so! Let me look, let me look!"

The box was brought to her bedside, and she was satisfied.

"Then the notes are burnt also. How could it happen? Here are lucifers; one of these must have done it. Sarah," she said to the nurse, "I sent you to the box for my Concordance the Sunday after I came home; you must have rubbed the lucifers in hunting for it.'

Mrs. L—— put the contents of the box back, and carried it out of the room, saying that she should consult her husband on his return, and see what he thought of it. Mr. L—— returned home two hours after, and Mrs. L—— communicated what had transpired during his absence. Next morning they examined the box and its contents, and found that the fire had scarcely extended beyond the tickets. The box itself was unsinged, and only a few papers were burned. It is needless to state the painful conviction that was forced on the minds of both respecting the whole affair. "Two fires in one house in a month!" said the servant, who had been taxed with going to the box. "It is a very strange business, *I* think. I was brought in for the blame about the fire up-stairs, and now I have set light to the box, it seems;" and in her indignation she talked to her fellow-servants of leaving, lest some still more serious charge should be fixed upon her; but she thought again, and felt that she could not leave her little nursling.

Marie seemed in such a state of excitement that her friends feared to endanger her life by entering on an investigation at that juncture: and as her uncle was expected, they resolved to await his arrival and communicate the whole to him. She saw that they did not believe her, and the following evening she re-iterated her statement to Mrs. L——. She spoke rapidly, and uttered several palpable falsehoods. "I have the numbers of the notes," she added, "for my uncle taught me always to keep them. Look, I have found one," she said, as she called Mrs. L——'s attention to some figures in her pocket-book, set down something as follows:

$$\begin{array}{cc} 1 & 4 \\ 2 & 8 \\ & 7 \end{array}$$

"You do not mean that *that* is the number of a note?" said Mrs. L——.

"Yes, I do," she said; "it is my random way of putting it down. It means 14287."

Mrs. L—— could not bear to hear any more. She laid her hand gently on Marie's shoulder, and said, "Do not say any more about it now, dear Marie."

"Do you mean that I am not telling the truth? Am I not to explain?" said Marie, almost fiercely.

"I mean that under your present feelings, you may say much which you will be sorry for afterwards. You should learn caution and self-distrust from the past."

And Marie replied with a look of black defiance which haunted Mrs. L—— long afterwards. It might have been the look of a murderess.

The next morning Marie asked to speak to Mr. L——.

"He is just going out, and has a busy day before him," said Mrs. L——.

"Do ask him to come in. I have written a letter to my un-cle, and I want him to post it for me."

"Have written a letter! When?"

"Last night, when you were in bed, I got up and did it. I kept up my fire, so do not be angry."

"But your uncle told you not to write till his retreat was over; and he is at Rome. Perhaps you will get him into trouble."

"Oh! it *must* go, *indeed* it must;" and Mr. L—— was called.

After some conversation, he persuaded Marie to wait her uncle's time, and at last gained her permission to read the letter. It was sealed and directed. The superscription was a long one.

Immediate.
If not at Manotté,
to be forwarded
forthwith
to the
Rev. H. C. Clifford.
Postage Paid.

The Very Reverend
H. C. CLIFFORD,
Grand Vicar, A.F.C.R.
Chateau de St. José,
Near Amiens,
France.

The principal object of this letter was to inform her uncle that through a sad act of carelessness, which from his acquaintance with her character he could well appreciate, she had accidentally destroyed three Bank notes, which were not her own property. That having collected this money for benevolent objects, her character was at stake, and she entreated him to extricate her from her distressing difficulty by forwarding the amount. It entered into minute details respecting her health and depression of spirits, and would not interest the reader.

CHAPTER X

A CORRESPONDENCE IN THE HOUSE.

MARIE gradually recovered, though she required constant watchfulness and medical attendance.

Mrs. L—— could not feel it right to pass over what had

recently occurred in silence, though Marie's precarious health and mental excitement were an effectual barrier to conversation. She wrote the following letter, and left it on Marie's desk one evening after bidding her good night :—

"January 31st, 1850.

"My dearest Marie,

"It is not my intention frequently to adopt the plan of writing letters to you, because I think it would rather tend to check the freedom of confidential intercourse ; but in this case I think it better to do so that you may more thoughtfully and calmly consider the subject of this, and also to spare both you and myself some of those painful feelings to which conversation about it would give rise. I fear, too, that in the excitement of the moment you might be tempted to say much that would hereafter be remembered with pain. It costs me an effort to write, and I would not do so if I did not love you, but I must prove my love in the best way, by being faithful to your soul.

"The circumstances attending your removal from Mr. S——'s caused us much grief. We hoped, however, that you had truly and deeply repented, and in the strength of God had begun a new life. Last week, however, our sorrow was renewed. I do not know when my heart has ached so much as it did then, and my dear husband felt scarcely less keenly. My cold furnished an excuse for seeming dull and poorly, and I tried to conceal my feelings as much as I could, knowing that in your then state of health any excitement was dangerous. I am sure you wish our happiness, but you could scarcely have marred it more effectually than by giving us such anxiety and distress on your own account. The *extent* to which you have deceived us, is known only to God and your own conscience. I believe that had you frankly confessed all on your return to us, the real truth would have been *far* less culpable than the series of falsehoods and artifices to which you were tempted to resort for the purpose of concealment. I do not wish you to confess to me *now*. Having delivered my conscience, I wish to bury the subject in oblivion, and hope that by a new course, you will so re gain our esteem and confidence that the past will never come to mind. But I do entreat you to confess to *God*,—Him against whom you have sinned. Return with deep contrition and repentance to Him. If you try to forget, and hide your sin from your own conscience or from Him, you will never have His blessing, and never know true peace. It will separate you from Him, destroy all confidence and joy in drawing near to Him, and at every returning illness or thought of a future life, there will be darker forebodings than at any period of your convent history. Your sin has been greater because committed against Him who not only lived and died for you, but who has appeared for you in so signally providential a way. Does He not seem to heap kindnesses upon you, as if to bring your ungrateful heart to repentance? How wonderfully He delivered you from your anticipated bondage! But as if that were not enough, He provided friends for you among strangers, and then inclined your uncle's heart towards you, and has now granted you all that could be imagined to contribute to your comfort and happiness in this life. And will you, dearest Marie, continue to grieve and vex His Holy Spirit? It is indeed folly and short-sightedness to sacrifice His smile and favor by yielding to this besetting sin.

"You may be assured that this is a crisis in your history. Your freedom from a state of dependence, and the prospects of comfort and earthly enjoyment now opening before you, will be used by Satan as a snare to lead you farther astray from God and holiness, unless sin is first purged from your heart, and you start anew in your heavenward course with most earnest and prayerful resolution henceforward to maintain a conscience void of all offence towards God and towards man. No day should close without self-examination and confession, and prayer for forgiveness and peace.

"I am rather jealous of your love of verse-making, lest it should rob you of that precious evening season which ought to be given to the examination of your own heart, and your preparation for judgment and eternity. Let that time be sacredly and conscientiously devoted to God, and I think you cannot then go far astray.

"If you ever hope to see your kind uncle favorably inclined to a purer doctrine than that which he has been taught to hold, there must be the most exemplary conduct on your part. What responsibility may rest on your soul as it regards *his* soul, if you should prove a stumbling-block in his way. What misery, too, would you bring upon him, if you fell into open sin, and brought disgrace on yourself. Surely *he* deserves a better return for a lifetime of kindness. *We* are but the friends of a day compared with *him*, and therefore I speak not of *our* claims upon you, but I am sure you would like to be the source of happiness to us all; and remember that can be not half so much by personal kindness and proofs of affection, as by letting us see you walking in the fear of God, blessed by Him, and a blessing to others.

"I have had my fears lest you should be too much elated by the change in your circumstances, and lest that should induce carelessness about higher and greater things. *I* find, and I think, dear Marie, you will find it still more forcibly true in your case, that you can never be happy without the love and esteem of those whom you love. You may be happy, in sickness or in poverty, with loving friends and God's sustaining grace; but if *unloved*, your life will indeed be desolate. And we cannot love you for *money*. The possession of thousands would make no difference in our feelings towards you, or our estimate of you. I think you must have been conscious of late, that with all our anxiety to be kind and careful of you, there has been less warmth and 'empressement' in our manner to you under your improved prospects that when we thought you penniless. That is just because we then regarded you as sincere and guileless, and loved you dearly for your *own* sake alone. Will you not allow us to love you again as warmly? to feel the same complacency, the same confidence,—to meet your look with unrestrained and answering looks of pleasure and affection? Seek mercy and help of God, and we shall soon be as happy in you as we have been.

"I wish you would look out in your Concordance for all the texts which regard truth and uprightness. Make it one of your evening exercises. You will then see what supreme importance is attached to these things in the Word of God, and find how *He* regards them.

"I trust you will also set out with an anxious desire to live not unto yourself. I do not like to hear you talk *too* much about yourself. And do not indulge in frivolous conversation, such as various things you like or dislike in the eating way, little maladies and sensations, fancies in the way of dress, &c. I do not mean that there is any harm in occasional reference to such things, but it is a poor sign when we can talk of nothing else. I want you to awake to your responsibilities as an immortal creature, as one signally favored by God and bound to unusual devotedness, as one who is now her own mistress, with time, abilities, advantages, at her own command, and with a life held by an uncertain tenure. You know not how soon you may be called to give in your account. Oh! that you may do it with joy and not with grief.

"I hope you will spend your money thoughtfully, and as accountable to God for this newly entrusted talent. That you will try to conquer those habits of disorder and thoughtlessness, which, as your uncle justly observes, may seriously affect your interests and influence and character, in ways you little anticipate. You *may* be *very* happy now. It rests in great measure with yourself, for God has placed within your reach nearly all the things which constitute earthly happiness. Oh! that you may, dear Marie, have wisdom to know in what your true happiness lies, and to act accordingly.

" I do not expect or wish any answer to this letter, but I shall hope, or fear, according to the spirit in which I may perceive that you have taken it. I wished to write before we commenced our morning studies, in the hope of dismissing from my mind the burden and restraint which so many painful thoughts have imposed. May God forgive you, dear Marie, as I do, and restore to you the sunshine of His countenance and forgiving love. So often prays

"Your anxious and affectionate friend,

"J. L——."

Marie wrote two notes in reply to this letter. One has been lost. The other, which is similar in purport, remains, and is here inserted.

"Thursday.

"My dear Mrs. L——,

"I have tried for the last week or two to speak to you personally, but have as yet found it quite impossible. I need not tell you how painfully I have felt your altered manner towards me. It has and *does* cause me much misery. Though you are equally kind and attentive to me as ever, yet I can but feel conscious that my affection is not returned. I am sure you must have noticed that many times in coming to kiss you I have hesitated, for I felt as if it was an effort on your part to show me that expression of affection for me.

"I never at any period of my life stood so much in need of both maternal sympathy and counsel; and I am sure, that did you know all my feelings you would not wound me by increasing coldness of manner. It would be an infinite source of comfort to me, could I openly express to you all I feel on the past. Unreserved communication would, I am convinced, tend to our mutual happiness. I fear you do not feel the same liberty in telling me of what is wrong as you once did, now that circumstances are changed. I am sure it will both grieve my uncle and myself if such is the case; for who can I now look to for parental care, if you shrink from this? I would much prefer speaking to you personally than resorting to this mode of intercourse; reserve is *very* painful to me. I *do* wish to throw it off, and be able to be as frank with you as with my own dear mamma, for I feel both your affection and displeasure equally the same as with mamma's. I am sure I could not endure much longer in my present state of mind, for my spiritual conflict is great. Added to this is the change in you, and my own great bodily weakness. I feel as if I was not a welcome guest. I could often burst into tears, and sometimes find it difficult to restrain them, when I look at you and see that my affection is not reciprocated. It is this, with my present weak state, that makes me anxious to see my uncle, for I do want to be fully reconciled to you. I *cannot* live with you under a sense of your displeasure, for I love you *too well* not to notice or care for it. If you will pardon the past, and receive me again to your favor, I hope then to be able to say all I wish, and for the future to be as frank with you as I was with my dear mamma and uncle; for I have and do miss much that open intercourse that existed between the latter and myself.

"Educated and trained as I have been in a circle, in which I do not hesitate to say I was much loved by all those with whom I was more immediately connected, though I was never spared when in the wrong, I can but now feel very sensitively the want of that love and affection you once bestowed upon me; and more particularly now that I am afflicted, and also separated from those I so dearly love. I grieve now, and feel much the loss of a mother, for I am so very desolate and alone now that I cannot meet you as I once did.

"I am quite conscious that there are many faults in which I may often displease you ; but if you will always tell me of them at the time, I will try to do all I can to correct them.

"I do trust I shall be able to say all I wish, and that this may be the last time I shall ever have need to adopt this means of conveying to you my feelings.

"With kind love, I am still

"Your affectionate

"MARIE."

Mrs. L—— was far from being satisfied with Marie's notes. The main topic was slurred over, or rather altogether omitted, while there was something of the tone of an injured person in reference to her alleged treatment. She frequently intimated, however, to Mrs. L——'s sisters, that she could explain all, had she but courage to do so, and that it would relieve her of an almost intolerable burden. She was again ill, and it was attributed to her state of mind. Many opportunities for the disclosure were afforded her ; but her resolution always failed, and each attempt was followed by increased nervous excitement. Week after week passed, and threw no light on the disappearance of the money. The conjecture to which the family most frequently reverted was, that she had been too liberal in her gratuities to a poor sick servant out of place, with whom she had become acquainted, and that being ashamed or afraid to acknowledge that she had exceeded her resources, she had been tempted to greater departures from rectitude to conceal the fact. She reiterated the assurance that it could be explained, and that when she had told her uncle all, he would clear it up for her. She proposed sending him a full statement by letter ; but as he was not then at home, and there was no certainty of a letter reaching him, her friends thought it better not to risk a communication involving her character, to the uncertainties of the continental post.

Mr. L—— having received a letter from Marie expressive of intense mental suffering and religious despondency, lent her what he deemed a suitable book. It was returned with the following note:—

"Saturday.

"My dear Mr. L——,

"I return you the book, with many thanks for your kindness and interest. It is an excellent little work, but I am sorry to say that I have *not* derived the good from it that you might have anticipated. The fault I know is *mine*, but I feel my mind in that state that would rather seek for something to charm than encouragement from the promises of God's truth. I wish I could have a conversation with you on the subject. I do indeed feel grieved you should have so much trouble and anxiety on my account. I *can never* repay you, but I trust God will; and earnestly do I hope and pray that if I ever again regain the favor of God, and be as I *once* was, happy with a sense of His favor, that you may then have the happiness of seeing me more consistent in all my Christian duties. I think I could open my mind to you if you would not feel reserved. I wish you always to be open and faithful with me, for I have now no other friends to guide and advise me. I am convinced it is my present unhappy state of mind that is preying upon my health, for I cannot sleep or rest when alone. If you have ever departed from God, you can enter into the distressed state of a backslider. I cannot hope, or look for mercy. I hope you will not be displeased in my writing to you, but it is and would be a relief to me to speak freely with you upon this subject. I have tried a time or two to do so to Mrs. L——, but somehow I feel too timid, having never said much to her on the subject of religion.

"I hope you will bear with patience all I have said, for I

am in need of both your prayers and counsel, for I am *very un-happy.*

" MARIE."

As Marie requested to see Mr. L—— alone, he called her into his study. She spoke in the same strain as in her notes, and wept much when giving expression to the mental agony which she was enduring. She attributed her errors in great measure to her defective education. She said that she had been taught to regard sin as committed against the Church or against her fellow-creatures, and that after making acknowledgment and reparation she had been absolved, and the subject dismissed: that she had never been taught to regard sin as committed against God, or to entertain any fear of displeasing *Him.* She spoke of what had occurred before her return from ————, but did not refer to the money burnings, and when Mr. L—— made a distant approach to the subject, she arose from her chair and rushed out of the room.

CHAPTER XI.

THE UNCLE'S ADMONITIONS.

MARIE's friends were rather amused, and Marie appeared to be not a little annoyed, at the graphic delineation of her character, contained in the following letter :—

(TRANSLATION.)

†

I. II. S.

" Manotté, 25th January, 1850.

" My dear Marie,

" I am just about to terminate all my arrangements before quitting this place to commence my six weeks' retreat.

Having an hour to spare before dinner, I embrace the opportunity to fulfil my promise of writing to you. I hope that my
dear Marie will receive with humility of mind the faithful advice and reproofs that I am about to give her. Let me assure
you, my dear child, that those are our friends who frankly tell
us of our faults, in order that we may correct them. It is then
because I love you that I write thus plainly as in former days.

"In the first place, I was not thoroughly satisfied with your
last letter. Not that there was in it any particularly offensive
expression, but the whole tenor of it convinced me of what I
have been well capable of ascertaining by experience, that light-
ness and thoughtlessness are still the weak points of your character. There was in the letter a frivolity which could not but
have struck a stranger, and was to me most displeasing. The
writing was truly characteristic, displaying so little care, part of
a word being forgotten, and so many et ceteras, that had I not
known you, and the letter had been placed before me, I should
instantly have said, ' the writer is a careless person.'

"I had formed a very favorable opinion of you after your
previous letter, though regretting the sentiments there expressed : the whole exhibited serious thought and strong intelligence. There was also a measure of consideration which led
me to believe that you were much improved in this respect.
Do not think me too severe if I give you pain ; it is for your
good. I fear that you do not regard this subject in its proper
bearing : it is a more serious matter than you believe it to be.
It is a fault that will cause you much sorrow, now that you are
entering upon the world. Now that I am upon this subject, I
will give you an incident which was the result of your folly, but
which I have never before told you. Do not think that I am
displeased with you for this : I tell it you that it may be a lesson to you, and that you may act with more prudence and
caution for the future.

"You recollect that two years since I remitted to Madame

D'H—— the sum of £80 to pay Monsieur Dupois for his medical attendance while you were ill in Paris. She then paid him, and gave you the receipt, in order that if she were absent, you might give it me, as I was shortly expected. A short time after, Madame D'H—— having asked you for the receipt, you replied very composedly, 'I had entirely forgotten it, and I fear that I have lost it.' This was certainly a most sensible reply where £80 were involved. In consequence of your departure from Paris, and other circumstances, it was forgotten, though Monsieur Dupois had been requested for another receipt a few days before his death, which was very sudden. Monsieur Dupois not having generally been in the habit of receiving his payments in person, had forgotten to enter the sum as paid. At Christmas twelvemonth I received a second medical account; and as the receipt could not be found, I had to pay the money over again. Some weeks after, the receipt was found in Paris. You had used it for a wool-winder. Now who but a person so careless as yourself would have done this? The money was of course returned. When you were with me you had a similar misfortune, though that was excusable, for you were then but a child; but that should have taught you a little wisdom. I speak of the roll of valuable papers with which you lighted the fire in your boudoir. Was it £30 or £40 that I had to pay for the loss of one paper?

"I will not enumerate other similar incidents, and only mention these to show you the consequences of your forgetfulness. I wish you to rise above such follies, and to act with a thoughtfulness and discretion worthy of the good sense with which God has liberally endowed you. Think how your dear mamma would be grieved if she knew that you had not yet lost this deeply-rooted habit. It is so sad that all who become acquainted with you should so soon discover this fault. I should be truly glad to learn, when I come to see you, that you are trying to overcome it. I know that this will be an affair of time. If you are resolved to make the experiment, you must not be discouraged if you do not immediately succeed, for you must not expect at once to conquer a habit so firmly rooted. You must do as I have often told you to do, 'Think twice before you act once.' This maxim will preserve you from many dangers.

"There is another thing against which I wish to warn you. It is your rash disregard of your health. I hope you do not give Mrs. L—— any trouble on this subject. You know well that you have often been to blame here. When you see that they care for you, the least that you can do is to remain passive, and not to retard your cure by your own folly. Recollect that if we thus voluntarily destroy our health, we are equally responsible with those who terminate their lives by violence. I hope that you are very submissive to the wishes of Mr. and Mrs. L—— in this respect. Their conduct and kindness to you has secured my respect, and has induced me to make the concession I have done, for I was convinced that they had no motives of interest in offering you their friendship when you apostatized from the true Church. I pray daily to God for them, and hope that he will reward them for their good deed, by converting them to the true faith. I hope that in all things unconnected with religion, you will act according to their wishes, and that you will do nothing without their approbation, for you are too prone to act on the impulse of the moment. I do not think that you are headstrong—far otherwise; but you must acknowledge that you are sometimes rash in your decisions. With the consciousness of this defect, I recommend you to be always open and frank with your good friends, for from what I know of Mr. L——, I have a great opinion of his conduct and judgment. The lively interest that I take in you has naturally led me to obtain every information respecting him, before deciding to make any permanent arrangement for you. He is the first Protestant in whom I have placed confidence. Some days since, in writing to Mr. L——, I stated to him my wish that you should continue your education. If you do not acquiesce in my proposition of sending you to a good school for a year or two, which I believe would be the best thing for you, I shall be very glad if Mrs. L—— will superintend your studies according to any plan that she thinks best; but that can be settled when I reach London. I much wish you to go through a course of English, in order that you may be able to write and speak that language with ease and elegance. I wish you to resume your Latin and German. My wish that you should not continue your studies at home, is caused by the fear that you will not apply your mind daily and constantly; without which you cannot be expected to make great progress.

"Wilton, your dear mamma's maid, died on Thursday. I went to see her. She spoke of you with much affection, and said, that one of her most earnest desires in this world was to see you once more. She knows not what a change there is in you, for it is still a secret from the servants.

"Arthur C—— is here for his health. He has left college for a time, and will have a private tutor instead. Before closing my letter, I shall mention the arrangements that I wish, if possible, to make before the end of the year. My first proposition is to invest in the funds without farther delay, (after my retreat) a sufficient sum to yield an annual revenue of £200, which I have thus appropriated. I propose that Mr. L—— should have the same sum annually as Madame D'H—— received, viz. £100 per annum for board and English instruction : £40 will suffice at present I think to spend in clothes, amusements, &c. The remaining £60 would be for medical fees, books, education, &c. If any part of this sum remain at the end of the year, it can be set aside as a fund for exigencies. The investment of the money, which is a subject you do not understand, will be confided to two trustees, a Catholic and a

Protestant, perhaps Captain Kenyon and Mr. L——. The reason why I select a Catholic is, that if you should return to the true faith, your Protestant friend would be free to give up his charge to Captain Kenyon. I do not think that it would be good for you to be without any restraints. I know that this would have a bad tendency, and it is for this reason I appoint trustees. I do not think that you would wish it otherwise. If I cannot at present succeed in making the addition I before mentioned, you must be content, at least for a time. You must not be too eager, for you well know my peculiar position, and that I cannot be too prudent if I would not defeat my object. I have placed the affair before the General in as favorable and as simple an aspect as possible. I must not forget to say that I have entire permission to fulfil my promise at the end of the time before mentioned; but on account of your delicate health, and my aversion to your taking a situation, I wish at once to place you in independent circumstances. I am sorry to inform you that your apostasy has brought much censure upon me. I have been blamed for not having taken measures to prevent it. This costs me many sleepless nights. At times when I think of you I am in an agony of feeling. Oh! why cannot I efface you from my memory? You are truly my cross in this world of sorrow. You have poorly repaid me for all the anxiety that you have cost me. How cruelly are we deceived when we expect our reward from men!

"I advise you to reply carefully to the enclosed questions, for they will have to be examined by other persons than myself. Be prudent. I would not deceive you.

"That you may seriously consider all that I have said in regard to your conduct, and that I may still have the happiness of seeing you an ornament to your sex, is the sincere desire of

"Your faithful and attached friend,
"H. C. CLIFFORD.

"You or Mr. L—— will hear from me at the end of my retreat, after which you will soon see me."

QUESTIONS PROPOSÉES.

"1°. Si l'Eglise Catholique n'est past la vraie église, où était l'Eglise Chrétienne avant l'époque de Luther?

"2°. Si la vraie Eglise n'existait pas pour quelque siècles antérieurs à cette époque, comment a-t-elle été corrompue? et comment cela peut-il être accorde avec les mots du Christ: 'Les portes de l'enfer ne prévandront pas contre elle?' "

Enclosed with Marie's letter was the following to Mr. L——.

(TRANSLATION.)

†

I. H. S. ·

"Saturday Morning.

" Sir,

"Since writing to Marie, the thought has occurred to me, that if you do not know the contents of her last letter you will be dissatisfied, under the supposition that she has expressed herself improperly.

"I wish to destroy this impression by informing you that there was nothing greatly amiss in her communication. Perhaps you will think me too severe in my remarks; but, sir, I who have been accustomed from Marie's infancy to analyze her feelings, thoughts, and character by her letters and by other means, can understand her well, and her last letter confirms my conviction that she is as careless as ever. She attaches much importance to a reprimand from me, and I have therefore ventured to speak to her very faithfully. She will tell you, I am sure, all that I have said to her, and if she appears sorry, a word of advice from you will give effect to my remarks. I am assured that you will see with me the importance of destroying this propensity, for with her prospects this constant thoughtlessness will be a source of great evils. If she do not gain the ascendency over it now, there will be no hope for her subsequently.

"I know Marie's disposition to make light of this defect. Whenever you see a tendency to do this, I advise you to reprove her severely. From what Marie has said, I believe that you and Mrs. L—— have much influence over her. From my position in life, I have had great experience in human character, and I must say I have always found that Marie's requires cautious management. The first and most essential thing is to gain her entire confidence, in order that she may be able frankly to avow her difficulties and her faults, in order that all reserve may be avoided. She has always been in the habit of writing to me in this way, frankly confessing all her faults; and I, in return, have given her advice or reproof as the case required. I cannot now attend to this; but it is my wish that the same sentiments may exist between Marie and her good friends. If, in consequence of her delicacy and timidity, you have hitherto been unsuccessful in this respect, the best means to attain it is always to speak to her very frankly as circumstances call for it. She has too much good sense, and you love her too much to offend her by so doing. If you act thus, she will amply repay you with the greatest affection. My late sister and myself always found that she preferred being reproved when alone.

"I have not now time to revert to business, as the courier will soon start. I beg to apologize for the liberty I take in writing to you, but I wished to say thus much with Marie's letter. I will not revive this subject again without your permission.

"Marie's letter will explain to you my present plans.   With respectful compliments,

"I am your devoted servant,

"H. C. CLIFFORD."

CHAPTER XII.

MARIE'S OCCUPATIONS.

As Marie's health improved her spirits returned.   She again joined the domestic circle, and mingled in their occupations. The impression of the past was to some extent effaced; and though none could feel the same confidence in her as formerly, and none could altogether forget that there was a painful mystery still unexplained, it ceased to be continually present to their memory.   Her precarious state led them to treat her with a measure of tenderness and indulgence which would not have been granted to one in vigorous health.   They knew not how short her stay on earth might be, or how sudden her removal: and who has not felt, in similar cases, an anxiety to avoid the cold look and harsh expression which might be recalled with pain when too late to be forgiven?   They regarded her as a child specially committed to their care by Providence, and not to be lightly cast off or too severely treated.

There was, moreover, another tie between Marie and her friends which it is difficult to explain in so many words.   It partook of a feeling as deep and tender, perhaps, as any of which our nature is capable, though less dwelt upon, and it may be less understood than other affections, namely,—the love we bear to the creature we have saved.

The child walks abroad on some winter's morning, and picks

up a little robin perishing in the cold. He warms it in his bosom, and carries it tenderly to his home; and by-and-by the dim eye brightens, and the bird begins to flutter, and to pick the crumbs from the hand of its benefactor, and warble forth its thanks. Is it not dearer to its young deliverer than the lively canary or gay paroquet which hang in his window in their gilded cages ? Why ? Because *he has saved it.*

The Christian missionary lingers near the scene of some savage conflict which he has vainly sought to avert. He sees a babe which has dropped from the arms of some slaughtered or captive mother. He rescues it from the spear or the flame, and folds it in his arms, and hastens with it to his home: and dark though its skin, and offspring of heathen and savage though it be, it is reared as tenderly as his own children, and is almost as dear to him as they—because *he has saved it.*

We hear much of the love which belongs to earthly relationships, but perhaps there is no love more delightful in its exercise than this. It seems to take its impulse from the love of Him who came to save—that love, the joy of which he himself describes in the beautiful parable of the shepherd rejoicing over the recovered sheep.

And *something* of this mingled with the feelings entertained for Marie, by those who fondly deemed that they had been the means of saving her from a life of misery. It required much, very much, to break through *such* a tie.

And finally, if Marie had been guilty of one grievous delinquency, there were many exhibitions of character which they could not but love. Her virtues appeared to be *her own ;* her faults those of the system in which she had been brought up. Grateful for every act of kindness done to her, and ready for every act of kindness she could render back ; patient and cheerful in illness ; warm-hearted, affectionate and sympathizing ; uncompromising in the expression of her opinions, and frank almost to excess in the avowal of her thoughts and failings;

they came to think of what had occurred as something apart from herself, and originating in some peculiar mental state arising from disorder of the brain. No fellow-creature in trouble, no poor person in distress, could come under her observation without calling out her ready sympathy and active efforts. There was a poor man of the name of Wood occasionally employed about the house, who shared largely in her thoughts and attentions. This poor man had a bad cough, the sound of which she said went to her heart, and that she could not but contrast his circumstances with her own. She made him two flannel waistcoats; she bought a gown for his wife, and worked hard at some frocks for his children; and more than once she made a quantity of rice-milk for them on her own fire, that she might be sure of having it nicely done. She excelled in fancy work, and spent much of her time in working for bazaars for charitable objects, and in making little presents for her friends. She wrote letters of sympathy to such as she knew to be in affliction, and of advice to her younger friends; and no scheme of kindness or of friendship could be proposed in the family, but she must take the first and most active share in its execution.

In conformity with her uncle's wishes about her education, Marie set apart two hours every morning to study with Mrs. L——, and commenced a course of English reading and composition. For the choice of masters in other languages, she was to wait her uncle's arrival. She occasionally practised, but in a very irregular way. She sadly wanted method and quiet perseverance; and her disorderly habits occasioned no little annoyance to the family. There was also an increasing measure of restlessness, and a looking out for excitement, which interfered with the pursuit of duty, and the tranquil enjoyment of life, and occasioned perpetual anxiety to her friends. This latter tendency found for a time some healthful exercise in preparing the answers to her uncle's questions, and set her reading and thinking to good purpose. She had scarcely commenced her undertaking, when she received the following letter :—

†
I. H. S.

Convent of St. Marie, Maggioré,
2d February, 1850.

" My dear Marie,

" Duties of an important nature have interrupted my retreat, and compelled my immediate presence in Germany, where I shall be detained for three weeks, after which I hope to finish my retreat.

" In consequence of this unforeseen event, I cannot see you until after the Easter services. I believe that it is better you should be made aware of this now, rather than disappoint you later.

" I shall be obliged if you will send me your replies to the questions I sent you. I wish particularly to have them before again entering on my retreat. Send them to me therefore between the 16th and the 24th instants. I leave it entirely to your honor to reply to them, without the aid of your friends. It is the commencement of a series of subjects to which I wish you to reply from time to time.

" Having so much to say in my last letter in the way of re-proof, I forgot to mention that it is probable that Mr. and Mrs. Kenyon will visit Manotté during my absence. I have packed all the things which belong to you, in order that Mr. and Mrs. K. may take them with them to London, and thence send them to you. There are five boxes. The first has been opened, and is a great wooden box, with iron bands. Inside the lid, nailed under a piece of leather, you will find the keys of the other boxes. In the tin box, No. 2, you will find all the principal articles of value, that is to say, the jewels of your beloved mother, her watch, and other things. You will also find there a little tin box, in which there are letters and papers requiring much care. It is for this reason that I have separated them. You will find the key of this box in the ink bottle of your desk. Do not open it while you examine the papers, lest it should meet with some accident. I do not wish them to be used for wool winders. I have put in this box a bank note for Mr. L———. I believe that it will be better for you to give him the papers, for I fear that you cannot be trusted with them, especially in the state of excitement in which you will be when you receive them. I have burned a great quantity of letters of little importance, written by you to your mamma. I have found one packet of letters that your mamma had tied together —the correspondence which passed between you during a sorrowful period when you were in England: I mean to say the two months which you passed under our great displeasure. I thought it better to destroy these, with the exception of the two last,—the confession and the reconciliation. You know that I rarely allow myself to be carried away by my feelings; but in reading several of her letters written at different periods, and above all those already mentioned, I was much moved, so forcibly did they bring to mind the loss which you had sustained in losing such a parent. I fear that this will be not only a temporal, but also a spiritual loss, involving the loss of your soul; for if she had lived, you would never have apostatized from the true faith. How can you think of her, and be happy? Few persons have had the happiness to possess such a mother, for she was truly one of the excellent of the earth. You knew not her real value, being too young to appreciate the integrity and honor of her character. She had had much mental suffering, of which you never knew the extent. It was a painful effort to collect these things, for they recalled one whom I strive to forget; and this sorrow was doubled when I thought of you, and of your sad position. Oh! think of your mamma, and then tell me whether you can still remain estranged from the true faith.

"I shall be very glad to receive a letter from you with the questions. I hope that the remarks I made last time will not hinder you from writing freely to me. I shall be sorry if that is the case, for it will defeat the object I have in view of judging of your character by your letters. My dear child, do all you can to correct your youthful follies, for strangers will not bear with so much patience and goodness the thoughtlessness so strongly indicated in all that you do, as those who have watched over you with so much interest from your infancy. I well know how little capable you are of sustaining a severe reproof, so for the sake of your own happiness try to destroy this propensity, which obscures so many noble traits in your character.

"You will say that I am always preaching on the same subject. I can imagine the expression of your countenance when you hear again the old song, but I know that when the cloud has passed, my dear Marie will appreciate all that I have said. I hope that I shall not again refer to this subject, except to express my pleasure in your having entirely corrected it. I shall know from Mr. L—— when that is, and then, as an encouragement, I shall present you with £50, with which to buy anything that you please in memory of having conquered so embarrassing an enemy. When you have passed three months without one careless action, and are capable of acting in all respects with discretion and reflection, then you will receive the gift; but it must be steadily carried out in your most important duties, and in your daily occupations. Bear in mind the proverb which you know so well. When you write to me, tell me how you spend your time, and how Mr. and Mrs. L—— behave towards you. I know that they are very good to you, but have they sufficient interest in all that concerns you, to point out your faults and counsel you to avoid them? Tell me frankly what sort of person Mrs. L—— is. Give me particulars, that is to say, as to her dispositions and character. I have seen her, but I cannot judge at sight. Do you feel any reserve with them, and can you speak to them freely on all subjects? I wish particularly to know all your feelings in this respect, and if there are any difficulties which I can remove. Above all, tell me if your health is improved. I hope you will not visit much, for I have a decided objection to your going into society. Do Mr. and Mrs. L—— visit a great deal? I suppose you were delighted with the escape of the apostate Dr. Achilli. Your sentiments correspond with his.

"You must not write again after the next letter until you have had tidings of me. Next Thursday is the anniversary of poor Earnest's death. It causes me regret when I think that I neglected him, my regard being concentrated upon you.

"I leave here at seven o'clock this evening. It is time now to assist at confession. I left my retreat last evening, though I am still in the convent. I am, my dear Marie,

"Your affectionate relative,

"H. C. CLIFFORD.

"Address to me—Duchess of Bellini's, Palace of Bellini, near Strasburgh, Germany."

Marie shed tears over some parts of this letter, but as a whole it afforded her much gratification. As will readily be supposed, she manifested much girlish pleasure in anticipating the arrival of her boxes. Her thoughts took a pensive turn when remembering how much there would be to recall her parent to mind, but the expected arrival of her own property was mingled with no such associations. She planned many gifts for her friends, the servants, and the poor. The coins she should sell to purchase a piano for herself. Then from her first quarter's pin money and incidental fund, she proposed buying furniture for her own little room, to which she longed to return. There was in it a recess in which she had ascertained that a little iron bedstead, long enough for her, would stand, and this would leave the area of the room vacant to be fitted up as a boudoir. She proposed buying a pretty carpet, an ottoman, and a handsome chest of drawers and bookcase, also a flower-stand; and she spoke to the gardener about procuring her some choice flowers. She anticipated many a pleasant hour in the opening spring, but her friends often doubted whether those bright visions would ever be realized.

CHAPTER XIII.

MARIE'S ANSWERS FOR THE GENERAL OF THE JESUITS.

Marie finished answering the questions, and accompanied them by a lengthened reply to her uncle's letters. With the exception of a few suggestions in the arrangement, and a few verbal alterations, the answers were her own, and her friends were not a little pleased with the way in which she had accomplished her task. Her letter went into minute detail on all the topics of his last, and being very lengthy, is here omitted.

QUESTION I.

" If the Church of Rome is not the true Church, where was the true Church before the time of Luther ?"

In order to answer the first question, it is necessary to ascertain the true meaning of the word 'Church.' There are only two senses attached to it in the Bible. The one applies to any congregation or body of Christians meeting in one place; for example, the Apostle Paul speaks of 'the Churches of God in Asia,' 'the Churches in Macedonia,' 'the Churches of Achaia,' 'the Churches of Galatia,' 'the Churches of Judea,' 'the Churches of Ephesus.' In the last chapter of Paul's Epistle to the Romans the following references are made :—1 ver. 'Phœbe, a servant of the Church in Cenchrea;' 4 ver. 'All the Churches of the Gentiles salute you ;' 5 ver. 'Greet the Church that is in their house ;' (the house of Aquila and Priscilla) ; 16 ver. 'The Churches of Christ salute you ;' 23 ver. 'Gaius, mine host, and of the whole Church, saluteth you.' In his 1st Epistle to the Corinthians, 1 ver. we find it thus addressed :—'Unto the Church of God which is at Corinth, to them that are sanctified in Christ Jesus, called to be saints, with all that in every place call upon the name of Jesus Christ our Lord, both theirs and ours.' At the close of this Epistle we again find, 'The Churches of Asia salute you, Aquila and Priscilla salute you much in the Lord, with the Church that is in their house.' 'Salute the brethren which are in Laodicea, and Nymphas, and the Church which is in his house.'—Col. iv. 15. In the 1st Epistle to the Thessalonians reference is made to those who became 'followers of the Churches of God which are in Judea.' In addressing Philemon he again says, 'And to the Church in thy house.' The Apostle Peter, in closing his 1st Epistle, v. 14, writes, 'The Church that is at Babylon, elected together with you, saluteth you.' The Apostle John, in the Apocalypse, addresses 'the Churches of Ephesus, Smyrna, Pergamos, Thyatira, Sardis, and Philadelphia.'

The second application of the term Church in the Scriptures is to the whole body of true believers, gathered out of all Churches, and forming one catholic or universal Church in Christ Jesus, recognizing him as their only head. 'And he is the head of the body the Church, who is the beginning, the first-born from the dead, that in all things he (Christ) might have the pre-eminence.'—Col. i. 18. 'Gave him to be the head over all things to the Church.'—Eph. i. 22. 'Unto him be glory in the Church by Christ Jesus throughout all ages, world without end.'—Eph. iii. 21. 'As Christ also loved the Church, and gave himself for it. That he might sanctify and cleanse it with the washing of water by the word. That he might present it to himself, a glorious Church, not having spot or wrinkle, or any such thing; but that it shall be holy and without blemish.'—Eph. v. 25, 26, 27.

Let us now proceed to the question itself—'If the Church of Rome is not the true Church,' &c.

The Church at Rome, when first formed, *was* a true Church, being founded or built upon Christ alone; but it was not the only Church, or even the first Church. The first Christian Church was formed at Jerusalem, and owed its origin chiefly to the preaching of the Apostle Peter. The Church at Antioch was formed before that of Rome, and was the first place where the disciples were called Christians.—Acts xi. 19-26. The Churches in Asia Minor, Syria, and Greece, if not formed *before*, were contemporary *with* the Church at Rome.

It is a remarkable fact, that while in most of the Apostle Paul's Epistles he addresses the Church at each place by name, in his Epistle to the Romans no direct reference is made to the Church at Rome.

Taking the *Bible* as our *only* guide, we find nothing to lead us to suppose that the Apostle Peter ever preached at Rome or even visited Rome, his mission being chiefly among the Jews. There is no mention of either Rome or the Romans in his history or epistles; being indebted for our chief information concerning the Church at Rome to the visits of the Apostle Paul. If he visited Rome, as some historians seem to infer, there is no evidence of his having sustained any official relation to that Church.

The question again asks, 'Where was the true Church before the time of Luther?' The true Church is composed of all true believers, from the time of the Apostles down to the present day

After the Church departed from the simple principles of

Christianity, and substituted the forms and customs invented by man in their stead, we find that through all ages of Church history, however corrupt, there has remained a true Church of God, preserved from the degenerate mass, though concealed by their obscure position. It was thus that the band of the Waldenses and many others, like those in Elijah's time, would not bow the knee to Baal.

From the writings of the most inveterate opponents of the Waldenses we find the following statements :—Bishop Sylvester says, 'The sect of the Waldenses is the oldest of any ; some even trace them up to the Apostolic age.' The Archbishop of Turin writes thus, 'There must have been great and powerful reasons why this sect has continued so many centuries ; and this, notwithstanding all sorts of people armed with the greatest power, have from time to time labored in vain to extirpate them, for they have ever invariably triumphed contrary to all human expectations, and have always been found invincible.' These are the sentiments of their persecutors—the Roman Catholics.

In the eleventh century, the Albigenses, Leonists, the Picards, and the Arnoldists are mentioned, as keeping themselves pure from the erroneous doctrines of the Church of Rome. Then the Lollards formed another part of the Christian band or true Church.

In the twelfth century, the Waldenses drew up a confession of their faith, which is precisely the same as made by the Christian Church of the present day, so that in the great fundamental truths of the gospel the Church of Christ has *ever* been one. The following is a brief summary of the Waldensian confession :—

" I. They acknowledge the Bible as the only rule of faith.

" II. That there was but ONE Mediator, and that no invocation ought to be to Mary or the saints.

" III. That purgatory was a fiction.

"IV. That there are but two sacraments—baptism, and the Lord's Supper.

"V. That the mass was to be rejected.

"VI. That all religious ordinances of human institution, as Romish fasts, festivals, monastic orders, pilgrimages, and such ceremonies, are to be rejected.

"VII. Disavowing the supremacy of the Pope.

"VIII. That the traffic of indulgences and the law of celibacy are inadmissible.

"IX. That they who hear the Word of God and do it, are the Church of God."

Though this faithful band of true believers were severely persecuted through a period of three centuries, all endeavors to extirpate them were fruitless; and before the year 1525 the Waldenses succeeded in banishing the Romish priesthood from their valleys, and had the whole Bible translated in the Waldensian language, for, prior to this, they had only the New Testament in their native tongue.

About this time, the year 1521, Luther, the bright star of the Reformation, emerged from the dark cloud of Popery, after spending many years of severe mental conflict. He,—guided by the unerring Word of God and the counsels of one of the secret disciples of Christ, Staupitz, a monk in the monastery of Erfurth,—became the honored instrument in the hands of God of rescuing the countries of Britain, Germany, and Switzerland, from the influence of that corrupted Church—the Church of Rome; and caused a purer light to shine upon them—the light of God's truth, the Gospel.

From these facts it will be observed that the true spiritual Church was preserved previous to the Reformation, and the Church of Rome has *no* claim to the exclusive title of the true Church.

QUESTION II.

" If the true Church had ceased to exist before the time of Luther, how had it become corrupted prior to its fall ? and how may this be reconciled with the words of Christ—" the gates of hell shall not prevail against it !" (signifying the Church.)

The first clause of this question has been already answered in the latter part of the first query—' that the Church of Christ had *not* ceased to exist prior to the time of Luther.'

The second part of the question is, ' how had it become corrupted ?'

1st. By departing from the true and certain Word of God and substituting the traditions of men ; as Christ himself said to the Pharisees, ' Making the Word of God of none effect through your traditions.'—Mark vii. 13. And as the Apostle Paul says, ' Beware lest any man spoil you through philosophy and vain deceits, after the traditions of men and after the rudiments of the world, and not after Christ.'—Col. ii. 8.

2d. Mixing the ceremonies and doctrines of Judaism with Christianity.

We have a striking proof of this error in the conduct of the Apostle Peter. ' When Peter was come to Antioch I (Paul) withstood him to the face, because he was to be blamed. For before that certain came from James, he did eat with the Gentiles ; but when they (the Jews) were come, he withdrew and separated himself, fearing them which were of the circumcision.'—Gal. ii. 14, 15.

The Church at Rome, when she was freed from persecution, and had received into her communion one of the heathen emperors, Constantine, departed still further from the simple worship of God, and substituted many of the pomps and ceremonies of Judaism. Crucifixes also became objects of adoration, relics were sought after and worshipped, as, in the days of

Ahaz, the brazen serpent became the idol of the children of
Israel.   The repeated observances of fasts and festivals ; priests
clothed in costly and gaudy vestments ; the sacrifice of the
mass in the place of the sacrificial offering of the Jews ; the use
of incense, holy water, &c.   So that the primitive simplicity of
Christian worship was gradually lost in the variety of human
inventions and ordinances.

These ceremonies became so numerous, that even in the days
of Augustine, about the year 400, we find him thus com-
plaining,—'that even the Levitical ritual was not so burdensome as the new ritual of the Christian Church.'

3d. The third cause of corruption was accommodating
Christianity to the idolatrous propensities of the nations.   The
general propensity of the world is to idolatry.   The Church of
Rome, in departing from the first principles of the Gospel, not
only corrupted the purity of her faith, but substituted rites and
ceremonies to meet the taste of the heathen world.   In the
place of their heathen gods, she supplied them with images or
idols of the Virgin and saints.   Take as an example the Pantheon at Rome, which was dedicated to Jupiter and all the
heathen gods : papal Rome reconsecrated it to the Virgin and
saints : so that it has served the two purposes of pagan and
papal idolatrous worship.   In the first, every heathen might
worship his favorite god : in the latter, his patron saint.   This
was the case with many other heathen temples : one idol was
exchanged for another.   In a letter written by Pope Gregory
to Melitus, he advises him thus : 'I have long been cogitating
upon the matter of the English people, and the result is this :
that the fanes of the idols that are in them ought by no means
to be demolished ; but the idols that are in them ought to be
destroyed ; the temples, meanwhile, sprinkled with holy water,
altars constructed, and relics of the saints deposited.   In the
same manner let this be done : as these people have been in
the habit of slaying many cattle in the sacrifices to their

demons, so far for their sakes ought there to be some solemnity, the object of it only being changed.'

All such idolatry is in direct opposition to the Word of God, and has in all ages of the world caused His displeasure. There are numerous instances of this recorded in the Old Testament. The following is one selected from many. By the command of God, 'Hezekiah removed the high places, and brake in pieces the images and brazen serpent that Moses had made; for unto those ways the children of Israel did burn incense to it.'—2 Kings viii. 4. Hezekiah feared God, therefore sought to banish idolatry from his kingdom.

In the New Testament, idolatry is equally condemned: the Apostle Paul exhorts all to flee from idolatry, 1 Cor. x. 14, and to renounce idolaters, 1 Cor. v. 11.

The falling away and declension of the Church was foretold by the Apostles. 'Let no man deceive you by any means, for that day shall not come, *except* there be a falling away first, and that man of sin be revealed, the son of perdition; who opposeth and exalteth himself above all that is called God, or that is worshipped; so that he as God sitteth in the temple of God, showing Himself that he is God. For the mystery of iniquity doth already work: only he who now letteth will let, until he be taken out of the way. And then shall that *wicked* one be revealed, whom the Lord shall consume with the spirit of his mouth, and shall destroy with the brightness of his coming: even him, whose coming is after the working of Satan, with all power and signs and lying wonders.'—2 Thess. ii. 3—9. 'Now the Spirit speaketh expressly, that in the latter times some shall depart from the faith: speaking lies in hypocrisy. Forbidding to marry, and commanding to abstain from meats, which God hath created to be received with thanksgiving of them which believe and know the truth.'—1 Tim. iv. 1—3. These predictions cannot apply to any other part of the Church than the Church of Rome. In the Apocalypse we have again striking prophecies concerning this Church. In the 17th chapter we find her thus described : as ' a woman sitting upon a colored beast which had seven heads and ten horns.' The 9th verse gives as the explanation the seven heads are seven mountains on which the woman sitteth. The city of Rome is built upon seven hills, over which the woman (Popery) reigneth. In the dress of the woman we have the two great colors (scarlet and purple) of the Church as worn by her prelates.

The Church of Rome is a corrupt and fallen Church, having left her first love. The people of God are earnestly exhorted to forsake her: 'Come out of her, my people, that ye be not partakers of her sins, and that ye receive not of her plagues. For her sins have reached unto heaven, and God hath remembered her iniquities.'—Rev. xviii. 4, 5. It is evident that these predictions likewise can apply to no other Church than the Church of Rome.

The closing clause of the question is, ' if the Church had become corrupt, how may it be reconciled with the words of Christ ?—"The gates of hell shall not prevail against it." ' It has been already proved that one portion of the Church had become corrupt, but not *the* Church, for that must ever remain pure. We have strong proofs of the possibility of the falling away or corruption of any particular Church, in the second and third chapters of the Apocalypse. The first Church there addressed, is the one at Ephesus. After commending them for their labor and patience, he says, 'Nevertheless, I have somewhat against thee, because thou hast left thy first love.' The Churches of Pergamos, Thyatira, Sardis, and Philadelphia, are each reproved for their spiritual declension. These passages from Holy Writ are quite sufficient to prove the possibility of a Church departing from the first principles of the Gospel, and consequently becoming a corrupted Church.

The last sentence of the closing question is, ' The gates of hell shall not prevail against it.' The previous answers are quite enough to prove that the gates, or deliberations of hell, have never yet prevailed against God's truth.

As soon as the Christian Church commenced its career, severe persecutions by heathen Rome seriously tried it. The efforts of Papal Rome seemed for a time to succeed; but the Church soon burst forth with greater brightness.

In the ninth century the counsels of hell again seemed to prevail; but a small band of true worshippers were found in the retired valley of Piedmont. Through a period of three centuries they endured increasing persecution : thousands were put to death. Did the gates of hell then prevail? No; for in the fifteenth century we again find them a flourishing Church.

This corroborates the fact that God has in all ages preserved his Church. The gates of hell could not be said to prevail.

It is cheering to learn that while tribulation and destruction were spreading in every direction, a branch of the true Church remained, whether amidst the Alps, or elsewhere, serving God in Spirit and truth, proving the fulfilment of our Saviour's promise, that 'the gates of hell shall not prevail against it.' Nor shall they so long as the world exists. And when the consummation of all things shall come, the Church of Christ will then be found gathered from every people, nation, tribe, and tongue, and will form one triumphant Church above, ascribing glory to 'Him that hath loved them, and washed them from their sins in his own blood.' 'To Him be glory and dominion forever and ever. Amen.'

MARIE.

CHAPTER XIV.

THE MIDNIGHT BELL.

THE mental effort required in answering the questions, and the excitement occasioned by her uncle's letter of February 28th, appeared to be too much for Marie, and another illness followed. One night in the beginning of March, Elizabeth was roused from her sleep by the sound of her name; and the faint light from the gas-lamp in the road, showed her Marie standing by her bedside half covered with blood. In the first moment of alarm she had rushed up-stairs, and not liking to disturb Mrs. L——, had come up to her sister. Elizabeth covered her up, led her carefully down, laid her on her bed, and did all that could be done for her till morning broke, and medical advice could be obtained. A bell was fixed from the head of her bed to the rooms up-stairs, so that she might in future give the alarm on the first symptom of illness. Several times during the following fortnight, in the dead silence of the night, the sound of that bell raised the family from their slumbers, and one or all would hasten to her assistance. "Oh! Mrs. L——, I can never stand this," said Marie, faintly, as, on the seventh occasion of the kind, Mrs. L—— stood by her side. "It must be my death before long." In the morning she asked to speak to Mr. L——, and entreated him to write to her uncle immediately, and hasten his coming, or she feared she should not live to see him. She also requested Mrs. L—— to lend her the manuscript of her book, as she wished to make a few corrections while she had sufficient strength remaining; but Mrs. L—— did not think it well to attend to this request. Mr. L—— went to her medical attendant to ascertain his opinion, and was relieved to find that he was far from being so much alarmed as themselves. He saw no ground for breaking in upon the uncle's retreat. He said she would soon rally, and be as well as before; and so it proved.

At this period, and indeed throughout her illnesses, it may be truly said, that every means that skill or kindness could suggest was fully tried. A variety of medicine, ice, leeches, &c., were resorted to, as the case required. She was not for some time allowed to take animal food, but poultry and fish, calves'-feet jellies, new-laid eggs, and vegetables (cooked according to her directions in French fashion), were provided for her. Her friends had great difficulty in inducing her to be sufficiently careful of herself, or to take her medicines regularly. She was a perfect child in this respect. Mrs. L—— had often to stand by her some minutes, persuading and reasoning, and at last was obliged either to show or to feign displeasure before she could be induced to take her medicine. Sometimes she would say, "I cannot take it *just now:* only leave me a little, and I promise you to take it presently."

Marie had recovered from her recent attack, and the alarm of her friends had subsided. Ten days passed over undisturbed, and again the dreaded midnight bell was heard. Another day, and the same cause of alarm occurred early in the evening. The family tried to persuade Marie to keep her bed for a few days, as the bleeding so invariably recurred after the fatigue and excitement of the day. But Marie could never be kept in bed if it was possible to rise. She *would* get up, and mingle with the family, and talk more rapidly, and laugh more heartily than any, and flushed and excited as the day closed in, they scarcely felt surprised when again summoned to her aid. When the bleeding had ceased she all but fainted, and was then slightly delirious. He friends became increasingly anxious, and resolved on having a consultation respecting her case, feeling that, in the event of a sudden and distressing termination, they should wish to have no cause for self-reproach, or for the reproaches of her uncle.

Marie strongly objected; but her objections were overruled, and the 25th of March was appointed for the consultation. She seemed much entertained with the anticipation. "Indeed Mrs. L—— you must not sit at the foot of my bed," said she, "or I shall laugh outright. They will tell me to count, and draw a deep breath, and tap here, and listen there, and give a rap here;" and she playfully suited the action to the word. The doctors came, and with their process of investigation just realized Marie's lively description. She caught Mrs. L——'s eye and laughed. In vain they told her to keep still. She shrank from every application of the stethoscope to her tender chest; and after various unsatisfactory efforts to hear what they wanted to hear, and to know what they wanted to know, they retired to another room. Mr. and Mrs. L—— were called in to hear the report. "As well as we can ascertain with so fidgetty a patient, we are happy to state that disease appears to be in a very incipient stage, and if her strength can be kept up, there will be no cause for alarm. Had it not been that several members of her family have died from similar causes, we should see no ground for apprehension. She may live twenty years, if no violent cold or strong excitement bring her life to a speedier termination." All unfavorable symptoms gradually disappeared after this visit, and sanguine hopes were entertained of her complete recovery.

Marie expressed some anxiety to obtain her uncle's offered £50, and requested Mrs. L—— to keep a journal. This was done, somewhat to the amusement of all parties; but its details are too exclusively domestic for insertion.

There was one bad habit of which frequent intimation occurs in the journal, and which seemed incurable. The postman's knock operated like an electric shock; and let the wind and weather be what they might, or half-a-dozen other hands ready, neither argument nor reproof could prevent her from running to the door to see if there was a letter from her uncle. The postponement of his long anticipated visit continually added to this excited feeling, and her friends ceased to struggle with her respecting the interdicted practice.

About this time, Dr. Achilli arrived in England. Marie eagerly entreated permission to be allowed to attend the meeting held to welcome him in Exeter Hall. She was sure that if she had a fly from door to door, was cloaked up and had her respirator on, she *could* get no harm. Her friends could not consent to her encountering the cold and excitement. She then expressed an earnest wish to meet him in private. She said that he must know much of the Jesuits, and would probably know her uncle. To gratify her, Mr. L—— went to Dr. Achilli's, stated her case, and invited him to dinner. Dr. Achilli cheerfully agreed, and a day was to be fixed as soon as Marie was considered equal to the interview. But fresh symptoms of oppression on the chest postponed the meeting, and the time never came.

One day it transpired that Marie had posted a newspaper for her uncle, directed to him at Rome. She persuaded Elizabeth to write the direction for her. It was a copy of the " *Christian Times*," containing a full account of Dr. Achilli's meeting, and of his previous imprisonment. Mr. and Mrs. L—— took Marie to task for so inconsiderate an act. Her apostscy having already brought suspicion on her uncle, the receipt of such a newspaper was as likely a step as she could take to compromise his character in the estimation of his Order. Marie only laughed, and could not be brought to take any serious view of the matter.

9*

CHAPTER XV.

THE UNCLE KNOWS ALL.

EARLY in March Marie received the following letter, which agitated her extremely. Having caught sight of its drift, she exclaimed, "Oh! my uncle knows all," and hastily left the room. It was long before she returned, and then tearful, flushed and agitated, she put the letter into Mrs. L——'s hands. She wept much for days, refused to eat, and said she could not sleep.

(TRANSLATION.)

I. H. S.

"Gand, February 28th, 1850.

"My dear Marie,

"If a severe illness had not prevented me from quitting Bellini, at the appointed time I should unfortunately have missed your letter, which did not reach till two days after date.

"I have been suffering from quinsy with a slight attack of inflammation, the consequence of a cold which I caught in travelling. I kept my bed in Bellini for ten days. My doctors feared lest it should turn to bronchitis. I hope it will soon pass off, for I have no more time to spare for taking care of myself, —it makes so great a breach in my arduous duties.

"I was very well satisfied with the care and propriety of your last packet. I shall not now make any farther observation on your replies than to commend you for the trouble which you have taken to please me. Though the sentiments were erroneous, the care and thoughtfulness were the same.

"The news of your indisposition gave me real sorrow. I am very uneasy about you. If money could save you, I am sure you know me well enough to believe that there is nothing I would not do to prolong your life.

"You have not yet received your boxes. Captain Kenyon wrote to me to say that they should wait a few days until a certain event relating to their eldest daughter had taken place, after which they would immediately leave Welby for Manotté. They will only remain there three weeks, so you will receive your boxes before I see you. I mentioned in my last letter that I had sent you money in your desk. You are also sure to find some Bank notes in your mamma's desk.

"There is one part of your letter which has occasioned me much solicitude. You say that you are becoming reserved. I had already discovered, though I have not liked to tell you of it, that you are not so frank with me as formerly. I have been much pained at your concealment of your recent error. I know to what extent you were culpable, and also to what extent you were injured. I am more inclined to pity than to blame you. I well know your thoughtless and ardent temperament, and can therefore enter into your feelings, and the temptations of a false world from which you have hitherto been preserved.

"I must tell you, my dear Marie, that the late affair has greatly distressed me. I feel so grieved that you should have again fallen into the sin which caused your mamma and myself so much sorrow some years since. It is not your natural disposition, for there have been but two periods in your life in which you have fallen into this lamentable fault. At other times you have been as remarkable for the contrary. I believed that you would not again have fallen into this snare, and I hope sincerely that the painful remembrance of the past will prevent your again yielding to so sad a temptation. I shrink from wounding your feelings, but if I did not love you, I would not give myself the trouble of warning and counselling you. I have often wished to mention this circumstance to you, but I could find no occasion for doing so, until, in your last letter, your remarks made me think that there was something which you wished to tell me, but were hindered by reserve, and I then determined to speak to you faithfully. I feared that in consequence of your timidity you had ceased to confess frankly when you had done wrong. This has induced me to say so much upon this point to Mrs. L——. I knew all that had occurred, and as you did not unfold the matter to me, I apprehended that you had become reserved. You say that you love Mr. and Mrs. L——. Why then can you not open your mind to them? If their love is sincere, I am sure they will not think the less of you, but will rather return your confidence with increased affection. I well know that unless your love for a person be very great, you cannot give your confidence; but I think that from what I hear that your affection is mutual, and yet you say you are reserved with them? I cannot understand it. Try by all means to conquer it, for unless you do so, I foresee incalculable evil to your naturally frank disposition. Is not pride at the root of this feeling? I propose to speak with you at length upon past circumstances. I have much to say to Mr. L——.

" Your exact description of the character of Mrs. L—— has pleased me much. One thing especially has given me pleasure; it is that she is firm and decided. Your easy disposition requires firmness. I do not like her the less for not retracting what she has once enjoined. The hymn is very good and very pretty. There is nothing in it to reprehend.

" Your anxiety to know the secret of my communications with Mr. L—— has a little amused me. As 'suspense is really worse than reality,' I leave to Mr. L——'s discretion the care of enlightening you upon the mysterious affair. If Mr. L—— thinks it well to tell you, his decision will be mine.

"I am thankful that Mrs. L—— endeavors to convince you of the importance of moving about gently. I suppose she occasionally trembles for the safety of her doors, chairs, tables, &c., when these articles find themselves under your gentle touch.

"I hope that you apply yourself to your studies. Wh· progress are you making towards the promised reward? · you more advanced than you were yesterday? I shall not put up with childish excuses.

"I hope to be with you by the 17th of April. Before that time Mr. L—— will hear from me. If the Kenyons should invite you during my stay in London, I wish you to refuse the invitation, but do not say that it is at my desire.

"I do not wish that your first introduction into your family should be as an object of curiosity. I know that A———C—— much wishes to see you, but I cannot bear the idea of your being distressed by the sight of any one of the C——'s. I would rather wait for more favorable circumstances, which will probably restore to you the favor and attention of your relations.

"I must now conclude, for I have other letters to write, which must all be closed in another despatch for England by this evening's courier. I leave here to-morrow.

"Present my compliments to Mr. and Mrs. L——, and accept the most ardent wishes for your happiness, of

"Your attached and faithful friend,

"H. C. CLIFFORD."

After the permission here given, Marie was gradually acquainted with her prospects, and to the relief of her anxious friends, she manifested far less elation and excitement than they had anticipated. The expectation did not seem to lay hold of her half so much as had the immediate provision proposed by her uncle. His last letter, and the reproach still resting on her character, seemed to occupy her thoughts, almost to the exclusion of any other subject.

The other letter, which came by the same post, was to Mrs. L——.

(TRANSLATION.)

†

I. II. S.

"Gand, Feb. 28th, 1850.

"Madam,

"After your goodness in sending me particulars respecting my dear niece Marie, I feel that it is needless to apologize for the liberty that I take in writing to you.

"The deep interest that I take in Marie's temporal and spiritual welfare, induces me to make some remarks, and also to give you some advice as to the manner of guiding and rightly directing her character. There was in Marie's last letter a remark which caused me much uneasiness. She said that she was becoming reserved, and that she could not frankly express what she wished particularly to tell you. She frankly avows that it is her fault. There is in Marie a degree of timidity, and a disposition which requires much encouragement. She is extremely sensitive, and a look of approbation or of displeasure on the part of those whom she loves, is sufficient to render her happy or miserable. She is very firm and faithful in her attachments. Few persons love so ardently as she does. I have seen and known many young persons who were much attached to their relations, but I never met with one whose love surpassed that of Marie. She watches every look, and the consciousness of having displeased her mother was more than she could bear. That alone was generally a sufficient punishment.

"I mention this solely to show you how great the influence which may be acquired over Marie; and I am well convinced that there is no one so competent to exercise it as yourself

From what she says to me, she appears to pay much attention to what you do or say. For this reason I wish you to endeavor to gain her entire confidence, in order that the great evil of reserve may be avoided. In the first place, never shrink from the necessity of pointing out to her faithfully what has been unsatisfactory; seek for a frank explanation when she has done wrong, and always mention your reasons for every cause of displeasure. Sympathy is the great key to gain her heart and confidence. I have always regarded her as a grateful and generous girl. Selfishness finds no place in Marie. She is, it is true, childish in many things."   *   *   *

    *   *   *   *   *   *

Marie tore up the other sheet of this letter to light a candle.

CHAPTER XVI.

MARIE'S POETRY AND ESSAY.

It has already been intimated that Marie had some taste for poetry, and her verses, though not of the highest order, were easy and pleasing. She wrote fluently and frequently. A few specimens written about this time may suffice.

TO LILLY ON HER BIRTH-DAY.

March 10, 1850.

I've seen two lovely roses grow,
    United on one stem,
And summer's heat, and winter's snow,
    Were shared alike by them;
To full maturity they'd grown,
    And flourished on that bough alone.

Seasons have passed; at length I've seen
  A tender bud appear;
But oh! so fragile it has been,
  That while with anxious care
I've tended it, I've feared each day
Lest all its beauty should decay.

How often then with lively joy,
  My treasured tree I viewed,
The pair have seemed to fancy's eye
  With human powers endued,
Bending with kind parental care,
O'er the young bud they hoped to rear.

Would you my simple song improve;
  Reflect, dear child, how you,
By tender parents' watchful care,
  Are kindly cherished too!
From infancy's first feeble breath
They've shielded you, and will till death.

And they have offered fervent prayer
  That, through a Saviour's blood,
Their child the early marks may bear
  Of one belov'd of God;
And they be favored to behold
Their child a lamb of Jesus' fold.

But verse can ne'er the love express
  With which their bosoms glow,
The full deep stream of tenderness,
  Increasing in its flow;
Their many kind parental cares
For you, dear " child of many prayers."

Oh! make their inmost souls rejoice,
  Yield to your parents' God
Yourself, a " living sacrifice"
  Through the atoning blood;
May you, my darling, live and grow,
A cedar in the church below;
Then, filled with peace, and joy, and love,
Reign glorious in the church above.

MARIE.

LINES TO ELIZABETH.

Why should a giddy world pursue,
  With such intense desire,
Joys which no sooner meet the view
  Than quickly they expire?
And why so fondly, closely cling
  To earth-born friends and ties?
The dearest may conceal a sting,
  To wound the sweetest joys.

When Spring o'er fair Creation's face
  Her budding beauties poured,
I joyed; and when Sol's warmer rays
  Those beauties had matured,
Still more I joyed; but soon the cold
  Autumnal blast swept by:
Stern Winter followed, and behold
  Scenes desolate and dry.

And thus it is with all below,
  Where'er our footsteps range;
For scenes of happiness and woe
  Alike are stamped with change

E'en friends, aye *bosom* friends, with whom
　　Our hearts were closely joined,
Too often in the soul's deep gloom,
　　Prove faithless and unkind.

Yet were it not so, were each heart
　　Sincere and free from guile,
And were we, my belov'd one, blest
　　With friendship's faithful smile ;
Yet death, whom none can long withstand,
　　Will snap the closest ties ;
And snatch, with unrelenting hand,
　　Earth's treasures from our eyes.

Then since all worldly joys decay,
　　And fairest scenes are changed,
And dearest friends are snatched away
　　By death, or grown estranged :
Let us, my dear one, fix our eyes
　　On more substantial bliss,
Nor trust to aught beneath the skies,
　　For happiness and peace.

MARIE.

THE STAGES OF LIFE.

I've looked on infancy, pure and bright,
When clad in its robe of simple white,
And I've loved to look on the brow so fair,
For fancy could trace gay visions there,
Visions though fleeting, perchance, and vain,
Yet bearing along in their joyous train
　　　　　　Much that was lovely.

I've looked on childhood's laughing face,
And marked with delight each dimpled grace,
The sparkling eye, the prattling tongue
Just lisping forth its imperfect song;
The winning love; the endearing smile;
I've marked them all, and have felt the while
              Much of true pleasure.

I've marked the child when swift-winged Time,
Had borne him along to the youthful prime;
And have marvelled much to behold the face,
So pure in its infant loveliness,
Oft wearing the trace of sadness now,
While frowns o'ershadow the once calm brow,
              Marks of humanity.

I've watched him still as his course he ran,
And have seen him rise to a perfect man,
And his brow was more wrinkled, for time and care
Had planted many a furrow there,
And his voice had lost its joyous tone,
He had sought but the world, and that alone
              Now was his portion.

I've marked in another how infancy's grace,
And childhood with mirth's expressive face,
And youth with its feelings fresh and warm
Have passed into manhood; but yet a calm,
Purer and holier still than that
Which once on the brow of the infant sat,
              On him hath rested.

'Twas not that his life had less of woe
Than falls to the lot of man below;

'Twas not that affliction within his heart,
Had thrust less keenly her barbed dart;
'Twas not that to him the weight of years,
Brought no addition of toils and cares,
          That he was peaceful.

Oh no! but his heart, by grace divine,
Was daily laid on Jehovah's shrine;
And though sharply and sorely affliction's dart
Pierced once and again his bleeding heart,
He knew 'twas God, and his soul was calm,
While the hand that smote applied the balm,
          Sweet balm of healing.

And I've thought when the contrast I've surveyed,
(As sunshine is bright compared with shade,)
How bright are the characters divine
On the features of the saint which shine,
Compared with the many and anxious cares,
Which the wrinkled brow of the worldling wears,
          Speaking of anguish.

I love pure infancy's artless glee,
I love young childhood blithe and free,
I love the vigorous fire of youth,
I love bold manhood with brow of truth,
I love old age as with stealthy pace
He steals along to his resting place;
But the settled peace and the calm repose,
Which should sweeten life as it nears its close,
 Dwells not on the brow disturbed by care,
Those only the sweet expression wear
          Who rest in Jesus.   MARIE.

.arie thought she would write some essays for uncle's inspection on his arrival, and that through them she would make him better acquainted with her views. The following unfinished attempt has been found among her papers. She was diligently collecting the evidence from the New Testament on the subject here chosen, and in particular the frequent and open appeals of Christ and His Apostles to the testimony of Scripture, when illness again compelled her to discontinue her studies.

(UNFINISHED) ESSAY

On the Reasons for concluding that God intended all Men to search and read the Bible.

The Church of Rome uses as a plea for withholding the Bible from the great mass of her adherents, that God only intended it for his prophets, apostles, and their successors in the ministry of Christ. It is the purpose of this essay to prove from the Word of God that He not only intended, but commands *all* men to read for themselves that book which is alone able to make them wise unto salvation.

The adaptation of the Scriptures to the most unlearned and humble capacity of man, as well as to the intellect of the wise and profound theologian, is in itself a proof of this. Each alike may read and understand the gracious truths they proclaim ; and while they both read of that love that brought the Son of God from his throne to take upon himself our nature, and at last to give his life a ransom for us, they can each with the Psalmist exclaim—' How sweet are thy words unto my taste ; yea, sweeter than honey to my mouth.' Even the little child is not forgotten : while the greatest philosopher can gain knowledge from the Bible, it equally entertains and arouses the sympathy of the little child. If God had not purposed that all men should search the Scriptures, would he thus have provided for the spiritual wants of all his creatures ? If he intended them only for the learned and great of the earth, the difficulty arises, How is it to be ascertained who are sufficiently learned to read and understand the Word of God ?

The second proof is, that the Scriptures themselves enforce the duty, and also show the benefit resulting from the search. Moses, in speaking to the children of Israel, commanded them as follows :—'And thou shalt teach them diligently unto thy children, and shalt talk of them when thou walkest by the way, and when thou liest down, and when thou risest up ; and thou shalt write them upon the posts of thy house and on thy gates.'—Deut. vi. 7, 8, 9.   This command was not restricted to the tribe of Levi, through whom the priesthood descended. The whole house of Israel were not only to read the laws of God, but were commanded to teach their children diligently. And this must not suffice ; they must also give all possible publicity to the Word of God.   We are told in 2 Chronicles xxxiv. 29, 30, 31, that the young 'king Josiah gathered together all the elders of Judah and Jerusalem, and the king went up into the house of the Lord, and *all* the men of Judah and the inhabitants of Jerusalem, and the priests and the Levites, and *all* the great and *small*, and he read in their ears *all* the words of the book of the covenant that was found in the house of the Lord.'   Here the learned and the unlearned, the rich and the poor, the young and the old, were alike summoned to hear the Word of God.   We read of no distinctions. Even the inspired writer prepared his heart to seek the law of the Lord, and to do and to teach in Israel statutes and judgments.—Ezra vii. 10.   In the book of Nehemiah we find that the people gathered themselves together, and desired him to bring them the book of the law of Moses. 'And Ezra the priest brought the law before the congregation both of men and women, and *all* that could hear with understanding, upon the first day of the seventh month, and he read therein.'   *   *
*   *   *   *   *   *   *   *   *

CHAPTER XVII.

DELAYS IN UNCLE'S ARRIVAL.

The genial weather with which the month of April opened allowed Marie again to venture out of doors. Her rapture was great when, for the first time after her winter's imprisonment, muffled up, and protected by her respirator, she was permitted one sunny morning to pace round the little garden plot in front of the house. She was soon fatigued, and glad to come in and rest. In another day or two she was able to take a short walk along the Terrace, and gradually to extend it to the immediate neighborhood. She leaned heavily on the arm of her friends, who took it in turn to guide her feeble steps. She was allowed to vacate the back parlor, and again to have a room up stairs.

Finding a walk of any length attended with much fatigue, Marie asked Mr. L—— occasionally to hire a conveyance for her, and she took several rides. She was well assured that her uncle would consider this a very legitimate appropriation of a part of her "incidental" balance. On one occasion she requested Mr. and Mrs. L—— and Elizabeth to accompany her to Hampstead, and ordering the driver to stop on the brow of the hill, she alighted, and took them by a retired and circuitous path, till they stood in front of the little Catholic chapel, and thence to the convent where she had been nursed after illness. Nothing could exceed her exhilaration of spirits as she again caught sight of her former abode, and rejoiced in her present liberty.

In April Mr. L—— had occasion to visit Staffordshire. Marie requested him to make inquiries about the place where, from her recollections of what her aunt had said, she imagined her property to be. He looked in all the guide-books and county maps for the house and village she named, and made many unsuccessful inquiries.   At length, falling in with a party of travellers at an hotel at Burslem, he met with one who knew the village of T——.   "There is a servant here," said his informant, "who lived at the house, and can tell you all about it."   Mr. L—— saw the maid, and from her obtained full corroboration of all Marie's impressions, as well as additional particulars, though, from consideration for Marie's uncle, he did not feel warranted in pursuing the inquiry farther by going to the place.

About this time the following letters came from Mr. Clifford :—

(TRANSLATION.)

✝
I. H. S.

" NICE, March 23d, 1850.

"My dear Marie,

" You will be surprised to find that I am here instead of resuming my retreat.   On account of the state of my health, the air of Nice was prescribed for me by my physicians.   The General wrote that he desired I should repair hither directly for some weeks' recreation ; and I do not therefore propose to complete my retreat until the autumn.

" After I had fixed the time to see you, in order to settle your pecuniary affairs, I found I had neglected to consult Mr. L—— as to whether it would suit him to see me at that time.   I have written to him in order to obtain a reply before quitting this place.   I have thought much of you during the last few days. Having no particular occupation to engage my thoughts, they have naturally turned to you.   The events of the past year appear to me like a dream.   I can scarcely believe in the reality of what has transpired.   The subject of my last letter often sorrowfully presents itself to my mind.   Yes, I sometimes even weep when thinking how the sad results of absence from the confessional have manifested themselves in your case. This circumstance has caused me much anxiety, and though I sympathize with you, I should not prove my love by passing lightly over this affair. It is too grave, too serious to be trifled with. I wish you to feel the disgrace and the punishment you have brought upon yourself. I have therefore resolved, though it will deprive me of much pleasure, that if Mr. L—— cannot answer my questions satisfactorily, I will only see you once for some months, and Mr. L—— and I can meet elsewhere. I know that this will give you pain. It is severe, and I wish it to be so; but it is my great affection which, after much consideration, induces me to act thus. As I was walking to-day, I considered how I could sufficiently impress upon Marie her error and my disapprobation; and this mode of treatment seemed to me likely to have the most salutary influence. I do not for an instant wish you to think that my regard is diminished. It is rather increased, for your fault makes me more anxious. When you write, tell me frankly the feelings and conduct of Mr. and Mrs. L—— with regard to this occurrence. I have special reasons for asking this, especially with regard to Mrs. L——. I am very glad to have had the opportunity of mentioning this before seeing you in person, both to relieve my own mind, and to enable us to understand one another when we meet. I hope that you will seriously ponder over the past and the future. Be always on your guard, lest you should again fall into the same snare. Above all things avoid the gossip of the world. Let charity govern your conversation. Never speak maliciously of the faults of others. I think you would be in danger of giving way to this temptation: I mean that of animadverting on the conduct of those who surround you. I believe that your dear mamma sometimes reproved you for this failing, for you know that calumny is a sin against which Catholics are very much on their guard.

"I much fear that your answers will appear with replies

in the *Tablet*. I wrote yesterday to the General to oppose it strongly, and I believe that I shall succeed. I tell you that you may be prepared if you should hear of it. I had not the least idea of such a thing, so do not blame me, for I am entirely innocent. No name will be mentioned, and this may perhaps reconcile you to it. When you write, pay the postage, and direct the letter to the post-office. Write frankly and fully.

"Tell me about your health. Is it better or worse? I wish you were here. The weather is splendid, and the town is full of visitors. So many English families are here. What will you say when you hear that I dined last Saturday with a dignitary of the Anglican Church. We met for the first time in an excursion on the water. We held many arguments. He is opposed to the high-church party, so you may imagine that we differed widely in our opinions. He is perfectly well-bred, and I enjoy his society, and that of his family. He has five daughters. I felt inclined to speak to them of you, but thought it better to be silent.

"With my love and most earnest prayers for your happiness, I am,

"Yours very affectionately,
"H. C. CLIFFORD."

(TRANSLATION.)

†

I. H. S.

"NICE, March 23d, 1850.

"My dear Sir,

"I feel that it is necessary to apologize for not having asked, if the time fixed for my visit was convenient to you. I am glad that the alteration in my own plans allows me to arrange according to your time and convenience.

"I shall now be free until the end of the month of June. I

can, if that is more agreeable to you, see you at any time that you may fix after the 16th of April. I should myself prefer remaining here a little longer on account of my health, the climate and the season being favorable to me, and I think that it will do me a great deal of good. Marie will not want money, as I have sent £50, and £25 in the desk. I leave it to Mrs. L——'s discretion to supply her.

"Have the goodness to write to me as soon as possible how you wish the deeds to be prepared. I shall reflect upon the matter, and then you can perhaps, with my consent, employ your own solicitor to prepare them. For special reasons, I do not wish to engage the family solicitor. I propose to give Marie without any restriction, a sum sufficient to realize an annual income of £200. I shall be obliged if you will take the trouble to ascertain clearly the amount that will be required. Captain Kenyon says £3500. All that I shall be permitted to do will be to give the money. I cannot in any way act legally, and must therefore request you, on Marie's account, to take upon you that part of the concern which relates to her affairs. When I come I may possibly have to employ a good deal of your time, for it will require several days finally to arrange all. I have not had any farther correspondence respecting the affair in Staffordshire, for the old lady will probably not live long; so I should prefer that Marie were free from all obligations until she received her own right. I rejoice that poor Marie is sheltered; for several members of our family have wronged the orphans of my dear sister; but my greatest joy will be, in spite of all. to see the only and beloved child of a dear sister raised above all their disdain and negligence. I only want an increase of wealth, to present her with a dignity worthy of the C——s. They cannot then, in point of etiquette, do otherwise than receive her with suitable respect. I hope that Marie will not widen the breach by imprudent acquaintances. She must be very prudent in these matters. If Ernest, the brother of Marie, had lived, he would have had the entire property; and now if the actual heir die without issue, and Marie married and had a son, he would be the heir. I intend to procure all the deeds when I come to London, in order that we may examine them together. You will perhaps be a little surprised that I, a Catholic, should be so confidential with you; but you will be more surprised when I tell you, I am grateful that Marie, having been guilty of so inconsiderate an act as her apostasy, has fallen in with a family so kind and so prudent as your own. She might have connected herself with persons who would have taken no interest in her health or spiritual welfare. From what I know of Marie's dispositions, I cannot hope that, without a great change indeed, she will ever change her habits, and therefore think it well worth while to preserve her from the evils to which a situation would expose her.

"It consoles me to know that she is so well protected, and with persons who love her; for I am certain that she loves you all ardently, and I believe that you have great influence over her. I am amused with some expressions in her last letters, particularly those which relate to Mrs. L——. She seems to have acquired much power over her. I have laughed heartily in reading that you were very indulgent, and Mrs. L—— strict, but equally kind. Marie easily discovers when persons give way to her; but the more firm they are, the more she esteems them. I hope that she attends to her duties, and tries to be more thoughtful.

"When you write to me, I shall regard it as a favor, if Mrs. L—— or you will frankly tell me your opinion of the circumstances which occurred at Mrs. S——'s. I wish, above all, to know how Marie was betrayed into them, and whether she has expressed penitence; also what you think of the plan I have proposed in the letter to Marie. I can realize her peculiar temptations with a sympathy which none but myself can feel. I shall be at the same time the last person to treat the affair leniently. I have never excused her when she has done wrong. I love her too well for that. She feels my displeasure so heavily, that I think this would have a good effect upon her. If we decide to follow out this plan, we can meet in town, or at the apartments of Captain Kenyon, which are not far from your residence, being near the Park. I particularly wish to know all that relates to her health, and her conduct, and also whether you wish me to say anything to her with regard to it. I entreat you to be frank with me ; for the next year or two will be of great importance to Marie, either for good or for evil. I am desirous that she should be all that is excellent, and an ornament to her sex. There is much to admire in her, and also much to regret ; and I am certain that, if well guided and restrained in her follies, she will eventually become all that we could wish. You cannot be too firm, for she is very thought-less and inconsiderate in many things. I believe that Marie is too prone to place herself on a level with her inferiors and with servants. Though she has been brought up to conduct herself towards them with suitable consideration and kindness, she is apt to depart from the dignity so essential to gain their respect. This very freedom will convince you that she does not like any-thing haughty or overbearing. I have mentioned this in order that you may guard her against it.

"Oblige me with a confidential reply to this letter, clearly stating how you wish the money to be invested, as well as the legal form of investment. I can then give you my reply. If I approve it, the documents can be prepared immediately, and some time may thus be spared ; or, if you wish it, they can be left till my visit. Fix the time most suitable for your own arrangements. If April will not suit, I should, on account of my delicate health, prefer remaining here this entire month, if that agree with your arrangements. I leave it entirely to you. As Mrs. L—— sent me so complete and so judicious a report before, I hope that she will pardon the liberty I take in requesting another. This will give me occasion to speak to Marie respecting every part of her character which requires correction.

"With respectful compliments to Mrs. L——and to yourself, I am,

"Faithfully yours,
"H. C. Clifford.

"P. S.—Have you spoken to Marie of the affair in Staffordshire?"

Here was another proposed delay in the long talked of visit. Mr. and Mrs. L—— were almost as sorry for the postponement as Marie, but it seemed unreasonable and unkind to urge Mr. Clifford to leave immediately. Mr. L—— therefore suggested the second or third week in May.

The replies of Mr. L—— and Marie to the foregoing letters have not been preserved. Mr. L——'s was a short note only, as, by his desire, Mrs. L—— sent a fuller reply, which was enclosed in his own. Her letter was as follows:—

"C—— Terrace, April, 1850

"Sir,

"It will give me much pleasure in any way to diminish your anxieties with respect to Marie, though there are many things which might be answered in a personal interview which cannot be so well committed to paper.

"The circumstances which occurred prior to her leaving caused us, as you may suppose, equal surprise and regret. We felt, however, that many extenuations might be offered. She appeared overwhelmed with sorrow, and after a week or more of reflection on her part, and admonition on ours, we indulged the hope that she was in the state of mind which we could desire. It was at this juncture that I wrote to you, and having advised Marie to communicate fully with you on your then expected visit, I did not think it necessary to refer to so painful a subject. Subsequently to this, however, other circumstances transpired which led us to doubt the genuine character of her repentance, and raised for a time a barrier between us which was painfully felt by us both, and to which she doubtless referred in her letter to you. The absence of the restraints of her former position, and subsequently of the friendly watchfulness exercised by ourselves, would account for much of what has been so painful; and not having her mind fully possessed with that holy fear of offending God, that hatred of all which he hates, and that ever present sense of His observing eye, which *pious* Protestants are accustomed to cultivate as the best safeguards against sin, she was left for a time to err without restraint. Both Mr. L—— and myself earnestly sought to bring her to a perception of the evil of sin as committed against God, and entreated her to make full confession to *Him*, and to seek His forgiveness. Her chief regret in the first instance seemed to be that she had grieved *us ;* but this was very far from satisfying us, and we trust that a deeper and more enlivening principle than that of affectionate regret has taken its place. Her mental sufferings have evidently been great, and we attributed her recent illness in a considerable degree to them. She seems now to have rallied, and to be again more herself and more tranquilly cheerful than since her return to us. And here allow me to thank you for the kind suggestions contained in your letter to myself. They fully accord with my own views of her character, though my impressions of the evil of the error into which she had fallen, may possibly have made me too stern in dealing with it. I am very sure that it proceeded from anxious desire for her best welfare, and that no one but yourself takes so deep an interest in her as I do. So singular were the steps by which she was led to us, and so peculiarly did she seem to be entrusted to us by Divine Providence, that we have felt her almost as much our own as if she had been given to us in infancy, and the tie which binds her to us as second only to that of our own children. Her own affectionate and grateful disposition has bound her still more closely to us, and far, very far, would it be from my thoughts ever to be unkind to her, or to be so harsh with her faults as to repel her confidence. I trust that all cause for anything like severity has passed, and I may here add that we should be greatly concerned were you to carry out your idea of seeing her only once. The painful excitement so severe a decision would occasion might be dangerous to her health, nor do we think that it could answer any good end in regard to her character. It would restrain those free communications on her part which are so desirable, and tend to diminish your salutary influence over her."

After entering into details respecting her health, education, &c., the repetition of which is unnecessary, the letter concludes :—

"I think I have gone through all the points which come within my department, and assuring you of the intense desire I feel to see her attain to all excellence and happiness,

"I am, sir,

"Yours with much respect,

"J. L——."

CHAPTER XVIII.

NEW TRAITS OF CHARACTER.

The proposed arrangement of her affairs naturally engaged much of Marie's attention, and the forethought and acuteness which she displayed, would have done no discredit to one in training for the legal profession. There was one stipulation in her uncle's letters to which she strongly objected, namely, the power Captain Kenyon was to have of choosing another trustee, in the event of Mr. L——'s death. She wished that right to be vested in herself, lest Captain Kenyon should choose one who might give her annoyance. She wished also to have more absolute control over the money. She wished when she came into possession of her estate, to be able to appropriate the £4000 to an object she had at heart. It transpired that this summit of her ambition was to build a chapel of her own, as a memorial of her deliverance from Popery. Mr. L—— should preach in it, she said. It should be built in some neighborhood, of his selection, and his favorite idea should be carried out of having the greater part *free*. Her friends smiled at her fancy; but Mr. L—— reminded her that it would be departing from every principle of honor and uprightness, to employ money which her uncle had appropriated to her individual comfort, in diffusing sentiments directly opposed to the views which he conscientiously held.

Marie suggested one difficulty in reference to the completion of the trust deed, namely, that her uncle, as a Jesuit, was disqualified for transacting any legal business, and would not be allowed to add his signature. At her request, Mr. L—— went to his solicitor for advice on this point, and was advised that Marie could herself sign the money over to the trustees. She laughed heartily, asking what was to prevent her taking sole possession at the time, instead of transferring it to others; but Mr. L—— told her that it would probably be lodged at a banker's, in her uncle's name, till she had actually signed the transfer. In speaking of her uncle, she said she had but one impeachment to bring against the uprightness of his conduct, and that was his having kept her in ignorance of her prospects. Her supposed destitution had induced her to yield to his wish for her to be a nun; and she would forever have regretted it, when acquainted with what might have been hers.

10*

There was a measure of restlessness about Marie which often distressed her friends, and sadly interfered with the comfort of the household. By her account there was always something wrong either with the children, or sisters, or servants. One Sunday evening she wrote a long letter to Mrs. L——, too long indeed for insertion, to prove that Lilly had on one occasion three months before, been guilty of equivocation. "Owing to my own failing," she wrote, "I do feel the more keenly for Lilly. I love her so well that I tremble at the bare idea that she should suffer as I have done. If I have sinned, do not think me the less anxious on her account. No; if possible, I feel more alive to her danger." She went on to request that the matter might be thoroughly investigated, that the servants might be questioned, and that she might be present. Mrs. L —— found this letter on her table one Sunday evening, when retiring to rest, and did not see Marie till the next day. She then spoke to her in reply—"Marie, you tell me that your uncle disapproves of writing letters in the house, and in this case it was quite unnecessary. I cannot yield to your wish in this matter. It is three months back, and I doubt whether either the servants or ourselves can remember all the particulars of so trifling an occurrence. It was to me that Lilly spoke, and my conviction is that she said nothing but the truth. Were it otherwise, I should not punish a child of her age for what happened three months ago. Should it happen again, and you tell me *at the time*, I promise you it shall not be passed over. No one could regard any departure from truth more seriously than I." Marie was anything but pleased with this reply, and intimated as much. "I do wish, Marie," said Mrs. L——, " that you could let things go on more quietly, especially on Sunday, when, of all times, we desire to be in peace. You keep the house in a constant state of commotion. It is bad for you, as well as for us, to be in such perpetual excitement. You neither rest yourself, nor let others rest." Marie was highly offended at this plain speaking. She rose, left the room, and rushed up stairs. The sisters could not prevail upon her to come down from the cold room, and Mrs. L—— went up to endeavor to pacify her. After some persuasion she yielded so far as to be led down stairs, but she would eat no dinner that day.

Mrs. L—— had often been much concerned to see the growing jealousy that Marie appeared to feel in reference to Lilly. It seemed strange that she should be jealous of a child; yet so it was. When she and Mrs. L—— and Lilly were alone, she could not bear Lilly to be noticed. She would monopolize all the conversation, and pay no attention to the child's patient efforts to win a word or look from her mother. If at length Mrs. L—— broke off for a moment to satisfy her little girl, she seemed annoyed. She neglected no opportunity of placing Lilly's failings in as prominent a view as possible, and there was a look of unmistakable satisfaction on her countenance when the child was reproved. It is true that there was no love lost between them. Lilly had at first been as warmly interested in her case as a child could be; but by degrees she seemed fully aware that, with all Marie's professions of attachment, her accession to the household was no addition to her happiness. She dared not engage in open warfare, but she kept as much as possible out of Marie's way. Little Arnold, too, did not at all fancy her boisterous caresses; and when he had kisses and smiles for every one else, he screamed when she attempted to take him: and when she tried to kiss him, would most unscrupulously slap her in the face. Sarah would have it that Marie pinched him, according to the practice of certain soi-distant mothers, who adopt this method to work on the sympathy of a benevolent public; but of course no one but Sarah entertained the foul slander. The family attributed Marie's growing restlessness to the circumstance of her uncle's delay, and to her own heart being ill at ease ; and they treated her with forbearance and indulgence.

One other feature in her character was so frequently developed, as to call for a passing notice. This was *curiosity*. No visitor could call, no letter be received, but Marie must know the history and business of the one, and the purport of the other. So completely had she become identified with the family interests, that there were few things which they ever thought of concealing from her. If by chance they withheld any particulars, a playful inquiry, a warm expression of interest, or a straightforward question, would generally attain her object, and put her in possession of the whole story. The inquisitiveness which from any other quarter would have been annoying in the extreme, was in her accompanied by so much winning naïveté that they seldom felt disposed to give it a check.

If sometimes staggered by the contrarieties in Marie's character, they could not but love the ready benevolence which manifested itself on the most trivial occasion. One instance may suffice as a specimen. Marie was taking one of her daily airings, and with slow and heavy step leaning on Mrs. L——'s arm. As they walked down Westbourne Terrace, a poor woman crossed the road from one of the side streets, another Meg Merrilies for stature and sinewy frame, thin, gaunt, aged, with a look of starvation and misery in her countenance, and a heavy load of wood on her head. She had picked it up in the unfinished houses, and she hurried on, as if to reach her wretched home while enough of her failing strength remained. "Oh ! look at that poor creature," said Marie ; and instantly her hand was in her pocket, and a sixpence out, and she bade Lilly run after the object of her pity. The poor woman, who was no beggar, turned round and gazed as if transfixed, and at length curtseying her gratitude, hastened on.

About this time Elizabeth went to visit some friends in the north. They had heard a distorted version of Marie's story, and were somewhat prejudiced against her. Elizabeth exerted herself with all the earnestness of a true friend to set Marie right in their opinion. In this she was entirely successful, and they soon became deeply interested. She made a passing reference to the subject in writing to Marie, and received a long epistle in reply, from which the following is an extract :—

"C—— Terrace, April 12th, 1850.

" My dearest Elizabeth,

*   *   *   *   *   *   *   *

" The tale about the young lady and the convent is really true. Mrs. L—— has a letter written by Lady B—— on the subject. It appears the young lady is a convert from Popery ; her father, a bigoted Papist, is resolved to remove his daughter (she being under age) from the influence of Protestants, and place her in a convent. To make this step appear less arbitrary, he will yield the point if she collects by the 20th of April, £2000 worth of old stamps. I forwarded mine yesterday by rail to Reading, and enclosed the young lady a note stating who I was, and also presented my sincere sympathy, having passed through a similar ordeal. I gave her my address, so perhaps we shall hear more of her.   *   *   *
*   *   *   *   *   *   * I am truly glad you have not been pestered for a recital of my history. I am sorry your friends in the north *still* regard me with suspicion. Happily for the Protestant cause I have as yet exercised my *Jesuitical* powers to little purpose, having *not yet made one addition to the Church of Rome.* If they had no agents more zealous in their cause, the whole concern would soon be broken up. I do not wonder they should regard anything belonging to so horrid a system with suspicion ; but they cannot abhor it as much as myself, having been so nearly made their dupe. I have suffered enough with them, so do feel somewhat pained that any should still suspect my principles. *I never was de-*

signed for a Jesuit, having so little tact in anything, let alone the tact required in a Jesuit. My uncle though one of them is not less dear to me. They do not know all about him and his struggles with obedience and love, or else they would feel differently towards him. I feel perfectly indifferent as to what others think about us, having the testimony of a clear conscience. My answers do not much resemble the answers of a Jesuit. I must say this dear E., and I say it with pain, that I have met with more of the treachery of Jesuits among professing Christians than ever I did in the seventeen years spent amongst them. I do not hesitate for a moment to make this statement. It is not their religion I blame, but the want of it. It is an awful thing to be only a professor in name without the power and reality of religion. I have learnt a great lesson from the painful circumstances of the past—the immense importance of Christian consistency. Earnestly do I hope and pray that I may not prove a stumbling-block in the way of another. My desire is that I may daily become more humble and watchful, and that, if it should please God to spare me, I may by my consistency and usefulness adorn the doctrine of Christ my Saviour in all things; and that if I am spared to possess wealth I may prove a faithful steward, remembering for what purpose it is given me. So that at last when I have done with the things of time, I may hear the glad news—'Well done good, and faithful servant, thou hast been faithful over a few things, I will make thee ruler over many things.'

"I am looking forward to our journey to the sea-side with great pleasure, the time will soon be here."   *   *

     *   *   *   *   *   *   *   *   *

CHAPTER XIX.

ATTEMPTS AT CONFESSION.

MARIE continued the custom of welcoming the postman, and the point had long been tacitly yielded. One day she took from the postman's hand two letters which she said were both for her. One was in deep black, as was usually the case with her uncle's letters. She locked herself in her room, and remained there some time. She returned to the dining-room with heightened color, and expressed her regret that she could not show Mr. and Mrs. L—— the letter which she had just received from her uncle. There were one or two things which he had mentioned to her in confidence, and which it would not therefore be right to show. He was still so delicate that he was about giving up his office for a twelvemonth, and taking up his residence in Yorkshire. She was sure that there was a great deal passing in his mind. She did not at all despair of seeing him a Protestant before he died. At any rate she thought that he would soon cease to be a Jesuit, and become one of the secular clergy.

On the 6th of May Mr. L—— himself received the following long letter. A brief note for Marie accompanied it.

(TRANSLATION.)

†

I. H. S.

"Nice, April 25th, 1850.

" Sir,

"I received your letter last Monday, and I should have replied to it by return of post if I could have done so.

"The day after the receipt of your dispatch, I caught cold in an excursion on the water, since which I have been confined to my room. I have suffered much in the throat, and for some days I was unable to speak : I could take nothing but liquids. My medical attendants said that it was a severe attack of bronchitis, but not dangerous, not being attacked with cough. I am under severe treatment, and suffer much from the constant application of caustic to the throat.

"My illness could not have happened at a more unfortunate juncture, for L am most anxious to see you as well as Marie. My surgeon tells me that my great anxiety retards my recovery. I have other very pressing and important affairs which require my presence in Yorkshire; in consequence of which, and of my anxiety to see Marie, my patience is severely tried. We must hope that all is arranged for the best by the great Disposer of events. I hope to go out to-morrow, and to be able soon to leave here for England.

"Before entering on the subject of your last communications, permit me to offer to you and Mrs. L—— my best thanks for the interest that you have both evinced in a person so dear to me as Marie.

"We will conclude all matters of business before entering upon circumstances equally sorrowful to all parties concerned. I write now confidentially, being assured that you will not abuse my confidence. I am much obliged to you for having taken the trouble to see your solicitor. The best investiture of the money would be to lay it out on mortgage, for I cannot exceed £4000 ; but the difficulty about this would be that Marie could call in the money at her pleasure, or if vested in the power of trustees, it might be eventually a source of contentions and losses for them and for Marie. I know that she would not do anything dishonorable, but in case of a disagreeable circumstance, I wish to ensure them and Marie from all uneasiness. The funds would meet the difficulty.

"With regard to the employment of my signature: after

having seriously considered the affair, and consulted with Captain Kenyon, who is now at Nice, we have come to the conclusion, that for the safety of the trustees, and to avoid all trouble in the event of my death, it would be most desirable to obtain a brief, empowering me to act legally. I have no doubt that through interest I could obtain this permission. I had not foreseen the difficulties which would probably arise from the absence of my signature, until Captain Kenyon pointed them out to me. He refused to be a trustee unless I invested the money, and legally transferred all power to the appointed trustees. We perfectly agree with you as to the way in which the deed is to be drawn up, except that in the event of Captain Kenyon's death, he alone would have the right of choosing a successor, in order to secure a Catholic trustee. I think this is not unreasonable. You alone would have the power of acting so long as Marie remained Protestant. Another stipulation is that Marie at her death could not make any bequests in favor of religious objects. If she die without heirs, she may bequeath it to any friend, or to objects tending only to the moral benefit of man, without regard to religious interests. Considering my peculiar position, you will not fail to see the propriety and honor of this restriction; for if I consented otherwise, it would be at the sacrifice of principle and conscience, which I am sure you would wish to consider. Captain Kenyon leaves me to-morrow to obtain the dispensation. If we cannot succeed in this we can have recourse to the plan proposed. My only anxiety is to exempt the trustees from any future disagreement. Above all I wish to protect you as a Protestant, and I am sure that Captain Kenyon desires it equally.

" As to the affair in Staffordshire, any day may decide it, for it is not probable that my aunt will live long. She is now seventy-six years old, with all her limbs paralyzed. You will receive immediate intelligence of her death; for Marie, being the eldest, her presence will be necessary before anything can be done. I think that it would be only proper for Marie to write to her. She once saw her when visiting me.

"I now come to a more disagreeable subject, and one which, for poor Marie's sake, I could wish forever to bury in oblivion. Before entering into detail, it is necessary to request you as a favor not to make known this part of my letter. I have always made it a rule to hold sacred every important communication, and this is the first time that I have violated confidence. Nothing could have induced me to do so, if I had not believed it to be justice to Marie, and for her own happiness. The circumstances to which you make indirect allusion in your letters have been fully confirmed by Marie in a letter which I received from her yesterday. I cannot express the feelings called forth by her two last letters—especially by the last—and I rejoice that, by her frank and sincere communication, she has become doubly dear to me. She has written to me in defiance of every one, and expresses her deep regret that the state of her mind and feelings obliges her to break a promise that she had made to you. Taking into consideration her extreme sensibility and her mental sufferings, you will not, I am sure, blame her for wishing to confide her causes of distress to one who so well understands her every feeling. I am extremely thankful that she has not waited for a personal interview; for if I had then heard all for the first time, I fear that I should have spoken with haste, and have caused you pain. Your letters have disquieted me a little; but after the receipt of Marie's last letter, all the mystery was explained. I much regret that you did not think it prudent to permit her some time since to write to me fully and freely. This would have spared poor Marie and yourself much needless pain. I gather that she has suffered in some respects very unjustly. I cannot recall having ever felt anything more strongly. I have always been the last to excuse or extenuate Marie's faults: but I must frankly confess, and I am sure that my candor will not displease Mrs. L——, that though she has acted from the purest and most elevated motives, she has still judged Marie rather too severely. I wish I were at liberty to give you the substance of her long and interesting letter, which it took her the greater part of three nights to write. This must be very bad for health; for she tells me she sometimes sits up for several hours, saying that she feels it a relief to give vent to those feelings when alone, which she has controlled throughout the day. I burned her letter immediately, or I could perhaps have sent it to you; for had you read it, you would have loved her still more tenderly. Marie's reasons for avoiding an explanation proceed from another motive, and from a higher source than those which had been attributed to her: and she was afterwards restrained, or rather frightened, from confiding an explanation by rather too much coldness and severity. Now do not think that Marie utters a murmur or a complaint. On the contrary, in giving me a recital of everything that has passed, she mentions it to show her deep anxiety that Mrs. L—— should treat her with justice: but I immediately discovered the cause of Marie's reserve. She is very timid. I have seen her suffer so much from fear in going to the confessional that she has been obliged to have medical advice. It is physical. Her mamma was the same, though she possessed great strength of mind. It will be long before Marie conquers this. Some years since I took the same course as Mrs. L—— has done, but I had reason to regret it. I have a copy of Mrs. L——'s letter to Marie, which, with the exception of one remark, is very praiseworthy, and manifests a faithful spirit. The phrase in question I will mention to Mrs. L—— in person. It weighs much upon Marie's mind.

" It is as much Marie's purpose as my own to enter fully into all the circumstances of the past. Marie is most anxious to do so, and she says that she hopes to have some conversations before my visit. I much disapprove of the habit of writing letters in the house. Marie tells me that she has written twice

to Mrs. L——. I hope that she will not do so again. I lay
great stress upon this, as tending to increase those feelings of
reserve which will destroy one amiable feature in her character.
I have not for a length of time been so struck with any letter
of Marie's as with the last. She has given me a full and sincere account of all that has occurred, from the commencement
to the close, before and since her return. It was a pleasure to
find that she was not only very frank, but very sincere, and truly
humble in her avowals, without any disguise, or in any way ex-
cusing herself, even when I well know that she might justly
have done so. I had learned all from other sources, and was
therefore able to judge impartially. Her expressions of regret
when she has erred, are genuine and profound, and her feelings
towards Mrs. L—— and yourself, are those of most ardent
gratitude. Her great anxiety is to be placed on the same footing as before. She deeply feels the absence of that look of
complacency which once met her own. I could never have believed that Marie could have loved any one but a parent to the
same extent as she loves Mrs. L——. It would be well for
her happiness if she loved less ardently. She anxiously awaits
my visit as the means for an entire reconciliation, and I am
deeply grieved that this illness hinders me from seeing her, for
I cannot bear the idea that she is suffering so intensely. I
tremble for her health as much as for the state of her mind.
Under the constant effort to stifle her feelings, the mind must
in the end give way. Marie suffers more for a long period after
the trial, than even during the trial itself. You have perhaps
discovered that though she is very thoughtless, she is disposed
to dwell much upon her troubles. After her mamma's death
every one trembled for her. For more than a year she fell into
a state of despair. She rarely laughed, and it was with difficulty that she could be drawn into conversation. I am very
uneasy about her on this account, though I know that she
struggles against it. Do not leave her too much alone.

"This and other considerations have a little altered my plan with regard to Marie. * * * * But before arranging anything, I must know what you think about the propriety of introducing Marie into a circle where the past is unknown. I cannot proceed further before having your sincere opinion. Mrs. Kenyon much wishes to have Marie with her for some months, but I cannot consent to this until the Staffordshire affair is settled. I have had some idea of placing her with my new friends, the clergyman to whom I have before made allusion. I have told them all about Marie, and they intend to see her on their return to England. I am certain that they would willingly receive her for a time, after which, if agreeable, she could return to you. Do not consult Marie on this subject, but give me your own impartial judgment. I hope that Marie will soon be reconciled to Mrs. L——, or rather that the reserve which exists between them will soon be destroyed. Without this she can never be happy. I hope that she will endeavor to say to Mrs. L—— what she has written to me.

"The affair of the newspaper was truly a piece of folly, and has caused me much vexation. The General is well aware of its having been sent. Marie was immediately suspected, and I was very glad I did not then know it, for I could deny the handwriting. I beg that she will never do it again. This was beyond a joke, for if it had been known that Marie had sent it, I could not have answered for the consequences—above all the interlineations about Dr. Achilli. Speak to her seriously on the subject.

"I thank yourself and your circle for all the kindness shown to Marie during her severe illness, and of which she speaks in most ardent terms. I will pay the medical fees, and also Marie's notes, when I see you. She cannot have her boxes until I come. I shall pass through Manotté on my way to London, for great alterations are being made there. I am having flues carried through the house to keep the library aired without any one going into it, during my absence from Manotté. I must remain there some days. I cannot until the receipt of your letter, and the return of Captain Kenyon, leave for London, for nothing can be done without him. If I were well the affair would still have to be postponed, on account of his absence. We shall return together. I hope to leave in a few days, for I am now extremely anxious to arrive in London as soon as possible.

"The affair of the *Tablet* was stopped. I am too fatigued to write to Marie. Assure her that weakness alone prevents me. It will be necessary for you to write almost by return of post, for I shall be ready to leave before if Captain Kenyon succeed, and my strength return. I am sorry that the sea has been recommended for Marie; I should prefer her remaining quiet, at least for the present. There are many reasons which thus influence me.

"I must not forget to express my approbation of your having taken the opinion of a second physician. I fear that this complaint will be fatal to Marie. It was the opinion of her first medical attendant some years since.

"I should have enclosed a five-pound note for Marie if I had one at hand, but I have only an hour left before the post goes, and cannot obtain one in time. It did not occur to me till a moment or two ago.

"I shall not stay more than a fortnight in London. Captain Kenyon and you can conclude the affair after I have given you the legal power. If it is agreeable to you and Mrs. L——— I shall be happy to pass my first evening with you. This will give more time for conversation than we could have in a formal visit. I shall not write again until I am on my way to London. I shall give you due notice. The deed cannot be prepared until I see how I ought to act.

"I beg you not to delay your reply. You need not pay the postage of the next letter.

"Present my sincere thanks to Mrs. L—— for her amiable letter, to which I shall reply verbally.

"With my respects, and hoping that your health is re-established,

> "I am, dear sir,
>> "Yours faithfully,
>>> "II. C. Clifford."

On witnessing the receipt of this letter, Marie informed Mr. and Mrs. L—— that she had written to her uncle, and gave them her reasons for doing so. She then inquired whether he had mentioned it. They replied that he had. She expressed her surprise that he should violate her confidence; and to clear him in her estimation, they thought it better to show her the letter: her *own* communication of the fact having released them from the obligation to secresy.

After breakfast, when left alone with Mrs. L——, Marie placed in her hands the note to herself, which was as follows :—

(TRANSLATION.)

†

I. H. S.

"Wednesday.

"My very dear Marie,

"I have only a few moments left before closing my despatch, and cannot therefore say more than a few words.

"Mr. L—— will explain to you the reason of my long silence with regard to your first letter. In reply to the last, I wish to tell you that you have not only my free and entire pardon, but my warmest sympathy. I need not tell you what a weight you have removed from my mind by your frank and sincere avowal. There is, however, one remark which has rather wounded me. It is where you allude to our treatment of you at another period. How can you make reflections on maternal counsels and treatments? I will convince you of your error when I see you.

"I cannot close without the expression of a wish that the late sorrowful events may serve as a warning to you to the close of life. I wish you to repeat all that you have told me to Mrs. L——. Try to overcome your timidity before my visit. I shall be well pleased if you do so.

"I am very glad that you have received the intimation of your change of fortune with so much self-control. I hope that when you possess riches, you will prove a good stewardess. They are given you for the good of others, and not for your own indulgence. Do not dwell too much on the past, and above all do not continue the habit of sitting up alone at midnight. As I hope soon to see you, I shall leave the subject of your letter for a personal interview. I wish you to write to my aunt Charlotte. Mrs. Kenyon will enclose the address in this letter.

"I beg that you will speak, not write to Mrs. L——, and do it immediately.

"I am truly sorry that time compels me to be so brief; and letter writing does not at all agree with me. With my most earnest wishes and constant prayers, I am ever,

"Your faithful and attached relative,

"H. C. CLIFFORD."

Mrs. L—— inferred from Marie having shown her this note, that she wished to prepare the way for making the long-talked of communication respecting the burnt notes, and she gently referred to the subject. As usual Marie hastily left the room, and rushed up stairs. Mrs. L—— stayed in that room all the morning, hoping she would return, and once went up to invite her down, but in vain. She stayed up stairs till dinner. Resolved to bring the matter to a point, when dinner was over, Mrs. L—— followed Marie into the back parlor, closed the door, and sat down by her side. "Marie, your uncle wishes you to speak to me, and he says that you wish it yourself. What is it that you would like us to know?"

Marie's cheeks flushed, and she said, "I would rather leave it till my uncle comes, Mrs. L——."

"But he wishes you to get it over at once; and if it would relieve your mind, if it can be so easily explained, it is a great pity that you should postpone it."

"Yes, indeed! it *can* be explained, Mrs. L——," said Marie, in the indignant tone of an injured person.

Her manner roused Mrs. L——, and for the first time she spoke in direct terms of the one interdicted subject. "Do not talk to me in that style, Marie. No one has injured you but yourself. Your uncle's words imply that we have treated you with injustice and severity, but you well know that has not been the case. Had it been any one else, we should long since have insisted on investigation and restitution, but we feared for your *life*, and were silent. Where there has been nothing said, nothing done, there can have been no severity."

Marie lowered her tone. "I think you mistake my uncle's words, Mrs. L——. I feel persuaded he would never say that. I have always told him the very contrary."

"Yes, he does," repeated Mrs. L——.

"Well, shall I show you the copy of the letter I wrote to him?

"If you like to do so, and prefer it to speaking."

"I will think about it," said Marie.

Mrs. L—— requested a sight of the letter she had once written to Marie, and continued, "Your uncle proposes your removal from this house. And now, lest you should think we are anxious to detain you, I must tell you frankly that nothing but the deepest interest in you would have enabled me to bear the anxiety and confinement of this winter. You are no longer unprovided for; and if you can be as safe and as happy elsewhere, I would not wish to keep you here one moment longer."

Mr. L—— was not aware of this conversation, but he, too, wrote in the same strain to Mr. Clifford, and said that while it gave him much pleasure to be of any real service to Marie, and neither he nor Mrs. L—— shrank from any trouble on her account, the moment her true interest could be promoted by any other arrangement, he should cheerfully be relieved of so responsible a charge.

CHAPTER XX.

REHEARSAL OF A DEATH-BED SCENE.

MARIE had gained strength so rapidly, that the hopes of her friends had risen high. May had come—bright and cheerful May! the time so anxiously anticipated for her uncle's visit. It was long since the midnight bell had roused the sleepers in the upper part of the house, and they had ceased to fear it. About one o'clock on Tuesday morning, the 7th of May, Mrs. —— was awakened by Marie's bell, and her blood ran cold a not-to-be-mistaken signal. The conversation of the afternoon rushed back upon her mind, and reproaching herself for having suffered an impatient word to escape her, she hastened down. She found Marie in distress, without light or water, having, as was usual when left to herself, forgotten to light her little lamp. In about an hour the bleeding ceased, and she sank into a tranquil sleep.

On Tuesday she seemed almost as well as before. On Wednesday morning Mrs. L—— was again summoned. Oh! that bell! It sounded like a premonitory death-knell. Never was it heard without a fearful apprehension that Marie might have bled to death almost before they could reach her. Never had she who first heard it dared to wait for dressing, even in the coldest weather. Mrs. L—— was indeed alarmed when she entered Marie's room. There was more than a quart of blood in the basin, and she lay deathlike and speechless. Her limbs were cold, her upper lip was swollen, and her mouth was drawn on one side. Presently there came on a convulsive twitching of the mouth and hands, such as Mrs. L—— had before witnessed on two sorrowful and well-remembered occasions. And could it be that poor Marie was indeed going when her uncle was so near, and when her prospects were so bright? Was she "to die and make no sign?" The sisters were away, and Mrs. L—— durst not leave her to call Mr. L——. She resolved to ring loudly if the alarming symptoms became more decided, and watched in intense anxiety for the issue. One wish was uppermost—that Marie might live to give more assured evidence of repentance for the past, and of a prepared state of mind. Gradually Marie revived, and a reaction commenced. Her head and hands became as hot as before they were cold; her face flushed—her pulse beat quickly—her mind wandered. She called for her mamma—called for Mrs. L——, murmured complaints that they did not come to her. By degrees she became more collected, recognized Mrs. L——, took a dose of medicine, and in another hour fell into a calm sleep. She was tenderly watched and waited upon that day and night.

At eight in the evening Elizabeth's knock was heard at the door. She had had a hurrying day, and had had neither dinner nor tea. She had been to the Strand in the morning on an errand of kindness, and back to Queen Square. Thence she had been to the Hall of Commerce to assist in arranging the tables for a fancy bazaar on the morrow. She had left the sale-room at seven to come up to C—— Terrace, and must return to Queen Square that night, and be at the Hall of Commerce early in the morning. "My dear Elizabeth," said Mrs. L——, "how could you think of coming here to-night? You will be quite knocked up." "I could not be easy without, I was so afraid I might never see poor Marie"—again, she would have said, but tears choked her utterance. She soon recovered herself, and went into Marie's room. "How kind of you!" said Marie, and she too was moved, and she turned her head on her pillow and wept. Elizabeth stayed an hour with her, settled her comfortably for the night, and then started off. She did not get back to Queen Square till past ten. The shops on the road were shut when she entered the Square, and it looked darker and drearier even than usual. She reached her friends without adventure, and thankfully retired to rest.

Marie did not attempt to leave her bed on Friday; but she said she must write to her uncle; and, propped up with pillows, she wrote almost without pausing for nearly three hours. Her friends did not see her letter till three months afterwards, and were not aware of its contents.

After expressing her deep sorrow and anxiety on account of his illness, she writes—

"I know not how to thank you sufficiently for the deep anxiety and solicitude you have evinced towards me, and also for your very sympathizing and affectionate letters. Your last has tended in some degree to tranquillize and soothe my agitated mind. Before answering your queries, I must first express my vexation—I cannot say sorrow—that the newspaper should have caused you so much annoyance. Had I foreseen this I should not have sent it. I have too much respect and veneration for so dear a relative to play any jokes with you. I certainly must say, this increases my feelings of indignation against a system that holds men like yourself in bondage; mere slaves to the caprice of fallen man."

She then enters at great length on the subject of her " reserve and timidity," the distress which it causes her, and the impossibility. of overcoming it ; the kindness of Mr. and Mrs. L——, and her wish, with his permission, to make them some handsome present in acknowledgment of the past year ; her intense desire for his visit, which is to set all right ; her misery at lying under false accusations, and her comfort that *his* confidence in her remains unshaken. As the letter occupies two sheets of foreign post closely written, one other extract may suffice.

" Mrs. L—— said, ' she could ·not bear to see my pale, unhappy face.' I longed to tell her it was not the amount of remorse that she supposes makes it pale. Oh, how could I have borne with such a load as that when often near eternity, not knowing any night might be the last ? Hardened, indeed, in crime I must have been to have existed under it. I was truly grieved to find that Mrs. L—— does, in some degree, think me ungrateful in not reposing confidence in her ; but what have I to say ? I cannot confess a sin of which I am innocent ; and their confidence is so far gone, that to assert my innocence would make them think still worse of me. So, as I said, I would rather bear the blame of a fault, than the disgrace of denying one. So I must leave my case for you and God to plead. You say you wonder I could have restrained my indignation at being supposed guilty of such an act. Oh ! dear uncle, after what had passed, it little becomes me to indulge in feelings of indignation. I deserved punishment for my sin of ingratitude and departure from God ; so I have received this reproach as such. I have been made to feel the bitterness of departing from Him, and also the sorrow sin entails upon us. I wanted something to humble me, and this has had the desired effect, though the trial has been a *very, very* sore one. You can little fancy what I have endured in the estrangement of one I so dearly love.   *   *   *   *   *   *   *   *   *   *   *   *   *   *   *   *   *

"Accept my best love and heartfelt wishes for your recovery, and prayers that you may reach here shortly and safely.

"I am, ever dear uncle,

"Your grateful and attached niece,

"MARIE."

CHAPTER XXI.

TRIFLING CIRCUMSTANCES LEADING TO GREAT EVENTS.

MARIE was much fatigued with penning so long a letter to her uncle, and she experienced the usual results of an additional excitement in a return of the bleeding on Friday night. It was but slight, and soon subsided.

With the exception of the previous Thursday morning, Mrs. L—— had seldom left her. Visits to the congregation, committees, and the claims of friendship, had long been in great part set aside, to keep watch over her of whose life they could not be assured from hour to hour. A claim of kindness and affection, more imperative even than Marie's, obliged her to leave home on that Saturday afternoon for a few hours. She hastened to the relative who needed her sympathy, and again with all possible speed returned home.

Marie's door was closed. Mrs. L—— knocked, and received no answer. She hesitated to knock again lest Marie should be engaged at her devotions. Wishing to be satisfied that all was right, she gave another gentle tap. A feeble and indistinct sound induced her to open the door. With a sickening of heart she beheld Marie faint and bleeding. Her clothes and

Bible were stained, and apparently in an almost lifeless state she could not call for help. There was a large fire in the grate, and the room was oppressively hot. To throw open the door, take off the fire, lighten the clothes, bathe her with Eau de Cologne, and apply salts, was the work of two minutes. It was some time however before she was able to take the prescribed medicine. It was pitiable to see her exhaustion, and the low fever and delirium which followed. From this too she recovered. She was not again left that night. The servants were very sorry that they had closed her door, and left her in the evening, but it had been at her request.

Marie wrote the following note to Elizabeth before her attack on Saturday.

" My dearest Elizabeth,

"I feel quite overcome with the kind expression of your love and affection in this my season of affliction. It was more than I could have expected from any other than a relative. I cannot express sufficiently my thanks, but accept all that is possible for me to convey.

"I had another return last night about ten : it lasted for more than an hour ; I do not feel so *very* weak, for another is coming on, my chest being still very tight. I am in bed. Mrs. L—— is calling to see you this evening, so I could not resist the temptation of writing. Do come to-morrow, you will cheer me for I am so low spirited. When I am alone I begin to fret. I am so anxious to see my dear uncle, I sometimes fear I shall never see him again, thinking God will take me very soon. I *cannot* long rally over these attacks, for I have no strength to stand against them. It does grieve me to give so much trouble to you all, but I cannot help it. I hope God will reward you all, *I never* can. Mrs. L—— is so kind to me, you can little fancy my feelings towards her. I never loved any one but mamma and uncle so dearly.

"I had such a kind letter from my uncle, I will tell you about it to-morrow.

"I cannot write more, so good-bye, and accept the dearest love of your poor and affectionate

"MARIE."

"Saturday Afternoon,
     "May 18th, 1850."

Elizabeth came back to take the place of nurse on Sunday afternoon and evening. Marie spoke of death as if anticipating its near approach, and asked Elizabeth to repeat many favorite verses bearing on the subject. "Which is the happiest death to die?" "Deathless principle arise:" "O the hour when this material:" "There is a world we have not seen:" "Can angel spirits need repose?" and "In heaven there's rest." Also in very different strain, Miss Jewsbury's "Lost Spirit," for which she asked twice.

The medical attendant came, and ordered leeches to relieve the oppressive tightness of which she complained. Elizabeth, who was a capital nurse, as usual put the leeches on for her, changed her dress, made her bed, and saw her comfortably settled before the family returned from evening service. She then went back to Queen Square.

The cause for alarm soon passed away. In two or three days Marie was able to dress and recline on the sofa. On Friday and Saturday she was able to take a little walk. On Monday evening she walked out with Mr. and Mrs. L——. Aided by an arm of each she went at the rate of about a mile an hour, as far as Kensington Gardens. There she rested; and declining the offer of a conveyance, managed by slow degrees to reach home on foot. Each day she gained strength, lengthened her walk, and acquired a somewhat firmer step.

Marie was now able to return to her favorite occupation of fancy work, and she exerted herself to finish a variety of articles which she had long been preparing for a bazaar in ——. It was for the building of the church for which she had some time before collected £10. She was very anxious to cover a table at this bazaar, and she asked all her friends for a contribution. She bought her wools and silks of some honest tradespeople of the name of P——, who had recently started in business nearly opposite. They had several children, and being a new neighborhood, they had a great struggle to make their business answer. Marie expressed much sympathy in all their troubles and anxieties, and would often sit half an hour in their shop, endeavoring to cheer poor Mrs. P——. She employed Mrs. P. to finish and ground a piece of work for her, but this proved rather an unfortunate order. The husband was a hair-dresser, and he had a waxen figure in the window to indicate his employment. This figure had cost £2. Mrs. P—— rose at four o'clock one morning to get Marie's work done by the specified time, and opened the shutters of the shop. The morning sun came with full power on the window at that hour, and poor Mrs. P——, engrossed in her employment, did not observe its effects. She had been working about two hours, when a boy ran in, exclaiming "Your wax head is melted away." She looked up, and to her consternation saw that it was too true. The head was indeed gone, irrecoverably.

Marie comforted the poor couple by the promise of an ample equivalent as soon as her uncle arrived. Many were the promises which she made, and the hopes which she held out to the various objects of her interest and sympathy, so soon as her uncle's arrival should put her in possession of her anticipated resources.

On Thursday morning, May 23d, Marie took a long walk with Mrs. L——, and surprised her friend by the information that she had an engagement in town that afternoon with Mr. K——. This was a valued friend in the congregation, who had throughout shown Marie much kindness, and to whose daughter she was much attached. Mrs. L—— was vexed at her thought-lessness.

"Why did you not tell me this morning, Marie? We are half-way there, and could have spared so much time and fatigue. Now we must return to dinner, and go over the ground again."

"O! but I am going alone."

"What! when you can only just creep along with our help? What would your uncle think of us if we could be so careless of you? Suppose you were taken ill in an omnibus, or fainted in the street?"

Marie *must* go that afternoon, for Mr. K—— would be staying at home for her, and she *must* go alone, for "it was private business," she said laughing, and Mrs. L—— was to know nothing about it.

"Then," said Mrs. L——, "I must take you to the house, and leave you there, and return again for you;" and so it was settled.

On Friday Marie stated that she had made another appointment, and must go to town again. It happened to be very inconvenient to post off to town without notice on two successive days, but rather than let her go alone, Mrs. L—— again accompanied her.

On Saturday Mrs. L—— went out on some little business in the neighborhood. As she returned, she met Marie coming from the house of a friend and neighbor. She ran up to Mrs. L—— with a quicker step than for many a day, and eagerly exclaimed, "Oh! Mrs. L——, I have had a note from my uncle. He will soon be here. He may be here to-day or Monday; for he says that perhaps, like the Irishman, he may be with me before his letter. It is a very short note, as he says he shall so soon see me."

Marie's glee passed away in the afternoon. She told Elizabeth and Selina that her uncle insisted on her speaking to Mrs.

L——, and said, that if on his coming he found she had not done so, he should not let her stay. They advised her at once to summon resolution, and get it over.

Marie was able to accompany her friends to morning service on Sunday (May 26th). On her account they had a fly, and she requested that the man might drive through Brook-street, and let her have a peep at Mivart's Hotel, in case her uncle should be there. In this she was indulged, but, as was to be expected, gained no information from the exterior of the house. Before service she passed to Mrs. L—— a few lines in pencil :—

"Dear Mrs. L——,

        "Can I have a little conversation with you in the vestry this afternoon, after your class?"

Mrs. L—— wrote in reply below,

        "Yes, dear Marie, if it is not on a subject that will unfit us for the evening service. You know best."

Marie went with Elizabeth to dine at Mr. and Mrs. K——'s. Mrs. L—— expected her in the vestry, but she did not come. She was seized with a violent headache in the afternoon, and obliged to leave the table and lie down. She asked for a mustard plaister at the back of her neck, and Elizabeth put it on, and tried cold applications to her forehead. She returned to the evening service, but unable to bear the heat, was obliged to go out. She went up to the minister's vestry, and with the door open below, was able to hear the sermon.

On Monday evening Marie requested Mrs. L—— to walk out with her. Her step was slow and feeble, and she was very silent. Mrs. L—— tried to converse in order to lessen Marie's restraint, but met with no response. They were out an hour and a half, and walked about three quarters of a mile. At length Mrs. L—— brought her home, and leaving her at the door, went to take a brisk turn for exercise. On her return, the servant informed her that Marie had been very ill: that she had fallen down senseless on the stairs, and that as Sarah and she with difficulty raised her, and carried her up, she had faintly uttered, "I wanted to speak to Mrs. L——, and I could not." Mrs. L—— ran up, and found Marie pale and cold on the drawing-room sofa. She said she had been seized with a violent palpitation of the heart. Of this in a slighter degree she had often complained. She said that her mamma had died of disease of the heart, and she apprehended that this, rather than disease of the lungs, would carry her off.

This was the third time that illness had followed Marie's attempts at making the communication respecting the burnt notes, which the uncle required. On the first occasion she had ruptured a blood-vessel; on the second, had suffered from intense headache; and on the third had been attacked with palpitation of the heart. Mr. and Mrs. L—— therefore told her that it had better be postponed till his visit, the near approach of which was now so anxiously expected.

On Tuesday morning Marie joyfully announced the receipt of another note from her uncle. He and the Kenyons were to come by the packet on Thursday. He would send her boxes under the care of Roberts on Thursday evening, and he would himself come on Friday at six, and, if convenient to Mr. and Mrs. L——, spend the evening with them. He wished her to be ready to accompany him on Monday to Staffordshire, and return to town on Wednesday. He expressed his regret that she had not written to her aunt, and it was to atone for this neglect, and place her on a footing of equal interest with her cousins, that he wished to take her. If she felt afraid to trust herself with him alone, perhaps one of the Misses —— would go with her.

Marie asked Elizabeth if she would accompany her on this important journey, and Elizabeth signified her willingness to do so. Much conversation passed as to how far she would conform to the usages of the Catholic family under whose roof she would rest; and she stated her resolution not to be present at prayers.

The arrival and contents of her boxes was another fruitful topic of speculation; but these lighter thoughts soon passed away, and she gave utterance to mingled emotions of a tenderer and more serious character, in the prospect of soon seeing her much loved relative.

CHAPTER XXII.

THE SCENE BEGINS TO CHANGE.

Thursday came at last, the day so long and anxiously expected. After breakfast Marie requested Mrs. L—— to go to town with her, and purchase a new dress, as she wished to look neat when her uncle came. She had long had a wish for a lavender French merino, which she said had been her uniform at Amiens, and her uncle had always liked it. Mrs. L—— objected that it would soon be too warm for the season of the year. Marie replied that she could then put it aside till the warm weather was over. In short nothing would do but this merino, so they sallied out. At the first large shop to which they went, the greater part of the merinoes had been packed away to make room for summer stock, and there was no lavender merino to be found. At the second shop it was the same, but the master produced a French de laine of the veritable shade; and Marie, captivated by the sight of the long-desired color, said that would do just as well as the merino; and with the eagerness of a child, she insisted on carrying the parcel herself. Thence they proceeded to a dressmaker's in Berners' Street, where a number of hands were employed; and Marie was fitted, and the dress promised by twelve o'clock the next day. On leaving the dressmaker's, they walked along the quiet streets. It was early in the day, and they could converse undisturbed. "I have been thinking a great deal about the visit to Staffordshire," said Marie. "I am not sure whether I ought not to make up my mind to go alone. I feel some uneasiness about taking Elizabeth with me."

"Why so? You do not think that anybody would do her any harm?"

"Oh! no, I could trust my uncle for that matter. He would never do anything dishonorable. The Jesuits would never choose *him* to do any underhand work. But I look at it in this way. My uncle is very pleasing. He has just those qualities which Elizabeth would appreciate. He is a perfect gentleman, and highly intellectual and intelligent. There is nothing on which he cannot converse. It is part of the education of the Jesuits to make themselves agreeable, and it is natural to him besides. Elizabeth could not but admire him. And I am sure he would be pleased with her,—with her wit, and grace, and disposition to please. He would think her a convert worthy of his efforts. Then she would be introduced into the most refined Catholic society, where no outrage would be done to her feelings and opinions, and she would see everything to advantage. He might even go so far as to plan some Catholic connection for her. I do not know young ———, but perhaps he may be a fine elegant young man. He would feel quite justified in trying any such scheme. He would think he was saving her soul, and he would spare no pains to make some atonement for the loss of me. I should never forgive myself if I were the means of bringing any evil upon her. I would rather run all risks myself than incur *that* danger."

Mrs. L—— was much struck with the forethought and prudence evinced in these remarks. There was, indeed, a strange combination in Marie. Reckless and wilful as she appeared at times, almost even to childishness, she could treat subjects of real importance with an amount of consideration and sagacity unusual to her years. Mrs. L—— so far agreed with her as to propose that Elizabeth should consult her father very fully on the subject, and that the responsibility of the decision should rest entirely with him. They then parted—Marie to go to Mr. K——'s, on her "private business," and Mrs. L—— in another direction,—to meet at home at five o'clock.

At half-past five Marie returned. The back-parlor was cleared for the reception and unpacking of the cumbrous boxes. Marie changed her dress, that Roberts might have no remarks to make on his return to his master, and took her tea quietly. She said that there would be considerable delay at the Custom House, and that Roberts would probably attend his master and the Kenyons to their hotel before he brought her things; so she did not at all expect them before seven or eight o'clock. As the evening wore on she became restless and excited, watched at the window till dusk, started at the sound of every cab, and ran to the door at every ring. Eight, nine, ten o'clock came, and no boxes. She began to despair, but at that moment a ring was heard at the bell, and presently a man's voice in conversation with the servant at the gate. Mrs. L—— ran up to the drawing-room window to see if it was the expected arrival. Was it Roberts? No; it was only Wood, come to fetch some broth for his children.

Marie bore the disappointment better than could have been anticipated. She said she should now expect them the first thing in the morning, as her uncle would not send so late. Probably there had been delays at the Custom House, or they might have come by a later packet. Her friends commended her fortitude: they supped and retired to rest.

The family rose on the Friday morning with something like an impression that Roberts and the boxes might arrive before they were ready to receive them. They met at breakfast. One of them gently opened Marie's door, and saw that she still slept. Exhausted with excitement and expectation, she had slept longer than usual. The postman brought a long letter to Mr. L——, which he read with deep attention and then put it in his pocket. Elizabeth had *her* letters too and did not observe him, but the wife did, and wondered.

She had forgotten it, however, when an hour afterwards he called her into his study, and put the following letter into her hand :—

" Marseilles, May 24th, 1850.

" Sir,

" It is with deep regret that I impose upon myself the painful duty of acquainting you of the very dangerous illness of the Rev. H. C. Clifford, the niece of whom is now under your protection.

" For the last six months we have been apprehensive that he was gradually declining in health, though he himself was unwilling to acknowledge it; and it was not until he was absolutely compelled by serious indisposition, that he could be prevailed upon to retire for a time from his very responsible and arduous duties.

" Since the severe attack he had a few weeks ago, his medical attendant and myself have endeavored to dissuade him from his purpose of attempting for the present to come to England ; but his extreme solicitude to see Maria overcame our persuasions. We therefore left Nice last Thursday, intending to be with you on the 1st of June ; but unhappily our worst fears were realized. He was very much fatigued with the journey here ; but on Sunday he was seized with dangerous spasms of the heart. Dr Rouchetti stated there was considerable enlargement of the heart, and also bronchitis in a severe form, which opinion has been confirmed by two eminent physicians, and to-day give but little hope of his recovery.

"Under the present circumstances I feel it my duty to inform you at once of his present condition, to relieve you from the suspense of expectation, and also to remove your anxiety in reference to the settlement of Maria's affairs in the event of his death.

"From respect for him, and the great esteem I had for Maria's mamma, I shall consider it a privilege to do all I can to carry out the kind and generous intentions of Mr. C. towards his niece, though she has justly forfeited the notice and friendship of her relatives by her late step of apostasy.

"I deeply sympathize with my esteemed friend in his great anxiety and sorrow for one so dear to him as Maria. She is now the chief object of his conversation and solicitude. During the past night he was delirious, and spoke much of Maria. From his incoherent expressions, and other little circumstances that have previously occurred, Mrs. Kenyon and myself can but think that Maria is laboring under some trouble or depression of mind. What it is we of course do not know; but if it is anything we can remove or alleviate, we shall feel a pleasure in doing so, in order, if possible, to remove Mr. L——'s anxiety.

"Last night we had great difficulty in persuading him to remain in bed, as he fancied he heard Maria in the next room crying, so he wished to go and comfort her. You can imagine how much we were distressed to see him in such a sad condition. Mrs. Kenyon tells me that he received a long letter from Maria a few weeks ago, since which he has been most impatient to see her. I wish it was in any way possible for Maria to come here. I suggested it to Mr. Clifford before I commenced my letter; but he would not consent to it, as such a step in Maria's case was quite impossible.

" The last few hours he has been more calm and collected, which cheers us a little.

" We sent express last night to Paris for his usual medical attendant; so we are looking forward with extreme anxiety for his arrival.

" I had, at the request of Mr. Clifford, an interview this morning with an English solicitor residing here, and have instructed him to draw up the deed which will entitle Maria to receive her uncle's intended gift, and also to enable you and myself to act as joint trustees. Mr. Clifford is very anxious to settle this matter immediately, knowing that Maria cannot claim anything after his decease. The document will be drawn up agreeably with your wishes with one exception, that we shall each have power to nominate our successor.

" Mr. Clifford wishes me to come to England at once to complete the business; but I cannot yet determine upon my course till there is some decided change.

" I had a long conversation with him yesterday about Maria, but to-day he says but little. He desired me not to write to her, fearing the shock would have a serious effect upon her health, to say nothing of the disappointment she will have to endure. We leave it to your discretion to acquaint her of the melancholy news. She *must* be prepared for the worst, though we would hope that God in his goodness will again raise so valued a relative. I expect that some of the C——'s will arrive here in two or three days.

" Mrs. K—— has just brought me in a message from Mr. Clifford to Mrs. L——. He begs that she will endeavor to persuade Maria to overcome her reserve, and also to tell Maria that he has perfect confidence in the truthfulness of her statement, whatever others may have thought of her; and if he is never permitted to see or write to her again, that he has freely forgiven the past, and hopes that she will for the future treat Mrs. L—— with that entire confidence to which she is so justly entitled.

"I think he feels great anxiety as to the effect riches will have upon the unsuspicious character and disposition of Maria.

"I am not at all aware of Maria's pecuniary resources, or whether she is in want of money. Mr. Clifford has been reserved upon this point, so do not know whether he has made a remittance lately; but should she require any, if you will kindly supply her I will settle with you should Mr. Clifford's death occur. Maria will soon be in the possession of her own property, for her aunt cannot possibly continue long. I shall write to you again in the course of a day or two.

"Mrs. Kenyon and myself will be glad to have a few lines from you in reply to this, stating how Maria receives the painful intelligence. With the kind regards of Mrs. Kenyon to Maria, in which I desire to unite,

"I am, sir,

"Yours truly,

"CHARLES W. KENYON.

"P. S.—Please direct for me here, to be left at the post-office till I call."

"I think this is a trick," said Mrs. L——, when she had read it.

"Why should you think so?" said Mr. L——, and he looked as reproachfully at her as it was possible for *him* to look, for her want of charity.

"For three reasons," she replied. "In the first place, there is bad spelling, of which no person such as Captain Kenyon is represented to be could be guilty. In the second place, it is not a gentleman's hand; it is more like the hand of those writing-masters who profess to cure bad writing; and, in the third place, when I have had a doubt, for doubts *have* crossed my mind since the discovery of Marie's falsehoods, I have always thought that the plot would break up in this way: and that the uncle would be taken ill and die, just when on the point of making his appearance."

" And will you set these vague surmises against all the internal evidence of the uncle's letters ?   Have we not posted them to all parts of the continent, and in due time received answers, and none have been returned ?   Oh ! no, no, you must not allow yourself to admit such unworthy suspicions."

He reminded her at more length of the features of genuineness about the letters ; the character of a priest maintained throughout, yet overborne by strong affection for his sister's child ; the fidelity of his reproofs to *her*, and the extenuations offered to *them ;* the gentlemanly language employed in all pecuniary matters, without any concession unsuitable to a Catholic or a man of business ; and at length he so succeeded in re-assuring her, that her first sceptical impressions were removed, and deep sympathy for Marie's overwhelming disappointment took their place.

Then how to communicate the tidings to her was the question.   They agreed that it would be better to keep her in suspense for a day or two, and so prepare her for the shock ; and they resolved that all should go on that day as if the uncle were still expected,—the drawing-room should be arranged, the tea service got out, books such as " Elliot's Horæ Apocalypticæ," and others bearing on the Popish controversy should, as Marie had stipulated, be removed out of the way, and Elizabeth allowed to go and consult her papa about the Staffordshire journey as if nothing had happened.

Marie rose about ten.   " Is there no letter for me ?"

" No, not any."

" Then I am afraid something has happened to keep my uncle.   He would certainly have sent this morning to account for the delay, for he would know what suspense I should be in." She could not eat—she could not settle to work—she wandered about the house pale and restless.   The new dress arrived, but she would not put it on; she had no heart to do so. They dined, and Elizabeth went off to meet her father who was then in London. Marie had ceased to expect her uncle, having received neither note nor boxes. She waited, however, till the appointed hour of six was past, and then she put on her things, and said that she would go out a little way alone, and try to walk down her excited feeling.

She did not return till half-past eight, and looked much exhausted. She said she had been to Kensington Gardens.

"Oh! Marie," said Mrs. L——, "how could you think of going there alone, and at *this* hour. What would your uncle say?"

"He will hear of it then," said Marie, "for I met Mary L——, one of my school-fellows at Isleworth, and we walked up and down, and had a long conversation together. She says they were talking about me at Mrs. Frederick ——'s the other evening, and she heard that my uncle was reconciled to me, and everybody was very much surprised. She talked so much and so fast, that I could hardly follow her. She asked me all about the people I was with, and wanted to know what could have made me turn Protestant. I told her I would write to her, for I did not feel in spirits to go into it all then. I did not tell her of my disappointment, for I thought he might not like them all to know that he was coming here. She says she is going to Cheltenham—6, Suffolk Square—on Monday, for six weeks, and I am to write to her there. She will call on me when she comes to town." Elizabeth returned in the midst of this narration. "What! no uncle, no Roberts, no letter! What could it mean?"

CHAPTER XXIII.

STARTLING DISCOVERIES.

The day to which all had so anxiously looked forward had passed over. The heads and hearts of all were variously exercised. For once they thought and felt apart, and yet all were conscious that an extraordinary crisis was at hand. Mrs. L—— rose first. Oh! what a dead weight was on her spirits when she woke. All Marie's past trials seemed nothing to the one now before her. Repeatedly disappointed, and now warmed up to the highest pitch of expectation,—all her fondest affections drawn out towards her only remaining relative,—her own life hanging on a thread,—how were they ever to break to her tidings which in all human probability must be her death-blow? She tried to meet Marie with an appearance of hope and cheerfulness, but it was hard work; and when her husband prayed with reference to Marie, in a way which she alone understood, she could not restrain her tears. She concealed them, however, and she stole a glance at Marie on rising to see whether it had occasioned any emotion or inquiry on her part; but Marie looked out of the window, in dreamy abstraction, and her thoughts were evidently far away.

Marie said after breakfast, that she should take a walk, her usual recourse when agitated, and she went up stairs. Mr. and Mrs. L—— resolved to show the letter to Elizabeth, and they called her into the study. She read the first sentence, and exclaimed, "How strange! I read this very sentence in Marie's handwriting the other day."

"When? where?" said Mr. and Mrs. L——, anxiously.

"At her desk when she went out for a walk. I told her I should sit and write a note there. I tried to pull the desk out, and something obstructed the movement. I looked behind to find the cause, and in the little vacancy between the top and bottom of the desk there was a paper. It was the copy of a letter. I pulled it out and read this."

" And why did you not tell us ?"

" Because I did not read any more, and so there was nothing to tell."

" But why did you not read it all ?"

" Because I thought it would be dishonorable. I was ashamed of having seen that."

" Oh ! not in such a case," said they both. " With any ground for suspecting deception, we are perfectly justified in reading such a paper. What a pity you did not read it through ! Why what could you think of it ?"

" I thought it very odd, and I felt puzzled. But I remembered hearing something about the uncle being ill a little while ago, and I supposed it was about that. I wondered he should have been so very ill, and I not have heard of it; but then I had been away some time. I thought it was a letter you did not wish me to see, and that when you had given it to Marie to read, she had taken a copy of it."

" Well, that is the most suspicious circumstance that has turned up yet," said Mr. L——, and they looked at one another, and felt as if they could hardly get their breath.

" Think it over again, Elizabeth," said they. " Can you recollect nothing else ?"

" No," she said, " but I am sure about this sentence, and part was crossed out and altered."

" Well, read the letter, and see if anything occurs to you."

" Nothing more," said she when she had done, " except that my eye caught the word ' solicitor' farther on. She will soon be going out, and I will have a hunt for the paper."

" Are you sure," said Mr. L——, " that you read that sentence ?"

"Oh, yes! it is so fresh in my mind. It struck me the first instant I read it again here, word for word."

"She will be down," they said, "and if she hear us in conclave, she will think that something is going on. Nothing must escape us. We must talk it over again by-and-by."

They agreed that Mrs. L—— should propose walking with Marie, and keep her out while Elizabeth instituted a search up stairs. At that instant they heard Marie pass down stairs. The sisters left the study, and she ran up, calling for Mrs. L——.

"If you will wait a minute, Marie," she said, "I can walk with you."

Mr. L—— was standing at his door. Marie stopped.

"Mr. L——, how pale you look!" she exclaimed.

"Do I? I am not very well this morning."

She began speaking to Mrs. L——, and again stopped to look at him.

"I cannot help looking at you. How very pale you are."

"I have the headache, but perhaps I shall be better when you see me again. Go and get your walk."

She and Mrs. L—— went, and Elizabeth ran up to her room. The letter was gone from its hiding-place, nor was it to be found among her papers. Elizabeth went to her brother to tell him of her ill success. He had been pondering the subject over, and he could not but think that her memory might have deceived her in reference to that one sentence. It seemed to him far more easy to suppose that she had retained some incorrect impression, than to imagine that all was false. Elizabeth herself taxed and retaxed her recollection till she became quite bewildered, and began almost to think with him that she might have been mistaken. Not so Mrs. L——. Elizabeth's exclamation had been so fresh and genuine, that she felt more confidence in her first vivid impressions, than in her subsequent perplexities; and she tried to reassure Elizabeth.

Marie went out again after returning with Mrs. L——. She did not come back till dinner was half over. "I am very sorry to be so late," she said cheerfully, "but I have been doing a good work. You shall hear." She threw her bonnet down, and seated herself at the table. "I walked to ——, and as I came back, I called in at Mrs. P——'s, for some purse-silk. She had none of the right shade, so I went down to the shop opposite the ——. I met Mr. R——, and he told me that Mrs. R—— was so low and weak, that it would be kind in me to call upon her. I found her on the sofa. She was doing a crochet collar, and she could not manage the pattern, so I stayed and put her right. Mr. R—— asked me to dine with him, but I said you would wonder what had become of me." They asked her many questions about Mrs. R——'s health and appearance, all which she readily answered. They heard and doubted ; but there were as yet no *proofs* against her. They could only watch and wait. They resolved to let her go out unrestrained, and give her full scope, assured that the progress of events must speedily bring her truth or falsehood to light.

In the evening she went out again, and again stayed till half-past eight. Elizabeth and Mrs. L—— determined in any case to take all prudent precautions, and they ran up stairs to make the most of the time during Marie's absence. They again examined her room, taking care not to alter the position of any papers or other articles. They searched under the carpet, at the top of the bedstead, up the chimney, felt over every part the mattresses, but could discover nothing of a suspicious character. Yet here and there, amidst what now appeared to them the *studied* confusion of drawers and boxes, were pious effusions and expressions of attachment to Mrs. L——, written on various scraps of paper, and left as if by accident in various places. Thence they went to Mrs. L——'s room, and were relieved to find the copies of the manuscript safe in their hiding-place. There were no fewer than three copies of this production : the

12

original in Mrs. L——'s and Marie's writing, and two copies which she afterwards had taken, one for her uncle and one for the publisher. Elizabeth and she now thought it better to divide them, and hide them in different places. The few articles of jewellery and plate were also deposited in the most unlikely hiding-places, and rubbish of all sorts carelessly thrown over them. Mrs. L—— gave her husband all the "uncle's letters" which Marie had asked her to take care of, and he placed them in his study, under lock and key. They resolved to keep a sharp watch on all her movements, without appearing to do so, and never to leave her in the house alone.

Marie was extremely anxious to go with the family on Sunday morning, but Mr. L—— persuaded her not to do so. Marie endeavored to prevail upon Elizabeth to go and hear her brother, but Elizabeth assured her that she could not think of leaving her alone when she had so much to make her anxious and depressed, and they went to a neighboring place of worship.

In the evening Marie was seized with a sudden desire to attend the Catholic chapel in St. John's Wood, or the one at Paddington Green. Elizabeth thought that she must have some plan, and would have gone with her, but through an oversight there was not sufficient time, and they again went to a Protestant place of worship.

On Monday morning, Marie was up in good time, and breakfasted with the family. The postman's knock was heard. There was a letter for her in a strange hand. She opened it, and read the first sentence—"my uncle," "change," "out of danger." "What is it?" "O take it, take it!" and trembling excessively, she dropped the letter.

Mrs. L—— picked it up. "Give it to me," said Mr. L—— and he read as follows:—

"Marseilles, 28th May, 1850.

"My dear Marie,

"I am requested by your uncle to write to inform

you that there is a slight change for the better, though he is not yet out of danger.

"I deeply sympathize with you in your great disappointment, and it is equally felt by your dear uncle.

"Dr. Martigny has arrived here from Paris. On the 24th (the day on which Mr. Kenyon wrote to Mr. L——) he gave but little hope of his recovery, but this morning the two physicians have given a more favorable bulletin.

"Mr. Kenyon is daily expecting a reply to his letter from Mr. L——. I will write again in a day or two, to give you every information.

"Your uncle desires his sincerest love, and with kind sympathy from Captain Kenyon and myself,

"I am, yours sincerely
"Constantia Kenyon."

Marie appeared to be in the greatest agitation and distress. She rushed out of the room, and went into the back parlor to give vent to her feelings.

"Does not that look like genuine feeling?" said Mr. L——. The others answered with a look of incredulity. They conded, however, that the note was in a lady's hand, and that its sententious brevity was not Marie's style. It was more like that of a woman of fashion.

Marie returned in a short time. "Now, Marie," said Mr. L——, "I may tell you what I did not think it well to tell you before. On Friday morning I received intelligence of your uncle's illness, but we thought it would be such a shock to you just then, that we would wait for the next letter before saying anything to you about it. As this morning's note is more favorable, I do not mind telling you."

Marie was all anxiety to see Captain Kenyon's letter, and Mr. L—— gave her the first part. She was dwelling on the details all the morning, and then retired to her room to write to her uncle.

Anxious to ascertain how far Marie was telling the truth, Mrs. L—— went to call on Mrs. R——. She rang at the gate. The servant came out, but did not offer to open it.

"How is Mrs. R——?"

"Better, thank you, ma'am, but she is still very weak."

"Can I see her?" The girl looked surprised.

"No, ma'am! she has not been dressed yet."

"Oh! very well. I hope she was not fatigued after Miss —— (Marie) left her on Saturday."

"Miss who, ma'am?"

Mrs. L—— repeated the name, and added, "The young lady whom you have seen with me."

"No one was here on Saturday, ma'am. Mistress has not seen anybody yet."

"I thought Miss —— had called on Saturday."

"She called once a long time ago, but not on Saturday. It is quite a mistake."

Mrs. L —— left her kind regards. She had learned what had already been suspected, that Marie had been on some other errand on Saturday.

Mrs. L—— returned home, and communicated the result of her call. Marie was still writing in her room. She re-appeared at dinner, but did not eat. Mrs. L—— had once begun to sketch Marie's face in an album. That afternoon she asked Marie whether she should finish it, in case her uncle should wish for it. Marie sat. Mrs. L—— was struck with the altered expression. She could not catch the animated happy look of former days. A shadow seemed to have fallen upon it. Some might have called it pensiveness or sorrow, but to Mrs. L—— there appeared a restless, deep, absent, plotting look, which altered the whole character of her countenance. The features were there, and yet the face scarcely seemed the

same. While sitting for her picture Marie asked Mrs. L——
to return her all her uncle's letters, as she wished to arrange
them, and also Mrs. L——'s admonitory letter to her. She
had made the same request a few days before. "Mr. L——
has them," was the reply. Marie applied to him on his return home. He evaded a direct reply and changed the subject.

Marie was increasingly anxious to watch for the postman.
She went out for a walk at five, and came in about six. Happily, she had just missed him. She went out again to meet
Mrs. L—— and Lilly, but missed them also. Mrs. L——
came in first, and Elizabeth opened the door, and took her up
stairs to be unheard by Lilly and the servants. She said, "I
am so thankful Marie was not in when the postman came. He
brought a paper of inquiry for the Rev. S. L——, to know
whether he had yet received a letter, signed Charles W. Kenyon, dated Marseilles, May, 1850, posted in Vigo Street, and
directed to 5, C—— Terrace. He would not give me the
paper. He said that the letter had been inquired for at the
post-office on Saturday morning."

No more convincing proof was needed by the sisters that
Marie was playing a deep game. They had not informed her
of the arrival of the letter till Monday morning. How then
could she be acquainted with the signature and date on Saturday morning unless privy to its contents?

Mr. L—— came home and heard the tale. He too was
convinced of Marie's falsehood, but more perplexed than ever
as to its motive and extent. He still thought "the uncle" was
true, but that Marie, weary of restraint and anxious for a change,
had invented some false tale for *her uncle*, and a fictitious correspondence to deceive *them*. If, indeed, the tale of the uncle
should be a fiction, he was satisfied that she must have some
able accomplice,—that the "uncle' letters could never be the
invention of a girl of twenty-five He could suppose Captain

Kenyon's letter to be her composition, but he could not believe her capable of such a series as Mr. Clifford's. Sometimes he thought that Marie had received Captain Kenyon's letter at the door, had opened and read it, and frightened at what she had done had re-posted it, and had thus become aware of its contents. The wife and sisters entertained no such hopes; but as the evidence of the past was still incomplete, they endeavored to prepare him for the future, and to fix in his mind that if there was no Captain Kenyon, there was no uncle. Of this they felt convinced that there would soon be proof.

CHAPTER XXIV.

MARIE IN UNCONSCIOUS CUSTODY.

In commencing this chapter, we must bespeak the indulgence of the upright and truth-loving reader for the family at C—— Terrace. For the next fortnight they were compelled to act a part to them entirely new, and to conceal their suspicions from Marie till they had traced out all her movements. Convinced that such ability in intrigue could proceed from none but a Jesuit source, they felt that had she suddenly left them at this juncture, they would constantly have had before them the idea of other Jesuit plotters and spies haunting their every step,—of some conspiracy, the object of which yet unfulfilled was to be attained in some new way. They feared too that if she found they were tracking her, she might resort to some desperate means to have her revenge. Perhaps they wronged her in their thoughts, but who can wonder after having *so* trusted and been *so* deceived if the reaction in their minds led them to suspect her even too far. The mother had fears of another kind. All past indications of indifference or dislike to the children rushed back upon her recollection, and she felt that life dearer than her own might depend upon her silence. Throughout this exciting period they never gave utterance to a falsehood, but they kept up their apparent belief in Marie's fictions, and talked as fluently as if they received them to the letter.

It was a great relief to Mr. and Mrs. L—— that Elizabeth was still with them. The atmosphere of her country home was too damp for her in the winter, and several circumstances, among which Marie's doubtful state of health was prominent, had detained her in town longer than she had intended. Warmly sympathizing with her brother and sister in a trial so new and strange, and ready to blame herself for the unconscious part she had taken in fetching Marie from the convent, she exerted herself to the utmost. Her sleepless nights testified to the extent of the effort, but no one would have detected it by day. Her ready tact and courage never failed, and keeping up a lynx-eyed watch under every supposable manifestation of sympathy, she contrived to out-manœuvre Marie herself.

To return to Monday evening. Marie, unaware of the postman's visit, came in to supper. The family stifled their emotions, and talked with her as usual. She took a little milk only. She had scarcely eaten at all for several days, and they urged her to take something more, but she shook her head. She was too anxious, too sad to eat. Mrs. L—— carried up her candle for her, and she retired to rest.

They chatted a little in an undertone in the dining-room, and tried to lay plans for the morrow.

"We must consider what to do about the postman," said Elizabeth, "for he will come again in the morning."

"I will have an early engagement," said Mr. L——, "and go out to meet him."

Elizabeth went into the hall, and fancied that Marie was listening over the banisters. They felt that it was not safe to prolong the conversation. Marie's door was open when they went up, but she closed it soon afterwards.

Mrs. L—— went up stairs, and stood by the side of her beautiful boy. His little fat rosy cheek rested on his dimpled hand, and the expression of sleeping innocence and peace seemed to rebuke her fears. She dared not take him into her own room, lest any unusual proceeding should arrest Marie's attention,—still less did she dare to put Sarah on her guard. She could only commit him to the care of his heavenly Guardian, and she thought of Hankinson's beautiful lines,* altering the pronoun only,—

> " I bent me o'er my infant child,
> And marked that in his (her) sleep he smiled;
> I could not tell from what bright thought
> His cheek that ray of gladness caught,
> Yet doubted not his angel's voice
> Had bid my little one rejoice:
> And when with all a parent's fears,
> I pore into the gulph of years,
> 'Tis sweet to think of Him whose hand
> Caressed the infant race,
> What time with voice divinely bland,
> He spake those words of grace—
> ' The children's angels always stand
> Before my Father's face.' "

More than once that night she started from her sleep, and fancied that she heard the boards creak, and that Marie was stealthily crossing the room : it was only Lilly turning in her crib, and the door was locked. Once she dreamed that she was lying on the drawing-room sofa asleep, and that Marie, expressing a fear that she was fatigued, held a smelling bottle to her nose. She thought she tried to push it away, but in vain, and opening her eyes, beheld Marie with a look worthy of

* " The Ministry of Angels."—Seatonian prize poem.

Madame de Brinvilliers, eagerly holding the bottle fast to her nostrils. She struggled violently and awoke.

Morning came, and baby and all were safe. Marie had an engagement with Miss K——. Mr. L—— had his engagement still earlier, and he met the postman at some distance from the house. He then went to the branch post-office to ascertain who had been making inquiries; and was thence referred to the General Post Office in St. Martin's le Grand. There he learned beyond a doubt that it was Marie, and that she had been there on Saturday morning, at the hour when she represented herself to have been with Mrs. R——. He went to a bookseller's for a "*Court Guide*," and found the addresses of all those who bore the name which Marie had asserted to be her mother's. He looked at the Peerage Book, and found her statements of lineage and intermarriage in that family, for the most part correct. He searched for a Captain Kenyon, but could find no such person. He looked in guide books for Welby Hall, the Kenyon domicile, but could find no such place. He went to the residence of one member of the family, with whom Marie claimed relationship, but he was not in town. He returned as much in the dark as ever. Indeed he seemed so confounded and paralyzed by what had transpired, as to be quite at a loss what course to pursue. Mrs. L—— urged him to take some friend into his confidence, and confer unitedly on the steps which should be taken. It was indeed too oppressive a weight to bear alone. Single-minded and unsuspicious, he was not the one to track a rogue, or to be very adroit in what more resembled the calling of a Bow Street officer than of a Christian minister. He yielded to her wish, and promised the next morning to go and communicate the whole to Mr. K——.

After bidding Marie good night as she passed her door, Mrs. L—— went up to Elizabeth's room. " What is Marie so busy about at Mr. K——'s ?" said Mrs. L——.

Elizabeth hesitated. "No harm," she said at length.

"No good, I am afraid," said Mrs. L——, "tell me."

"Marie told me in confidence, but I think you ought to know now. She is collecting money from the young people in the congregation, to make S. (Mr. L——) a present. I believe it is to be Dr. Arnold's Works, nicely bound, as she had heard him say how much he should like to have them."

"Then, indeed, I shall go to Mr. K——, and put a stop to it at once," said Mrs. L——. "The poor things will all be cheated out of their money. She wants it to pay for her fictitious letters, I do not doubt."

"But if you interfere she will find it out."

"No; Mr. K—— will contrive that:" and fearing to remain longer together they parted.

On Wednesday morning Mr. L—— started on another journey of inquiry, intending to consult Mr. K—— by the way, and return home at three o'clock. Marie went out, and was absent about an hour and a half. On her return she wrote letters to Mary L——, Mrs. Kenyon, and to her uncle, and put them into Mrs. L——'s hand to read.

The letter to Mary L——, grounded on their meeting in Kensington Gardens, stated in full her reasons for becoming a Protestant. Mrs. L—— silently remarked that Marie, though requesting an answer, had given no address, and had merely signed herself, "Marie." It was directed and posted to 6 Suffolk Square, Cheltenham. Whether there is any such place, the reader may possibly know.

The letter to Mrs. Kenyon is not of sufficient interest to merit insertion. An extract from the letter to her uncle may suffice.

"June 5th, 1850.

"My very dear uncle,

"I need not tell you of the great sorrow the intelligence of your serious illness has caused me. The disappointment of not seeing you was hard to bear, but to hear you were ill, and so far distant too was much greater. I do trust that God will, in his infinite and boundless mercy, again restore you. We cannot understand the purposes of God in these dispensations, but we do know that He designs them for some good and wise end. I do pray that whether it please God to remove you or not, that you may be enabled to cast all your care upon the sinner's *only* Rock, the Saviour; and if death must soon be your portion, may it find you 'ready the summons to obey:' it will then usher you 'into the dwelling-place of God,' not to the dark regions of purgatory. Bear with me, dear uncle, in saying this much : I cannot refrain from doing so, for the Word of God tells me 'there is no wisdom, or device, or knowledge in the grave,' and that 'there is no other name by which men may be saved than the name Christ Jesus.' No mediator or mediatrix can save you in a dying hour. I know, dear uncle, it does not become me to preach to one so much wiser and older than myself, but my love to you will not permit me to refrain from persuading you to inquire into the realities of religion."

*   *   *   *   *   *   *   *   *

Mrs. L—— could scarcely suppress her indignation at the desecration of all sacred things with which this letter abounded. She returned it without a remark, and left the room. The propriety of giving publicity to such hypocrisy may be doubted, but it seems necessary to the full exhibition of Marie's character. This letter is but a specimen of what she had been in the habit of writing to her friends for a period of many months.

The most direct way of proceeding at this juncture was evidently to write to the family whose name Marie had employed. Mr. L—— had hesitated, for he still clung to the idea that the uncle was a reality, and that it would not do to indicate suspicion of him without positive proof. Mrs. L—— resolved to meet the difficulty by writing to Lady ————, whom Marie had claimed as her cousin, and enclosing a *bona fide* letter to the uncle, requesting her to forward it. To avoid Marie's observation, she took the pen and ink to her room, locked her door, and standing at her drawers with an open bonnet-box beside her, wrote the two notes. Marie came and tried the door. Mrs. L—— quickly and quietly transferred the writing apparatus to the bonnet-box, and threw the door open. Marie merely came to ask a question and withdrew. Mrs. L—— finished the notes, and waited till nearly post time to consult Mr. L——. He did not return, and she resolved to run the risk of posting them herself.

      " To Lady ————.

" Madam,

      " May I request your ladyship kindly to direct and post the enclosed to the Very Reverend Herbert Constable Clifford, of Manotté, near Amiens, but of whose present address I am ignorant. The letter relates to his niece Miss M—— L—— G——, the daughter of his late sister. She has been for some time residing with us, and the letter is of immediate importance.

" As a perfect stranger, I owe you many apologies for thus troubling you, but as the object is connected with the interests of a member of your family I hope to be excused.

" I enclose stamps for the value of the foreign postage, and am, madam,

              " Yours respectfully,

                    " J—— L——.

" 5, C—— Terrace, ————,
    " June 5th, 1850."

The letter to the uncle mentioned the fact of Marie's inquiries at the post-office, and requested him to explain the circumstance. It was merely written to meet the possibility of his existence, of which Mr. L—— still entertained a latent hope.

Elizabeth took the letters to the post-office. Marie heard her go out, and ran to the window to see which way she went. Elizabeth had turned in a different direction, and gone to a more distant post-office than the one opposite.

Mr. L—— returned home soon afterwards, but Mrs. L—— did not *then* acquaint him with what she had done.

CHAPTER XXV.

THE SISTERS ENDEAVOR TO KILL THE UNCLE.

IT was Wednesday evening, June the 5th. The postman knocked at tea-time, and Marie rushed out to open the door. It was a letter to Marie from Mrs. Kenyon. "Oh dear! it's bad," she said, as she glanced over it. She passed it to the others, and hastily left the room. The letter ran thus :—

"MARSEILLES, May 31st.

"My dear Marie,

"I truly regret that I cannot at this time give you so favorable a report as my former one. Your uncle has had a severe relapse, and since yesterday has been quite unconscious.

"I grieve, dear Marie, to tell you that I fear there is but little hope of his recovery.

"I am sure what I am now writing will be a great trial to you. The loss will be almost that of a second parent, but I trust God will sustain you in your affliction.

"Your dear uncle has spoken much of you, and you seem

to have been constantly in his thoughts.   Dr. Rouchette says that the next twenty hours will decide a change.

" As a small matter of consolation to you, will you pardon me saying that your dear uncle's death, should it occur, will not affect your pecuniary prospects.

" I have promised your uncle that should you ever express a wish to return to your friends my house will be open to receive you.

" Allow me, dear Marie, to urge upon you affectionately one little matter that has distressed your uncle very much, namely, that reserve which still exists between Mrs. L—— and yourself. I am sure you would be glad to do anything to relieve his mind, therefore at once comply with his request ; it may be his last.

" He has written a letter to you and Mrs. L——, to be forwarded in the event of his death.

" I strongly advised your coming to see him, but he opposed it for reasons which he said he had before explained to you.

"Captain Kenyon will write to-morrow. With my sincere sympathy and kind love, I am,

" Yours affectionately,

" CONSTANTINE KENYON."

The sisters were rather encouraged by this letter. They were most anxious for the winding up of the drama, as their present position would have been insufferable for any length of time. What would come next, they could not imagine. Perhaps some person in the shape of Captain Kenyon with papers for Mr. L—— to sign. Nothing could be done till the uncle was either better or worse; and as the latter course was more decisive, they resolved, if opinions could have any influence not to hold out the slightest hope, and bring his life to as speedy a conclusion as possible.

They went to Marie. She sat with the back parlor door open, in an attitude of distress and agitation, but said she could not weep. She feared that all was over when Mrs. Kenyon wrote, that this letter was designed to break it gently to her, and that the next would inform her that he was no more. " Did they think so ?" " Indeed it did seem too probable. They should so view it were it their case. At any rate the event must have taken place before now, as the letter had been six days in coming."

Elizabeth felt so disgusted at the part Marie was acting, and so weary of acting her own, that she said she would go to the evening service at the Lock chapel and endeavor to calm her mind. Marie went to her own room. She complained of head-ache, and said she should lie down. Mrs. L—— slipped out with Mr. L—— for a little air. They met Elizabeth coming from the Lock, and he related his adventures. He had been a long round without success. First he went to the Horse Guards to get a sight of the Army List. No Captain Kenyon was there ; but as no record was kept of those who had sold their commissions, this was no *proof*. Thence he went to the Catholic booksellers and publishers to try to obtain a list of the Catholic clergy, but could find no list of those in England, far less of those in France. At length one bookseller suggested that he might obtain the information he needed at the Jesuit's house, —— Street, Berkeley Square. He went, but it was a festival day. The priests were engaged in their services, and he could not see them. He was told to go again the next morning. Mr. K—— undertook this errand, and he returned home.

They supped. Marie could neither eat nor talk, and retired before the others. They dared not indulge in lengthened con-versation lest it should awaken conjecture. Mrs. L—— had been in the habit of going into Marie's room the last thing, lighting her " Albert," and seeing her comfortably settled. " You must not omit your nightly visit," said Mr. L—— ; " and you too, Elizabeth, should look in." They went up. Marie was seated on a chair by the bedside. Her desk was drawn close, and the Bible lay open upon it. She sat with her head bent on her chest, in an attitude of deep despondency. "Are you not going to bed, Marie?" said Mrs. L——. She shook her head. "Come, let me help you to undress."

"It is of no use, I could not sleep."

"Perhaps you may if you try. At any rate you will get cold and tired if you sit up."

"I will in a little while, but I can get no sleep till I hear that my uncle is better. If I could but cry—but I feel too stunned and stupified to shed tears. To see one dear object after another taken from me—and now last of all my uncle, who has of late become so very dear! What do you think about him?"

Mrs. L—— and Elizabeth never suffered any hope of the uncle's recovery to pass without a check. "Well," said the former, "I do not think it kind to nourish groundless expectations. If this is a relapse, and he has been twenty-four hours unconscious, there does not seem to me the shadow of a hope that he will recover. If I were you, I should try to prepare my mind for the worst."

"He did once rally though from a similar illness. I cannot give up hope yet."

"Well, do get to bed soon."

Mrs. L—— was about to take her leave. Marie did not seem ready. At length she jumped up, threw her arm around Mrs. L——'s neck, and said, "To-morrow I hope to comply with my uncle's last request."

"Ah! indeed you have been long enough in coming to that resolution. Do you not regret it now?" said Mrs. L—— in an admonitory tone. Elizabeth caught sight of herself in the looking-glass laughing, and she withdrew through the half-open door. Mrs. L—— followed. They closed Marie's door, and went into Mrs. L——'s room. They retreated to the other end of the room, and burst into a fit of laughter which they in vain endeavored to stifle. They were by the bedside, and they buried their heads in the counterpane, lest Marie should hear the sound. It was well for them that they *could* laugh. Their minds were kept on so unnatural a stretch, that it was a relief when circumstances prompted to relax into a laugh ; and distressed, shocked, horrified, as they were at the discovery of Marie's wickedness, and painful as it was to them to act the part they were compelled to act, there were some incidents so truly ridiculous, that the transition was not so difficult as might at first be imagined.

Marie appeared at the breakfast table on Thursday morning, and expressed much anxiety for further tidings respecting her uncle. The postman brought no letters for her. She retired to her room, and was heard to groan frequently. In the course of the morning she returned to the sitting-room, and took up her crochet-work, but frequently put it down as if unable to proceed. Elizabeth proposed that she should take a little walk. "Not yet," she said. "She felt too poorly, and had not sufficient energy, not having slept till daybreak." She spoke at intervals of the subject that engaged her thoughts.

"Where will your uncle be buried, Marie?" said Elizabeth.

"Wherever the General may appoint," she replied. "I do not know whether he will be buried according to secular or monastic vows, as he was thinking of becoming a secular."

"But if he should die at Marseilles, as you fear?" said Elizabeth.

"It will not be at Marseilles certainly, but whether it will be at Rome, Amiens, Manotté, or Yorkshire, I cannot tell. The Kenyons will accompany the body, and it will lie in state for a week. I should think it most probable that the funeral will be at Manotté. Mamma is buried there, and I am sure that it would be his wish to lie with her," she added in a tone suited to the occasion.

Mrs. L—— was glad on some pretence to make her escape from the room. She feared lest she should catch Elizabeth's eye, and one of her merry glances would have betrayed the whole. She ran up-stairs, and Elizabeth soon followed her. They locked themselves in Elizabeth's room, and again, though under their breath, indulged in a hearty laugh. The idea of the honors paid to the supposititious body was so exquisitely absurd, that it was too much for their gravity.

As the day wore on, and two other post deliveries passed without a letter, Marie expressed a rising hope that her uncle might be a shade better. Her poor mamma had rallied for two months and gone off suddenly at last. Perhaps *he* too might rally. This hope gained strength, and the sisters perceived that their patience must be kept in longer exercise.

Some doubts were *now* for the first time suggested, whether Marie had really come out of the convent at all. Elizabeth was quite sure that she saw her *go in* on the day when she first walked back with her. In order to be more fully satisfied, Mr. L—— and she went to S——. The door of the Catholic chapel was open, and they went in. It all answered to Marie's descriptions. The altar and the altar-piece, the confessionals and the names of the priests. They looked for the side entrance through which she had spoken of making her escape. There it was, the lobby and the little court leading to the convent at the back; and they came away fully satisfied that she had indeed been there.

After Marie had withdrawn for the night, Mrs. L—— remained to say a few words to Mr. L—— respecting the letter to Lady ——. It must be confessed that she had some few misgivings about having made so important a movement without his sanction, and she did not go directly to the point.

"Are you going out to-morrow morning, dear?" she asked.

"Why?"

"Because I want you to open the door for the postman. You can keep the key of the house-door a little longer in your pocket."

"What for?" said he, rousing up.

"Because I expect a letter which I do not wish Marie to see."

"From whom?"

"From Lady ——;" and she told him what she had done.

If woman is unequal to the lengthened process of reasoning by which profound and sagacious man arrives at his conclusions, she certainly often comes as by intuition much more speedily at the same result. In this case Mrs. L—— was quite sure that her husband must eventually see the necessity for writing to Lady ——, though it might have been a week or more before he had so decided. She could not expect him to express *approval* of the course she had adopted, lest it should become a precedent. What thoughts were passing in his mind did not appear, but she conjectured that he was not sorry. At any rate he did not reprove her.

"How will you manage it;" she said, "will you keep the key of the house-door in your pocket in the morning, instead of putting it back in the door when you come down?"

"Leave it to me, I will manage it better than that."

Mr. L—— was down before Marie was in the morning. He drew the top-bolt of the house-door, and removed the chair which stood in the hall. They breakfasted. The postman knocked, and Marie rushed out. She could not reach the bolt, and while she ran to get a chair, Mr. L—— opened the door, and took the letters in, but there was not one from Lady ——.

On the previous day, Mr. S—— had placed in Mr. L——'s hands, a correspondence between Marie and Messrs. Cameron and Viall, 50, Oxford-street, of whom it appeared that she had obtained a velvet mantle, and some other articles. Her notes to Mr. Viall were full of the most atrocious falsehoods; but as they are not characterized by any particular interest or ability, they are omitted.

CHAPTER XXVI.

THE UNCLE DISAPPEARS.

It was Saturday morning, June 8th, just a week from the discovery of Marie's treachery, and though every day brought additional evidence of her falsehood, the *proof* of the non-existence of her uncle was still wanting. This, Lady ————'s answer could alone supply ; and as the postmark would betray the correspondence to Marie, the anxiety of the family lest it should fall into her hands was extreme. They could not adopt the same precautions two mornings in succession. This morning, for the first time, they breakfasted without a fire, and the servant, from the force of habit, had brought up the kettle and placed it on the cold hob. Marie, as usual, established herself between Mrs. L—— and the fireplace, in full view of the window. "Marie," said Mrs. L——, "I should be obliged to you if you would sit on the other side. In the cold weather I was glad for you to have the warmest seat, but now the fires are done with you will be more out of the draught on the other side. It is rather inconvenient for you to sit here, as I have to go round you to get at the kettle."

Marie dared not raise an objection. Looking extremely disconcerted, she took her seat on the other side of the table where she could not see the postman's approach. Mrs. L—— saw him coming, and went out before Marie was aware, but the much desired letter was not in his budget.

Marie expressed her full persuasion that she should receive some intelligence from the Kenyons that day. She watched eagerly at the window for the eleven o'clock post. The sisters conjectured that she was anxious to intercept any unwelcome communications from Mr. Viall, or returned letters from the continent. Some conversation arose as to the medium through which Mrs. Kenyon transmitted her letters, as they bore the English postmark. Marie always said that her uncle's letters were for greater security enclosed with his church despatches, and posted in London. Mrs. L—— expressed some surprise that Mrs. Kenyon's letters should come in the same way; as church despatches could not be going so often, especially while the uncle was so ill. Marie replied that the Kenyon letters were sent under cover to Mrs. Frederick ——, a relative of the family. Mrs. L—— expressed surprise that she should write on such thick paper. "Oh!" said Marie, "*they* would never think about postage."

As she stood at the window watching for the postman, a lady unknown came to the door. Marie thought it must be Mrs. Frederick ——, and was in a state of appropriate excitement; but the lady was a stranger who had mistaken the house.

Marie went to her room, and was writing letters till dinner. She intimated to Elizabeth that she intended to disclose the long talked-of secret to Mrs. L—— by letter, as she found it impossible to speak. She was at her post of observation for the three o'clock delivery, but received no letters.

Cheered by Mrs. Kenyon's silence, Marie became conversational at tea time. Turning to Elizabeth she asked, " Did you ever read a book called 'Elizabeth ; or the Exiles of Siberia ?' "

" Yes," said Elizabeth, laughing, " before I was born."

"The Archbishop of Paris gave it to me," continued Marie, " when I was a child. Mamma did not approve of it. She and my uncle had a dispute about it I remember, and they told me to go out of the room. I believe mamma did not like it, because there was something of love in it."

After waiting the arrival of the six o'clock postman, Marie went out for a walk. She came in about eight o'clock, and ran up to Mrs. L—— in high spirits. "My uncle is better. I have had a letter from Mrs. K——. I met the postman in B———— Terrace. She says that Captain Kenyon is quite worn out. He sat up with my uncle six nights. The General has been to see him, and he sat up with him one night. I am not to write to him for some days. The T——'s are to go and nurse him at Manotté. I cannot show you the letter yet, for Mrs. Kenyon has made an offensive remark, which has offended me very much. I shall have another letter on Monday, and then, perhaps, I shall be at liberty to show it to you." Mrs. L—— was putting away some things in her drawers, and did not trouble herself to bestow much attention upon Marie's communication. They all met at supper, and Marie repeated the contents of her letter to Mr. L——. He advised her to go to some church near home in the morning; and Marie retired to rest.

When she had been heard to shut her door, Mr. L—— turned to the sisters. " Would you believe it ?" he said, " she has not had a letter at all. I met the postman myself, and he said, ' That young lady, sir, came up to me just now, and asked me if there were any letters. I told her there were none, and if there *had* been any, I should not have given them to her after what happened last week.'"

On Sunday morning, Marie appeared absent and uneasy at breakfast.

" How silent you are, Marie !" said Mrs. L——, " any one would have expected you to be quite in good spirits at your uncle's recovery."

" I was thinking of Mrs. K——'s remarks," said Marie, " I feel very much annoyed at them. I think it most unwarrantable," added she in an indignant tone.

Mrs. L—— signified her intention of staying at home. Elizabeth went with her brother, and returned to relieve guard in the evening. Marie wanted to hear some new preacher, and mentioned a variety: Mr. Noel, Mr. Nolan, and Dr. Cumming,

—the Catholic Chapel in St. John's Wood, or Mr. Fisk. On consideration, some difficulty occurred in the way of each; and mentioning the old sensation of tightness on her chest, she determined on staying at home. She urged Elizabeth to go to the Lock; but Elizabeth pleaded fatigue from her long walk through the Park, and said she should stay at home with her. They sat reading some time, and then Marie went to her own room. About eight o'clock, Elizabeth heard Marie tapping, and went in. "I have been trying so long to make you hear," she said faintly. She had had one of her old attacks, and a quantity of blood was in the basin. Elizabeth used Eau de Cologne and vinegar, and Marie was soon herself again. She said it had relieved her. She came down to supper on Mr. and Mrs. L——'s return, and ate heartily of cold meat. They were glad when she was satisfied, and withdrew.

On Monday morning Marie hurried over her breakfast; and rising from table, stood and watched for the post. Mr. L—— sat on one side of the table, and Elizabeth on the other, in such a way that she could not pass without violence; and Mrs. L—— being near the door, went out to take in the letters. There was no letter from Lady ——, but there was another from Mrs. Kenyon. Marie read it, and said it was good news. Her pocket was always full of letters. She pulled some out, mixed them together, and then handed over one which she said had arrived on Saturday night; but which was, in fact, the one just received. As she had herself given the substance (see page 286,) its insertion is unnecessary. Marie went to her room to write a reply to this letter; and having finished, brought it to Mrs. L—— to read.

It was a most convenient circumstance for Mrs. L—— that Marie imagined her to be offended by her continued "reserve," that is, by her postponement of the explanation about the burned notes. It furnished an excuse for the absence of former cordiality. Thoroughly sickened of Marie's hypocritical letters, she declined reading the one now offered her. Marie reddened violently, and expressed disappointment and vexation. "I do not like half-confidences, Marie," said Mrs. L——. "When you have told me *all*, I will read anything you wish me to read." The letter was left lying about for some days; but was not read by those for whose eyes alone it was written, till some time afterwards. It is very lengthy, and not of sufficient interest to merit insertion.

The postman came at three o'clock on this day (Monday), and wonderful to say, Marie was up stairs at the time. Elizabeth opened the door, and glad she was that it had so happened. The long looked-for letter had come at last. Lady —— wrote from Paris, and her absence from home had caused the delay.

"Hotel ——, Place Vendôme,
"Paris, June 8th, 1850.

"Madam,

"Your letter, and one enclosed to the Reverend H. C. Clifford, was forwarded to me to-day, with some postage stamps, wishing me to send it to Mr. Clifford, which I should have great pleasure in doing, but I am not aware what Mr. Clifford it can be, or to whom you allude. I only know —— —— and —— —— of ——.

"I should be very happy to forward this letter, if I knew where; and I will keep it, with the stamps, until I hear from you what you wish to have done with it; and remain, madam,

"Your obedient servant,

"—— —— ——."

This letter was decisive. Mr. L—— doubted no more. "You had better write again," he said, "and give Lady —— fuller particulars of Marie's fictitious pedigree." Mrs. L—— did so.

In comfortable ignorance of a correspondence so fatal to all her plans, Marie continued her indefatigable efforts to keep up the deception. While Mrs. L—— was writing to Lady ————, she was writing to Mrs. L——, and produced the following epistle :—

"5, C—— Terrace,
"Monday, June 10th.

"My dearest Mrs. L——,

"I had written a long letter to you on Saturday last; but owing to Mrs. Kenyon's recent letters, I shall defer the subject of it, feeling assured my uncle will be able before long to see you himself, so I much prefer waiting till his visit, as I shall not feel timid or afraid of saying what I wish when with him, having the assurance that his confidence in me remains unshaken; and I rejoice to say that I feel within myself the consciousness of not being quite so undeserving of yours, as you appear to think me. Nothing less than this, and my love and affection for you, would have enabled me to bear the coldness at different times of the past five months. Very different reasons and motives have influenced my silence than those of impenitence or distrust; and my uncle's extreme anxiety that I should overcome the timidity that has hitherto prevented me from speaking, arises from his consideration for my happiness; and also the confidence he has in the candor and truth of my explanation, leads him to suppose you would have the same. He felt desirous after all I had said to him, that I should mention it before his visit, so that he might know how it was received; for he justly remarked that if you loved me, which he was sure you did, you could not, or would not doubt my sincerity. I, however, feel that I have lost your confidence, so I cannot hope to regain it by any explanation or vindication of my conduct. I would sacrifice anything again to occupy the same place in your affections I once did. If I act sometimes

13

strangely and closely, it is this feeling that influences me; and I am thrown so much upon my own thoughts, that this alone makes me restless and unhappy. I have not now the coldness of one alone to bear, but your sister is now cold and shy towards me. I feel it now the more, because it was so different when my uncle was expected. The grief and disappointment has been my *own*, for I had been anticipating his visit with extreme delight, thinking it would render me happy with you, for I shall never be so while you think of me as you do.

"I much wish that either you or Mr. L—— would write in a few days to my uncle, should he continue to improve, and give him your statement and opinion. He will then write in reply, and it will be settled in some way. You will find that he will not screen me or spare me, where I am deserving of blame; for no one is more severe with me than himself when reproof is needed.

"I will now take the opportunity of mentioning one little matter which I did not intend to name till my uncle's visit. In one of his late letters he remitted me a sum of money for pocket money; since which I have sent the £5 to the Bible Society.

"I am extremely sorry you should have thought I do not take your advice so readily as I once did. I have mistaken you, and thought you did not wish me to consult you. I have felt this much myself, so we have misunderstood each other.

"May I ask or beg that all unpleasant feeling or embarrassment may cease between us? It shuts up all the avenues of confidential friendship. Let the matter be at once submitted to my uncle, and do not longer let me be an object of suspicion or conjecture. If you or Mr. L—— write to him, he will soon decide it. The reason he did not do so when he last wrote, he was fearful of violating my confidence in him. He would be glad, I am sure, if you were to do so, for he feels the reserve and unhappiness that exists between us most painfully. He knows from experience what it cost me when a similar timidity and reserve existed between him and me some years ago, but I overcame it ; and since then I have now the happiness of thinking that I have never concealed a fault intentionally from him, though I have ever dreaded his displeasure.

"I have never yet ventured to ask you if it is your wish that I should remain with you. A separation from you would be one of the greatest trials I could endure. I should still be acting very ungratefully to you, were I to stay longer than would tend either to your happiness or comfort. I have felt this very painfully of late, particularly as my affairs have been so long delayed. I feel as yet a dependent upon your hospitality, upon which I have no claim, though I know it will not always be so ; though I must ever remain a dependent upon the kindness of others, having no social or near ties to whom I can look for either sympathy or love, with the exception of my uncle ; and I must continue almost an alien from him, for I can never live with him,—and if he recovers I can but seldom see him. I often wish I was the poor dependent of last year, rather than what I am now, for then I possessed both your smile and affection; but now, though the expected heiress of wealth, I am without what I most value—your esteem and confidence. Wealth is poor compensation to me, compared with that. I value only the smile and approbation of God and those I love.

"When all coldness and estrangement is removed I shall bring up the matter myself: but I can never be led into conversation by shyness or reserve.

"I was suggesting to Mr. L—— that it would be well if I was to go from home for a few days.

"I should be glad to have your letter to me when you have done with it ; for my uncle desired me to keep it till he came.

"In conclusion, may I beg that as far as I am concerned the affair be buried in oblivion, and all explanations rest with my uncle, for he is the most proper person to plead my cause. He

is in possession of everything that has transpired since coming
to you, and also of the correspondence that has passed between
us ; for in writing to him I felt determined to withhold nothing
from him.   I confessed in what I was wrong, and stated everything as it then stood, and left him to draw his own conclusions.   With warm love and gratitude,

> " I am, ever
>
> " Your affectionate and attached
>
> " MARIE.

" P.S.—I hope this letter will not agitate you ; but I
thought it better to write and relieve your suspense, and also
inform you of my wishes, for I could not express them
verbally."

Mrs. L—— was inexpressibly shocked at the lie about the
Bible Society. , Marie did not pretend to have refunded the
money collected for the church.   *That* could have been refuted,
but it was very easy to point to any anonymous £5 in the
Bible Society list, and say, " That is mine."   Worse than the lie
of Ananias and Sapphira, Mrs. L—— shuddered at the provo-
cation she was offering to the truth and justice of offended
heaven.   She returned no reply to Marie's letter that day, and
indeed scarcely took the trouble to speak to her at all.

CHAPTER XXVII.

PROGRESS OF DISCOVERY.

MR. L—— was engaged from home the whole of Tuesday,
and Marie favored the sisters with much of her company.   She
used her utmost endeavors to persuade them to walk out.   She
was very obliging, and begged to be allowed to do some work

for Lilly and baby. She kept a sharp lookout for the post, and after post time had past went to her room to write.

Relieved from her presence, and with two floors between, the sisters indulged in conversation.

"I hope," said Elizabeth, "that she will not be ill just now. What should we do if she were laid up?"

"Do not fear," replied Mrs. L——, "it would not suit her plans to keep the house just now."

"You do not mean," said Elizabeth, "that her illness is all make believe."

"I cannot help thinking so, now that everything else turns out to be fictitious. Remember she has always been taken ill when alone, and always at night."

"Very true," added Elizabeth, "and last night when I did not pity her she soon got well. She came down to supper half an hour afterwards."

"And she ate a hearty supper of cold meat, and went out in the rain the next morning. Do you think any one who had really ruptured a blood-vessel on the lungs would eat a hearty supper directly afterwards?" suggested Mrs. L——.

"But how *can* she manage it?" asked Elizabeth. "Have we not really seen blood come from her mouth?"

"I cannot tell how," said Mrs. L——. "Perhaps she has some way of putting blood in her mouth, or perhaps she has some way of bleeding it at the time. We must try and find out."

They could come to no conclusion on the subject that day; but once on the scent, and their perceptions sharpened by recent exercise, they did not despair of getting at the truth.

As dinner was coming up, Marie reappeared. Mrs. L—— took the opportunity while Elizabeth was out of the room, to make short work of Marie's note of yesterday. "Marie," she said, "I do not wish to answer your letter in writing, as your uncle so decidedly objects to it; but it shall be as you say, 'We can let the matter rest till he comes.'"   Marie ran up stairs as soon as dinner was over, and wrote as follows:—

"My very dear Mrs. L——,

"I fear my letter of yesterday has grieved you, though I did not intend that it should.   I wrote under feelings of excitement, so perhaps have expressed myself more warmly than I ought to have done to one so kind as you have been to me.

"I confess my fault in acting so strangely as I have of late by my great reserve.   Whilst in bed last night I reflected on my own disrespectful conduct towards you in treating you with such ingratitude by my moroseness.   I have felt very miserable about it all day, and so think it best to at once acknowledge it.   If you will forgive me I promise that my conduct in future shall be very different.   I feel determined to overcome it, for it has caused me so much misery.   I feel the double pang of conscience, for I am not only behaving unkindly towards you, but disobeying a dear relative in being so reserved with you.   But I have fancied you were very cold with me and did not feel interested in my different plans and pursuits, so have avoided mentioning them.

"Do please relieve me from my present anxious state in assuring me of your forgiveness, for I do feel so distressed with the humbling sense of my conduct and ingratitude towards you.

"I have acted very wrong during the past week for which I am truly sorry ; such an occurrence shall not again take place so far as I am concerned. Do forgive me, and let me feel that I am again reconciled to you, for I do feel very unhappy.

"From your distressed

"MARIE.

"P.S.—I came in to speak to you this afternoon, but my

feelings would not permit me to do it without agitating both of us."

As Marie seemed so anxious to get a note, Mrs. L—— wrote in reply—

"Dear Marie,

"I am not offended with you. You have done nothing to offend me. To say that your notes are satisfactory would not be the truth, for they contain neither confession nor explanation, and of course leave the matter just where it was. One inference only can be drawn from your silence, namely, that the explanation you have given to your uncle is one which you know I shall not believe; and I have but one request to make—that you will not again refer to the subject till you are resolved to speak the truth, the *whole* truth, and *nothing but* the truth. That you may be delivered from the snares of the evil one is the wish of her who has ever desired to be

"Your sincere and faithful friend,

"J. L——."

Elizabeth was out at tea-time, and Marie referred to Mrs. L——'s note.

"I am sorry, Mrs. L——," she said, with a slight toss of the head, "that you should think me capable of telling my uncle what I knew you would not believe."

"Then why all this mystery, Marie? If all is fair and straightforward, why is there so much difficulty about an explanation?"

Marie was silent. They took their tea without another word; and Marie, glad to escape, went up, and put on her things to go out. She returned at half-past eight, and said, "Good night."

Mr. L—— came home. He was glad to find that Marie had absented herself.

"Mr. K—— met me at the railway station," he said, "to tell me that the veritable Captain Kenyon is discovered. Miss K—— has found him out."

"Indeed! Well done, Miss K——; and pray who is he?"

"A writing-master in —— Street. Mr. K—— told his wife and daughter of Marie's affair. When he mentioned the application from the post-office, Miss K—— immediately said that she thought she could throw some light on that subject. When she and Marie were out collecting, Marie stopped at the stationer's shop in —— Street, and telling Miss K—— to go on to a friend's, said she would rejoin her there. Instead of doing as Marie had directed, Miss K—— turned back and followed her. The side door was open, and Marie was ascending the staircase. Miss K—— waited some time, and then saw Marie coming down with a letter in her hand. Marie joined her at the door of the shop. They made one or two calls, and Marie posted the letter in Vigo Street. Mr. K—— went with his daughter to take a review of the shop, and found that the name on the side door was ——, writing-master. So we shall pay a visit to the writing-master in due time, and learn particulars."

It was half-past eleven, and they went up to rest. Mrs. L—— looked in at Marie's door. She was still up, sitting at her desk, with her writing apparatus before her. She was talking to Eliza, the cook, in a piteous tone, and groaning at intervals. Mrs. L—— was afraid of her practising on the servants. "Marie, your uncle does not like you to talk to the servants;" and she called Eliza out. "It is quite time for you to go up stairs, Eliza," she said." "What does Miss G. want you for?"

"Nothing, ma'am; but," added she, in a voice of sympathy, "Miss G. says that she was taken ill by the canal side to-night, and brought up a great deal of blood."

Mrs. L—— did not express much concern; and the girl seemed to think her mistress had become strangely unfeeling.

On Wednesday morning, at breakfast, Marie said she had been thinking whether she could not send some one to Manotté for her boxes.

"Surely you would not entrust any poor man with the care of such valuable articles?" said the others.

"No; I meant some confidential person, such as Mr. King, for instance."

"He would not understand the language, or find his way about the continent," they replied; and she ceased to urge her proposition.

After breakfast Marie set off to meet Miss K——. Elizabeth, as usual, embraced the opportunity to search her room. She ran down stairs to her sister. "I have made one discovery," she said : "a box of dead leeches."

"She can have no honest use for them," observed Mrs. L——. "It is long since any were ordered for her, and those were always put in a jar of water in the back kitchen. I will go to the chemist's, and find out when she had leeches."

Mrs. L—— went, and bought some trifle. "When did Miss G—— have leeches here?" she inquired.

"She came for some one day last week."

"What day?"

"Oh! I recollect," replied Mr. N——; "it was Saturday evening."

"Saturday evening! and it was Sunday evening that she threw up blood. Then she puts leeches in her mouth," was the instant conclusion of both the sisters.

"But how can she get enough?" asked one.

"Probably she mixes it with water; and that would make it look like blood from the lungs. Dr. —— said that it was very thin blood. Then, I suppose, she calls us in; and the

13*

little which we see coming from her mouth, is from the leech-bites," said the other.

" How can she lower her pulse to deceive the doctors ?" was the next question, and not quite so easy a one to answer.

" You know she is very familiar with the prescriptions which have been ordered to check the rapidity of the circulation. She has often talked about ' Digitalis,' and other medicines, as very lowering. She may take a large dose when she knows the doctor is coming," was the most probable conjecture.

A subsequent examination of the chemist's book showed that Marie had several times had leeches on the sly, and that the dates corresponded with her illnesses.

Marie was out all day collecting with Miss K——. To avoid the loss of the money Mr. K—— had arranged that instead of paying their subscriptions at once, the young contributors should meet on an appointed day and pay it all in together. Marie had therefore received a few shillings only. For these she had made Miss K—— receipt the book, and she had kept the money. All unknown to Marie, Miss K—— was going about with her in the capacity of jailer. A gentle, timid, lady-like little thing of seventeen, it was amusing with how much self-possession and adroitness, she came out in her new character.

During Marie's absence a second letter was received from Lady ———.

" Hotel ——, Place Vendôme,
" Paris, June 11th.

" Madam,

          " I have this moment received your letter, and fearing you may be further imposed upon by the person whom you say is now under your roof, I am anxious to let you know that not one word of what she has said respecting our family is correct, and I am quite convinced there is no such person as the Rev. H. C. Clifford. The statement respecting Mrs. Frederick —— is also incorrect, but any information you may wish to have respecting her, you will learn from ——— now residing at ———. The T——'s are also in town, who will, I have no doubt, be able to contradict the statement respecting them.

"I have enclosed the letter and postage stamps, and remain, madam,

"Your obedient servant,

"——— ——— ———."

Marie returned home to tea. At six a Captain Kenyon letter, addressed to Mr. L———, arrived. Elizabeth turned it over, and could not suppress the inclination to have a little innocent amusement at Marie's expense.

"What a vulgar seal!" she said. "It looks like a bread seal. Is this the Kenyon crest?"

Marie examined it in her turn, seemed much annoyed, but said nothing.

Elizabeth took it again, and said, "It is not at all like a gentleman's hand. I am sure I feel no anxiety to see this Captain Kenyon."

Mr. L——— came in, and the letter was read.

"MARSEILLES, June 11th, 1850.

"Sir,

"I should have written to you yesterday, but was prevented by indisposition.

"I have been daily expecting a reply to my first letter, for we have felt very anxious to know how Marie bore the disappointment, but I presume more important duties came in the way.

"You will be happy to hear that Mr. Clifford is rapidly improving, though he is still very weak and feeble. The very excruciating pain he has endured seems to have quite prostrated his energy and strength, and I fear it will be some time before he recovers himself.

" We all gave him up last week, for no one thought it possible he could survive such a relapse.

"I had proposed leaving here this week in order to reach home by the 15th, that being my rent day ; but Mrs. Kenyon is not willing to leave Mr. C. until he is so far convalescent as to be removed to Manotté. Owing to the excited state of France I do not deem it prudent to return home without her. So I shall probably remain with Mr. C. till he visits England. He has resigned his office in the church for a year, which period he intends spending chiefly in Yorkshire.

" As he is now so far recovered as to be able I trust in a few weeks to see you himself, I have from prudential as well as religious motives, declined settling any business in reference to Marie. Nothing but his death would have quieted my religious scruples in transactions of this nature.

"You are no doubt aware that Mr. C.'s love and affection for his niece had induced him to act contrary to religious principles and obedience. To avoid this I have frequently offered to take Marie till she comes into the possession of her own property, which cannot now be long, but he firmly opposes it.

Mr. C. requests that you will send him Marie's account. If she goes to the sea-side, which he leaves entirely to your discretion, he will most likely join her for a few weeks, so that it will enable him to spend more time with you and Marie, and it will also benefit his own health. He wishes to know where and when you are going.

" Marie must spend a few days in Staffordshire soon. She may now write to her uncle. Mrs. K. will write to her again in a day or two.

" With kind remembrance to Marie and respectful compliments to yourself,

" I remain,

" Yours truly,

" CHARLES W. KENYON."

"Why, Marie, this letter is dated June 11th," said Mrs. L——, "and this is only the 12th. It never can have come from Marseilles in a day."

Mr. L—— thought this was coming rather too close to the point, and turned it off. Marie had had as much as she could bear, and possessing herself of the unfortunate letter she left the room.

"We will go to I—— to-morrow," said Mr. L—— to his wife, "and Elizabeth can keep guard at home."

<hr>

CHAPTER XXVIII.

CONVENT DISCLOSURES.

It remained to be ascertained how much there was of truth in Marie's convent story, and Mr. and Mrs. L—— had purposed putting it to the proof by a journey to I——. Mr. L—— had been completely upset by the disclosures of the past ten days, and on Thursday morning he was scarcely able to rise. To avoid further delay he thought it better for Mrs. L—— to go without him, and proposed that in her way she should call on Mr. K—— and request him to accompany her as a witness.

As Mrs. L—— was going out she encountered Marie at the dining-room door. "O! Mrs. L——," she said, "where are you going? How nicely you are dressed!"

"I am going out for the day. I have several calls to make. Perhaps I may see ——. Have you any message?"

"Yes; tell him I have a very bad headache. It is just like what I had before the brain fever in Liverpool," she said, looking up with half-closed eyes.

"Very well; I will tell him."

Mrs. L—— passed out, and Elizabeth followed her with a parcel of open newspapers in her hand. In these she had concealed the album which contained the sketch of Marie's face. She slipped it under Mrs. L——'s mantle, and escaped Marie's observation.

Mrs. L—— called on Mr. K——, who readily consented to accompany her. They crossed Hungerford Bridge, and took the train to I————. They walked through the quiet village to the still more quiet convent, with its high brick walls, and large sheltering trees. They rang at the little gate, and a thin, sedate-looking person in black, slid back the tiny shutter, and peeped at them. They asked for Madame ———— (Reverend Mother, or Mother Julie, as Marie designated her alternately), and the lay sister conducted them to the house. An old piano was going in the hall, and several young people were round it. They were shown into the reception room, of which Marie had talked so much, and which she said that it had been her office to keep in order. It was a respectable old-fashioned room, but without one sign of the grandeur of which Marie had so frequently boasted.

They waited a short time, and a lady appeared. She was dressed in a black cap, with a quilling of crape round the face, a black gown, and a little black shawl, or rather handkerchief, crossed in front and pinned. Mrs. L—— rose, and asked if it was Madame————.

S.—" No ; Madame ———— is not here at present. Perhaps you can tell me what you wish."

Mrs. L.—" We called to make some inquiries about a young person who was educated here. She was afterwards a governess in the family of some friends of ours, and left on account of ill health. It is necessary that she should find another home ; and as our friends were not fully satisfied, we thought that, perhaps, you would favor us with a little information respecting her."

S.—" What is her name ?"

Mrs. L.—" M—— L—— G——."

S.—" I do not know that name."

Mrs. L.—" Perhaps she was here before you ?"

S.—" Oh, no ! I have been Superioress of this convent for a number of years. I am quite sure that we have had no one here of that name."

Mrs. L.—" She states that she was twice here : on one occasion, for a period of two years ; and that she has been seventeen years in convents of your order. She says that she used to write letters for Madame D'H——" (Very Reverend Mother).

S.—" That cannot be, for Madame D'H—— never has any one but a religious person to write for her. She cannot speak English, and she never comes to England."

Mrs. L.—" It is just possible that this young person may have changed her name. Perhaps you may recognize the handwriting," producing a specimen.

S.—" This is the handwriting taught in our schools, certainly."

Mrs. L.—" She says that Madame de la R——,* who died last June, and who joined your community when she became a widow, was her aunt."

S.—" Madame de la R—— was never married, and she is still living."

Mrs. L.—" Perhaps you would know this young person's portrait. I have brought it with me."

S.—" No ; I do not know this face. I am sure she was never here."

After a pause the Superioress added, " Perhaps you will allow me to take it out of the room for a few minutes, to see if any one else can recognize it."

---

* This was the aunt mentioned in the uncle's first letter, the announcement of whose death occasioned so much emotion. Marie went into mourning for her.

The lady left the room,—the piano ceased, the voices in the hall dropped, and a quiet debate appeared to be going on. In a few minutes she reappeared.

"No, we do not know the person; but we think that Madame —— (Reverend Mother), who is now at S——, would be able to tell you. She may have been brought up there."

Mrs. L.—"I did not know that there was any school at S—— except the poor school."

S.—"Oh, yes! there is a very large school for an inferior class of pupils to those who are brought up here. Madame —— will be here to-morrow, or you could see her at S—— this evening, if more convenient."

They thanked her, and returned to town by the next train. They went back to Mr. K——'s, and thence hastened to S——.

It was nearly eight o'clock when they entered the outer gate in the street, by the side of the Catholic chapel; and passing through the little court, or garden, to another entrance, they rang the bell. A novice in her white cap drew back the little sliding panel, and inquired their business.

"We wish to see Madame ——. We will not detain her many minutes. We have been to I——, expecting to find her there, or we would not have come at so late an hour."

The novice withdrew, and presently another came, unlocked the door, and showed them into a little room close to the gate. The floor was covered with oil-cloth, and there were a few wooden chairs.

Presently a third person appeared, and led them into another little room adjoining the first. It was carpeted, and a little better furnished than the other. It looked out into the large court-yard, where several nuns with measured steps were passing to and fro. A large range of building surrounded this court; but they had scarcely observed thus much when another messenger came up to ask the name of each. The names were given and she withdrew.

Finally, Madame ——, the Reverend Mother, appeared. Mrs. L—— again stated the case as at I——, and asked if Madame —— could oblige her with any particulars respecting Marie.

"O yes! She was with us for a month about a year and a half ago."

"Only a month! She says that she was seventeen years in convents of your Order, and that she had been for the two last years a postulant."

"She was not with us longer than a month or five weeks. She was introduced to me by the Reverend ——, a priest in Liverpool, as a young person who had become a Catholic, and was very much persecuted by her Protestant friends. She was obliged to leave home and wanted an asylum, and he said that it would be kind if I would take her."

"She says that she was six weeks in your Liverpool convent, and two years at I——."

"She never set foot in our Liverpool convent. I brought her to town with me the same night, and we made her up a bed in the little parlor, because the house was full. She *wanted* to go to I——, and she was there for one day, but I sent her back again, for we have none but young ladies there, and we only employ persons of confidence."

"She says that she has been in convents of your Order at Amiens, Manotté, Paris, Chateâuroux, Carrouge, Nice, and Limerick."

"It is very true that we have convents at all those places, but she has never been in them."

"I should like to be quite sure that it is the same. Do you know this portrait?"

"O yes! That is she certainly."

"Will you kindly tell me why she left you?"

"Yes. After she had been with us a little while she became restless, and said that her temporal affairs required her return to her friends. She showed me some sort of deed and a lawyer's letter, and said that she should lose her property if she did not go."

"And how did she go?"

"She said that a friend of her family lived in ———— Street, and that if she went to her, she knew that she could soon get back to her relations in the north. I sent, but probably the lady had moved, for no such person could be found. She went out another day, and came back saying, that she had found her friend, and that she would come for her at half-past six o'clock. I offered to send a responsible person to ascertain that it was all right; but she said there was no occasion, as she was quite satisfied. A lady came in a cab that night, and she went. As her health was delicate, and she did not feel well enough to do anything, we were not on the whole sorry that she decided on leaving."

Mrs. L——— thanked Madame ————, and rose to leave. The lady requested that her *name* might not be brought forward, and Mrs. L——— promised that it should not. "She was a very well-conducted young person while with us," added Madame ————, "I have nothing to say against her."

Madame ———— moved with them to the gate. The key had to be sent for. The gate was unlocked, and they parted.

On Mrs. L———'s return to C——— Terrace, she found that Marie had had another attack of illness. Elizabeth gave her an account of the whole transaction, which shall be inserted in her own words.

"During the afternoon Marie complained much of headache, and seemed very depressed, restless, and anxious. She wandered about the house, looking out of the window and settling to nothing. Tea came in. It was a very quiet solemn meal, and few words were spoken on either side. While reading to Lilly, Marie darted out of the room and hurried up stairs. I remained and enjoyed a quiet half-hour by myself. Wanting something at the top of the house I ran up stairs, and hearing a muffled groaning as I passed Marie's room, I peeped in. Marie was lying on her bed, and Sarah standing by her side looking the picture of commiseration, and bathing her face with cold water. The basin stood in the chair full of blood. 'Oh! Miss ———, Miss G—— has been so ill—thrown up all this blood.' Looking at it in anything but a sympathetic frame, I said, 'Yes, it is more than usual;' and well I might say so, for to my apprehension it would have needed pretty well all the blood she possessed to fill that basin. Thinking it a pity that Sarah's feelings should be worked upon, I told her to leave, and that I would attend to Miss G——. Sarah looked very much as if she thought that I had left my compassion down stairs, and reluctantly obeyed. The vinegar bottle was on the mantel-piece. I poured some into a tumbler, glad to give her what I knew would be anything but pleasant.* She drank this, but still continued very faint and scarcely conscious.

"I was determined to seize the opportunity, and if possible to find the leeches which had caused this dreadful rupture. I opened a drawer, and said, half aloud, 'Oh, how very untidy! I shall set these in order for you, Marie :' and drawing a chair to me, most energetically set to work. A degree of consciousness seemed to return, and in a very feeble voice she said, 'No, you need not do that. I will as soon as I can. Leave it for me.' Seeing I was resolved, she yielded, and continued her subdued moaning. The drawers being finished, but no discovery made, I turned with increased zeal to confer a like benefit on the desk. The water, Eau de Cologne, and vinegar had failed to revive her; but what they could not do, this sudden movement on my part at once effected. Rousing herself in a moment, and raising her head from her pillow, she leaned forward and said, 'Don't, pray don't take all that trouble. I will do that myself.' Not appearing to notice her, I set to and

* Acids were ordered to stop the bleeding. Marie generally had lemons, of which she was rather fond.

very soon made a clearance. I arranged every corner most
carefully, routed out everything, and satisfied myself that what
I was in search of had yet to be turned up from some other
hiding-place. So large a loss of blood had of course left her
very weak. Her head was very bad, and as ' brain fever was
coming on,' I found it very easy to persuade her to undress.
To add to her comfort I shook her pillow and put the clothes
smooth, taking care to feel in every direction for what I longed
to find, but all to no purpose. Then I folded up her clothes
with double care, and felt in the pockets, but was again disappointed. All my toil had been for nothing. I lighted her
lamp and bade her good night."

Not long after, Mrs. L—— returned and went up. Marie's
door was open, and Eliza, the cook, was in attendance, changing
the wet cloths which Marie had directed to be placed on her
forehead. The servant saw her mistress and came out. "Miss
G—— is afraid she is going to have brain fever, ma'am. Her
head is so bad."

Mrs. L—— went in with the candle in her hand. "So,
Marie, you have been ill again, I hear."

"I can't bear the light," said Marie in a faint voice, and
pulled the curtains round her.

Mrs. L—— withdrew ; and presently Marie sent to inquire
if she had brought her a prescription.

"No; she had not done so."

Then came a message requesting that Eliza might sleep with
her. This was permitted, and a charge given to Eliza not to
let Miss G—— talk, as it would be so bad for her head. Last
of all came Sarah, and with much compassion in her countenance, as if wishing to make one more effort in Marie's behalf, said, " Miss G—— says she has thrown up some of her
lungs to-night, ma'am."

The sisters looked at one another, and broke out into a
hearty laugh, and Sarah, surprised and puzzled, said no more.

CHAPTER XXIX.

CROSS PURPOSES.

THE unprecedented loss of blood and anticipated brain fever of Thursday evening having failed to call forth any demonstrations of sympathy from her former friends, Marie came down the next morning much as usual. She went out and paid Mrs. P—— a visit, and on returning wrote the following note :—

"My dear Mrs. L——,

"If you will allow me to go from home for a few days, it is my determination now to confess and explain all the circumstances that cause us both so much misery. I cannot endure any longer your cold and embarrassed look. *It is torture of the most agonizing kind to me.* I prefer being away when I do it. I think I can feel more freedom than if I had to meet you directly after. I may then hope the subject will never again be brought up, but be buried in oblivion.

"Mrs. Y—— has invited me several times. I can write and offer now to accept it. Miss K—— is going from home.

"I have written to my uncle, telling him of the present state of things, so I hope you will soon have a reply from him.

"I am, with love, your distressed

"MARIE."

"Mr. and Mrs. L—— fancied that Marie might intend to decamp, so they agreed to prevent such a movement. She was then working in the dining-room. Mrs. L—— went to her. "Marie, I think it would be a very good plan for you to go to Mrs. Y——'s, but I do not think you ought to go without ascertaining whether it is convenient. Suppose you write by the half-past one post, and you will get an answer either this evening or to-morrow morning."

Marie seemed uneasy. This evidently did not meet her views, though what they were is unknown. She could not, however, raise any plausible objection, and after a little hesitation she rose, and wrote the note to Mrs. Y—— as requested.

Mrs. Y—— was a friend in the congregation who had been very kind to Marie. It happened that her spare room was occupied, and that she could only invite Marie for a day. This did not suit the inclination of the latter, and she declined.

On Friday afternoon, Marie wrote some lines in commemoration of little Arnold's birthday, and sent them to Mrs. L——. Elizabeth was present when she composed them, and saw her scribble the rough copy, altering and amending, and asking Elizabeth to help her about a short line or a bad rhyme. They were undoubtedly her own, and are here inserted to show the entire self-control with which she could govern and direct her thoughts in the midst of the plots and anxieties of the period.

TO S. ARNOLD L——,

ON THE FIRST ANNIVERSARY OF HIS BIRTH, JUNE 14th, 1850.

> Smiling boy of twelve months old,
> Now my gladsome eyes behold
> Thy birthday! and with rapture I
> Wish thee, dearest, every joy.
> Thou art but an infant now—
> Joy sits smiling on thy brow;
> Yet we sometimes tears may trace,
> Rolling down thy dimpled face,
> E'en in infancy to show,
> All is not serene below.

No; for infancy has cares,—
Childhood is not free from tears;
Manhood,—trouble still is seen;
Age,—and still unchanged the scene.
Sorrow, grief, distress, and pain,
Mark the fleeting life of man!

This dear infant is the soil
Thou art planted in awhile;
This is the ungenial clime
Thou must dwell in for a time.
Dost thou from the prospect shrink;—
Yet I would not have thee think
All is barren, and no flowers
Grow upon this globe of ours:
No; though happiness is sought
Oft by those who find it not;
Though comparatively few
Gain the prize which all pursue;
Though unruffled streams of bliss
Flow not in a world like this:
Yet there's much of peace and joy
In religion's paths, my boy.

Shrink not, then, in terror back,
Follow in the Saviour's track:
He whom now we dimly see,
Once became a child like thee;
He was nurtured here below,
Suffered agony and woe;
On the cross resigned his breath,
Made a sacrifice in death.
Darling! may thy infant days
Be devoted to His praise;

If maturer youth be thine,
Still pursue the track divine ;
Manhood, if thou'rt spared to see,
Live as for eternity ;
And should age with stealthy pace,
Steal the beauty from thy face,
Placing wrinkles there instead,—
Then, dear, may thy hoary head
Be a crown of glory bright,
While thy spirit, ripe for flight,
Patient waits, till freed from clay
It mounts to realms of endless day,
And there beholds with full delight,
The glories of the Infinite.

M.

Saturday was Mr. L——'s quiet day, and Marie's affairs had to stand over till the next week. Mr. K—— went to Mr. S——, to arrange a meeting at C—— Terrace for their final settlement, on the following Tuesday, and Mr. A'B——, a legal friend, of character and standing, kindly expressed his willingness to be of the party.

Mr. and Mrs. L—— were out in the evening. When they reached home, Marie opened the door, and eagerly informed them that there was a bulletin in the " *Tablet*," of her uncle's recovery, and she showed them the printed scrap which she had cut out, as she said that " M'Shane wanted the paper back for another reader." The notice ran thus :—

" We are happy to state that the Reverend H. C. Clifford, who was attacked with spasms of the heart at Marseilles, and whose alarming illness excited the most serious apprehensions, is now in a fair way of recovery, and is able to proceed to Paris, whence it is anticipated that he will shortly remove to his own chateâu at Amiens."

"Does not that almost stagger you?" said Mr. L—— when she had gone up stairs. The sisters recommended him to go to the "*Tablet*" office, and try to obtain a sight of the hand writing.

On Sunday morning Mrs. L—— took Marie to the service at a neighboring chapel, and in the evening they all went together to their own accustomed place of worship. Mr. L—— no longer opposed Marie's wish to go. He was anxious that she should hear the voice of warning yet once again before she should leave his house, never more to enter it. He had never preached for any *one* individually before; but that night he preached for *her*, and for her alone. He took as his text, 2 Pet. ii. 21: "For it had been better for them not to have known the way of righteousness, than after they have known it, to turn from the holy commandment delivered unto them." He preached with all the pathos and earnestness which the conviction that to her he was making one last appeal, naturally called forth. The congregation insensibly caught his emotion, and many were in tears. Several subsequently made the remark that they felt that he must have some individual case in view, and they asked themselves, "Is it I?" And *one* there was who felt as if the concentrated emotions of many months had been crowded into that hour, and the pent-up feelings of the last distressing fortnight could no longer be restrained. She wept uncontrollably, and could scarcely refrain from sobbing aloud. And Marie sat near her, not unobserved by some. *She* did not weep. She looked uneasily round, and her restless eye wandered over the congregation. Did she wonder why her friend was so moved? or would she remember and interpret the signs of sorrow that *she* had caused, in days yet to come?

Monday, the 17th, was a tolerably quiet day, and the sisters have no clear recollection of the morning's occupations. They remember a little incident which passed at dinner time, which may amuse the reader by the way. Strange were the transi-

14

tions from the pathetic to the ridiculous which that never-to-be-forgotten period presented.

" What a beautiful painting that is, and *so* like," said Marie, looking up at Mr. L——'s portrait, as she sat at the dinner table. " I hope Mr. William Harling will be in town when my uncle comes. I would give anything for such a likeness of *him*."

" Mr. Harling is very clever, dear," said Elizabeth. " I dare say he could do your uncle from description. How should you describe him ?"

For once Marie's ready tongue seemed to be at fault, and the only thing she could get out was, " He is very dark. He has a very black beard."

" And dark eyes ?" asked Mrs. L——.

" Yes, very dark eyes."

" Is that all ?" said Elizabeth. " What is his nose ?"

" I hardly know how to describe his nose. He always wears Roman collars."

" Oh, well ! we will soon make your uncle up, dear," said Elizabeth : " a black beard and Roman collar. Mr. Harling will have no difficulty, I dare say."

Marie turned a scrutinizing glance on Elizabeth, but could read nothing in her countenance ; and they passed to another subject.

In the afternoon Marie went to her room, and wrote a long letter, which she said was for Mrs. L——, and contained the long-talked-of explanation. Elizabeth sat with her and worked—professedly to keep her company, but really to watch her, and prevent her giving them the slip. Marie rose from her desk, and going up to Elizabeth, kissed her, and thanked her much for all her sympathy and kindness. She did not know what she should have done for the last few days, had it not been for her. " I knew it was the last day," said Elizabeth, " so I had been doing it with double zeal. I thought I was very like

Judas in accepting the thanks and kisses, but I could not well refuse. I suppose she saw that I did not respond very warmly, for she soon marched back to her desk and her writing." She talked of going to ———, to see a young convert from Popery; and Elizabeth arranged to go with her, but she afterwards gave it up.

Mr. L—— had been to town. He returned at eight. The house was being painted and pointed on the outside, and the men had .left the scaffolding in such a position as to seem to tempt the entrance of thieves. Mr. L—— called his wife and sister out, and they looked up at the house as if talking of the danger; and there, safely out of Marie's hearing, he communicated the result of that day's inquiries. "I have learned two things," he said. "First I went to the ' *Tablet*' office, and tried to ascertain who had sent the notice. I was disappointed to find that it was published in Dublin, and that the people at the London office could throw no light on the matter. When about to leave, I thought I would ask to have a look at the paper. I found the paragraph, and at its conclusion read this clause—' We think it right to add that this notice has been sent to us anonymously.'* This was why she cut the paragraph out, and returned the paper to M'Shane. Did you ever hear of anything more daring, than a girl of her age sending a fictitious advertisement to a public paper?

"Mr. K—— and I then met by appointment to go to the writing-master. We left it to the last, on the supposition that if he was an accomplice, he might play us false, and give her warning. We went up to the top of the house, and entered a room fitted up with desks for writing. A stout old gentleman in spectacles made his appearance, and asked us to be seated.

* Any reader who doubts the truth of this story may be satisfied by referring to the "*Tablet*" Newspaper of June 15th, 1850. Being quoted from memory there may be some slight verbal inaccuracy, but the substance is the same. See page 312.

We commenced the conversation by assuring him that we had come in a friendly spirit, though on somewhat disagreeable business. A letter, signed Charles W. Kenyon, had been traced to his house, and our object in calling was to request that he would communicate all he knew respecting it. The honest bearing of the old Scotchman at once disarmed all suspicion, and convinced us that he had been as much Marie's dupe as any one else had been. He said that a young lady called on him, and stated that a friend of hers had sent her from Marseilles some letters in the Italian language, which, as he did not understand English, he had requested her to translate, and he wished them to go to his correspondent in a gentleman's hand. As she seemed to be a respectable young lady, and there was nothing objectionable in the letter, he had written it according to her orders. A few days after, he received the following note :—

"'Please Mr. ——— will you write this letter directly, and post it by the next post. I will call for the copy this afternoon. By so doing you will oblige,

"'F. H. Affre.

"'Direct the envelope Reverend ———.
"'Please to seal the letters with your seal.'

She called in the afternoon, as arranged in her note, and his suspicions being excited by the repetition and apparent strangeness of the commission, he sent his boy to follow her, and see whither she went. The boy saw her enter a shop in Regent Street, and returned. Still feeling dissatisfied and suspicious, he made a special entry of the occurrence in a book, which he produced and read. Thus the mystery of the Captain Kenyon letters was explained, and the honest Scotchman cleared of all suspicion of collusion."

Mr. L—— having finished his tale, they went into the house. Marie went out for a short time, and they took advantage of the opportunity to make some arrangements for the morning. They placed pens and ink on the drawing-room table, and strong salts in readiness for real or pretended fainting. Fearing that when accused she might rush up stairs and do mischief, they resolved to lock all the bed-room doors on the arrival of the gentlemen, and they put a mark on each key. They looked out boxes and cord in readiness for packing her clothes. They planned to finish breakfast only just before her examiners arrived, in order to keep her in till they came; and they agreed to send the children out for a long walk till all should be over. Last of all, Mrs. L—— requested the tradespeople to send in Marie's bills at ten o'clock the next morning.

Marie supped with them, but withdrew at an early hour.

"Has she any suspicion?" said Mr. L——.

"Not the least."

"Well, it has been a regular game of chess for the last fortnight, and with all her cunning, she is check-mated at last. One cannot help feeling some sort of satisfaction in such a conclusion, after having been duped for so long."

Elizabeth found Marie writing when she went up. It appeared to be the same long letter which she had been writing in the afternoon. Elizabeth thought that it really might contain some confession, and that she would do all she could to encourage it. The night was a cold one, and the servants were gone to rest, so she herself lighted Marie's fire, and fetched her a new candle. Then devoutly hoping that the house might not be burned down before morning, she bade Marie "good night."

CHAPTER XXX.

THE TRIAL MORNING

TUESDAY, June 18th, dawned in almost cloudless beauty. Marie came down to breakfast, little thinking of the dark cloud which was louring over *her*, preparing in one short hour to burst upon her. She had arranged to walk across the Park to Mrs. Y——'s, and Elizabeth was to accompany her. As soon as breakfast was over, she ran up stairs to get ready. In a few minutes more she would have been off. A knock was heard at the door. Elizabeth ran up to her, "Marie, a gentleman wants to speak to you."

She turned pale. "Who is it?" she asked anxiously.

"It is only Mr. K——."

Marie seemed relieved, and went down to the drawing-room.

According to pre-arrangement, while Mr. K—— engaged her in conversation, Mr. S—— and Mr. A'B—— arrived. Mr. L—— was watching for them, and he opened the door before they knocked. They ascended the staircase as noiselessly as possible, and opened the drawing-room door. There they stood! Mr. S—— in whose family she had lived, Mr. L—— whose kindness she had abused, Mr. A'B—— with whose professional character she was well acquainted, and Mr. K—— their confidential friend. Why had they all assembled at *that* hour to confront *her?* She saw it at a glance. She bent her head, and there she sat, calm, modest, self-possessed, without any of the excitement so well feigned in earlier days. She did not faint, she did not move. In former days the slightest incident would throw her into a state of excitement which alarmed her friends. Now, when any one else would have been agitated, she sat unmoved. If there was a struggle within, there was no manifestation of it without. Her examiners betrayed more emotion than herself.

Two of the gentlemen placed their chairs between Marie and the door, and they all seated themselves in silence.

Mr. L—— spoke. He said he had invited these friends to be present, while he entered upon matters too important for conference with her alone, and wishing them also to hear any explanation which she might have to give.

He then stated, that two facts had come to his knowledge. Her previous acquaintance with the contents of Captain Kenyon's letter, and inquiries for it at the post-office ; and her correspondence with Mr. Viall, full of mis-statements which had come into his possession. " Can you," he inquired, " explain either of these ?"

Marie seemed about to maintain the veracity of her statements to Mr. Viall, till assured by Mr. K—— that the whole matter had been thoroughly investigated, and that such asseverations were useless. She was silent.

Mr. L—— repeated the question, whether she could explain these circumstances.

A scarcely audible " no" dropped from her lips.

" It now becomes my painful duty," said Mr. L——, " to tell you that there is too much reason to fear that you have been an impostor from first to last."

Marie raised her eyes, and without manifesting the slightest emotion, gently said, " It is too true, sir."

The whole party looked at one another in amazement at her unparalleled self-control.

" Well, then," said Mr. L——, " it only remains for you to tell us who you are, where you came from, and what have been your motives for acting in so extraordinary a way ?"

With great firmness Marie replied that there were some circumstances connected with her early history which she must decline to communicate. Indeed she would rather die than

reveal the circumstances under which she had left her family.
Thus much she would say, that she was a native of M——;
that her father was a surgeon; that he and her mother died
when she was young, leaving her to the care of an only brother: he treated her unkindly, and she had long since left him.
For two years before coming to London, she had had a situation at ———— Hall, near C——, and the charge of two little
girls. Their mother and father dying, they were sent to the
care of their guardian. Being again thrown upon the world,
she had had recourse to the expedient of going into a convent.
Growing tired of its discipline, and having heard of Mr. L——
in the north, as a man of benevolence and kindness, on coming
to London, she determined to find him out.

"Well," said Mr. L——, "if I were to express what I think
of your conduct, it would only give you pain, and under present
circumstances do little good. I presume that you have no uncle?"

"No."

"How were his letters managed?"

"I wrote them all myself in your house, and had them translated and rewritten by Mr. ————, a teacher of languages in
———— Street."

"Then am I to conclude that the money you received for
the church went to pay Mr. ———— ?" (the translator.)

"Yes."

"And we have every reason to believe that your illness was
feigned."

She showed a little emotion, and seemed about to deny it.

"Oh!" said Mr. A'B——, "Mr. L—— has been to Dr.
———— (mentioning a shrewd physician to whom the case had
been submitted) and he knows all about it. You had better
say nothing more."

She was silent.

"Can you refer me to any parties who will authenticate your
statement about being in a situation?"

She gave the names of two parties.

"Is your brother living?"

"Yes; the last I heard of him was that he was practising as a veterinary surgeon at S——."

"Of course you can no longer remain under my roof. What can you do?"

"I will emigrate," she said with emotion.

Her apparently artless tale had worked on the sympathies of the visitors, and so great was the power she was capable of exerting over the judgments and feelings of others, that their abhorrence of her imposture was forgotten in pity for her *apparently* unprotected and destitute condition. There was a short conference among them, and they all agreed that she should not be turned out without shelter, but that an apartment should be taken for her, while they should consider whether any plan could be devised for her emigration.

Mr. L—— said that she must not be surprised if, after the deception she had practised, he suspected all her movements. He thought it right, therefore, to warn her that if she absconded while they were making inquiries, he should advertise her in the papers.

"Oh! Mr. L——, you cannot think that I should do that."

She then said, "I shall leave the house directly; I cannot bear to see Mrs. L——." She proposed taking a walk while an apartment was being provided for her; and it was settled that a note with the address should be left at a shop near, and that she should call for it.

How were Mrs. L—— and her sister engaged during this interval? No sooner were the gentlemen ushered into the drawing-room, than they both ran up stairs, locked all the bedroom doors, and pocketed the keys, and then locked themselves in Marie's room. They emptied out her drawers, and carefully packed her clothes. These they found all neatly washed up, as if in readiness to abscond. Then they turned out her desk, and just inside her portfolio, they found two letters carefully copied out, and evidently all ready to take with her. She had doubtless been writing these when Elizabeth was in the room the day before. One professed to be a letter from her uncle to Mrs. L——, and the other one from him to herself. In one of the little drawers they found a sealed enclosure, on the outside of which was written, "Private Papers." They had often seen this when her desk stood open, and she had told Selina that it contained a confession and explanation for Mrs. L—— to read in the event of her death. Between the bed and mattress they found two novels, a class of books of which she had always professed a perfect horror. These were "Misrepresentation" and "Agincourt." On opening a China-box on the drawers, they found some dead leeches and blood in a state of putrefaction. They must have been standing there some time, but the pretty box in which they were hid excited no suspicion. They found a small glass tube about two inches in length, curved, and with a very small opening at one end. It was such as she had once told them was used in France for the application of leeches to the mouth and nostrils. The new dress which had been obtained by a trick, they kept back, and the velvet mantle, of which she had defrauded Mr. Viall, to return to him. The mantle and bonnet which Mrs. L—— had given her, they left out for her to put on. They had the boxes corded, and her name attached; and as they doubted whether she would get any dinner that day, they cut a few sandwiches for her, and put them in her basket. They brought her boxes down, and were seated in the back-parlor before the conference broke up.

Mr. L—— came to them, and briefly told them what had passed. "She says she cannot meet *you*, so I have come to ask you to keep in this room." He returned to the drawing-room, and Marie hastily ran up stairs. Doubtless she was eager to ascertain if her letters had been discovered. Desk, drawers—all were empty. They heard her go to the closet on the landing for the velvet mantle. That too was gone. In another minute she rushed down stairs as for her life, opened the hall-door, banged it after her—she was gone!

The gentlemen came down stairs, and the letters found in her desk were read. From the first sentence in the uncle's letter to Mrs. L——, in which he apologizes for employing an amanuensis, it is evident that she was giving ———— the slip, and about engaging another translator. These letters have not the advantage which the others gained by the French translation, so effectually concealing as it did the peculiarities of her style; but considering the difficulties by which she was hedged in on every side, it must be conceded that they are not inferior in ability to their predecessors. Mr. A'B—— expressed his high admiration of the talent displayed in the whole series, and declared that in all he had ever read in romance, or met with in his profession, nothing at all approached the realities of this extraordinary case.

The letter from the uncle to Mrs. L——, found in her desk, was as follows :—

I. H. S.

" Madam,

"I much regret that illness compels me to depute a second person to write for me. On account of this I shall not be able to comply with poor Marie's request, in entering fully into the detail of the event which has caused so much embarrassment to both parties.

" I have received two letters from her which have both grieved and seriously displeased me. I never felt so really angry with her before. I hope you will never think that I should for any motives screen or palliate her faults; but you can sympathize with me when you remember my peculiar relation or position to Marie. If I take her part when I may think she is not to blame, designing reasons are likely to be attributed to me, though I feel sufficient confidence in you and Mr. L—— to believe that you would not entertain such a suspicion; but I am well aware of the fact that some few officious friends have questioned my sincerity to Marie. On the other hand I feel it is my duty not only to reprove her when in the wrong, but I must also exonerate her from unjust conjectures.

"I have no doubt you have been much tried with Marie's reserve; you cannot be more displeased with it than I am, but still you are not right in doubting the truthfulness of her statement and confession to me; she did not tell me what you could not believe. I have had too much experience of human nature and character not to discover the slightest prevarication, and more especially with Marie. There was one part of her letter alluding to a subject which has caused me many sleepless nights. It will be sufficient to explain what I mean when I say the newspaper affair. I am convinced from her evasive statement some other party was privy to it. I strongly suspect one of the servants, or some very improper friend. I have charged Marie with the equivocation, and am much displeased that she has not answered me satisfactorily. Marie was most frank and sincere in her confession to me. I have not taken her testimony alone, but have had other sources of information that corroborated all she said. I do feel grieved that you should have taxed her with insincerity to me after she had performed so painful a task. Whatever may occur between you and her I hope you will never question the truthfulness of her confessions to me. Few, considering Marie's altered position, would have written so frankly, so I do wish to commend her where praise is due; she is most anxious that I should give you the full explanation of all that has transpired, but I do not now deem it prudent, but will leave it for a personal interview, providing she does not do so herself before my visit. I fear now to hazard such a communication under the present circumstances; suffice it then to say that Marie is not exempt from great blame, nor yet is she guilty to the extent you perhaps suppose her, so I hope the impression will be removed that no satisfactory explanation can be given.

"I must clear her from one very unjust circumstance with which she was indirectly charged by your sister a few months ago. I mean an event that occurred the day after Marie's return to you. She has felt this most painfully. I should have taken more notice of it were I not aware of Marie's failing in being so sensitive, and being also possessed of so lively an imagination. From the conversation that passed I concluded that the expression used by Miss —— was not intended to convey any specific charge to Marie. I could understand it either way, or have placed the more favorable construction upon it. I cannot suppose for a moment you entertain such a suspicion; if I thought you did I should then feel obliged to endeavor to clear Marie from it. Such a conversation as the one alluded to, has, I am sure, done much to lead to her reserve. She has never been accustomed to anything like taunting, and I have always found such a system is attended with very bad results to an open disposition. No one ought to reprove Marie but you and Mr. L——. I beg you will not think that Marie has been making any complaints, for in relating all that passed she had to mention the conversation in question: she could not omit it, and she spoke in the most glowing terms of the kindness shown to her by your sisters, particularly by the one mentioned.

"I perfectly concur with Mr. L—— that this is a crisis in Marie's life, therefore the deep interest I take in her will induce you to bear with me in a few remarks and suggestions. In the first place I think it will now be well that the circumstances that have caused so much misunderstanding be left till Marie has quite overcome the reserve—I mean as far as she is concerned. I shall give you a full explanation, but let nothing more be said to her about it. When she recovers herself she will be the first to tell you, but while she is so timid with you the evil is only progressing. In the next place do not yourself be afraid of speaking openly to her; she thinks you are afraid of her, so it would seem the timidity and reserve is mutual. I know from experience what this feeling is, for she once behaved as strangely to me for nearly six months. I was very distant and cold with her, though it was a great struggle to me. The late venerable Father Affré advised me to take an opposite course, which was to affectionately expostulate with her and gently to invite her confidence. I did so; she did not then confess her fault, but in a few days after she came to me in my study and with deep penitence acknowledged her error. I spoke seriously to her, since then that confidence has remained unbroken.

"I have been much distressed to hear that she has lately fallen into the same sin; she mentioned the incident. I cannot tell how to account for it, for it was not her besetting sin: she was remarkable for many years for the contrary. If confidence were restored between you I am sure she would be preserved from it. Marie must be able openly to confess her faults and be checked in them; she has never had free license before, so that if she has not a confessional of one kind she must have of another.

"I think it is now time to adopt some stringent measures for the checking of this sin, and also the reserve. I purpose sending her a very stern letter. I much regret it, for my late letters have been so very severe, and I am rather doubtful of the result of such severity.

"In the first place, I must strictly prohibit any letters being written or received without your sanction. I was not a little astonished when I heard that there was no restraint in this. I forbid any plans or purposes being carried out without your knowledge, and I shall in future expect her to account to you for money spent. In these restrictions I beg you will kindly give me your prompt assistance; tell Marie they are my commands.

"She expressed with deep contrition her consciousness of having treated so good a friend as yourself with great ingratitude. I think a fearful struggle between good and evil is going on now with Marie. I should esteem it a kindness conferred upon myself, if you or Mr. L—— would take the trouble to speak seriously on her present temptations and the sinfulness of her errors. Nay, may I go still further, in appealing to your feelings as a mother, and beg that you will still feel a mother's interest in Marie. In the name of one who is now no more, I would plead for her dear and beloved orphan child, whom she loved with the tenderest affection; and it cost her many a bitter pang, when, in her last hours, she thought of Marie's lonely position should she enter upon the world. She knew how unfit Marie was to contend with its temptations and snares. Let this consideration induce you to bear with Marie's failings. She will not I am sure long continue so reserved, for she seems to have suffered so much, that she will be thankful for any measure that will break the chain asunder. I do heartily sympathize with her in her present state of feeling and her alienation from you. She is thrown so much upon herself, that it tends to make her both irritable and unsocial; but you could not have acted differently, if you are to prove your love by faithfulness and disapprobation of her faults. My esteem for you has been doubly increased by your conduct to Marie; and while I may think that you have perhaps judged her rather too harshly, I must attribute that judgment to your own high sense of virtue in abhorring that which is hateful in Marie.

"I was much pleased with her answer to Mrs. Kenyon, though she has, I fear, lost her friendship and notice; but I quite think Mrs. K——'s interference merited Marie's remarks.

"Marie is very anxious for my permission to show you my

late letters. I am sorry I cannot grant her request. I said several things in confidence to her, and consulted her upon one or two little matters that I wished none but herself to know for the present. Such communications are not likely again to pass between us.

"I have been much amused with Marie's great annoyance, that Captain Kenyon's letters should have given you an unfavorable impression of him. She was vexed at his bad spelling, &c. I should think it too ridiculous to notice, did I not consider it right, in justice to Mr. K——, to endeavor to remove that impression. There is no one amongst the circle of my friends and relations whom I more sincerely esteem than Mr. K——. I respect him for his high moral worth and gentlemanly conduct and deportment. His incorrect orthography does not arise from want of education, for he is a man of considerable intellectual attainments; but it is from an extreme degree of nervousness, which produces often an absent state of mind, and which absence is considerably increased by excitement. He rarely ever writes letters at all, and frequently have I known him to write part of one sentence, forget what he has said, and he has completed it with a totally different subject. I read over his second letter, fearing any blunder of this kind. I hope ere long to have the pleasure of introducing him to you and Miss ——, when I think the latter will say, Captain Kenyon *is* a gentleman, though his seal and letters are so ungentlemanly. I am now joking, so hope no offence will be given.

"If Marie has not yet written to acknowledge my remittance, please see that she does so directly. I should have sent more, but I trust to see you soon, and there is £75 in the boxes. I could not send one of my servants with them, for nothing could be removed during my illness, as the General sent a person to Manotté, who will remain till I am able to go there. I think Marie forgets how peculiarly I am situated, or she would not be so impatient. She may by such impatience defeat my plans, and cause me much censure. She has got a strange fancy now: she fears that you would wish to part with her, which fear distresses her very much.

"I was much annoyed to hear of Marie being seen alone at the time and place, by her old companion and schoolfellow, Miss ————. It has gone the whole round of the family, with the addition that she looked dull and miserable.

"I should feel obliged by Mr. L—— forwarding me Marie's account, and also acquainting me of his plans for the sea. If he writes in a few days he may direct for me here. I should feel favored by a few lines from yourself about my dear Marie.

"Please present my very kind regards to Mr. L——, and say I hope he will not think I have taken a liberty in again addressing you. With my most respectful compliments, I am, dear madam,

"Yours faithfully,
"H. C. CLIFFORD."

The "Private Papers" when opened, proved to be her Will, bequeathing the imaginary articles in her non-existent boxes to various members of the family.

"I, Marie Lucille G——, now residing at the house of the Reverend S—— L——, ————, near London, do will and bequeath the following articles to my several dear friends, they being my own property, left me by my mother, Marie Constable G——, who died in Manotté, France, on the 7th of August, 1844 :—

To my uncle, the Reverend Herbert Constable Clifford, of Manotté, I leave my late mother's desk and contents, her portrait, books, and all the diamonds and jewels belonging to my late grandmamma, Marie Talbot Clifford.

My own desk made of porcupine quills, I bequeath to my dearest friend, J—— L——.

The jewels belonging exclusively to my late mother, to be disposed of as follows :—

My uncle to select any he may particularly desire as family relics.

To E—— T—— a ring, and cameo brooch, and diamond crucifix, and bracelet.

To S—— T—— a brooch and ring.

To the Reverend S—— L—— my late mother's watch, seals, and gold guard.

To J—— E—— L—— my own miniature, enamelled Geneva watch and gold chain, my pearl ornaments, and coral necklace, and ruby crucifix.

To S—— A—— L—— my silver mug, and silver case of spoons and forks.

To S—— H—— a ring.

To S—— S——, second son of T—— S——, Esq., my gold pencil case, or some other token of love.

To the Reverend W—— F—— and his wife, a ring and brooch.

To T—— S—— and his wife E——S——, each a trinket.

The rest of my jewels, clothes, books, boxes, &c., I leave to J—— L——, wife of the Reverend S—— L——.

Each of the servants to have some trifling token of remembrance of me. The coins to be sold, and the proceeds to be expended on a font for ————, left as my last dying legacy, and a suitable inscription to be put upon it.

This is my last wish and will, signed by me on this, the fourth day of March, 1850.

Witness."

The codicil which follows refers to articles really in her possession.

" The Bible given to me by S—— T——, I leave for my dearest uncle, and also the book called the ' Anxious Enquirer.

My first little Testament I bequeath as my *greatest* earthly treasure, to Lilly.

My work-box to Miss T——.

A Bible to Miss S——.

My ' Cruden's Concordance' to Miss K——.

The copy of ' Young's Night Thoughts' to Mrs. T——.

My smelling bottle to E—— P——.

One of my little books to T—— D——.

Hymn book to E—— S——."

CHAPTER XXXI.

MARIE'S TRANSMIGRATIONS.

AFTER the departure of their friends, Mr. and Mrs. L—— set out in search of an apartment for Marie. They at length found one at about a mile and a half distance, where the poor woman who owned the house appeared honest and respectable; and giving her a charge to attend to Marie's comfort, as a young person intending to emigrate, they agreed on the terms for her board and lodging, and turned their steps homeward. The address was left for Marie at the shop before mentioned, and her boxes sent to her apartment.

Mrs. King called soon afterwards to inform them that Marie had been at her house. Mrs. King not being at home, she asked to go to the kitchen fire, and there to the surprise of the girl, she emptied her pockets of a great quantity of papers and *burnt them all.* She went up stairs to wait, and found Mr. King* at his dinner. He was finishing on gooseberry pie, and

* This was a nursery gardener, who had brought Marie many presents of choice flowers during her illness.

she took some with great relish. Who else could have sat down to eat immediately after such a conviction ?

On hearing of this conflagration, the gentlemen regretted that they had not insisted on her turning out the contents of her pockets, but a mixture of gallantry and pity had induced them to let her off more easily than she deserved.

Very strange and sad were the feelings of those whom she had left. It was certainly a relief to be freed from the anxiety and watching of the last fortnight; but who can imagine the blank which she left behind ? The dream of eighteen months was over. She whom they had loved and cherished as a daughter had, as far as her place in their affections was concerned, suddenly ceased to be. They felt as if they had been keeping guard over a felon, and as if she had that morning been tried, condemned, and sent beyond the seas.

They could not bear to sit down and *think*. There was no bright spot on which they could rest in the past—no gleam of hope in looking forward to the future. There were several subjects of inquiry still remaining, and they resolved to busy themselves about these, and escape for a few hours from the desolate house. They started in search of the professor of languages, and found his rooms without difficulty. They were shown into a drawing-room, and presently a short, stoutly built German entered ;—a sturdy uncompromising person, a man of business, a man of the world, and as it would seem little likely to be imposed upon. " I have called on you," said Mr. L——, " in reference to some letters which have been sent to my house, written by Miss G——, and translated here."

" Oh, it is Mr. L—— I suppose ?

" Yes."

" Well, I am glad to see you. I was thinking of calling upon you to know if you can tell me about Miss Clifford, as she has not been here for some time."

" It is a Miss G——, not a Miss Clifford," said Mr. L——.

"No, it was a Mrs. or Miss Clifford who came here, and the letters she sent were to Miss G——."

Mr. and Mrs. L—— looked perplexed and puzzled.

"She was a short stout young lady," said Mr. ———, "and she came to me, and said she wanted some letters translated for her niece, a Miss G——, at Mr. L——'s, C—— Terrace. She asked me if I was a Catholic. I said, 'If you come to me on business I will attend to you, but if it is about religion, I have no time to talk on that subject.' She said it did not matter, only she thought if I were a Catholic I could better enter into the feelings with which she wrote these letters."

Mr. and Mrs. L—— could not yet make it out. Here was a new character appearing on the stage in the shape of a Miss Clifford.

Mr. ——— proceeded, "She told me that her niece had apostatized from the Catholic Church, and that she had been so angry with her at first that she had declared she would never write to her again, but latterly she had relented, and wished to try to bring her back to the true Church. Her niece did not speak English, so she wished the letters to be in French; besides which she should save her word by our writing them." He then produced two packets, one of Marie's English originals, and the other her orders to him to translate them. "I did them up," he added, "in case I might be out, as she said she was going to call; and I wrote the account outside, 131 pages at 1s. a page, £6 11s."

"But these letters were from a gentleman, a priest," said Mr. and Mrs. L——; "not from a young lady."

Mr. ——— was puzzled in his turn. He rang for his French assistant, a tall, grave young man, and they began to chatter away in French.

"Those letters, Miss Clifford's letters, were from a priest," said ———

"A priest! no," said the young Frenchman. "They were from a lady!"

"Why how could you translate these letters, and think they were from a lady?" said Mrs. L——; and she eagerly seized one of Marie's copies to show the impossibility of understanding the writer to be a lady. She ran her eye down a page. "There is frequent mention of the General," said she, "the General of the Jesuits."

"It does not say what general," they replied, "it might be a father or brother, a military general."

"Here he talks of keeping his retreat," she said again.

"Ladies have retreats too," they replied.

And true enough, as she looked down page after page, she saw that they would suit equally with either of Marie's assumed characters, an aunt or an uncle. To the Frenchman she was an aunt, to Mr. L—— she was an uncle. Like those cosmoramic amusements, which used to be in vogue when we were children, in which any compartments of landscape scenery, however variously placed, would form one perfect whole, so these letters were arranged to make up a consistent story in the character either of aunt or uncle, as the case might require.

"But how could you make out her writing to her niece from Ghent, and Marseilles, and Nice," asked Mr. and Mrs. L——.

"Why she wrote to me from those places herself," said Mr ——. "She called on me the first time, and afterwards she wrote to me from abroad, and she said that her letters were sent to England in other despatches:" and he showed her notes to him, which corresponded in their statements with the uncle or aunt letters which accompanied them.

"I am very sorry I have been done," said Mr. ——. "We poor professors have nothing but our time to depend upon. A great deal of time has been taken up about these letters. She only paid us thirty shillings. A shilling a page: that is not too much, I am sure: 131 pages, at one shilling a page, unpaid for: £6 11s. left to pay. Many a time we sat up

at nights to write these letters, because they were always wanted in such a hurry, and sometimes we put off lessons to get
them done. One hundred and thirty-one pages at a shilling a
page," repeated the poor professor in hopeless despondency.
" I am truly sorry I have been *done*."

To show the ingenuity with which Marie acted out her
character of a wealthy aunt, some specimens of the orders sent
to Mr. ——— are here inserted.

" Monsieur ——— will oblige Miss Clifford by sending by
the bearer the letter left by her last night.

" Miss Clifford hopes that her French letter was duly sent,
and she also desires to say she shall not forget Monsieur
———'s prompt attention to this commission.

" Portman Square,
  " Thursday Morning."

———

" Sir,

   " I saw my niece on Thursday, and was glad to find
you had written so promptly. I should have seen her again
to-day, but am unable from other engagements. I should be
very glad if you will translate the enclosed *immediately*, and
post it for me forthwith. I was unable to call or send yesterday, but I shall be returning in my carriage this evening
through ——— Street, at least I expect so : if not I shall be
at the Pantheon on Monday, so will call for the copies, and pay
you for the translations. I have not any stamps : if I send
for any I shall miss the next post, which I am anxious to avoid.

   " I was pleased with the neatness of your note, for we had
occasion to refer to it. I noticed one mistake in the direction
of the name, it was spelt thus G———, which was wrong, it is
G———, but that is of no consequence.

   " I wish my niece to have the letter at the latest on Sunday
morning, so you will oblige me by being prompt. If you are

not in when I call, will you please leave me a few cards of your terms, I may use them for you.

"I am,

"Yours respectfully,

"II. C. CLIFFORD.

" Westbourne Terrace,

  " Saturday Morning."

" Sir,

"I should feel obliged by your translating forthwith the enclosed letter in French. I wish you to send it by to-morrow morning's post. ———— Street will do.

"Please do not put 'signed' to the name, as I give you free permission to sign my name.

"Be particular in putting the day 'Wednesday morning.' I wish the same person to write this one that translated the other letter of mine.

"A sheet of plain paper with envelope sealed with black will do. I wish the postage paid. In calculating your charge for the other translation, I think the stamps sent will defray the expense. I have not any more by me, or should send them, but I shall either call to-morrow, or send my page for the English copy, so can then pay the remaining charge.

"I have mentioned you to some relatives of mine in London who wish for a French tutor. They will call upon you soon. By your *immediate* attention to this business you will much oblige,

Yours respectfully,

" II. C. CLIFFORD.

" Westbourne Terrace,

  " Tuesday Morning.

    " GREAT HASTE."

" Sir,

"The illness of a relative called me suddenly away, so that I could not call, or yet send. My time has been for the last week so much engaged with the Christmas duties, that I have been unable to attend to anything beyond them.

"I enclose you the sum for the last one, and desire you to copy out the enclosed in French. Please do it directly, and date it by the month as given, and post it from the City. Direct it from the given address. I am leaving London to-night for our country residence Manotté Park, from whence I came yesterday on business. I shall be up again on Saturday next, so hope to call for the copies.

"By attending to this *directly* you will oblige,

"Yours, &c.,

"Wednesday Morning." "H. C. CLIFFORD."

"Saturday, Feb. 3d.

"Sir,

"I have not convenient change by me before I post this letter, having only notes, or should enclose 10*s*. for the other letter; but will pay you for the two on my return home, or, if I see my cousin Mrs. Kenyon, I will direct her to forward you the money. I hope the last sum was correct.

"You will oblige me by translating the enclosed *immediately*, and forwarding it forthwith.

"It has struck me, that it perhaps might appear mysterious my requiring you to translate these letters; but it being in the way of your business, it is scarcely necessary to enter into explanations; but I would just say, that I pledged myself, under very painful circumstances, not to write to my niece. I being her only friend in our family, and she also not understanding much of the English language, I have spared her feelings by having them written in French : so the excuse has served both purposes.

"By prompt attention you will oblige

"Yours truly,

"H. C. CLIFFORD.

"Address to Miss G—— as before."

"Mount St. Benedict, Jan. 19th 1850

✝

I. H. S.

" Sir,

" Having a little nephew who is under our care, and who is now in rather delicate health, we have been induced to remove him from the public college where his education has been conducted for the last year. Feeling it unadvisable that he should entirely discontinue his studies, his uncle and myself have almost come to the decision of engaging a private tutor. We had some thought of having a priest, but have now given up the idea.

" As you have an establishment, it struck me that you might hear of some worthy young gentleman fully competent for the duties required. A sound English education, with a knowledge of mathematics. He must understand the Latin and Greek, German and French languages. Drawing would be another inducement, and it is indispensable that he be a member of the Roman Catholic Church. If you know of any one that is able to take this situation, I should be glad if you would communicate with me after the 12th of March, for I shall be engaged till then in religious duties. The tutor would have all the comforts and treatment of a gentleman, and salary would be no object to us, providing he was a clever, intellectual person. We shall reside in London, and trust that will be the home for the tutor and pupil during the summer months, so that we are not particular to a resident or daily tutor.

" When I come to London I will send my address, so that you may call upon us, which will be about the time stated, that is, when we have fixed upon our residence. I have desired my cousin, Mrs. Kenyon, to call upon you with this letter, having sent to her, and having deputed her to pay you your charges for translating, and also to receive the copies. If she does not call with the letter, she will do so, I dare say, a few days after. You can mention to her if you know of any person that will suit us, for we have a decided objection to advertising.

"Please translate the enclosed as soon as possible. —— Street post will do. I have discontinued black paper. I do not know if you have used it. Please observe the date given. By so doing you will oblige

"Yours truly,

"H. C. Clifford."

"Address Miss G——, &c., &c.

"P. S. I wish the letter enclosed in an envelope, so directed that my niece can hand it over to her friend, the party addressed."

----

†

I. H. S.

"Ghent, February 28th, 1850.

"Sir,

"Having been detained by illness much beyond my purposed stay, I have not been able to remit you the money for the translating of the two last letters. I shall be in England in the course of another fortnight or three weeks, so will enclose the money from Manotté, for I shall not come to London till April, when I hope to make arrangements with you for my nephew, for we have taken a house in town for the season. I should feel obliged by your translating the enclosed *directly*, for considerable delay will have ensued through the transmission of the letters from here to you. I have had to enclose them in another despatch, so that two delays will have occurred. You will really greatly favor me by attending to them *immediately*.

"The letter to Mrs. L—— I wish translated, and very *neatly* enclosed in a small envelope, sealed with a small black seal. The other letters I wish directed as usual to my niece, sealed with black.

"By your *immediate* and *prompt* attention to this commission, you will favor

Yours truly,

"H. C. CLIFFORD.

"P. S.—Use nice paper to Mrs. L——, and let the writing be carefully attended to. My niece's is not required to be particular.

"Address, Miss G——, &c."

---

†

I. H. S.

"Nice, March 23d.

"Sir,

"I really feel quite ashamed to put you to so much trouble, being so far distant; but being unable to return so soon as expected, on account of health, I am obliged to write again to my niece.

"I have enclosed you money for this letter. I cannot send more, for it would add to the postage, and I have to enclose this in another despatch for London; but I could not think of sending to you again without paying for this one. As soon as I come home, I will remit you the other. Please translate it *immediately*, for I want their answers directly, it being of *immense* importance.

"I should be glad if you would use black. I am obliged to use white, for I cannot purchase black here.

"Enclose the Reverend S—— L——'s letter in the one to my niece. By so doing, you will oblige

Yours respectfully,

"H. C. CLIFFORD.

"*Great haste.*"

CHAPTER XXXII.

THE BANDAGED ARM.

THE mystery of Mrs. Kenyon's letters was still unexplained. Well written, and in a lady-like hand, they formed the most perplexing subject of speculation that yet remained. On returning from the French translator, Mr. L—— went to the post-office opposite, to ascertain if Marie had ever attempted any tricks there. "Never but once," said the young man who kept it. "She wished to persuade me to post a letter without marking it. She said she wanted to play a joke on a young friend, and did not wish her to find out where the letter came from." He recollected the address, having once known the lady. It was a Miss H——.

Mr. L—— suspecting that some light might here be obtained on the unexplained mystery, went to Miss H——, a day or two after, and found that she and her sister kept a highly respectable boarding-school. He was shown into the drawing-room, and a ladylike, pleasing person appeared. He introduced himself by name, and apologized for his visit. "Oh! you have come about Miss D'Orsay," said the lady. Mr. L—— immediately saw that this was some new trick, and requested that Miss H—— would kindly acquaint him with all that had passed between Miss D'Orsay and herself.

Miss H—— readily complied. "One evening, about a month ago, a lady called on us, and stated that she was a niece of Count D'Orsay, and that she was now in England for the benefit of her health, under the friendly as well as professional care of Sir James and Lady Clarke. She said that she had both a French and English governess, but between the two, had not become perfect in either language; and she wished while in

England to have the advantage of improving in English. She had heard of us through her friends, the daughters of Colonel Watson, and thought that a residence with us would just meet her views. She said that she wanted two rooms for herself, and a little room for her maid, and offered us four guineas a week for our drawing-room floor. We had never thought of letting any part of our house before; but she was so agreeable and interesting, that we thought she would be a pleasant addition to our circle, and we agreed to meet her wishes. She spoke of several persons in fashionable life with whom we were slightly acquainted; and her *broken English*, and simplicity of expression, agreed with her account of herself. She had all the French animation of manner, and seemed very intelligent. We wondered at not having heard from her again, and felt anxious to do so, as we were about purchasing furniture for another room, to use instead of our drawing-room."

Mr. L—— inquired if Miss H—— could throw any light on some letters which had come to his house from a Mrs. Kenyon.

"O yes! we wrote them out for Miss D'Orsay at her request. Her arm was bandaged up in a nice cambric handkerchief, and she told us that she was now under Sir James Clarke's treatment for it. She then said that she had that morning received a letter from her friend Mrs. Kenyon at Marseilles, and that Mrs. Kenyon had enclosed a letter for a young friend of hers in that neighborhood; that Mrs. Kenyon could not write in English, and her friend Miss G—— could not read French, so Mrs. K—— had asked her to translate and send it. 'I would do it directly,' she said, 'but my arm is so bad, I cannot use it. If you would kindly write it for me while I translate, I should be so much obliged.' She took out of her pocket what appeared to be a French letter, and dictated while my sister wrote. As there were no matters of business in the letter, merely an account of the illness of a relative, we did not see any objection, and we corrected the mistakes, and wrote and posted it for her."

" And how was the next letter managed ?"

"She came again, very nicely dressed, with her arm still bandaged up, and said that she could not come to us so soon as she intended, as Sir James had ordered her to Hastings for a few weeks. She fixed to come to us the first week in August. She talked a great deal as before, and asked us to write another letter for her, as her arm, though better, was still too weak to guide the pen."

" And did you feel no misgivings as to the correctness of her story ?"

" No, not the slightest; but we afterwards had a letter from her, dated Hastings, the extreme vulgarity of which quite shook our confidence. We thought that no lady could be capable of penning such references."

" Well," said Mr. L——, " how could you be misled by that ? because, if she were capable of writing a letter from Hastings, she could write Mrs. Kenyon's letter and send it herself."

" O," said Miss H——, " I will soon show you how that was done;" and, producing a scarcely legible scrawl in pencil, Mr. L—— read as follows :—

" Hastings, June 5th, 1850.

" My dear Miss H——,

"Most gladly do I take up a pencil—*not a pen*—to fulfil my promise in scribbling a few lines to you, to tell you of all the troublesome disasters that have befallen me since my arrival at this outlandish domicile. I have made a change for the worse, not for the better; for I must tell you that Sir James Clark has been most unfortunate in his choice of apartments. In the first place, there are six noisy children. I have had ' *le bonheur*' of hearing the shrieks of two boys, while undergoing the penance of flogging from their ill-tempered papa. I felt strongly inclined to go out from my bedroom to the next one to interfere, for he was in a violent passion with the poor unfortunates. In the next place, I did not sleep through those horrible night intruders; this morning when I got up my eye was swollen quite up. I shall not remain here, for Lady Clarke thinks I must go to some other place; for if I go elsewhere in Hastings it will give mortal offence. Lady Clarke is returning this evening, so I hope soon to gain my dismissal from here, for it is so *very, very* miserable. My hand is so painful, I fear you will not be able to read this ' *billet doux :*' my little finger is now breaking out. I told Sir James about your decision, but he would not give me any answer, and he said it had better not be settled in any way till I returned to London; for he did not know yet whether he should have me in London for the summer : it depends upon my state of health after my hand is well. I may perhaps go to St. Leonard's if I do not stay here. I am sure to come to you for the autumn, if I don't for the summer. I am much annoyed at being sent from London so soon, for I am so dull when in strange places. I should like you or your sister to come down and see me when I am settled somewhere. Lady Clarke is going to London after dinner, so I shall get her to post this letter for me there, so as to save a post, for I am too late for the one here. The last is three; so it will be so long on the way if I leave it till to-morrow. Will you kindly write me the enclosed note, and address it to Miss G——: I received it this morning from London. I must now go and dress for dinner. Do not write till I write again, for I do not know how soon I may leave. I will write directly to you, and give you full particulars.

"With many thanks to you for your kindness to a lone female,

"I am, with love, yours sincerely,

"JULIA K. D'ORSAY."

By a comparison of dates, the first visit to Miss H—— appeared to have been paid on that same Friday when Marie professed to have met her friend Mary L—— in Kensington Gardens; and in all probability she then sought the deepest shade of those gardens, not to converse with a friend, but to bandage up her arm, and employ a stratagem worthy only of the meanest beggar.

In clearing a table drawer in the back parlor at C—— Terrace, another set of dead leeches were found; and the butcher added the information that she had a little time before brought him a phial to be filled with bullock's blood, which she said she wanted to put to the roots of a choice vine that her uncle had sent her from Provence. By the mixture of this with warm water, she could imitate blood from the lungs. It was subsequently ascertained that when feigning loss of appetite, she had supplied her wants from the larder and the pastry-cook's shop.

Her gifts to the poor, her presents to friends, and her contributions to fancy sales, were all found to have been left unpaid.

CHAPTER XXXIII.

TEMPORARY EXILE.

Mr. L—— and Mr. K—— made inquiries about the possibility of Marie carrying out her proposal to emigrate. They found that her outfit and passage would cost between £40 and £50. To this outlay no one appeared disposed to contribute. The congregation, indignant at the imposition practised on their minister, would more readily have paid the expenses of her prosecution. Mr. L—— and Mr. K—— went to her at —— Street, informed her of the difficulty, and asked if she could suggest any other plan. She said that her early governesses, Misses A—— and C——, had removed to Dieppe and set up an English school there, and if she could only get to them, she was sure of a welcome and a home. On a subsequent interview she stated that she had written to them and ascertained that they had removed to Ghent. It was agreed that her passage thither should be paid, and that she should go as soon as possible.

Letters were in the interval received from two parties to whom she had referred. One confirmed her statement of having been two years in a situation as governess. The other conjectured that the inquiry must refer to a relative, though the Christian name was different, and the surname was spelt differently, and he had not heard of her for years. As Marie spelt her name in four different ways, it was not easy to identify her. A doubt also arose whether she was indeed the person whom she had latterly represented herself to be, or whether she was personating some other character with whom she had come in contact.

A letter to her alleged brother at S——, was, after sundry wanderings, returned by the post-office as " not known."

The Roman Catholic priest, mentioned by Madame —————— on application confirmed Madame ——————'s statement.

On one point all were agreed, that whoever Marie might be, it was very desirable to send her out of the country ; and whatever might be her object in going to Ghent, no more feasible project for disposing of her could under present circumstances be suggested. It was arranged that Marie should leave by the steamer for Ostend, so as to take train for Ghent. Some suspicion as to her intentions being still entertained, her friends were anxious to be assured that she really went. It was not thought safe to entrust her with the passage money, lest she should appropriate it in some other way. It was therefore determined that she should go by herself to the packet, and that Mr. L—— and Mr. K—— should meet her there.

At half-past eight o'clock on Friday the 28th of June, Mr. L—— and his friend repaired to St. Katherine's Wharf. The scene was such as to awaken no ordinary feelings. It was an unusually wet and gloomy evening for the bright month of June. The day had been a brilliant one, and made the contrast the greater. Heavy clouds obscured the sun as he hastened to his setting, and heavy showers fell. The Thames was covered with thick mists; the masts of the shipping looked through like unearthly spectators; the gray tops of the Tower of London added their gloomy associations to the scene; the dark coming shades of night were already deepening the gloom; and the deep-toned bell of a neighboring church tolled mournfully as on the morning of some fearful execution: and, as if to complete the impression, an occasional flash of lightning gleamed in the sky, as a type of that light from heaven which had so wonderfully laid bare the artful imposture now brought to a close.

The two friends felt the influence of the scene. They looked down upon the steamer. The drops of falling rain echoed on the deck; and the busy crew, amidst harsh sounds such as sailors alone can utter, were taking on board, and depositing in the hold, large bales of merchandise. Pacing to and fro upon the deck in plain attire, friendless and unprotected, was seen a female form in strange contrast with all other objects. Could it be Marie, the frail girl over whom little less than a mother's love had watched, expecting every moment to be her last? Could it be she whose touching history had delighted so many hearts? It was: but, alas! how changed in circumstances, and character, and appearance. Such is crime. It may have its sunny day, but its evening will close as cheerlessly as Marie's.

Indisposed to have more conversation with her than necessary, the friends did not immediately go on board. The keen eye of Marie had been watching them as they lingered on the wharf, and fearing probably lest they should leave without re-plenishing her purse, she disappeared below, and soon the steward ascended the ladder with the following note. It was written on a fragment of soiled paper, torn out of an account-book.

"Please Mr. L—— do you wish to bid me good-bye ; and will the captain see me, or arrange for me to go to Ghent ?"

They went on board. Marie received them in the cabin with her recently adopted self-possession, and without any indication of anxiety in her countenance. Mr. L—— paid her fare, supplied her with pocket-money, and gave her a small book calculated to arouse conscience. Without one word of thanks, one expression of regret for the past, one sign of emotion, Marie received his last act of kindness and sad farewell, and hurried into the ladies' cabin.

Mr. L—— and his friend left the wharf. The mists yet hovered over the river : the deep toll of the bell seemed to proclaim the character of the occasion : the lightning, now more clear amidst the darkness, but still fitful and lurid, seemed to hover over the criminal. Will it be called weakness if he who had regarded her with almost a father's interest and a father's hope *wept*, and his friend sympathized in his emotion !

On the return of the vessel to London, the steward informed Mr. L—— that she had been landed at Ostend, and that he had seen her take train for Ghent.

In the month of August Mr. L—— and his sister were travelling on the continent. They stayed a night in Ghent, and availed themselves of the opportunity to inquire after Marie. They went to all the ladies' schools in Ghent, and made every inquiry at the post-office and elsewhere, but no such names as those of Mesdames A—— and C—— had been known in Ghent within memory of the present generation. What was Marie's motive for going, and how she obtained the means for returning, are questions still unexplained. She has since reappeared in London, and is believed to be still in some family at the West End in the capacity of a governess.

CHAPTER XXXIV.

WAS SHE NOT A JESUIT?

MARIE'S name has so far been suppressed, under the supposition that she may possibly belong to some respectable family, whom they would not wish to implicate in her disgrace. The circumstances, dates, handwriting, and portrait will, it is thought, be sufficient to lead to her detection wherever she may be carrying on some new imposition. She states her age to be twenty-six. She is short, and rather stout. She plays a little on the organ and on the piano, and excels in all kind of fancy-work.

Marie's transactions with the post-office may be explained on the supposition that some of her letters were sent without her own address, that others were recalled from the foreign post-offices, and that others when returned were intercepted at the door. The answers to the questions, page 188, and the letter mentioned, page 244, were the only two which came back after her departure. The fact that not one of the numerous letters to Manotté was returned has suggested the suspicion that she may have had some accomplice there to receive them. A long letter from Mrs. S—— informing Mr. and Mrs. L—— of various suspicious circumstances which had come to her knowledge, never found its way to them. The letter to Reverend Mother, referred to page 115, was posted by Mr. L.—— himself; but whether the one originally written ever went, or whether another enclosure in the same envelope was dexterously substituted for it, cannot now be ascertained.

Marie's statements respecting the Order to which she said that she belonged, page 17–20, are well worthy of investigation, though the writer cannot now vouch for a single particular of her convent history or of her escape. All that regards her introduction to the family at C—— Terrace, with the whole of the "Sequel" from page 115 to the close, is *literally* true.

Marie brought with her from the convent two rosaries, two crosses, a sealed wafer, said to have been blessed by the Pope, several little pictures of Mary and the Infant Saviour, Saint Francis de Sales, &c., with pious reflections, two medals with a figure of Mary on the one side, the "sacred hearts" of Jesus and of Mary on the other, and the inscription "O! Marie, conçue sans pêche, priez pour nous, qui avons recours à vous," and a third with the motto, " *Souvenir de mission.*"

Marie's imposture has been explained, but Marie and her object are still involved in mystery. The question naturally arises, Was it her own unaided project? Was she acting without the assistance or concurrence of any other party? retaining her own fearful secrets without a single confidant—living a life of plotting and guilt, and hazard, without one friend with whom to divide her anxieties? Had she sacrificed all human affections, and left herself without one to love, and by whom to be loved? It is difficult to imagine the case of a heart so utterly lonely and desolate—living among her fellow-creatures, and yet altogether as apart from them in all of interest and communion as if she had lived in some uninhabited desert. It would be difficult to find such a case even among thieves and assassins, of a being without one remaining tie—of one so entire in its solitariness and isolation, for—

> " There can be no companionship
> For loneliness of heart."

Then comes the second question. What could be her motive? Was it the mere love of deception and romance? We
can scarcely fancy that sufficiently powerful and durable to
carry her through for so long a period, and counterbalance all
the risks and terrors it involved. If it did, her case was unique.
Men do not lie and scheme without the hope of some great
ulterior gain.

Was it indolence? that rather than undergo the fatigue of
teaching children, she preferred to be nursed in ease and idle-
ness? Yet she exerted herself far more than if she had been a
governess. Her brain must have been always at work, plotting
and counterplotting; she was writing almost incessantly; she
sacrificed her rest at night; she gave up a comfortable salary,
and involved herself in straits and difficulties for want of money;
she underwent much punishment and privation in connection
with her fictitious illness; she sacrificed conscience and character: and the supposition of indolence furnishes a very unsatisfactory solution of the wonderful and untiring energy with
which she carried out her well-contrived and consistent story.

The conclusion can scarcely be resisted that there must have
been some strong concealed motive for her deception, which has
yet to be explained. It has been surmised by many that she
may have been a lay sister of some religious order, and employed by the Jesuits for some purpose of their own. If so, it
would account for the assumption of a character altogether the
reverse of her own, and so consistently maintained from first to
last; for the seeming frankness, conscientiousness, thoughtlessness, recklessness, and excitability which had no place in her;
for the system of lying and trickery in which she was so great
an adept; for her prying curiosity; for the religious garb which
she so zealously assumed; for her intimate acquaintance with
convent life, Catholic observances, and continental services; for
the wonderful self-possession which she manifested at her conviction; for *her anxiety to destroy all the papers which she car-*

ried about with her ; for the indifference with which she went off all but penniless to a foreign land; and the ease with which, without a character, she appears to have obtained a situation on her return. If she had a higher motive to sustain her,—if she had powerful protectors to fall back upon in the event of failure, her proceedings would no longer be inexplicable.

There is no apparent reason to doubt the truthfulness of the replies given by those who introduced and received her into the convent; but supposing the parties concerned to have acted in good faith, and from pure benevolence, even they may not have been made acquainted with Marie's object; and her brief refuge in the convent, may have been sought merely as a stepping-stone to its attainment.

It has been urged upon those whom she has deceived, that so extraordinary a development of character is too interesting a study for the mental and moral philosopher, to be consigned to oblivion. Other considerations might have silenced this and similar arguments, had not the conviction gradually, but irresistibly, forced itself upon them that Marie was only an agent, and her plot a part of some great system which may have been brought into action far more widely than Protestants are aware.

It must be obvious to all, that women introduced into families for Jesuit objects would be far more efficient than any out-agents could be ; and that feminine tact, combined with Jesuit cunning, could scarcely miss the attainment of any desired object. "If," remarks a popular French writer, "there is anything more dangerous than a Jesuit, it is a Jesuitess." How many governesses, or household servants, or even other "escaped nuns," whose story has been concealed from regard to their safety, may now be aiding the purposes of the Jesuits in this country, is well worthy of inquiry.

Supposing this to be the case with regard to the subject of this volume, it is far beyond the power of those who sheltered her to track the wily course of a Jesuit. In the absence of

positive proof, they do not wish to charge her deception on the
Jesuits; but they put it to the reader, whether the circumstances do not warrant suspicion. They can but bring the
facts—and facts which, with such convictions, they would not
feel justified in concealing—before the notice of the public, and
leave their Protestant countrymen to pursue their own investigations, and to form their own conclusions. It will surely be
conceded, that the agent in so extraordinary a series of plots,
has earned for herself the title *she assumed*, of "a Female
Jesuit."

THE END.